IT'S NOT THE END OF THE WORLD

SOPHIE RILEY

Copyright © 2026 by Sophie Riley

❀ Formatted with Vellum

*For my mother, who would go to the
end of the world and back for me.*

PART I
THE ROAD

CHAPTER ONE

YOU CAN'T BLAME me for not taking the end seriously at first. I was barely fourteen. The world practically ended for me every day.

There was a shocking quietness to it at the start. The patter of rain on the windows, the murmur of the TV, the muffled voices of our neighbors on the other side of the apartment wall. It was the end of October and the fog rolled low over the valley, the California air turning sober and sharp.

While Mom fried up some eggs, she sent me to the lobby to get the mail. There were bills, ads, a child support statement from my dad, and other boring adult things. But there was also another postcard from my brother. This one's edges were worn and bent, and it had an illustration of the Oregon coast on it, even though Preston's camp was further inland in the dry, craggy mountains lined with thin pine forests.

I flipped the postcard over.

Mom + Lay,

    Having a great time. We got to eat hamburgers yesterday (no cheese). It's getting

colder up here but it's not that bad yet.
Leaving the camp soon to go on another two
week hike in the woods. Now THAT will be cold.
Send warmth. And tell Dad hi for me next time
you talk to him.
      -Preston Wise

I slipped the postcard into the pocket of my baggy denim jacket and took the rest of the mail upstairs. Mom didn't get to see the postcards. My rule.

When I walked back into the apartment, Mom called over her shoulder from the kitchen. "Layla, would you get to these dishes? They've been in the sink for two days."

I tossed the mail down on the tiny table, right between our vase of fake lilies and Mom's pill bottles. "Yes," I grumbled.

"And brush your hair. I could tell you didn't yesterday."

"I *did.*"

I yanked my fingers through my brownish hair, letting strands flutter to the floor, and plopped down in my seat just as she turned around. She gave me a suspicious look and set down my plate of eggs. "Eat up. I have to get going."

"I thought you were off today."

"The hospital asked if I could come in for a few hours. I guess they're overloaded." She touched my head and headed off to her room. "Brush your hair."

I resisted rolling my eyes and scarfed down my breakfast. When I was done, I worked some stray food out of my braces—they were coming off in two days, and I couldn't *wait* to be a liberated, gorgeous, straight-toothed woman—and followed Mom to her room.

The TV was on in there, playing the news. Mom always got the news from the TV instead of her phone, acting like some old geezer even though she wasn't even forty yet.

"Are there more Band-Aids?" I asked.

"Same place they always are." She was in front of her mirror, twisting her long red hair into a bun. "Don't tell me you're wearing those horrible goth shoes again."

"Goth?" I laughed. "Mom. They're cute."

"They give you blisters. And goths wear clunky black shoes, don't they?"

I dug into the drawer of her bedside table, took out two Band-Aids, and sat on her bed to put them on the backs of my heels. "They're called Mary Janes, and they're very cool."

"I know what they're called, they're just impractical."

"Well, good thing I bought them with my money," I said. I held back from adding *at least I don't wear clunky white nurse shoes all day.*

I idly watched the TV as I stuck the Band-Aids on and was struck by a memory of my brother. That happened a lot since he'd been away. Memories would hit me so vividly it felt like I was standing inside them—this time, it was the day I insisted he take me out on his skateboard in the parking lot outside the strip mall. I got all scraped up on the pavement, and he took me home and put Band-Aids on my knees while I sat on the kitchen counter, trying not to cry.

I focused on the news.

The anchor was recounting a story that Mom had been following for a few days. Up in Siberia, the permafrost was melting because of climate change, surfacing well-preserved prehistoric creatures like mammoths and wolf pups and bison, once frozen deep beneath the ice. There were some American researchers up there, rushing to maintain their study sites and data as the terrain so rapidly changed. But that wasn't the story. The melting had also released some ancient pathogens, and all those scientists got sick. They'd supposedly been quarantined in Russia for a week now, and it was all very hush-hush.

Mom caught me watching. "If we weren't so overpopulated, maybe things like this wouldn't happen to the earth. Maybe another virus is nature's way of getting back at us."

I shrugged. "Jamal thinks it's a stunt by the Russian government to get people riled up."

"Jamal has an overactive imagination," she replied. "Just never about the right things. I mean, if this virus escaped quarantine, it could be serious. We've had lots of sick people in and out of the hospital the last couple days, and I've been watching the news, and—"

"Maybe if you stopped watching the news, you wouldn't have to take so much Xanax." I pushed off the bed to go put on my clunky black *goth shoes*. But as I walked out, I stuck my hand in my pocket and realized Preston's postcard wasn't there.

I glanced back at the bed; it had fallen out onto the comforter.

Mom followed my eyes and picked it up bitterly. "Layla Elizabeth Wise. I told you to stop hiding these from me."

"It's not like he ever says anything in them anyway."

I tried to snatch the postcard so I could put it with the others in a box beneath my bed, but Mom held it away. "I still want to see them. I like to hear from him."

"You don't get to miss him when it's your fault he's there."

Her brown eyes went cold. That look made my stomach a little upset, not because I'd upset *her*, but because now I was thinking about his camp, and that always made my stomach hurt. Camp made it sound like a fun summer away, swimming in lakes and doing archery. That wasn't what Preston's camp was. He'd been gone for months. He wasn't allowed to call home. Ever. His postcards made it seem okay, but they hardly sounded like him at all—they'd squeezed all the *Preston* right out of him like an overripe orange. And my parents were the ones who did that to him.

"I've told you, Layla," Mom said. "There are things parents have to do that kids just can't understand." She turned back to the mirror, postcard in hand. "You're going to miss the bus."

THE RAIN LET up by the time my bus pulled into the school lot, so before class started, I hung around in the bustling court-yard and sat on a damp bench with Jamal.

Jamal Hardy was a huge dork, but he was nice to be around, and he was the only person I could really stand. Mostly because he didn't care about stuff most other eighth graders cared about. He was still in Boy Scouts, he watched anime openly, and he wanted to be a storyboard artist when he grew up. I liked all that about him. He wasn't pretending for anyone.

He was pretty much the only person who could stand me, too.

"I don't know what should happen next," he said.

He was holding our comic book in his lap. Right now, we

7

were working on issue 3 of *Major Ursus*, a story about a military man-turned-bear who teams up with a wildlife biologist named Leah. Major Ursus was genetically transformed into a bear by the evil Sosna Syndicate, a Russian group that wanted to use him as a weapon and set him loose in the U.S. Only the experiment failed, and because Major Ursus retained his human heart, his love for Leah caused him to shift in and out of his bear form—just not at will. Together, he and Leah vowed to protect the forests from the Sosna Syndicate's horde of violent, engineered animal experiments.

"What do you mean?" I asked. "I thought Major Ursus and Leah found the secret base and were gonna find a way in."

"Yeah, but I'm stuck. I mean, Major Ursus is stuck in bear form right now, so he's huge. How could he possibly sneak into the base?"

"Maybe you shouldn't have made him stuck in bear form, then."

Jamal snorted. "That's the whole point of the last three chapters, Layla. They have to infiltrate the Syndicate and try to change him back because he's becoming less and less of a human. If he's not stuck in bear form now, then his whole arc won't play out."

To be honest, I didn't always care what happened in the comic. Jamal made up the story and drew the pictures, and I just colored them in. I was good at staying inside the lines when I wanted to. When Preston and I used to color as little kids, he was wild with it, scribbling in all the colors. But my coloring was as neat as a pin. It made me feel calm to zone out and turn my brain off for a while.

Maybe Mom could use some coloring books.

"Well, maybe Leah can turn him back with love or something," I muttered, because it felt like an easy answer. Jamal's brain was too big for me. None of my ideas ever worked. I was good at coloring, and just coloring, and that was fine with me.

Jamal stared at the pages in his lap, thinking. But then he

dropped the matter entirely and said, "I got us free tickets to that haunted maze in Sacramento."

I gasped. "Seriously?"

"Yep," he grinned. "Perks of being an Air Force kid, I guess."

"I'm *only* friends with you for your Air Force perks, you know."

"Right, because there are *so* many perks to living on a base." He rolled his eyes. "Anyway, we should plan our costumes. I was thinking—"

There was a loud, roaring swoosh over our heads. We looked up just in time to see two dark planes cutting through the fog overhead, flying so low over the valley that the school windows rattled. Everyone went quiet, staring upward.

"Those were flying pretty low," I observed. "Were they from the base?"

Jamal shrugged and turned back to the comic. "Probably."

The hush stayed for a moment before people began chattering again. Jamal was unbothered, already transfixed on *Major Ursus*, but a girl from our grade—who also lived on the base—skipped over and sat next to him.

Deepti was a tiny, dark-haired, perfect-nosed fairy girl who was somehow friends with everyone, yet still managed to be the meanest girl alive. She smiled. Unlike me, she'd gotten her braces off two months ago and couldn't stop showing off her perfect rack of teeth. "Hey, Jam. Hey, Layla."

"Hey," he murmured. He hated being called Jam, but it didn't matter if Deepti did it because she was pretty and he secretly liked the attention. I knew him well enough to understand these things.

"Where do you think those planes are going?" Deepti asked.

"Could just be a drill," Jamal said.

"They were going toward the ocean. That could mean Russia."

I had no idea, but I wanted to back up Jamal. "It was just a drill," I repeated.

She gave me a look that said *what would you know about the*

Air Force? Then she leaned into Jamal. "You know, my friend's great-aunt got sick, and they haven't been able to contact her for two days because she's in some quarantine unit thing. My uncle says it's about to get so bad that we'll be going under martial law any day now. Do you know what that means?"

"Of course he knows what that means," I snapped, even though I myself didn't. "He's thirteen, not three."

Jamal shrugged and kept his attention on our comic book. Then the bell rang, and Deepti rolled her eyes and sauntered off.

"Whatever this virus is, it better not ruin our haunted maze," I said as we gathered our stuff from the bench. "I feel bad for Preston. He wanted to go this year. I'll have to send him pictures."

I had sent him plenty of postcards, letters, photos, even some candy. Mom sent stuff here and there, but not nearly as much as I did. In August, I'd even taken my polaroid camera to school. It had been a super hot day, the first week back from summer vacation, and I wanted to send him a letter, but I had nothing interesting to say. So I'd taken pictures throughout the day, wearing the same bored, monotone expression in each of them—until a teacher took my camera away. They were terrible photos, but at least he'd know I wasn't having a ball without him.

"How long has he been gone, again?" Jamal asked. "Four months?"

It was October now. He'd been gone since late May. "Five," I said.

It was one of those camps where they send bad kids. It was called Jackpot Alternative Wilderness School—JAWS for short—but I got the picture pretty quickly that this was not a normal camp, and definitely not a normal school. I wasn't even sure they learned anything there.

Preston was fifteen when they took him, sixteen now. He got into trouble often, but last spring he'd gotten into *a lot* of trouble, and that was the last straw for my parents—even my indulgent divorcé Dad who lived a thousand miles away and was hardly around. Dad had called JAWS, and they'd sent two men in a van to come to our apartment in the middle of the night, bust into our bedroom, and drag Preston out of bed. He didn't get to take anything with him. He didn't even get to say goodbye. They dragged him down three flights of stairs and shoved him into the van, and we ran after in our pajamas while Mom kept saying, "I'm sorry, I'm sorry, I'm sorry."

She hadn't even warned me they were coming.

I still didn't like to think about it.

MY FIRST CLASS was English with Deepti. I was a few seconds late, but it didn't matter; our teacher wasn't in yet. The room was abuzz with conversation. I sat in my assigned seat in the middle, and beside me, Deepti and her friend Juanita were talking in low voices.

"It's only going to get worse," Deepti was saying.

Juanita rolled her eyes. "It's just another flu thing. Trust me, my mom's a pharmacist."

"Trust *me*. My uncle works really high up in the government. He told my mom that the Russians released it as a bioweapon, and the US is trying to hide it by saying it's a strain of influenza."

"Stop trying to sound smart, Deepti," Juanita said.

"What's that supposed to mean?"

"You also said your uncle works for the FBI, so which is it?"

"He *used to*. What does that have to do with anything?"

"I'm just saying, it feels like you're making stuff up sometimes just to act like you know stuff. Like when you said you had synesthesia and could taste colors."

"I never said that!"

I turned my attention to my book. We were starting *Where the Red Fern Grows*. Everyone complained about it, but I kind of liked it so far. I knew it ended horribly, though, because Preston had cried when he read it two years ago. He used to cry a lot when he was younger. Then he grew up and stopped having emotions.

"What do you think?"

I realized Deepti was talking to me. "Huh?"

"Your mom's a nurse, right? Does she think this virus is weird, too?"

I toyed with the corner of my book and shrugged. "She just works part-time in pediatrics. She said it's bloodborne, though. But I don't really know what that means." They nodded vaguely, becoming disinterested, so I shifted gears. "Hey, are you going to the haunted maze on Halloween?"

"Yeah, why?" Deepti asked. "Are you?"

I shrugged, trying to play it cool. The haunted maze was supposed to be super scary—so scary they made you be thirteen or older to go in. From what I'd heard, half the school would be there on Friday night. Mostly because half the school was Air Force kids who got free tickets.

"Of course," I said.

"Cool. See you there, I guess." Deepti's brown eyes flicked around. "Hey, where's Ms. Henry?"

The three of us looked to the front of the room. Ms. Henry's swivel chair still sat empty.

She never did show up. The principal dismissed us to the library a few minutes later but gave no explanation. I sat with Juanita and Deepti and colored pictures the librarian printed out, and I thought about what Preston was doing this very moment. I wondered if he was having more fun than I was. I seriously doubted it.

JAMAL CAME HOME with me after school. He hated being on the base. I didn't know why; it was like living in a small town where you knew everyone, and where everything was within arm's reach. But he'd been an Air Force kid all his life. Before moving to California two and a half years ago, he and his dad had lived in five different places.

When we got to my apartment door, our next-door neighbor Margie was waiting there. She was a short woman who often wore pastel dresses, kept her hair pulled back in headbands, and smelled like baby lotion—which all made her seem kind of juvenile. Today she held a package wrapped in plastic.

"Hiya, Layla, is Heather around?"

"She's still at work." I fished for my key in my yellow-striped backpack. "Did you need something?"

Margie gave me a shaky, nervous smile. She was in her late forties and lived alone, but spent half her time at our place. She and my mother liked to share Diet Coke and watch rom-coms to get their minds off the "horrors of the world." Sometimes I thought Margie was a bad influence on my mom, like her anxiety was rubbing off on her. Margie was just a jittery bundle of nerves and conspiracies.

"Well, I brought you two something."

I ran my tongue over my braces. "What?"

"Radiation vests."

I glanced at Jamal and nearly laughed. "For *what?*"

"In case of nuclear war, honey."

She shoved the heavy package toward me, and it slipped in my arms. "Uh, thank you, Margie, but I don't think—"

"Did you see the planes today?"

"Yeah?"

"They're going west. Russia could attack at any time."

"It could just be drills," Jamal said.

"Better safe than sorry." Margie patted my arm and cleared her throat. "Anyway. I'll be next door if you need me."

WHILE WE WAITED for my mom to get home, we worked on our algebra homework on the floor of the small bedroom I shared with Preston. Neither of our hearts was in it.

"What's the point if the world's gonna end?" Jamal joked. He was doodling human Major Ursus on the edge of his paper—a sturdy man with dark skin, a heavy jaw, and a buzz cut. He kind of looked like Jamal's dad.

"I wonder what your dad will say about the planes," I said.

"Why is everyone so worked up about it? They fly by all the time."

"I don't know. The air feels weird, I guess." I stared at my quadratic equation, sighed, and set my pencil down. "You'd believe him if he told you it was nothing, right?"

"Of course," Jamal said quickly. "I'd believe him no matter what he said."

His vigor didn't surprise me. He and his dad were closer than any father and son I'd ever met. Sergeant Hardy called him Little Cub. They had a secret handshake. They never argued.

They trusted each other to make decisions, and have integrity, and keep each other safe.

I was used to not trusting my parents. When my mom told me not to worry about something, I knew she was secretly up all night in her room, rolling over in bed, thinking about it herself. Like when she told me not to worry about her and Dad fighting, and soon after, he was packing his things and moving to Colorado Springs. Or when she told me not to worry about Preston, and later in the spring she was rushing to the hospital because he'd been drunk driving. And now his bed was empty, and every morning when I woke up, I was forced to think about it.

"Deepti thinks there's going to be a war or something," I said. "Margie thinks the same thing, apparently, considering she bought us radiation vests."

"That kooky old lady doesn't know what she's talking about."

"She's not *that* old."

"But she is kooky. She and your mom are bad for each other."

I laughed. "Yeah, next time Margie comes over, I'm going to drop one of my mom's anxiety pills into her Diet Coke."

Jamal doubled over in laughter. I pushed my math book aside, feeling airy and warm, like homework didn't matter, and nothing else did either. Nothing except lying on the floor with my friend at the last cusp of our childhood and pretending it didn't scare us.

It's weird how normal things are before they change. Before they end. One second you're a kid in your bedroom, hungry for dinner and neglecting your homework, and the next, it's like you're nothing at all. Like the world is spinning backward.

WHEN SHE FINALLY GOT HOME, I left Jamal in my room and found Mom standing at the kitchen counter, staring at Preston's postcard.

"Are you okay, Mom?"

She flipped the postcard back and forth, ignoring me.

"*Mom?*"

Finally, she huffed and turned around. "Didn't I tell you to wash the dishes?"

"Sorry. I'll get to them."

"You've had *hours* to get to them."

"I said I'm sorry and I'll do them. What more do you want?"

Her eyebrows were raised so high and severe that there were wrinkles across her forehead, and I wanted to reach up and smooth them out. She put the postcard down and reached for a pot in the lower cabinet. "Long day, Lay."

Jamal and I watched TV while spaghetti boiled on the stove. Only a few minutes later, Sergeant Hardy called Mom, and she put it on speaker so we could hear. He asked if Jamal could spend the night. This was unusual; our friendship was as platonic as they came, but we'd never had a sleepover. But Sergeant Hardy said there was a lot going on tonight, and if Jamal could stay until school in the morning he'd really appreciate it.

"I don't have any of my stuff," Jamal said. "I don't have clothes."

"You can borrow Preston's," Mom murmured.

"Thanks for keeping my cub out of trouble," Sergeant Hardy said. "Layla, you there? If you want, you can come over before your haunted maze on Friday. I'm making my special chili. I know you love that stuff."

"Yes!" I exclaimed.

We told him goodnight, and Mom hung up and returned to the bubbling pot in the kitchen. Outside in the October black, three more planes roared by.

CHAPTER TWO

"YOU'RE NOT GOING to school today."

Jamal and I were eating cereal at the kitchen table, already up and dressed, when Mom said this—Jamal looking out of place in one of Preston's middle school basketball t-shirts. "What? Why?" I asked.

"I'm worried about that Siberian virus. They haven't said it outright, but I know it's what's going around. Patients get this…" Mom motioned to her head, *"brain fog,* and this rash that eats at their skin. There haven't been any cases in pediatrics, but I filled in at the emergency department, and it was bad. These people start hallucinating, and the nurses have to sedate them."

"And that fixes them?" Jamal said.

Mom hesitated, hands wrapped tightly around her chipped yellow coffee mug. "No, it doesn't last."

"So what happens? They die?" I asked. Mom didn't respond. "You can say *die,* you know. How long does it take?"

"I don't know. I haven't seen any of them die yet."

"That's good," Jamal said.

"Well, I haven't seen any of them recover either." She pushed away from the table. "I have to go. I'm covering another shift."

"What if *you* get sick?" I said.

She dumped the rest of her coffee into the sink. "I won't."

"Then why are you so worried about us when you're the one at the hospital? No one at school has a brain rash."

"Layla, I'll be fine."

"Exactly. You'll be fine, so we'll be fine. We're going to school."

"What kid even *wants* to go to school?" she scoffed. "You're not going. Not with all this stuff going on. Jamal, I'll call your dad and let him know, okay?"

I rolled my eyes and set down my spoon with a clank. "Oh my god, Mom. Bad stuff happens literally all the time, everywhere. Dad says we can't let that stuff get us worked up, or we're giving in to fear-mongering."

"Frankly, I don't care what your dad says." She swept by and kissed me on the head. "I'll be home this afternoon. Lock the door, stay inside."

"Wait, my orthodontist appointment is still happening tomorrow, right?"

She turned in the doorway. "I'll call the office and make sure."

She was gone quickly. I went to the kitchen window and watched her down below, walking out to her white Volkswagen on quick feet. I sighed and looked at the clock. The bus would be here soon.

"This is dumb," I said. "I'm going. Are you?"

Jamal shrugged, took one more bite of cereal, and spoke with a full mouth. "I'm not scared."

"Good. Then let's go."

I grabbed my bag, shoved on my Mary Janes, and we went downstairs.

"I THINK I got it figured out," Jamal said as we walked through the school courtyard. He was hugging three multicolored *Major Ursus* folders to his chest, each of them holding different issues, with a pen tucked behind his ear. "Turns out the Syndicate knew they were coming. They capture them and keep them apart. It switches to Leah's perspective, so she has to escape and find out what happened to Major Ursus."

"Leah's perspective? That's new."

Jamal shrugged and adjusted the pen. "I'm getting tired of drawing bears."

He stopped me and swung open the folder to show me the newest drawing. It was of Leah and Major Ursus standing in the forest, mountains in the background. They were in front of a simple bunker door built into the ground, looking surprised— well, as surprised as Jamal could manage to draw a bear. Leah, on the other hand, looked normal. I liked how Jamal designed her. Long, golden-brown hair in a ponytail, eyes that were a little bigger than they would be in real life, a khaki outfit with boots. She looked kind of like me. I'd never asked him if he meant to do that. I didn't really want to know the answer.

The school felt emptier than normal. At first I thought I was imagining it, just a side effect of my mother's paranoia rubbing off on me. But when I got to English, there was still no Ms. Henry, and a number of empty desks.

"Deepti's mom made her stay on the base today," Juanita whispered to me.

We had a substitute come in, but he hadn't read *Where the Red Fern Grows*, so he just turned on this awful old movie adaptation of it, and we sat in the dark, staring glazed-eyed at the screen for the entire period. Some kids talked quietly, some went on their phones, some did other homework. I lay my head on the desk and rested my eyes, thinking if I hadn't been so stubborn, I'd be home lying on the couch right now.

My science class didn't have a teacher either, and the school didn't have enough subs to go around. They sent us back to the library. More kids trickled in from other classes and colored pictures and worked on homework, but when the bell rang for the next period, many of them stayed put, like they were scared of what they would find in their next classroom. Or wouldn't find.

I caught up with Jamal at lunch. All the lunch ladies were accounted for, and they'd cooked up some soggy chicken nuggets and dry mashed potatoes. Jamal and I always sat with other kids, but today, we were alone.

I glanced around the room, noticing the strange hush that had replaced the usual clatter of voices. A few kids had been picked up during earlier classes. They'd probably texted their parents, *no one is here, I'm scared, come get me.* I thought of what Dad had once said about fear-mongering, about how scared people were weak people. I hadn't really known what that meant, but I'd agreed anyway.

"Are people really this worried about the virus?" Jamal asked.

I took a heaping bite of mashed potatoes. "You mean the brain rash?"

He smiled a little at this, but his eyes drifted through the cafeteria and then widened. "What is *she* doing here?"

I turned and nearly spewed potatoes across the table. My mother was standing by the cafeteria doors, clutching the strap of her purse, eyes searching. Her gaze fell on me before I could try to hide.

"Oh god," I said.

She waltzed over, still in her scrubs, bun slipping down the back of her head. "I'm here to take you home," she said. "Both of you."

"Why?" I asked, but she just took my hand and pulled me up from the table. Jamal stayed seated, his face all mushed in confusion.

"Come on, Jamal, I told your dad I'd get you too," Mom said. "Do you need to stop at your lockers?"

She didn't explain why we were leaving. Not when we stepped out of the school, or got into the Volkswagen, or started for home. But it was clear that, in her mind, this had to do with the brain rash.

As we neared our neighborhood, we passed a gas station with a line of cars. Mom gripped the steering wheel tightly. I peered at her gas meter, just curious, and saw that the tank was only half full. In the back seat, Jamal sat among a few paper grocery bags.

"Why did you leave work?" I finally asked.

"I wanted to come get you."

I pointed to the bags. "You went shopping first."

"I picked up a few things on the way. Why does it matter?"

"Because this is weird, and you're making me think something really bad is happening, but you're not saying anything."

We stopped at a light and she clenched her fists against the wheel. "Did you stop to think that I've been at the hospital watching people suffer all morning and that maybe I just needed a minute of quiet?"

I didn't respond right away and turned to the window. Then I muttered, "Well, it's been more than a minute."

"Layla!"

"Okay, okay."

"I told you not to go to school today. Margie called while I was at the store and asked about you. And I said, 'Oh, Layla is at home.' And she said, 'No, I saw her get on the bus this morning with her friend.' Do you listen to anything I say, Layla? Ever?"

"Yes, Mom. Sheesh. Can we not do this right now? Jamal is literally in the car, and you're making him uncomfortable."

I looked back at him, but he just shrugged. I rolled my eyes.

Back home, we all carried the grocery bags up to the apartment. Inside, there was an old-fashioned yellow suitcase—the kind without wheels that you have to lug around—lying on the coffee table.

"What is that?" I asked.

"Margie made us a survival kit."

"It's not a kit, it's a suitcase," I said. Mom popped it open, and I leaned over her shoulder. Inside, there was a first-aid kit, a flashlight, rope, matches, one of those shiny silver thermal blankets, a pocket knife, and a mess of other things. "Margie just had all that lying around in her apartment?"

Mom closed it as soon as she had opened it. "Go do your homework, alright? I'll make you a snack."

"You're being crazy."

She straightened up and looked me dead in the eye. "No, Layla, I don't think I am. So many people came into the hospital that we had them in the hallways. We had to start turning them away. One of the nurses *died* in the emergency department." Mom's voice softened at that, and she squeezed her eyes shut. "I didn't see it happen, but I heard one of her patients freaked out on her and…and anyway, I had to leave." She looked at the suitcase. "But we got some supplies, so Margie thinks we should be okay for a while if things go bad."

"Go bad?" I looked at Jamal standing against the wall and tried not to laugh.

I'd seen this before.

About a year ago, Margie and my mom had been up late watching some talk show. I'd listened to their conversation from my bedroom. Margie had started talking about this farming conspiracy, how all the chickens and eggs were being treated with some weird chemical that would give people cancer, and I hadn't known what she was talking about, but she got my mom all worked up about it. My mom wouldn't let me and Preston eat eggs for a month.

Mom made firm decisions with cold, hard logic, and she stuck to them. But when her logic was flawed, so were her decisions. She'd get anxious thoughts and they'd stop her from being able to see clearly. I mean, the eggs were fine. And I was sure that this situation—whatever this virus thing was—would be fine too. It was just another one of her panic-mode moments. Thanks to Margie.

"I think it seems bad now, but it'll blow over," I said. "It's probably another flu thing."

"I don't know. Margie heard online that Russia has released this virus to weaken us," Mom said. "They're going to hit us with airstrikes when we're at our lowest. Or a nuclear bomb. Or an EMP."

I gave Jamal a deadpan look that said *told you*. His mouth curled, and he turned his face away. "An EMP? What even is that?" I asked.

"An electromagnetic pulse," muttered Jamal.

Mom nodded. "He's right. It can knock out everything that uses electricity. Lights, electric cars, phones, TV, internet. They'll cut us off from one another and wreak havoc. We wouldn't even know it had happened until it was too late."

"You can't be serious." I tried not to smile. "You're saying Russia is going to cut off our electricity and drop a nuclear bomb on top of giving us a virus? Sheesh, pick a lane."

But Mom *was* serious—very, very serious—and she didn't think I was being funny. Her arms were folded, her hair was in her face, and her eyes were cold and clear. "Something is off with all of this. I feel it in my gut, okay?"

"Well, I don't trust your gut."

"*Well*, the fact of the matter is, even if we don't know much about this virus, we need to be safe. We should stay home for a few days in case something happens."

I gawked. "What about the haunted maze tomorrow?"

"That's really what you're worried about right now?"

"I mean…yeah." Then my stomach dropped. "Wait, what about my appointment for my braces?"

"It got canceled."

I stared at her in shock, but she didn't say anything more. So now I couldn't even get my stupid braces off? After a year and a half of waiting, all because of this stupid, stupid virus?

I refused to cry in front of her, so I grabbed Jamal by the wrist, pulled him into my bedroom, and shut the door loudly.

"She's being crazy," I said. But deep down, I knew she wasn't. *All* of this was crazy, and it was happening so fast I couldn't keep up.

JAMAL HAD to sleep over again. Last night it had been fun, but tonight, something heavier hung in the air. We were both thinking it—if his dad was held up at the base, then something really *was* going on. We just didn't want to talk about it, because then it might become real.

Jamal and I didn't even have homework because nobody had been around to assign it. So we worked on the comic. He sat on Preston's bed, face pinched in concentration, while I sat on mine and colored neatly with my alcohol markers.

Mom made ham and potato casserole for dinner, and I didn't talk to her the whole time. I just stared at her, picking food out of my braces with my finger, impolite and unapologetic.

That night, when she and Jamal were asleep, I crept into her room and took her phone off the bedside table. I wasn't allowed to have my own yet—even though Preston had one at my age before he ruined it for the both of us—but sometimes I'd take hers to talk to Dad.

Dad was very different from my mother. He grew up an only child while my mom was the oldest of four. Maybe that was why he didn't get worked up about things like Mom, like he knew things would go his way, as they always did.

Dad had grown up in Colorado Springs and always wanted to move back, but Mom never wanted to. She'd grown up on a ranch in the north, and living outside Sacramento was as far from her childhood home as she was willing to go. I think the whole Colorado Springs thing was part of the reason they split up. Originally, Dad was going to stick around after the split and share custody, but when he got a fancy job opportunity in Colorado, he decided to go for it. He said Preston and I could visit whenever we wanted, but we never did. It wasn't that we didn't want to, it was just that flights were expensive, and Mom didn't like us traveling that far without her.

I'd never say it to Mom's face, but I wished we lived there. Dad had a real house, even bigger than our old one. He had the life he'd always wanted for us, we just weren't a part of it.

He was sort of a pushover, too. Like, if we didn't finish homework, Mom would launch into a speech about responsibility, like we'd self-destruct if we missed one assignment. But Dad always said we'd learn from our mistakes on our own. If we wanted to stay up late, sure—it was our choice if we wanted to be tired in the morning. If Preston got in trouble at school, fine— the world would go on.

He just didn't let things be a big deal. Sometimes it made him hard to talk to, but I'd always admired how he stared life down and somehow always got what he wanted out of it, and it never cost him anything. He was never weighed down. Even when they split up, he simply moved on. Went back to Colorado Springs, got a new place, started a new job with new people. He just knew how to accept things.

That's why I wanted to talk to him. I wanted a little sanity. If anyone could tell me that this was all being blown out of proportion and everything would be okay, it was Dad.

I went into the living room, plopped onto the couch, and dialed his number. It rang and rang. He never picked up. Feeling bitter, I flopped on the throw pillows and contemplated trying again. It was late, though. Nearly midnight for him.

I closed my eyes, phone to my chest, and found myself slipping into sleep. I thought about Dad, about Preston. I imagined another life, living near those snow-capped mountains, with a parent who never worried, never pushed.

I dozed for only a few minutes before I was awoken by buzzing.

I sat up fast, and the phone slid to the floor, its screen lit up.

I swept up the phone. I thought it would be Dad calling me back, but it was an unknown number. At least, unknown to Mom's phone. Not unknown to me. I knew that number, because I'd found it on the internet and tried to call it multiple times before realizing they'd never let me talk to my brother.

It was a call from JAWS.

If they were calling, something had to be wrong. I picked up immediately. "Hello?"

I expected to hear the gruff voice of the male counselor who always answered, and who always told me, *you know you're not supposed to call here. Only your parents can call, and only for emergencies. Now give the phone to your mommy and quit it.*

But instead, I only heard breathing on the other end.

"Hello?" I said again.

"Hello? Layla?"

My blood ran cold. It was Preston. "Pres, what are you doing? I thought you weren't allowed to use the—"

"I'm not. It's a long story—doesn't matter. Where's Mom?"

"Sleeping."

"Layla, I need you to listen to me." His words trembled; I hadn't heard his voice in months, but over the last few years, he'd grown hard and cold. Now he just sounded weak. Had they broken him, my unbreakable brother? "I need you to tell

Mom that she and Dad need to sign me out of here, okay? I can't do this anymore. If I have to go four more months, I won't—"

His voice cut out. I strained to listen. "Pres? Pres, what happened?"

I could hear scuffling on the other side, then his voice dropped to a whisper. "Please, Layla. Just tell them I need to come home, okay? Get me out. Please—"

"Hey!" someone else shouted. I heard movement and a strangled grunt, and then the call ended with a click.

I stared at the phone, shaken.

I knew I should wake up Mom and tell her, but my gut told me she wouldn't listen. When Preston's first postcard had arrived in the mail in early June, Mom and I had read it together, and I told her it wasn't *him*. It was his handwriting, sure, but it wasn't his voice. It was automatic, chirpy. The real Preston was sarcastic and brooding. He was also the type to hold a grudge, so the fact that he was sending postcards to Mom *at all* told me they weren't sincere.

As much as I liked to imagine he was happy, I knew he wasn't. After he left, I'd stayed up for hours at night, reading stories from wilderness therapy camps on Mom's heavy, old laptop. There were all kinds of camps out there, some religious, some not, but none of them had particularly glowing reviews.

The JAWS website had pictures of smiling boys in cabins, on hikes, swimming in lakes. It was a newer organization, so there weren't many stories online, but I'd found one buried in an online forum. A boy had been sent there to get help with an eating disorder. They had to hike miles and miles on excursions, rain or shine, carrying heavy backpacks. If he got in trouble or refused to participate in activities, they'd put him in isolation or give him strenuous tasks. They once left him on the trail because he refused to move, and he had to find his way back alone. He came out of JAWS worse than ever.

I'd tried to show Mom the forum. She wouldn't hear it. She just sat there, shaking her head, saying, "He needs help, and they'll help him. Ask your dad; he'll say the same thing. It's for the best."

But now, hearing Preston's voice tremble like that…I knew I'd been right all along.

I took Mom's phone and stood at her bedroom door, trying to muster up the courage to knock. I'd been asking for my parents to sign Preston out of camp for the last five months, and they never listened. Even if she *did*, she'd have to call Dad and talk to him about it. She always called him about this kind of stuff— even after the divorce—like she couldn't make choices on her own. Like she was still scared to displease him. She was always adamant that she could parent us on her own, but never when it counted.

I crept into her room. She'd fallen asleep on top of her covers, bathed in blue light from the TV. I didn't want to disturb the peace with another argument, but this couldn't wait.

"Mom?" I whispered. Then, louder, "Mom."

She stirred and blinked at me. "What? What time is it?"

My hands trembled, still clutching the phone. "Preston called."

She sat up. "When, just now? What's wrong?"

I blinked back tears and shook my head. "I don't know. He just…he said he wants to come home. It sounded like something happened, but he didn't get a chance to say it. I don't think he was supposed to be calling."

Mom sighed nervously and glanced at the TV. The news was on, volume low. I paused to watch, almost expecting something to happen. Some emergency message, some sign of lockdown, something that would tie together all the weird, stupid rumors I'd been hearing about planes and viruses and Russia. But instead, the news was covering a high school cross country meet that had happened earlier in the week.

"So what do we do?" I asked.

"We…we can't do anything," Mom replied. "He's there for a reason. If something happened, I'm sure it was justified. His counselors will take care of—"

"He sounded scared, Mom. I heard him."

"Layla, I can't..."

"Yes, you *can*. You can get him if you want. It's been five months; don't you think he's been punished enough?" I motioned to the TV, even though nothing notable was on it. "You're so worried about all this stuff going on, but you're just going to leave him there? Don't you think he should come home?"

She blinked at the screen, eyes shining in the dim light. She looked on the verge of breaking down, and it gave me a burning sense of satisfaction to see her upset about this. But when she saw me holding her phone, her expression hardened.

She slipped the phone from my hands. "You should go to bed."

"But—"

"I'll call your dad in the morning," she said. "We'll talk about it. Okay?"

I didn't want to say *okay*, because I knew what would happen. She would call Dad, Dad would call JAWS, and then he'd convince her that Preston was fine. They wouldn't do anything. They'd leave him there to rot. But just like everything else in my life, I had no say, so I stormed off to bed.

CHAPTER THREE

WHEN I WOKE UP, it was late in the morning. No one had even tried to get me up for school. I found Jamal glued to the TV in the living room while Mom cooked in the kitchen.

I rubbed my eyes and stood by Jamal. "Is she making you watch the news?"

"She's not *making* me. Stuff does look kind of weird." He muttered under his breath, "Stupid brain rash."

The TV was playing a public service announcement about the virus, NVS-1: Necrotic Viral Strain 1. I was actually relieved to see it spoken about on the news, but there was no real word on it, no talk of hospitals or hallucinations or violence. The only thing it said was that the state was imposing a shelter-in-place mandate to combat the spread, effective immediately.

"What does that mean?" I said.

"It means they want us to stay home," Mom replied, walking toward the couch. She handed Jamal a plate of sloppy mini pancakes. "Jamal, sweetie, your dad will be here this afternoon. Are you packed up?"

He nodded. I sat on the arm of the couch, and as if I'd plunged into cold water, I remembered Preston's phone call. It felt like it had been a bad dream. Mom was acting so calm, like it hadn't even happened.

"Mom?"

She was back in the kitchen. "What?"

"About Preston. Did you—"

"Your dad called up there this morning, and I guess he got in a little trouble for an argument with another kid. But they've taken care of it, and he's fine."

"But *Mom*."

"They're leaving for an excursion today. He's going camping." She nodded and offered a pathetic smile. "He's fine."

My chest burned. In my heart I knew he wasn't fine this time—that if he'd managed to get to the phone, he really needed me. But I didn't want to argue about it in front of Jamal, so I let it go. For now.

We spent the morning doing absolutely nothing. Mom sat on her laptop. Jamal lounged on the couch. I read a few chapters of *Where the Red Fern Grows*, but I couldn't focus on the words when the only thing in my head was Preston's voice echoing *Layla, I can't do this anymore*, over and over.

Sometime in the afternoon, Jamal and I dug some dusty board games out from under my bed and tried to distract ourselves. We'd only just set up The Game of Life on the coffee table when there was a hard knock at the door. Jamal jumped to open it.

It was Sergeant Hardy in his crisp, navy blue uniform. He immediately pulled Jamal into a hug. "Hey, Cub. I'm so sorry."

"It's okay." Jamal tugged him into the apartment. "We just hung out. It was fun."

Sergeant Hardy gave me a hug, too. Although I didn't have a dad around, he sometimes made me feel like I did. He was tough and a little scary if you didn't know him, with a stern brow, a shiny bald head, and eyes so dark they looked black. But his hugs were warm, his chili was amazing, and he had a big collection of historic stamps and coins that he let us look at whenever we wanted.

He didn't seem nervous—not that he ever did. That reassured me, because I was more willing to listen to him than anyone. "Is my mom being crazy about the Russia stuff?" I whispered.

Usually he'd smile, tease me a little. *Oh, Layla. Give the woman a break.* But he looked as serious as my mother. "Some things have gone down today. I think you and your mom should come back to the base with us."

The room felt colder. His words seemed to catch Mom off guard. "Why? Is it that bad out there?"

"I don't entirely know, and I can't disclose much anyway. But…you'll be safer at the base, whatever happens."

"Just for the night?" I asked.

He looked at me for a long few seconds before he shook his

head, and that reassurance quickly faded. I sat on the coffee table next to the yellow suitcase and the cards from our game, and I understood. Whatever was happening wasn't going to blow over.

Then something else occurred to me. "So what about Preston?"

Mom went pale. "They're so remote, I doubt anyone would get sick up there. Right?"

She turned to Sergeant Hardy like she was expecting confirmation. He shrugged stoically, trying to appease her, but he didn't sound convinced. "Maybe you should call the camp about their emergency plans."

"If something really bad happened, wouldn't they send the boys home?"

Sergeant Hardy shook his head. "I have no idea, Heather. I'm sure Preston is fine, but like I said, things are going down, and I'm not sure when or how they'd be able to get the boys home. I think you should call."

I glared. She looked between all of us, realized Sergeant Hardy meant *call now*, and took out her phone. We watched silently as she dialed the number and held it to her ear, but only a few seconds passed before she shook her head.

"Busy signal," she whispered. She hung up and tried again. Twice. Then she lowered the phone, all the blood gone from her face. "They aren't answering."

"But didn't Dad just call this morning?" I asked.

"It was very early." Mom gripped the phone tightly in both hands, and I could see it in her shifting eyes: the anxiety was setting in hard. "Maybe...maybe they all left for their excursion. Preston said they were leaving soon, didn't he? Maybe no one is there to answer." Mom nodded, reassuring herself, but I could tell she wasn't convinced.

Sergeant Hardy reached to pat her shoulder. "Well, there's nothing we can do now. I think you two should pack a bag, and—"

"I should go get him," she said suddenly. "Before things go bad."

The Hardys looked at her in shock.

But I must have looked really pissed off, because Mom scowled. "Don't give me that look, Layla. You've been wanting him to come home for months."

Sergeant Hardy spoke softly. "Heather, I don't want to scare you, but things already *are* bad, and they're only going to get worse. I don't know if it's a good idea for you to—"

"Of course I've been wanting him to come home!" I interrupted. "But he should've been home months ago. He should've never left! But now we're *all* in danger, including him, and it's your fault!"

She tightened her jaw. "That's why I'm going to go get him. I'll get him, and I'll bring him home, and it'll all be okay."

Sergeant Hardy expelled a breath. "Heather, listen to me. I'm not supposed to tell you this, but California is closing state borders tomorrow morning. If you leave, you might not be able to get back home. At least for a while."

Her eyes were pink, holding back tears. I could see that it was hitting her hard: she might not get a chance to bring him home at all. But she didn't deserve to cry over this. Over Preston. It was too late for that.

"I'll have to leave tonight, then." She looked at me. "Layla, I want you to go with Sergeant Hardy."

"No."

The thought of getting in the car with my mother, driving around like a madwoman with a survival suitcase, did not sound appealing. My mind was clouded with thoughts of Russia, of war, of bioweapon diseases and EMPs, and whatever other crap I'd heard. There were too many factors, too many confusing bits and pieces and dangly parts I couldn't fit together in my brain yet. On the base, it would be safe. There was cable TV, and chili, and *Major Ursus*, and bear hugs from Sergeant Hardy. There was the military. There was Jamal. I just wanted to crawl into bed and wake up and have it all be over.

But this was real, and only one thing felt clear: I wanted my big brother. I wanted him to be okay, and get out of that place, and be with me again.

"I'm going with you," I said.

Mom turned to Sergeant Hardy. "Mike, tell her to go to the base."

"I think *both* of you should come to the base," he said. "But I also think this is serious, and whatever happens, you should stay together. You might lose each other if you don't."

I crossed my arms and repeated myself. "I'm going with you, Mom."

She stared at me, eyes watering. Guilty eyes. But she didn't say no.

It was settled: we were going to Oregon.

Sergeant Hardy understood this and sighed. "You'll need to leave before nightfall."

He wasn't able to tell Mom anything he'd heard, so with only vague warnings, he wished us luck and headed out with Jamal; they needed him at the base. If we changed our minds, we only had to give him a call.

Before they left, Jamal darted to his backpack, pulled out his orange plastic folder, and shoved it into my arms. "I drew more pages," he said. "You have to color them while you're gone. Homework."

I held the folder to my chest and nodded, but I couldn't think of anything to say. Oregon was less than eight hours away—we'd be back in a few days at most—but it felt like I was leaving until the end of time. I didn't have any free arms, but I leaned toward Jamal. We weren't usually the hugging type, but he got the message and pulled me in.

"Stay safe," he said. "Stay away from the brain rashers."

"You too, I guess."

I felt Mom's hands on my shoulders, pulling me away from Jamal, away from one of the few places I felt truly safe. I could count those places on my fingers. The Hardys' home on the base. My bedroom when Preston was in it. My mother's childhood ranch, where we used to ride horses in the summer, back when we were young and still a family. And Jamal. Anywhere he was.

"We have to get going, Layla," Mom said. "Go pack."

The Hardys stepped out of the apartment, and Jamal gave me one small wave before his dad shut the door between us.

CHAPTER FOUR

WE DROVE IN SILENCE, the back of the Volkswagen packed with our yellow survival suitcase, overnight bags, paper sacks of whatever food Mom had scrounged up at the picked-over grocery store, and a few blankets. I held the orange folder tightly in my hands. It was late afternoon now, and we were heading into the hills.

The traffic had been heavy and anxious leaving town, with everyone trying to get home or get to stores before supplies ran out. But when we got to the country road that cut through the valley and wove into the mountains, we were practically on our own.

The mountains looked blueish in the distance, spread out at the end of a great green meadow. We passed the Kerrick Air Force base on our way out. Off in the field, I caught sight of a plane taking off and jetting into the blue expanse of sky. It had rained all day yesterday, but today was cloudless and bright. I glanced back at the city, just a blot in the distance behind us. I had such a strange feeling, but I couldn't pinpoint what. Then something dawned on me.

"Shouldn't we be going north? Oregon is north."

Mom was messing with her phone, eyes shifting between the screen and the road. "We'll go east first, then up through

Nevada. It's the same distance, but this will get us out of California faster. Darn it, this stupid phone. My map won't work."

"If we went north, we probably would've gone right by Grandma's ranch," I said.

"It doesn't matter. It's not her ranch anymore."

Mom tossed her phone down dismissively. I knew it was a touchy subject for her. Grandma was dead and buried, and the ranch had been taken by the bank instead of going to Mom like she'd always been promised. I shouldn't have brought it up.

I opened the folder to look over Jamal's new comic pages. He'd drawn them out but hadn't filled in all the speech bubbles. From what I could tell, Leah had snuck into the bunker alone and discovered more human-animal hybrids before realizing it was all a trap. She was captured and questioned by some henchman with glasses and spiky hair, but there was no sign of Major Ursus; he'd been captured separately. I reached into my backpack at my feet and pulled out my markers, which I'd grabbed as we scrambled to pack.

"You've sure been working hard on that comic book," Mom said. "What are you two going to do with it?"

I uncapped a blue marker and brought it closer to the page, but the car was vibrating too much. There was no way I'd be able to color if it would be this bumpy the whole time. I sighed and recapped it. "I don't know. Publish it, probably."

"Publishing isn't that easy."

"We'll figure it out."

Mom laughed to herself.

"What?" I said.

"It's just not that easy. Your dad tried to publish that sci-fi novel he wrote years ago and he didn't get any interest."

I grumbled and put the markers away. We were entering a more wooded area now, a sign that we were easing into the mountains. "Maybe I'll just become a publisher first, and then I can publish all my own stuff."

"Since when are you interested in publishing?"

"I'm not."

Mom was quiet for a second. "You put a lot of time into that comic."

"You already said that."

"I know. It's just that, at conferences, your teachers told me you don't always get your work done, so I thought if you took a break on the comic book, you might finish some of it."

"I thought you liked the comic book."

"Ursa Major is fine—"

"*Major Ursus.*"

"—but your grades matter more."

"Does that even matter right now, Mom? People are dying out there and you're worried about my math assignments?"

Mom had long since given up on her phone, but now her eyes flicked to the gas meter. "This will get us a little ways, but I couldn't fill up all the way. The gas station had a five-gallon limit because of the lines."

Typical of her to change the conversation when she knew she was wrong. I scoffed and put my feet up on the dash.

"Feet down, Layla." She glanced at my shoes. "Oh god, you really wore those awful things?"

I touched the toes of my Mary Janes together. "Yeah?"

"You can't walk ten feet without getting a blister."

"I'm sorry you rushed me out the door and I didn't have time to put on anything else, *Heather.*"

"Don't call me Heather. And what if something happens to the car and we have to walk across the desert?"

I laughed. "We'll be in Oregon by the middle of the night. We'll be fine. Then we can go home and I can do all my math homework, right?" Mom didn't say anything, but her hands tightened on the wheel. I ran my tongue over my braces absentmindedly. Then a horrible thought struck me. "Mom? If the world ends, how am I going to get my braces off?"

"The world's not ending, Layla. If it ends, that means we're dead, and your braces won't matter anyway."

AS WE HEADED toward eastern California and left the valley behind, the hills steepened and the pines swayed overhead. I expected the traffic to build, but we never reached a slowdown, even with the steady convoy of cars on the road. Mom said not many people would be heading down a remote road toward Lake Tahoe during a national emergency.

This area was dotted with campgrounds, hiking trails, and old gold rush towns. As we passed one campground, I saw a line of cars trying to leave, their blinkers on, waiting to turn out.

I was hit with another one of those sharp memories: camping here as little kids, Preston listening intently as Dad showed him how to start a fire. My skin getting burned by a stray ember. Preston dropping a marshmallow into the dirt and eating it anyway, laughing at Mom's expression of disgust. The world had felt bigger back then, like there was more of it. More time, more space, more fun.

"You know this area is where the Donner Party ate each other?" I said.

Mom sighed.

"It's true. They were pioneers who got stranded here on their way out west, and the winter was so bad that, like, half of them died, and the rest of them ate the bodies to survive. I learned it in school."

"I don't really want to talk about that," she said.

I rolled my eyes and put my feet back up on the dash. Up ahead, a gas station came into view, and Mom sighed in relief.

There was already a line of about ten cars there, but the station only had two pumps. *Last Chance for Gas* was written on a handmade wooden sign, nailed to the side of the small shop. The shop appeared closed, but there was a payphone, an ice machine, and a plastic display with pamphlets and maps outside. The whole place was surrounded by towering, autumn trees.

"This looks like it might take a while," Mom said, craning her neck to see the pumps over the cars in front of us.

In dismay, I spotted a grubby concrete outhouse off near the forest. "Can I get out? I have to pee."

"Be quick," Mom said.

I scampered out and ran over to the outhouse. I could smell the sewage from outside the wooden door. It was open an inch, but someone was inside, moaning. Must've eaten something bad. It didn't make me particularly excited to use this toilet, but I had to go.

I sighed and stretched my stiff legs while I waited. The sky was fading fast, pale gray-blue, the same color as Preston's eyes. I'd see him tonight. After so many months away, I'd finally see him. The thought filled my chest with warmth. I'd already been picturing how it would go: we'd drive up to his camp, and he'd come running. He'd be so happy to see me that he'd sweep me off my feet in a hug—he wouldn't even care that anyone was watching. He loved his little sister that much.

I snapped out of my daze. In the lot, Mom's car had only moved up one spot in the line, and now she was talking to another driver through her open window. She spotted me and waved. I waved back, shifting on my feet. I *really* had to pee.

"Are you almost done in there?" I said loudly at the outhouse door. No one answered. There was a strange sound aside from the moaning—almost like retching. I wrinkled my nose and stepped back.

Mom shouted at me from her open window. "Layla! Grab a map, would you?"

I took one last look at the outhouse door before I left my spot and ran over to the plastic display by the shop. The brochures immediately distracted me. Lake Tahoe, Virginia City, Bodie the ghost town. Preston and I always wanted to go to Bodie. Dad promised he'd take us one day, but that was one trip we never got around to.

I couldn't think about that right now.

I found a small road atlas and tucked it into my back pocket, then headed back for the outhouse. But the door was open wider now. A man was walking away, his blue baseball cap pulled low over his face, moving slowly like he was in pain. Or sleepwalking, almost. But something else was odd about him.

His head turned, and I realized what it was. His eyes were milky white. His skin was sallow, blistering off his cheeks like flecks of peeling paint. And his beard. It was glistening red, like he'd stuck his face in something dirty.

I was a pretty smart kid, and growing up with a mom as anxious as mine, I knew the signs of bad news. Kidnappers, human traffickers, drunk people, drug dealers, drug addicts, you name it. More importantly, I knew to stay away. To listen to that little gut feeling that tells you something is off—the feeling my mother felt almost all the time—and get out.

I abandoned the outhouse and ran back to the car.

"The guy up there said the pumps aren't working," Mom said as I got in.

The screens on the pumps were black. I peered at the overhang where two big, round lights hung down, but neither of them was turned on.

Breathing hard, I stole a glance at the dark outhouse and its open door; I still really had to pee. The bearded guy was gone, but I was *not* going back over there alone. "Hey Mom, can you park and come to the bathroom with me?"

She didn't question it. It was one of those womanly, motherly instincts, where girls just know to have each other's backs in the bathroom. She pulled into a spot in front of the shop, and as we headed toward the outhouse, I realized something was very wrong, I just couldn't place it until we got closer. That's when I saw a sandal. A sandal connected to a foot, peeking out from behind the outhouse door.

Mom pushed it open, revealing a woman collapsed on the concrete. I gasped and stepped back, but Mom immediately dropped to her knees on the grimy floor, nurse instincts kicking in.

When I saw the woman's face, my stomach rolled. Her skin was torn up, like someone had clawed at her, and there was blood everywhere. Streaking down her neck, dripping at her mouth, pooling beneath her in a dark puddle, spreading slowly. And her shoulder. It was like someone had shredded it apart, right down to the muscle, so bad her arm didn't even seem connected anymore.

The outhouse smelled sharp, like rust and innards. My stomach flipped hard, and I fought not to get sick. "What happened?"

Mom didn't hear me. She was checking the lady's pulse on her unmarred wrist, being careful not to touch the blood. Then she paled. "Oh my god," she said. She gingerly nudged the woman's head to the side to get a look at a half-moon-shaped gash right at the base of her neck. She looked up at me. "Does that look like a bite mark?"

Just as I started to connect the dots, somebody screamed outside.

We rushed out to find the bearded guy wrestling another man to the ground by the gas pumps, just yards from our car. They rolled on the asphalt, the bearded man vicious, feral, mouth gaping, the other man screaming in terror. What I'd seen on his beard—it had been blood.

People screamed and scattered from the fight, except for a couple in gym clothes who ran over. They managed to rip the bearded man away, but I didn't see what happened next. Mom grabbed me by the wrist.

"Come on," she said.

"But the lady in the bathroom—"

"She's dead. *Come on.*"

Instead of going to our car, we ran for the woods behind the station. The woods were thin and sprawling, not offering much space to hide, aside from a rocky outcropping jutting from the earth. It was just big enough to cover us if we crouched. Mom pulled me down. We pressed in close and listened to people scream.

It sank in what Mom had said. *She's dead.* The lady was dead. How had that happened? *When* had that happened? And what would've happened to me if I hadn't gone to get that map or run back to the car?

"What's wrong with that guy?" I whispered hysterically.

Mom was breathing hard, eyes dashing around the woods, looking for danger. "Just stay here for a minute until the police come."

"Did you call them?"

"My phone's in the car, but I'm sure someone else did."

We stayed for a few minutes, huddled up in the mossy dirt. Cars screeched away and people yelled, all of it echoing through the trees. I closed my eyes and covered my ears, and Mom held my shoulders with tight, bruising fingers.

Then suddenly the sounds settled. We stayed put for a few

more minutes, waiting for something else to happen. But it was over.

I took a deep breath, and Mom grasped my hand. We carefully moved out of our hiding place and headed back to the car. We passed the outhouse, and although I told myself not to, I couldn't help but peer inside.

There was no one in it. The woman was gone.

Mom tugged on my hand, keeping me moving.

Back at the gas station lot, things were quiet. Most of the people had fled, but I caught a glimpse of a few bodies on the pavement near the pumps. Mom steered me away with her arm around my shoulder and covered my eyes. "Just don't," she said.

When we got to the car, the back door was open and our groceries were gone, but neither of us paused to investigate. Mom just slammed the door, and we jumped into our seats.

As we sped away, I looked back at the bodies lying still on the pavement, covered in blood. It was the couple in gym clothes.

Mom jabbed at her phone while she drove. "Why won't this stupid thing work?"

I clicked on my seatbelt, feeling shocked. I'd never seen a dead body before. I'd never seen so much blood. I'd never seen someone attack someone else.

"Was that guy sick?" I whispered. My hands were shaking. "He was in the bathroom before. Did he...do you think he hurt that lady, too? Killed her, I mean?" I shook my head. "I don't think she was dead."

"She was."

"But she wasn't in the bathroom anymore. Where did she go?"

Mom didn't answer. She threw her phone into the cupholder between us and clenched both hands around the wheel. She drove for a long moment, staring straight ahead, breathing hard, then seemed to realize that we were on a random road, possibly going nowhere.

"Did you get that map?" she asked.

I drew the atlas from my back pocket.

Mom pulled over onto the gravelly shoulder and unfolded a page over her lap. She studied it carefully, squinting. But I couldn't hold it anymore. I got out and peed in the ditch.

"I hope I don't get poison ivy or something," I muttered when I got back in.

"Shh." Mom had the map pulled close to her face. "We're on a remote road. That means we might be safer, but we also won't have as many options for food or gas. We won't make it far on our tank, maybe another hour or two. But I say we keep heading east—"

"Mom?"

"—and see what we can find. There are campsites all around this area—"

"Mom."

"—so we can stop for the night and sleep, but we might have to sleep in the car."

"*Mother*," I said, "are you not freaked out by what just happened back there? Why are you being so calm?"

She lowered the map and looked at me. "I told you, Layla. I told you this was happening, and you didn't believe me."

"*What's* happening? You've said a million different things. How would you even know?"

She didn't answer.

With that, she pulled onto the road again and headed deeper into the hillside, the sun sinking low at our backs. After a few minutes of aching silence, she turned on the radio, but only a couple stations came through, all of them thick with static.

I still felt shaky, and my lungs didn't feel like they were getting real air. Mom glanced at me. "Are you okay?"

"Not really."

She breathed through her nose. "Let's just pretend this is one of our old roadtrips. Remember all those? We had so much fun."

I nodded. Of course I remembered. How could I forget the last time I'd actually felt happy?

"Yeah, so...let's try not to think about all this stuff and just pretend we're on a trip," she said. "We're just…going to Oregon. Right?"

I looked out the window. Easier said than done—and coming from her of all people. She thought about everything, all the time, too much. We weren't on a trip. We were going to pick up my brother from wilderness therapy, and there were violent *brain rashers* everywhere, and night was slowly closing in overhead, promising to seal us into the dark.

The road was winding, each side sheltered by trees so tall that I felt like a squashed bug. We didn't pass anything for a while, until finally, a slew of more campsite signs appeared. But Mom didn't stop. She said we had to keep moving until we found a working gas station, or we wouldn't make it over the border.

We crossed some puny, forested towns here and there, but if they even had a gas station, the pumps were out of service, the lights out, the lots barricaded. We pulled into one last town not far from the border, a little bigger than the others, but same deal. Even as evening settled, none of the lights were on. The power really was out.

"I wonder if that's why your phone isn't working," I said. As much as I didn't want to admit she was right, I couldn't help but think of our conversation earlier. "What if it was that thing?"

"What thing?"

"The pulse thing you and Jamal were talking about."

"An EMP?" she said. "Maybe."

"But wouldn't we have felt it happen?"

"No. It's just a burst of radiation. We wouldn't know until everything stopped working." Her eyes scanned the road. "We'll have to find somewhere to stay for now. In the morning, maybe things will work again, and we can call for roadside assistance. Here, let me ask this guy."

We were passing a shabby, vacant fish restaurant, where some dude in an apron was out on his smoke break. There were no cars in the lot; I wondered why he didn't just go home.

She asked him if there was *anywhere* to get gas, and he said probably not. "Maybe once you're over the state line into Nevada, but don't count on it."

My stomach sank, and by the ghostly look on Mom's face, I knew she was feeling the same thing. If we even made it over the border, it would be by the skin of our teeth.

Mom told him the situation, and he directed us to the nearest campground. "Power's out everywhere, they're saying," he said. "And you heard about all the stuff going on in the cities? People are going wild. You're smart to just hunker down for a bit. Call it a vacation."

He laughed, showing his yellow cigarette teeth.

We drove on.

CHAPTER FIVE

THE CAMPGROUND WAS DARK, the entrance enveloped by the imposing pines on either side. The tank was almost empty, and the car dinged at us, angry and hungry. I had a terrible thought that our car would die right there and we'd have to sleep in the middle of the road, but we made it to the ranger station. The ranger, a young guy who still had acne, told us to park in any open spot. The campground was nearly empty tonight.

"If you need anything, get it now," he said. "In the morning, I'm heading to another station and won't be back."

We parked at the closest site we could find, drawn in by the light of a campfire that was already raging. The car puttered to a stop.

Mom took the keys out of the ignition and sighed. "That's that. Thank god we made it."

There was a woman at the site beside us, gruff and boxy-looking. She had a single tent, lime green, set up right next to an aged, teal GMC Yukon, and was stooped in front of her fire pit, cooking a hot dog on a stick. She waved at us through the flames, smiling big.

"Let's just stay in the car," Mom said.

"But I have to pee again."

So Mom and I got out and went to find the campground bathroom, shivering the whole way, then hurried back to the site. Before we could get into the car and set up our makeshift beds, the woman was walking over.

"Hey there!" she said. "I'm Pearl. Need any help setting up camp?"

"Oh, no, we're just sleeping in the car."

Pearl laughed. She had wispy brown bangs and a thick, fluffy coat, her cheeks splotchy and beet red in the chilly air. "No tent?"

Mom shrugged and laughed nervously. "No tent."

"Shame. Well, do you need something hot to eat? And don't tell me you're cooking in the car, because I know you ain't!" Pearl laughed again, and it echoed across the trees, sounding like a rusty gate. "Come on, I don't bite, and I make a mean hot dog."

Mom looked at me. My stomach was grumbling because we'd skipped dinner, I'd barely eaten lunch at home, and our groceries had been ransacked in the panic at the gas station. I knew Mom had to be hungry, too.

"Really," Pearl said. "It's no trouble. I know things are strange out here right now, but I promise I got nothing to hide. So if you want something to eat, you're more than welcome to join me. If not, I'll leave you be."

She turned and strutted back toward the fire.

"I'm kind of starving," I whispered. "And cold."

Mom let out a long breath. "Fine. We'll warm up, but we aren't staying long."

We joined Pearl, sat on the ground, and introduced ourselves. "Heather and Layla. Such pretty names," she mused from her folding chair. "You're named for an evergreen plant, and Layla, you're named for the night."

Mom held a stick over the fire, turning her hot dog slowly. "I never knew Layla's name meant that. I just liked the sound of it."

We ate chips and baked beans. The deep forest lay at our backs, and the flames cast dancing shadows on the canopy above us. The leaves rustled, the fire snapped. The air was frigid, but I felt warm for now. Tonight in the car would be a different story.

Being on the base with Jamal, his dad, and a warm bed sounded pretty darn good right about now. I wondered what Jamal was doing. Probably reworking *Major Ursus* plotlines or pirating a scary movie on his computer. That's when I remembered it was Halloween. I should have been with Jamal at the haunted maze without a care in the world, but instead, I was here. Already missing home so much it ached. I stuck my hands close to the fire, letting the heat distract me.

Pearl raised a can of beer to her lips and looked at the sky. "Stars are bright tonight, aren't they? I grew up in Vegas. Brightest city you ever saw, and you could never see the stars. That's why I like it out here."

"You camp often?" asked Mom.

"Only all the time. I'm a retired technician, no spouse, no kids. Wouldn't have it any other way. What do you do?"

"I'm a pediatric nurse."

"And where are you two ladies heading?"

Mom hesitated, but I blurted it out. "We're picking up my brother from his wilderness therapy camp in Oregon."

"Making a little trip out of it," Mom smiled, but it didn't reach her eyes. It was the smile of a liar.

Pearl crunched on a chip. "What about you, little miss? How old are you?"

"Just turned fourteen."

"What an age to be. So eighth grade? Do you have a boyfriend? Do you play sports and whatnot?"

"Uh, no boyfriend," I laughed. "And I play volleyball, kind of." The truth was I'd been cut from the team. Not because I wasn't good enough, but because the coach said I didn't get along well enough with the teammates, and she couldn't have someone on the team who was critical at practices and wouldn't listen to instruction. Whatever that meant. "Mostly, I do other stuff. I like art, video games, movies."

"Favorite movie of all time?"

"Oh, I don't know. Have you seen *10 Things I Hate About You*?"

Pearl was just about to eat another chip. "Oh, I don't watch TV. Is it any good?"

"It's awesome."

I told her what it was about, and she laughed and nodded, but Mom was quiet. I didn't know why. I liked Pearl. After such a long, weird, horrifying day, it was nice to just sit and talk with someone normal. Someone other than my mother. Chatting with her about real life, I could still be a regular fourteen-year-old who talked about regular fourteen-year-old stuff.

When I ran out of things to say, the silence spread over us like a blanket, and Pearl took a long drink of her beer. Mom shivered and turned to me. "Do you need your coat? I put them somewhere in the back."

She'd put a lot of stuff in the back I hadn't thought we'd need, but I hadn't expected a seven-hour drive to turn into a night of sleeping in the car in the mountains in October. Maybe we *would* need that stupid survival suitcase after all.

"Yeah, thanks," I said.

Mom headed to our car, sinking into the shadows. Pearl sipped her beer. Her lips curled into a conspiratorial smile, and she tipped the can toward me, her eyes reflecting the firelight. "Want to try a sip?"

I laughed nervously. "Oh, uh, probably not."

"Mom won't know." She wiggled the can, and I could hear Mom opening car doors and rifling around far off behind me.

I thought of Preston. The first time I saw him drink alcohol was when he was fourteen, my age. I'd followed him out to the skatepark and sat on the rim of the bowl to watch him work on his tricks. He had some older friends, and I liked hanging out with them, because even though I was twelve, they didn't treat me like a baby. But one of them, Monty, had brought a six-pack of beer. I watched Preston pop one open with practiced confidence and take a deep drink like it was nothing. When it was gone, he crushed the can under his foot and caught my eye. He didn't have to tell me not to tattle—he knew I wouldn't.

When we walked home that day, he was the one who brought it up. *One beer isn't a big deal. You know that, right? I'm not, like, an alcoholic or anything.*

"One sip won't hurt, I guess," I told Pearl.

I took the can and raised it to my lips. It was gross, kind of sour and bitter, like drinking pine needles or something. I crinkled my nose and handed the can back. Pearl chuckled.

Mom returned moments later, holding both our coats. "What's so funny?"

"Nothing, just girl talk," Pearl said, scratching at her cheek. "Hey, you mind if I turn on my radio?"

"You have a signal?"

"Only emergency broadcasts get through now. I've been listening on and off all day. I wouldn't even have known anything was going on if that ranger hadn't told me."

We put on our coats and settled in to listen. Pearl had an old hand-crank radio. She turned it on, but it wasn't music. It was staticky and faint, hard to make out. I found myself leaning close to the fire to listen.

This is an official emergency alert from the United States government. Due to the ongoing viral outbreak, a nationwide state of emergency has been declared. Beginning at 7:00 AM local time on November 1, a mandatory lockdown will go into effect. All non-essential travel is prohibited under threat of arrest. Hospitals are at capacity; do not attempt to seek medical care unless directed by emergency personnel. Shelter in place and await further instructions.

My blood ran cold.

"How far are we from the border?" Mom asked Pearl.

Pearl stared into the fire, looking sleepy, probably from the beer. "Oh, I don't know, another hour?"

"Another hour," Mom echoed. She put her head in her hands. "Shoot."

"What's the matter?"

"We don't have gas."

Pearl was still looking into the fire, looking mesmerized. "Well, I could get you where you need to be. Or at least take you to a gas station. I was planning on leaving in the morning, heading back to Nevada, then who knows where else. Maybe Joshua Tree. Beautiful this time of year."

The broadcast had repeated, and I caught the end of it this time. *Avoid contact with potentially infected individuals. If you or a family member exhibits symptoms, isolate immediately. This message will repeat*, it said. Then the message started one more time.

Pearl picked up the radio and messed with the frequencies, finding nothing aside from the broadcast. Then a sudden voice cut in, corrupted with static. *If anyone can hear this, we're trapped on I-80 near the—we need help. Please, if you—* It cut out after that.

Pearl stared at the radio for a moment and switched back to

the broadcast, turning the volume low. "Well, I'll be. Looks like everyone's got their panties in a knot."

"You're not worried?" Mom asked.

"Why should I be?"

"Because there's a pandemic happening. It's making people crazy. We saw it."

Pearl nodded slowly, her eyes almost glazed over. "I ain't worried. Don't you worry, either. I'll get you to your gas station."

"Pearl, all the pumps are off. There is no gas."

Pearl leaned back in her chair and sighed calmly, like she hadn't even considered this was an issue. "You know, there was a couple from San Francisco camping here this weekend. They heard about a potential lockdown this morning before the power cut and decided to try to get back to the city. Not sure why. They're safer out here. I'm planning on staying a while, riding this out."

"You just said you were going to Joshua Tree," Mom said slowly.

Pearl frowned. "Oh. I did, didn't I?"

Mom and I exchanged a glance. Pearl's radio hissed with static. *This is an official emergency alert from the United States government. Due to the ongoing viral outbreak, a nationwide state of emergency has been declared.*

Mom's hand crept toward me. "We'd better be off to bed. Thank you for dinner."

"Anytime," Pearl said. "You let me know if you need anything else."

Mom's fingers closed over mine. As she pulled me toward the car, Pearl turned up the broadcast behind us. It was only after we climbed in and locked the doors that Mom whispered, "I think Pearl is infected."

"What? Really?"

"Did you notice her skin was rashy? I didn't notice at first because it was dark, but that's what happens as your skin starts to decay. Then I realized she seemed confused, too. It reminds me of the people at the hospital. The brain fog is an early sign before they turn."

"*Turn?*"

Mom locked eyes with me. "Remember how I told you the nurses had to sedate people?"

I nodded.

"It wasn't just because they were hallucinating, like I said. It was because they started getting violent. Like…they didn't even know what they were doing."

"Like that man at the gas station," I whispered.

"The one who killed the nurse was just a college kid, not much older than Preston. He was so sick, and when he started getting violent, they sedated him. Then his heart stopped and we thought he was gone, but…he wasn't. He came back, even worse than before. He…he turned." She chewed her lip and hit the car lock again, just to be sure. "Let's just try to sleep, okay?"

"But what happened to him?"

She looked away. "They had to put him out of his misery."

So they'd killed him. Like a rabid dog.

"Should we leave? You know, if she's…" I asked.

"And go where? We're better off locked in here. It'll be fine."

We reclined the seats as far as they would go, and Mom reached in the back for the blankets. I could still see Pearl, staring and staring into the flames, the crackle of the radio just barely audible in the distance. It wasn't comfortable, and it wasn't warm, and the darkness outside the windows was over-bearing, but I was mostly thinking about Preston now. Thinking about how if Mom hadn't forced him to camp, none of this would be happening. We'd all be safe in the apartment—or on the base with the Hardys—until this ended.

Somehow, it felt like if Preston hadn't been sent away, none of this brain rash stuff would've ever happened at all. It was karma, and it was Mom's fault. All of it. Everything in the whole world.

"Why'd you send Preston away?" I asked.

Mom was unfurling the space blanket from the survival suit-case. "You know why."

"I know what he *did*," I said. "But I don't know why that meant you had to send him away."

"JAWS is a tough place, but he's getting the help he needs. He gets to go camping and hiking, he's making friends, and—"

"Well, I think he's lying. They won't let us actually talk to him. He writes two sentences on a postcard every other week, and that's all we get. That place is terrible and you know it."

Mom put the space blanket over me, tucking it beneath my chin and around my shoulders. "Layla," she said slowly, "even if I'd wanted to bring him home earlier, I couldn't. We signed a nine-month minimum contract with the camp, and to break the contract early, both your dad and I had to sign. And your dad already paid for the camp in full, so he wouldn't do that."

"But I just don't get it. Dad never cared about what Preston did, and then all of a sudden he freaked out and shipped him off. Would you ship *me* off if you got pissed enough?"

She sat back in her seat and let out a long, tired breath. "What happened with your brother was very serious, and I'd hope to god something like that never happens to you. All of this was for his own good. You have to stop questioning me on everything."

I rolled onto my side bitterly, eyes out the window.

"We're going to get to him, okay?" Mom said. "We will."

I DRIFTED off to sleep eventually. I dreamed about Preston, and then I dreamed we were stuck outside in a snowstorm and Mom wouldn't let us inside. In the dream, we lived in a house. Dad's house, in Colorado Springs. The snow was up to my neck.

Sometime in the night, I was jolted awake by a deafening crack.

I sat up, heart pounding.

Mom was awake too, staring out the windshield. Across the site, the fire had died down, just embers now, a blur of orange through the condensation on the glass. I couldn't tell if Pearl was still out there.

"Stay quiet," Mom whispered. "I think that was a gunshot."

We lay there, listening, but there were no more sounds. Just the wind rustling the leaves, the distant call of an owl. Mom reclined in her seat again.

"It must've been a hunter. Try to go back to sleep."

But I couldn't close my eyes. The shadows seemed longer, the night colder. I didn't know what time it was, but I desperately hoped it was close to dawn.

CHAPTER SIX

MY FAMILY USED to be way more normal. At least, that's how it felt to me, though I'm not sure anyone can be entirely normal. But there was a time when my mom wasn't such a wreck, and my dad was still there, and I didn't stay up at night worrying about my big brother. There was a time when I didn't feel so alone.

Way back when, we lived in a real house. It wasn't that big, but we had our own cozy rooms and a backyard where Mom planted all sorts of flowers. She knew way too much about flowers. The amount of sunlight they needed, and the pH conditions of the soil, and how to prune them without killing them.

Her parents had taught her about them on the ranch, where the wildflowers were as plentiful as stars. Mom was smart; she started community college at sixteen and left the ranch to become a nurse, then met Dad right as she finished her degree. They married quickly and moved to the city, but she always missed the meadows back home. That's why she brought the meadow to our narrow yard. While Dad worked, she'd sit out there and lose herself in the garden.

It seemed like the only time Mom felt like herself was when we were on the road.

When I was young, California sprawled in my mind, longer

and wider than I could fathom. My parents thought taking us places would make us more well-rounded, but we never seemed to get off the West Coast. Dad said there was plenty to see right around us—no ritzy hotels or airline tickets needed. But Mom was happier on those trips, when she had a chance to escape the yard and the messy house and the endless days inside it. We'd go a few times a year, driving down the sun-bleached highways: sometimes west to the cliffside beaches, sometimes southeast to Yosemite, and often north through the mountains to my grandmother's ranch.

Grandma owned a trail riding business for tourists, with about twenty horses. It was perfect there, with acres of rolling pastures and wildflowers, and cold, clear lakes between mountain ridges. The sky seemed more vast than it did back home.

Mom never got along well with her mother—they always butted heads, Grandma nitpicking Mom, Mom being too wounded about everything—but she'd still take us up there often. She wanted us to learn to ride the way she had when she was a girl. To build character. To connect with something wilder. She dreamed that one day we'd move up there for good, that she'd inherit the ranch like she'd always planned, but for now, we'd visit when we could. We'd sleep in Grandma's creaking, wooden house and help her staff with the chores, and when tourists came for their trail rides, we'd walk around like we owned the place.

Preston had a knack for horses. He could ride any in Grandma's stable, even the stubborn old gray mare that didn't like anybody. He was gentle with them in a way he wasn't with anything else in the world. We used to talk about running the ranch together someday, and how we'd add on to the house, and breed the horses, and raise chickens. But that dream died quickly.

In the span of a year, Mom and Dad divorced, Grandma died of lung cancer she hadn't told anyone about, and the ranch was foreclosed. I grew out of the horse stuff pretty fast. I grew out of a lot of things that year.

Preston grew out of everything but his anger.

He wasn't always bad. He never really had been. He was lean and lanky, with wild golden-brown curls and elbows always scraped up from skateboarding. He liked to fix things, take them apart, and see how they worked. Everything was an experiment to him, even people. He liked to test boundaries just to see what would happen, just to see if he could get out of the mess he'd made. If he got something in his head, there was no talking him out of it.

No one really *got* my brother. He was a serious kid with a habit for trouble, but it was hard for me to see the bad in him. Not when I always saw so much good. He was rough around the edges, but he softened for me.

Sometimes I thought if we'd lived somewhere else, he would've been okay. Like if we'd lived on the ranch, we could've ridden horses and built forts and explored in the tall grass by the stream. But we didn't live there. We lived on the outskirts of a city where the population was swelling, rent kept climbing, and the schools were so crowded that they crammed kids into trailers and called them classrooms. Preston's playground was the skatepark, the abandoned strip mall on the edge of town, the patches of woods riddled with trash and needles.

He'd rarely let me tag along, but he'd often come home with new bumps and bruises, let me sit on his bed, and tell me about the crazy things he and his friends had gotten into that day. He'd tell me anything. He was the only one who did. Although his adventurous spirit only ever got him into trouble, he developed an instinct to look out for things, to protect. From a young age, that's just who he was.

Dad had never worried about him. Dad never worried about anything. Though he worked hard at his job, he still made time for us. He'd let us play hooky all the time, and we'd go to the arcade or to get sushi, or even go all the way out to the coast sometimes. I asked him why he had to work so much, and he said because one day he was going to buy us a big house with a swimming pool and a stable so Mom could have horses again. I believed him.

The last trip we ever took with him was to Virginia City when I was ten and Preston was newly thirteen. Preston got to bring his friend Monty, and Dad let them wander the town alone for the afternoon. Mom didn't like that. They argued about it while the three of us got ice cream, and my cookies and cream tasted like freezer burn and divorce. Mom and Dad split just three weeks later.

But on that trip, everything still felt okay.

We camped there for a couple nights. Preston and Monty taught me how to make a perfect s'more. They told me scary stories to freak me out before bed. And it worked. I lay awake that night, staring at the tent ceiling and listening to the summery buzz of the woods. Preston put his arm over me and told me none of it was real. And even if it was, he wouldn't let the ghosts get me. Not without a fight, at least.

My brother was always a fighter. He fought with our parents, he fought at school, he fought at the skatepark. Especially after Dad left. Because Dad was the one who taught him to stick up for himself, to hold his own, to do what he wanted. And then Dad turned around and did the same thing for himself, leaving us all behind.

Still, I never worried about my brother. I knew as much as he fought, he had things to fight for, too. He had me. So no matter how restless or angry he got at the world, I could always reel him back in.

But things change so fast sometimes you don't even realize it's happening. Suddenly you're alone, and even though you've grown, the world feels even wider and scarier than ever. Maybe it was a part of being fourteen. When you're fourteen, it feels like you're the only kid in the entire world who feels the way you do. Like everyone else has some guide that they didn't tell you about. I tried to be like my dad and Preston, not letting things get to me so much, but I knew deep down I was my mother. Hiding out in the garden of my own company, pretending the loneliness wasn't there, but not really trying to fight it, either. I guess I'd never been much of a fighter.

Maybe my family was never normal. But at least, back then, it was easier to pretend.

———————————

PRESTON GOT in a car accident in mid-spring, when the roads were slick with rain and his head was fuzzy from a night spent drinking by the river. He was only fifteen. He crashed Monty's car into a metal barrier, and the car flipped on its side. They both lived, but Monty was paralyzed from the waist down, and Preston was in the hospital for a week. Preston never forgave himself for that night.

It was so bad that Dad flew out from Colorado Springs, and he spent hours in that hospital room. Mom only let me visit once. She felt like Preston's delinquency would rub off on me somehow. As if I'd walk into the hospital, see him all banged up with a bandage over half his face, and go *oh, yes, I definitely want to drink alcohol and crash my friend's car.*

I sat in his hospital room and watched him sleep. When a girl from my class was in the hospital with appendicitis the year before, we'd all made her a card, but there were no cards for Preston. I found a scrap of paper and drew him a dog holding balloons, then crumpled it up because it was horrible.

Through the crack of the door, I saw Mom and Dad in the hallway, speaking in low voices. "He needs help," Dad said. "More help than we can give him."

"He can get help here. He needs to be with me."

"Heather, you're always adamant that you can do this on your own, but you have to admit this is getting out of hand. And I know I haven't made it any easier by moving, but I told you before that he could live with me—"

"What, so you could let him go off and do whatever he wants?" Mom said.

"He's already doing whatever he wants!"

"*You* raised him that way."

"I raised him to hold his own. And yeah, he's had his rough patches, but any real trouble he's gotten into has been under *your* care. You don't have a grip on him, and he's becoming a danger to you and Layla."

Dad happened to glance over and saw me listening. He quickly closed the door, sealing off the rest of the conversation, but I'd heard enough.

PRESTON WAS different when he got home from the hospital. For one thing, he had a new scar across his eye. He was grounded until the end of the century, and had to go to some alcohol education program, and wouldn't be able to get his license when he turned sixteen. But something else had changed about him. He was catastrophically quieter. He stopped talking to Mom, and he barely talked to me.

Though something had darkened in him, he wasn't dangerous. I knew he wasn't.

Dad stuck around for a couple weeks, insisting Mom needed help, but she was too stubborn to accept it. Their bickering was getting to Preston. Mom tried to be gentle with him, but he was constantly on edge, blowing up at her for the smallest things. The night before Dad was supposed to leave, it all escalated into an argument so bad that Mom took me to Margie's apartment next door, who made me sit on the couch and watch TV at full volume. It was the show *Castle.* I watched it blankly, feeling like someone had pulled a bag over my head.

When things settled, Dad came to get me. Preston had locked himself in our room, so Mom made me a bed on the couch. In the morning, Dad flew back to Colorado Springs, Preston emerged, and things became surprisingly calm.

I should've known it wouldn't last.

The night they took Preston was the worst night of my life. Worse than sleeping in a car, stranded at a campground with panicked people infected with brain rash. Worse.

It was a couple months after the car accident, just after he'd gotten his cast off. I was sleeping lightly that night, stretched out on top of my sheets since the third floor got so hot in the summer. A *bang* woke me up, the sound of a door flying open. Before I could even sit up, there were two men in our bedroom— big, gruff men in black clothes. I screamed, and Preston screamed, and they pulled him out of his bed by his armpits. He didn't have a shirt on, just shorts.

I cried out for Mom, thinking they'd broken in to take us, drag us away and kill us. But they didn't touch me. I stayed frozen as they pulled Preston into the living room, then I heard his voice cry, "Mom, what's happening?"

And Mom's voice said, "I'm sorry, I'm sorry. It's for the best. I'm sorry."

I leapt out of bed and ran into the other room just as they were hauling him out the front door. Mom pulled me close, like it would make me feel safe or explain it all away. Preston was still screaming as they took him down the hall, and people peered out from their apartments in their pajamas to see what all the racket was about.

Mom grabbed my hand and pulled me after them, down the stairs, and into the warm May night. We watched them shove Preston into a stocky green van in front of the complex. It had *JAWS* written on the side, which I'd soon learn meant Jackpot Alternative Wilderness School in Jackpot, Oregon. I didn't care what it was. It was taking away my brother.

The men slammed the door, and Mom kept apologizing, even after they drove off.

I sat on the ground in shock. Mom knelt and wiped my cheeks, hands trembling. "It's okay, baby. It's okay. I'm sorry—I told them not to go in there until I could wake you, but they didn't listen. They didn't listen."

I cried so hard that snot ran from my nose. Mom held me in the parking lot, and I let her, but I didn't want her. I wanted to understand what had just happened to my brother, and why she seemed to be a part of it.

I didn't think I'd ever be able to forgive her for it.

CHAPTER SEVEN

AFTER THE GUNSHOT, I didn't think I'd fall asleep again. But the next thing I knew, the forest was bathed in icy, gray light and the birds were singing. I rubbed my eyes and sat up stiffly, and that's when I saw the streak of red across the windshield.

I shrieked.

Mom gasped awake. "What, what happened?"

I pointed. The windshield was covered in frost, but there was something lying on the bottom edge: a furry, brownish lump and an unmistakable smear of blood.

"What on earth?" Mom said. It was hard to see outside with the frost, so she popped the door. "Stay here."

But I wasn't about to let her go out there alone. I shoved on my Mary Janes and climbed out after her. We circled the front of the Volkswagen and peered at the lump. It was a squirrel, torn up and bloody, most definitely dead.

"Maybe a hawk dropped it," I said, feeling sick.

"I told you to stay in the car."

Mom scanned the campground, the empty, small plots, the frosty grass, the vivid orange and deep green of the trees. The air smelled like smoke, but there was no one around.

"We should try to catch the ranger before he leaves," she decided.

As we walked away from the car toward the narrow road, I noticed something else: there was more blood smeared along the passenger door, right above the handle.

I tugged Mom to a stop. "Is that…?"

"A handprint," she said. She stared for a second, thinking the same thing I was—someone had tried to get in last night. She grabbed my arm. "Stay close."

We walked to the ranger's station, and in the daylight, I could see it was just a small, brown cabin along the road. Mom peeked through the window, but it seemed empty. We went around to the door in the back and yanked it open. Unlocked.

"Hello?" she called.

We stepped into an office that smelled like old wood and

smoke. Through a doorway, we could hear someone rifling around inside the next room.

"Hello?" Mom repeated, louder.

The rifling stopped, and the ranger burst into the office with a can of bear spray, cocked and ready. "Stay where you are!"

Mom and I stepped back, but at the sight of us, he relaxed a little. "You made it through the night," he exhaled. "Good. No, no—don't come any closer."

"What's your problem? We're not infected," I said.

"Can't be too careful."

"Well, then maybe you should lock the door, dummy."

Mom whacked me on the shoulder, then pleaded with the ranger. "Listen, we were just wondering if you have a working phone. A landline, maybe? A radio?"

He shifted, and I realized he had a duffel bag hanging on his shoulder. The bear spray was still aimed in our direction. "Phone line's dead," he said. His lips curled into something that was half snarl, half smile. "So is that lady from the site next to you, by the way."

Mom let out a little gasp. "Pearl? What happened?"

He breathed heavily, unsteady. "In the middle of the night, this guy ran to the station screaming somebody had attacked him near the bathrooms. I went looking, and when I found her, she was next to your car, blood all over her mouth. She chased me into the woods, looking...looking *wild* or something. I've never seen a look like that on a human face."

I glanced at his arm—not the one holding the bear spray, but the one resting over the duffel bag. The edge of a white bandage peeked out from beneath his khaki sleeve. I thought of the woman in the outhouse, the bite on her neck.

"I have," Mom said. "She was infected."

"Well, I shot her," said the ranger. "And I'm not afraid to do it again. I have to go." He cocked his head. "Step aside."

Mom put her hands up. "But—"

"Move!"

We skittered out of his way, and with one hand still on the

bear spray trigger, he backed out the door. "Don't try to follow me, you understand?"

"We weren't planning on it," Mom muttered.

After he ran out, Mom and I waited there for a minute, just to be sure he wasn't coming back. When the sound of his truck engine had faded down the gravel road, Mom squeezed my arm, turned to the desk against the window, and started opening drawers.

We dug through everything, searching for any line of communication. There was nothing, and if there had been, the ranger had taken it with him. All we found were camping records, bug spray, and first-aid. In the back bedroom there were two bare cots and a little stove. Everything else was gone.

"I think he got bit," I said. The words felt like rocks in my throat, hard to get out.

Mom was pressing the landline to her ear, listening for a signal, but she must not have heard anything. She slammed the phone back into its holder and grabbed the first-aid kit from the desk. "Let's go, Lay."

I followed her outside to the road. "Go *where*?"

"We have to find someone to give us a ride."

"Maybe we should try to get home," I said. "Maybe someone is going back that way."

"We need to get across the border. We have about two hours before the travel ban is set in place, so we need to get moving."

I stopped walking. "I want to go *home*."

Mom turned. "We can't. This is getting bad, and we don't know how long it'll last. If we don't get to Preston now, we might not get another chance. Ever." She walked on ahead, her feet crunching on fallen leaves. When she didn't hear me follow-ing, she stopped to look back. "I gave you the option to stay behind. You made your choice. Now come on."

We took the long way around the campground road, keeping our eyes peeled for anyone who could help us, but of the few campsites that were occupied, no one was out. There were some fires crackling, a dog tied on a long leash, a running car. But no one came out of their tents, their vans, their tiny, rusted campers. Everyone was in hiding. We did see one family urgently packing their stuff into a sprinter van, their little toddler boy sucking his thumb and watching us as we walked by.

"Hey, do you have a working phone?" Mom called out.

The father scooped up the boy with wild fear in his eyes, took his wife's hand, and darted into their van. They slid the door shut with a bang.

"Do you think everyone knows about the outbreak by now?" I whispered, feeling strangely watched.

"They must have heard the broadcast."

Back at our site, Pearl's fire was reduced to ash, but all her stuff was still sitting there, as if she wasn't gone. With a shiver, I wondered where her body was—where she'd been killed—and I had the sudden urge to hold my mother's hand. I quickly shook both thoughts away.

Mom stood in front of the fire pit, surveying Pearl's belongings. Her tent, her folding chair, her empty can of beer, and a hot dog package—all the leftover hot dogs eaten up by animals by now. My stomach got queasy.

Mom unzipped the tent, revealing a sleeping mat and a ratty old backpack. As she went through the backpack, I didn't question it. We were scavengers now. This is what it had come to in less than a day.

She pulled out a set of car keys. "I found a ride."

"We're stealing her car?"

"She's not going to use it, is she?" Mom left the tent and went to the Yukon. "I think she'd want us to take it. Go to our trunk; I put some cleaning supplies in there."

We spent ten minutes wiping down the interior of Pearl's car with disinfectant wipes. There wasn't much food, and most of it had been opened. Mom said not to touch it, or any of her other stuff, or we might catch the virus. I felt a pang in my gut when I thought of the beer I'd sipped from last night. A beer Pearl's mouth had touched.

"Mom, what's a bloodborne pathogen?"

"It means it's spread by blood or bodily fluids."

"Or, like...spit?"

"Sometimes," Mom said. "If the spit's been exposed to blood somehow. But you're more likely to get it from getting bitten, scratched, or punctured by something that's been exposed to the pathogen. With this virus, there's so much we don't know; it could spread in ways that we don't even see yet. We just need to be overly cautious."

She tasked me with grabbing stuff from our car while she took Pearl's stuff out, but all I could think about was that I was going to die. I was going to get the brain rash and *die*. All because I'd sipped a beer, which hadn't even tasted good.

"Layla, come on. We have to move."

We carried over our stuff and tossed it in the back of the Yukon. All we had were two backpacks, blankets, and that stupid, stupid, stupid yellow suitcase. Mom added the ranger's first-aid kit to it but removed a sharpened kitchen knife wrapped in a dishcloth. She put the knife in the cupholder beside her.

"Just to be safe," she said, turning the key in the ignition.

The gas tank was fairly full, enough to get us over the border and then some. Maybe the power would work in Nevada. Maybe *something* would work in Nevada. This was our silent hope, but neither of us voiced it as we left the campsite. I tried not to imagine Pearl's body in the woods, bloody at the mouth, eyes open, staring at the sky. It was too much.

We were just out of the campground, only a mile or so down the road, when we passed a smoking truck smashed into a tree. I sat up straight to get a better look and realized it was a park ranger's truck; I could just make out a ranger slumped in the driver's seat. It looked like the one from the station.

Mom pretended not to see.

AS WE NEARED THE BORDER, Mom needed me to navigate. I'd never used a paper map in my life, but I kind of liked the realness of it, even if it stressed me out. It was like we were two characters in an old movie, two girls in a stolen car, escaping something bad.

"I feel like we're in that movie Grandma used to like. *Thelma and Louise*," I said.

"They drive off a cliff in the movie," Mom said.

"Well, I've never actually seen it."

I moved my foot and realized one of Pearl's bags was still underneath the passenger seat. It was a small, black bag with something heavy inside. I opened it and pulled out a gun.

Mom gasped and swerved, then wrenched the wheel to correct it. "Put that down!"

"Well, I didn't know it was in there!"

"Obviously, Layla. Just put it down, *please*."

"Okay, okay," I mumbled, but instead of sliding the gun back under the seat, I reached back and tucked it carefully into Mom's backpack. "We might need it."

"I hope not."

"We can use it to hunt, at the very least."

"It's a handgun, Layla. Do you know how to hunt with a handgun?"

"I mean, I don't know how to hunt at all."

"Exactly. Don't touch it."

We drove south, closer to Lake Tahoe, trying to avoid Reno; with the mountains flanking it, there was no way around Reno, only through, and Mom was certain the highways were grid-locked. The detour would add an hour to our trip, but it would be safer to avoid the city.

I believed her; every so often, we'd pass a crash on the side of the road where cars had careened into guardrails or ditches, left horribly mangled. They were electric vehicles, I realized after a while. Whatever had happened to the phones and the internet had affected the electric cars too, making them crash mid-drive. I hated thinking that someone had done this intentionally, and that there was no way of knowing who.

The road twisted through narrow passes, carved into the

pine-covered slopes. We wound our way through, and I peered over the guardrails into the wooded ravines, and out at the lake when it came into view. In some stretches, the road tapered into one usable lane, clogged with more crashed or abandoned cars. Mom drove slowly, the asphalt crackling under our tires.

Other cars had been abandoned entirely, doors flung open, belongings scattered on the faded asphalt—we even saw a child's car seat toppled onto its side. In more populated areas, Mom had to drive slowly to weave through the mess. Some cars had shattered windows, like they'd been broken into, and it made me think of our stolen groceries, the panic someone must have felt to have been so desperate. One car we passed was on fire, just a burning husk.

But not everyone was gone. We drove by people here and there, wandering between cars and houses and buildings. From a distance, we couldn't tell if they were rashers or just lost, but we didn't stop to find out.

As we made our way along the Lake Tahoe shore towns, it was easy to imagine we were here under different circumstances. To swim, camp, go on a boat. The lake was deep blue under the rising sun, the pines tall and proud. It made me sad.

When we reached the state border at Kings Beach, traffic slowed to a crawl. Mom craned her neck to try to see ahead of the cars that stretched before us. "I see military trucks," she said. "I think this is some kind of border patrol."

They'd set up barricades along the road to keep people from cutting through, but as the Yukon crawled closer, we noticed the soldiers were just waving people through—they didn't even check our IDs, like they didn't care where we went, as long as it was before 7:00 AM. We crossed into Nevada with ten minutes to spare.

Once in Nevada, Mom pulled over on the shoulder of the road and snatched the map from me to get a better look. Then we were off again, curling around the lake and cutting through the forest.

As we moved further into the state, the terrain changed fast, from forested, snow-capped mountains to dry, sprawling desert covered in brush and stone. The landscape was sparse and unpopulated for a while. I closed my eyes and tried to sleep.

We made it to another town by mid-morning. The place was dead, everybody hunkered inside their homes, but at least the roads were empty. We checked a gas station at the edge of town —nothing. Mom stood at the dark pump, just staring at it, willing the power to come back on and the screen to come to life. Wind rattled the metal sign of the station shop. Desert dust blew at our feet. It was futile.

It was sinking in that we might never make it to Oregon, but I held my tongue from saying *I told you so*. I was a part of this now.

We lingered in the faded lot under the gas station awning and ate granola bars from the survival suitcase. Mom popped a Xanax while I looked out over the low, brown mountains. I'd always hated the desert. The parched earth, the blazing sun. It made me feel so small. Only the mountains far in the distance gave any indication that the desert could end.

"Does Colorado have travel bans, too?" I asked.

"All I know is what I heard on the radio last night. Why?"

"Maybe we should get to Colorado Springs." I saw the flabbergasted look on her face and backtracked. "After we get Preston, I mean. We could find Dad, and he could keep us safe until this ends. You said it yourself: you don't know how long it'll last."

"Do you know how far Colorado Springs is from here?"

"Dad has guns and a big house, and I think his rich friend has an airplane. It might be an option if we can't get back home. That's all I was saying."

Mom shook her head. "Let's just focus on one thing at a time, alright?" She started the car again. "We have to keep going."

"Do you not want us to be with Dad or something?"

"Why would you think that?"

"You never want us to see him."

She released a short, impatient breath. "It's impractical, that's all. He lives far, and that was his choice. We can't change that, especially not now."

She drove away from the town and back into the wilderness of the desert. We didn't pass many cars. It was a little surprising to me after what we'd seen by Lake Tahoe; I thought everyone would be trying to get somewhere. I guess there was nowhere to go. Nowhere to escape to. If the virus was in California and Nevada, it was surely everywhere by now.

I wanted to color my comics, but it was too bumpy, so I resorted to drawing on my arms in blue ink instead. Flowers, planets, tiny animals, and looping, swirling designs. Mom looked annoyed, but didn't stop me. With no music, nothing to read, and nothing to talk about, I was going crazy, and she knew it.

We eventually came to another town, if you could even call it that. It was more like a scatter of buildings with metal roofs and walls bent out of place. I was fairly certain most of the buildings were abandoned. Mom drove slowly. There were a few cars parked here and there, and a post office with a faded flag rippling out front, but no signs of life.

It was only when we were at the far edge of that town that I spotted a man. He was old and sunburnt, his hair bright white, and he was standing in front of a car with a very flat tire. He waved at us with his long, wrinkly arms as we passed. Not a hello wave, but a *please help me* wave.

Mom drove on.

"Mom, did you see that old guy?" I asked. "Maybe we should stop."

"That's not a good idea."

"I think he just needed help with his tire. He looked kind of weak or something," I said.

"He could be anyone. He could be waiting on the side of the road for someone to stop and then kill them. Do you want that to happen? Didn't think so."

"Not everybody in the world is evil, Mom."

"Yes, but right now, the way things are, everyone in the

world is potentially dangerous. *Everyone.* So I'm not taking any chances."

"You never do," I mumbled.

She scoffed. "What's that supposed to mean?"

"I mean you're always so quick to think the worst of people."

Her face hardened. "Just drop it, okay?"

"Fine."

It was quiet for a second. The engine grumbled and the tires spun, and Mom breathed in and out through her nose, trying to be calm. She often did that when she was stressed. Breathe in deep, let it out slowly. She'd been doing it a lot since we'd left home.

"You just don't know how the world works," she said quietly. "You're a kid. It's a mom's duty to protect her kids, okay?"

"Right, like you did such a good job protecting Preston."

"*Layla.*"

"I'm just saying. You're acting like you're doing this amazing thing by going to get your kid, but the only reason you're out here is because the world is falling apart. You didn't care enough to bring him home before. You and Dad made up your minds about him, and you threw him away. If all this brain rash stuff wasn't happening, you'd let him rot at JAWS for another four months, right? Can you at least admit that?"

"JAWS was an intervention for—"

"For his own good, yeah, yeah. Whatever," I said. But then I was hit with a horrible thought. I'd been having a lot of those lately, and it was turning me into my mother. "What if he isn't even there?"

Mom didn't respond right away. She stared on ahead for a long moment, squinting in the eastward sun. "What?"

"What if they took the kids somewhere else? You know, since they're minors? What if they took them to a town or a military outpost or something? Or…what if he's infected?"

"Why would you even say that?"

"Because what if? He could be dead for all we—"

"*Layla Elizabeth Wise,*" she snapped. "Stop it. I'm serious. I'm trying really hard to hold it together here, and you can't get in my head like that. We're going to find him. So stop saying stuff like that. Please."

I folded my arms and slumped in my seat. "I'm just trying to be realistic, Mother."

She didn't reply. Her silence was thick and burning, like smoke.

I wanted to say so much more, but I didn't have to. She already knew what I was thinking. Things felt bad, in the kind of way you know they're only going to get worse, so the least I could do was shut my mouth.

PART II
THE DESERT

CHAPTER EIGHT

WE RAN out of gas in the middle of the desert.

We had no choice but to stop at a neglected farmers market on the side of the road, because it was the only building we'd passed for miles. As we got out of the car, Mom muttered about checking for someone who could help us, even though we both knew it was unlikely. I kept thinking, *I bet that old man had a working phone and a big jug of gasoline and he was just waiting to give it to the first person who helped him with his flat tire.*

The market was a small wooden building painted green, with a red-striped awning that stuck out against the barren landscape. The awning flapped hard in the wind, faded from years of over-bearing Nevada sun. Beneath the awning, there were crates for produce, but they were all empty aside from a few pieces of sun-rotted fruit. Flies buzzed by our ears.

"Looks pretty hopeless to me," I said. I could feel a blister forming on my heel, but I didn't reach down to adjust my shoe until Mom turned her back.

"Let's look around anyway," Mom replied, walking toward the crates. "What else are we going to do?"

She scoured the stands for salvageable food while I went into the building to search for a payphone in hopes that something, somewhere in this hellscape worked. I found one in the back near a row of empty shelves, hanging beside a tattered map on the wall. Overhead, high, grimy windows were left open, letting dust blow in. I held my breath as I picked up the heavy black phone, but no sound came through.

I glanced at the map. It was a dusty, white picture of the entire state, and there was a small, blue star toward the north. *You are here.* The closest big town was called Winnemucca.

Mom walked in, holding a plastic package of something orange. "I found dried mango," she said. Her face scrunched. "Any luck?"

I put the phone back into its holder and shook my head.

MOM HAD FOUND a pamphlet by the cashier's counter that read *Winnie's Wild West Escape.* It was a faux Wild West town, complete with mini golf and a hotel, just a mile or so up the road. It sounded promising—more than being stranded at an empty farmers market, at least—so we gathered our stuff, left the Yukon behind, and started walking.

My feet were killing me by the time Winnie's Wild West Escape came into view. It was a gated venue, but the gate was wide open, creaking back and forth. Beyond it, there was a newly paved street with rows of buildings on each side, all novelty storefronts or restaurants with raised wooden porches and saloon doors. Nobody was around. It would've felt like we were inside an old cowboy movie if it weren't for a bright sign saying *Gold Rush Mini Golf* up ahead.

"Look," Mom said, pointing past the sign.

She was referring to the building that stood imposingly at the very end of the street. It was built of wood with wraparound porches on all three levels, designed to look weathered and old even though it didn't seem fully finished; there were construction vehicles abandoned in the sun beside it, and a pile of gravel out front instead of any landscaping. A large banner hung off the side that read, *Coming Soon: Winnie's Wild West Inn.*

"Let's see what we can find here, and then we'll check out the inn. It might be a good place to stay the night," Mom said.

She stepped up onto the nearest porch, her white sneakers tapping on the smooth planks of wood. The porches were so new they didn't even creak, but even so, everything was covered in a layer of desert dust. Mom wiped a clean spot onto the nearest window so we could look inside.

There was a darkened neon sign hanging down that said *Last Stop Cowgirl*. It was an upscale Western boutique; all the displays were still stocked with cowboy hats, glossy leather boots, feathered jewelry, knit shawls. I spotted a particularly pretty tan hat hanging from a rack with a turquoise band braided around it.

"Can we go in?" I asked.

"Not right now. We need to find someone to help us."

"Find *who*? Nobody is here."

Mom ignored me and walked down a few storefronts to a novelty mercantile. The door was locked, but the large front window was shattered, so she carefully stepped inside. I peered in after her, working a piece of dried mango out of my braces that I'd eaten on the walk over. Many of the shelves were empty; it had only been a few days and everyone was already scavenging. We were no better.

That being said, who cared if I nabbed a cute hat?

While Mom was hunting around in the mercantile, I backtracked to the boutique. I was prepared to break a window if I had to, but I was pleasantly surprised to find the door unlocked —whoever was here had left in a hurry. I checked the cash register first, but it was empty. I didn't really need valuables anyway, but it was my instinct to take what I could in this new world. That couldn't be the same as stealing.

Preston had shoplifted things before. He and I had stopped at the convenience store on our way home from school once, and he told me to ask the cashier where the bathroom was while he took two energy drinks from the fridge and tucked them into the pockets of his shorts. It was the only time I'd ever seen him steal, but he did it with such ease that I was sure it wasn't his first or last. That night, I was so amped up on caffeine that I stayed up all night sweating, and Mom thought I was sick. Preston stifled laughter while she fussed over me and took my temperature.

I moved toward the back of the store to the souvenir section. There were Nevada-themed snow globes and carved desert animals, cheap beaded jewelry, totem bracelets, woven baskets, fake turquoise keychains. Everything was supposed to look like it was made by local Native American tribes, but the tags on them said *Made in China*.

My Mary Janes rubbed against my socks as I wandered to the hats and shoes up front. I browsed the rows of cowboy boots until I found a pair that was my size, light brown with thin white embroidered flowers. I found a pack of thick socks, too, and sat on the floor to try everything on. The socks were soft and cushioned, and the boots were smooth on the inside. I grinned. They fit perfectly.

I tucked my Mary Janes into my backpack and headed for the door, but on my way out, I reached for that beautiful tan cowgirl hat I'd seen through the window, the one with the turquoise braid. It was a little big on me, but it was suede-soft and smelled like fresh leather. To top it all off, I grabbed a plastic gun from a bin by the door as I headed outside.

I crept back to the mercantile, stepped through the shattered window, and burst into the room with my plastic gun raised. "Stick 'em up!"

But Mom was nowhere to be seen. There was a staircase leading to the second floor, so I climbed up and found Mom putting jars of artisan pinto beans into her backpack like a madwoman.

I edged closer and yelled, "There ain't enough room in this town for the two of us!"

Mom jumped so violently that she dropped the jar, sending glass, beans, and water across the floor. "Damnit, Layla," she said. But when she looked at me, she cracked a reluctant smile. "Very cute."

I did a twirl. "I know."

"All you need now is a horse and a cow or two."

"I could've worn this to Grandma's ranch."

"She would've loved that." Mom brushed off her dusty hands. "Alright, you better go put that stuff back. We need to keep moving."

"Why? No one is coming back for it."

"Because it's stealing."

I gave her a look. "Mom, you stole someone's car this morning. Plus, it's, like, the end of the world. No one is gonna miss one hat. Especially because no one is ever gonna shop here again, probably."

Mom turned back to the shelf and took the last jar. "We don't know that. Things could go back to normal any day."

"Yeah, but you don't really believe that." I tossed the plastic gun into a nearby empty barrel labeled for peach rings, but I kept the hat and boots on.

Mom held up a metal canister. "I found some wildflower tea. *Made from real Nevada wildflowers.* Interesting, huh?"

"Ew."

"What, you don't want to drink flower juice? More for me." She slipped the canister into her bag and sighed. "Alright, there's nothing else in here. Let's go look for water. Stay close this time."

Despite her request, I couldn't help my curiosity. When we headed to a grill next door called *The Iron Skillet*, I discreetly slipped away again and wandered a couple storefronts down. I found myself inside an ice cream parlor with yellow wallpaper and a long wooden bar counter. Everything in the ice cream display was melted into a spoiled, goopy mess, but when I went behind the counter, I found a few bags of unopened toppings. Score.

Feeling accomplished, I took bags of chopped peanuts, rainbow sprinkles, and butterscotch chips and returned to the grill. I ran right into Mom in the doorway.

She was spooked. "God, Layla. I told you not to wander."

I beamed and held up the bags of toppings. "Look what I found."

"I'm serious. You could've been—" She shook her head, then took my wrist and pulled me toward the buildings across the street. "Forget it. Come on."

I rolled my eyes. "I was just trying to help."

"You don't need to help. You need to stay where I can see you."

We went into a saloon. I expected it to be untouched like everything else, but there were chairs overturned and glass on the floor. Like the rest of the place, it was wild west themed, complete with the head of a stuffed bear hanging over the bar in the back. If Jamal were here, I'd have teased him about it being bear-form Major Ursus after the Syndicate got to him.

Mom pressed a finger to her lips. "Something happened here."

"Bar fight," I joked. But she pointed to the ground, and I saw what she was seeing: a dark trail of dried blood, leading out from behind the bar, through the swinging doors that led to the kitchen. "Is that—"

"Yeah," she said. She took a careful step toward the counter, glass cracking under her sneakers. "Just…stay close. For real this time."

She found some large, novelty drinking containers in the shape of boots, complete with bendy straws, and filled them from the taps, which somehow still ran with cold water—Mom said maybe the pumps were powered by some automatic backup generator or something. We drank up, then refilled before heading back outside.

We sat on the porch and opened the bag of butterscotch chips for a snack. They were a little waxy, but they melted sickly sweet on my tongue. Mom put a handful in her mouth and smiled apologetically. "I have to admit, they aren't bad."

"Remember when we went to the boardwalk in Santa Cruz and Preston got those deep-fried Oreos and they made him throw up?"

Mom snorted. "Oh, geez. Don't remind me."

"Oreo chunks flying *everywhere*," I said.

"All the way down his shirt." She was laughing now, remembering it clearly. Preston had been ten or so and insisted on eating the Oreos before going on the Cyclone, but the second he got off the ride, he'd doubled over and barfed down his shirt. Mom had tried to take him to the bathroom to rinse off, but he'd run the other way instead, off the boardwalk and onto the beach, and charged straight into the ocean. Dad thought it was hysterical. He picked me up and plunged me into the water too, and we all swam like that, fully clothed. I'd thought Mom would be mad, but she just sat in the sand, watching and smiling.

I picked up another butterscotch chip and tossed it high in the air to catch it. I missed.

"Try me," Mom said.

I tossed one into her mouth, then she tossed one into mine. We kept going until we'd wasted most of the chips. In the grand scheme of things, it didn't seem to matter, because it had put us both in a better mood.

When the chips were depleted, we sat staring at the empty

bag. We'd scavenged every building in this plastic town and were hardly better off than before, which meant we were officially out of reasons to stay here. But if we kept moving as the sun went down, we'd be as good as bait on that long, empty road. Yet if we stayed the night at the inn, it would put another twelve hours of distance between us and Preston. Both options felt suffocating. I didn't have the energy to weigh either of them.

"What now?" I said.

Mom's eyes drifted down the street. "Want to go mini golfing?"

CHAPTER NINE

WE STEPPED INTO THE COOL, dark air and ducked around a banner by the door that read, *Grand Opening: Gold Rush Mini Golf. Strike it Rich!* We stepped onto the course. It was too dark to see, but I could feel the turf under my boots.

"So eerie. It still smells new," Mom said. "Oh, hang on." She set the survival suitcase down, clicked it open, and pulled out a flashlight. As she turned it on, the cold beam illuminated the course ahead of us, revealing painted canyon walls, a faux blacksmith shop, a covered wagon, and a cowboy mannequin smiling broadly just feet ahead of me, his legs splayed over the first hole. In the light, his plasticky face was cast in stark shadows.

"Ugh. Creepy."

"It's just for fun," Mom murmured, swinging the light around, but I heard the uncertainty in her voice. "We could use a little fun, right? We'll just stay for a few minutes."

We found a rack of clubs by the counter, which were still good as new. I chose a pink golf ball and Mom chose neon yellow. She tossed it in her hand. "Alright. You first?"

She held the light for me while I set up my ball and aimed my sights on the hole between the cowboy's shiny plastic boots.

"Just a light swing," Mom said.

"I know."

"I'm just reminding you."

"Mom, I know how to hit a ball." I gave it a gentle tap, but it only rolled halfway down the turf and bumped into the side barrier. I scowled.

"Well, you have to think about the angle, too. Here, watch." Mom handed me the flashlight, set up, and hit her ball perfectly between the cowboy's boots. It went into the hole with a clatter.

"What the heck?" I said.

She shrugged and went to pick it up. "The first hole is the easiest one."

The next hole was meant to look like a river, and you had to put around gold pan obstacles. Mom got it in two tries, but I didn't even count how many it took me. The following hole was inside the blacksmith shop, and then there was a rickety bridge built over a tiny canyon full of dynamite barrels.

I aimed across the bridge.

"Remember, light—"

But I was already taking an exasperated swing. I hit the ball hard, and it slammed into the side of the bridge, bounced wildly, then disappeared off the course and into the darkness. I heard it roll away and hit something. Mom swung the flashlight, and another part of the course came into view. It was a dark tunnel designed to look like a cave entrance, held up by precarious wood beams with a sign that said *Danger: Mines*. I spotted my pink ball rolling lazily on the floor outside of it.

"I suck at this," I grumbled, stalking across the course.

Mom followed close behind and peered into the mine tunnel as I scooped up my ball. "This hole is pretty cool. Want to try it?"

I sighed and put my ball on the edge of the turf, right at the mouth of the tunnel. "Why not?"

The tunnel gaped darkly before me. Mom held the light steady, and I noticed tiny gold nuggets embedded in the jagged stone walls, glittering faintly. I took a breath and lightly tapped the ball.

It rolled down into the darkness, a straight shot.

"Nice, Lay!" Mom said.

I tried not to grin as I followed after it. The tunnel was tighter than I thought, and without air conditioning, the air felt dry and hot. It smelled, too. Like chlorine, but also something sort of sour. I ignored the smell and inched down, my hands trailing the rough walls, the flashlight beam hitting my back. Then the room opened up ahead of me.

We entered a cave. It looked like there was supposed to be a water feature, but there was no water, just an empty basin and a spout.

"Cool," Mom said.

She was in a chirpy mood, all things considered. I found my ball, located the hole, and set up to make the swing.

Then *thud*.

We both froze and peered blindly toward the back of the cave, where it sounded like something had hit the wall—maybe just a shifting pipe or a piece of machinery. But then there was another sound. Something dragging over the turf, and a deep, wet rasp.

Mom swung the light around, and the beam landed square on the face of a boy. He wore a red polo, khaki shorts, and a nametag, but he wasn't normal. He *definitely* wasn't normal.

His mouth was full of sores, his skin sickly white and tearing away. He lurched for us, falling toward the harsh light. I couldn't even scream. I stumbled backward into Mom, and the flashlight went flying to the ground.

"Lay!" she cried.

I staggered and fell back into the basin. The cement scraped my hands and hurt my butt, but I hardly felt it. My attention was only on the rasher. In the lopsided light, the thing jerked toward Mom, swiping at her, his throat making that awful, strangled sound.

Mom lifted her mini golf club, let out a war cry, and swung down hard. It hit his skull with a *thwack*.

He stiffened and fell back.

Mom threw the club down. "Run!"

She scooped up the light and reached to yank me out of the

basin. My boots slid on the turf as we bolted through the tunnel, Mom pushing me from behind. I could hear him behind us, still rasping for air. We broke back onto the course, but we didn't stop. We leapt over the rickety bridge, dashed through the black-smith shop, and beelined for the exit, grabbing the yellow suit-case on our way out the door.

Outside, the light burned my eyes. We ran down the wooden porch, then onto the road. It was only when we'd made it halfway to the inn that we skidded to a stop to catch our breath.

"Oh my god," Mom gasped.

Her hand was pressed to her hip like she had a stitch in her side. I put my hands on my knees; I realized I still had the pink golf ball in my hand, and in disgust, I chucked it away.

"Are you okay? Are you hurt?" Mom asked.

I shook my head and pressed my hands to my eyes. "No, I'm fine."

She pulled me by the sleeve. "Let's get away from here, quick."

Evening was creeping up on us. We could either trek back to the Yukon or go check out the hotel, and the hotel sounded more promising. So we hurried to Winnie's Wild West Inn.

We got through a back entrance that had been left propped open with a cinderblock and found our way through a hallway into the lobby. As soon as we stepped in, I sensed that we were alone and felt immensely safer. The place was quiet, new. It smelled like drywall and bleach.

The lobby was meant to look like something out of a western film, with a wagon wheel chandelier, red wallpaper, ornate furniture. The furniture was still wrapped in plastic like it had only just been delivered, and there were unopened boxes on the floor. Mom picked up a flyer from the solid oak front desk. "Grand Opening, November 15th."

"Darn, we're too early."

Mom grinned. "Too bad, huh? We just missed it."

We decided to stick to the first floor and found an open room just down the hall. It had two queen mattresses under plastic covers, but there were no sheets or duvets on them yet. Mom set down her bags and pulled back the plastic.

"At least there won't be bed bugs," she said.

Our blankets had been left behind in the Yukon, so we set off on a scavenger hunt through the hotel, trying to find some bedding. We opened the boxes in the lobby, checked the maids' closet, searched behind the front desk. Nothing.

"Maybe the bedding shipment hadn't come in yet or something," Mom said.

"Sucks for us."

We found the kitchen, where the taps didn't run, but where Mom found a small tea kettle that made her absurdly happy.

Our futile search for bedding continued until we came across the pool. To our surprise, it was filled, waiting for families that would never come. Our spirits were lower now, but the water looked clean and relaxing, and we were tired from the last few days of camping and driving and running from rashers. We decided to dip our feet in.

We stripped off our socks and shoes, easing our feet into the cool water. The sky was darkening outside, and the pool house was a murky blue without lights. I stuck close to Mom, feeling her warm leg against mine. The white of her skin glowed in the rising moonlight.

We talked about the rashers. Mom said that the kid at the mini golf course had turned, which meant the virus had killed the mind of the person inside, yet somehow kept his body alive like a host. It was like the burning car we'd seen by Lake Tahoe: nothing more than a husk.

It was the first time I'd seen one of them so close. He still looked so *human*, even though his body was rotting. His skin had been riddled with dark, reddish-greenish patches, peeling away, overtaking him like mold overtakes a damp fridge. The sores around his mouth were putrid, and the blood had been thick and nearly black, seeping from the corners of his lips and trailing down his chin. He'd been twitchy too, stumbling like a puppet with its strings all tangled up. It was like his brain couldn't understand that his body was broken.

Somehow, his eyes had been the worst part. Milky white in the harsh flashlight beam, and so far gone.

"Do you think he could even see, or did he just like…smell stuff?" I asked.

Mom sighed and trailed her foot through the water. "I don't know. I don't think I want to know."

"So, when you turn, you're gone, right?" I said. "Like, your mind can't come back?"

"From what I could tell, the virus causes rapid body decay, so that must include your brain. Once you get infected, it only takes about twenty-four hours before your body starts to shut down and you hallucinate. One day after that, your heart stops. That's when you turn. But by then, I think your mind is long gone." Her foot went still and her expression became blank, like she was slipping deeper into thought. After a moment, she added, "Of course, there's no way of knowing what's really happening inside their heads."

I looked at the pool ceiling, the rippling reflection of the water, and I thought of those white eyes. The eyes made it clear. It wasn't a *he* anymore. It wasn't a person.

AFTER THE POOL, we went to the lobby to start a fire in the fireplace so Mom could try to make some tea with her saloon water. As the tea steeped, she took the other packets out of the canister, spread them on the floor, and looked at them wistfully. Poppy, fireweed, evening primrose, balsamroot.

She didn't say it, but they reminded her of home.

That night in the room, we slept far better than we had in the car, curled under the space blanket from the survival suitcase and a few towels we'd found by the pool. We unintentionally slept in late, both of us exhausted from the last two days.

In the morning, Mom braided my hair as we tried to make a plan—we could either go back to the car and just sit there, or continue following the road on foot. There was really only one option.

We had a slow morning, trying to rest up. We ate some pinto

beans and chopped peanuts—which Mom called continental breakfast—and then walked back to the saloon to refill our water containers. By early afternoon, we'd left Winnie's Wild West Escape in the dust, with new boots on my feet, a hat on my head, and a hotel tea kettle shoved into Mom's backpack.

Ahead, the land stretched on and on, just brown earth and prickly plants and a low ridge of mountains in the distance. I felt exposed. "Where to now?"

Mom adjusted her grip on the survival suitcase and started down the road. "We just keep walking."

CHAPTER TEN

WE WALKED FOR MILES. Every so often a car would rumble past, but no one ever stopped for us. I wasn't sure why they would. We were just two more stragglers in a dying world.

My feet were aching and the sun was merciless, even for October. No wait—November now. I tied my jacket around my waist, but sweat gathered beneath the weight of my backpack straps. All around us, the Nevada mountains loomed. Some of them even had snow, which seemed impossible given how hot I felt.

We didn't say much. The silence was solid and heavy. I fell deep in thought, trying to process our situation. I kept seeing that rasher in the tunnel, mouth bloody and eyes white. And then I kept seeing Preston. I was imagining him on the other end of Mom's phone, hands shaking as he begged someone to come for him. I wondered if he even knew what was going on out here, or if he thought he'd been forgotten. Maybe they'd left for their camping excursion and he didn't even know rashers existed.

Every so often, I glanced at Mom, but she was always looking straight ahead. I wondered what she was thinking. If she was replaying it all in her head, too. It was hard not to.

My feet still stung with old blisters, and the soles of my feet had barely gotten used to the dull throb of walking. I moaned.

Mom side-eyed me. "What?"

"Nothing."

"Boots holding up okay?" she asked innocently. Her voice was scratchy—she hadn't said anything in nearly an hour.

"They're fine."

"Mhm," she said.

"Just drop it, Mom."

"I didn't say anything."

"Yeah, but you were like *mhm*, and that's the same thing as *I told you so.*"

"Are you implying I was right about your earlier shoe choice? I told you they'd hurt your feet."

I stayed stubbornly quiet. Mom laughed a little.

"Do you remember when you were little, and we went to Grandma's for Christmas? She got you those yellow rainboots, and you *refused* to put them on because you said they squeezed your toes. And I couldn't understand why because, if anything, they looked too big for you."

I cracked a dry smile. "But you never took out the paper that was stuffed inside them."

"Right," she laughed. "I thought you were just whining, but turns out I'd left the paper in your shoes."

"I loved those boots," I murmured. They were rubber with little ducks on them, and I would wear them down to the river that traced through Grandma's property. She'd take us into the slow, shallow banks to look for skipping stones.

"Whatever happened to the ranch?" I asked.

Mom sighed. "Some tourism company bought it, I think. I don't know."

It was supposed to be hers. All of it, hers. She'd counted on it from the time she was a little girl. As the oldest in her family, the land was hers to inherit, with the wildflowers, the hills, and the trail riding business, too. But it was gone now. Lots of things in her life had slipped between her fingers. Her promised ranch, her marriage, her son.

When Mom and Dad split and Dad sold the house, we'd gone up to stay with Grandma for a couple weeks. Mom was starting over; she'd have to find a new place for us to live and find a nursing job, even though she hadn't worked in over ten years. She didn't tell us, but she hoped that

Grandma would let us stay. That our new life could be on the ranch, for good.

She'd finally mustered up the courage to talk to her mother about it toward the very end of our trip. We were all sitting down to dinner, and the grandfather clock ticked on the dining room wall. She'd said, "Mom, what if we stayed?"

Grandma had become very solemn. Then she broke the news quickly and suddenly: she had lung cancer. She had for quite some time, but had kept it to herself to avoid the fuss. She didn't want to do treatment; she didn't want to try to hang onto the tail end of what had been a good life. She just wanted to go out the natural way. She didn't have much time left.

Mom had been so shocked that she just stared, clenching her fork, the clock ticking and ticking behind her. When the shock wore off, she'd quietly sent Preston and me upstairs. We shut ourselves into our room and listened to them argue through the door; we couldn't understand what they were saying, just that it was bad.

When Mom had come to tell us goodnight, her eyes were swollen and red with tears. She'd sat on the end of my bed and patted my leg, searching for words that wouldn't come. From the other bed, Preston broke the silence.

"So...we're not staying," he'd said.

Mom had shaken her head. "No. We're not."

Turns out Grandma had run out of money a while ago. The ranch was hardly hers anymore as it was, and she didn't want to leave something so shattered to our mother, not when Mom was barely on her feet as it was.

We left two days later, heading back to the city to stay in a motel until we could find an apartment. Mom had said she'd come up to see Grandma real soon, but she never did. Grandma died within two weeks, and shortly after, the ranch was gone. It all ended so quickly.

I looked at Mom now, walking with her face to the sun.

One of my earliest memories was a car ride heading north. Mom hanging her head out the window like she was breathing it all in. Like for a second, she wasn't in the car, wasn't in her life. She was somewhere else entirely, a whole other person with sun on her face, wind in her hair, wildness in her bones. Someone with places to go.

It made me sad to imagine what our life could have been. I had to stop thinking about it, so I just kept my eyes on the road.

<hr>

WE STUMBLED upon a property after another mile, just as the sky was turning orange.

The property was surrounded by a sprawling, barbed wire fence. A herd of cattle was out in the field, grazing in the dry, yellow grass, and in the distance, there was a white farmhouse, two stories, sitting under the shade of one tall, lonely tree.

I noticed there was a light on inside the house, and hope fluttered inside me. "Is the power back?"

"They probably just have a generator," Mom said.

We stood at the entrance to the long, dirt driveway. The gate was closed with a chain, but it looked easy to climb over if we needed to. There was a rusty sign hanging on it, the red letters reading, *No Trespassing. Violators will be shot.*

Mom squinted. "There's a truck parked by the house. You think anyone's home?"

"You're not seriously thinking of going up there, are you?" I pointed to the sign. "Can you read?"

"Well, it's not trespassing if we knock on the front door, now is it?" She straightened out my hat and took my hand. "If anyone asks, we live around here and we ran out of gas."

Mom pushed on the gate, and it opened just wide enough for us to squeeze through the gap. We walked up the long, dusty driveway, her hand crushing mine, and stepped onto the creaking front porch. The house was worn down, almost decrepit. I was about to say we should turn back when Mom lifted her fist to knock.

Before she could, the door swung open.

Two men with rifles stared us down.

102

CHAPTER ELEVEN

WE THREW our hands up instantly, and the survival suitcase hit the ground with a *thump*. "We're not infected!" Mom cried.

Neither of the men lowered their weapons.

The older one was gruff, his gray beard growing down to his rotund beer belly. His eyes were cold, unflinching. Beside him, the other man—more of a teenager, really—looked clammy. His eyes darted, and his fingers clasped and unclasped around the gun. He had long black hair and wore a dirty flannel over his t-shirt.

"We're not infected," Mom said again, slowly, like she was talking to a child. "I'm Heather and this is Layla. We just need help. We ran out of gas."

"Where you from?" said the older man.

I opened my mouth to say *California*, but Mom interjected. "Fernley."

"Oh yeah? Then why you up this way? Why ain't you home?" the man asked. The teen boy swallowed hard, locked eyes with me briefly, then looked away.

"We're trying to get to our family," Mom replied. "Like I said, we've run out of gas, and it's getting late, and we're wondering if you could help us. We can pay you."

She made the mistake of taking a small step closer, and the man jabbed his rifle at her chest. "Stay back!"

"Hey, we told you we're not infected," I said.

Mom shushed me. "Listen, we haven't been in contact with anyone for two days. We're just trying to get to my son."

"Well, where's *he?*"

"Camp, in Oregon."

The man snorted. "What, like summer camp?"

"No, not like summer camp," I said. "It's November."

The man stared at me, and for a second, I thought he might pull the trigger. But he coughed out a laugh. "You're funny, girl."

Mom smiled faintly, trying to keep him loosened up. She nodded toward the teen boy. "Is this your son? Imagine if he was miles away and you couldn't contact him. Wouldn't you try to get to him?"

The man looked at his son and made a grumbling sound. The teenager swallowed again, then lowered his rifle. "Where's your car at?"

"Down the road a ways, by a farmers market and that wild west place. We were wondering if you have any gasoline. Anything to spare at all."

"What make?" asked the man.

"What?"

"The car. What make is it?"

"GMC Yukon."

"Alright, give us the keys." The man cocked his head at his son. "Take Titus and go check it out, make sure they're not lying about the gas tank. I'll keep them here in the meantime."

"Titus?" I whispered.

"My horse," the teenager replied.

Mom gave him the car keys from the side of her bag, and he disappeared into the house, but the man remained put. "Assuming you ain't lying, we can take care of your car in the morning, but for now, you sit tight right here."

He cocked his head down the porch at two faded white rocking chairs, which overlooked the expanse of desert in front of the ranch. Mom and I glanced at each other, then went and sat. The man settled on the porch steps, and although he relaxed his gun, he kept his eyes on us.

"Just relax," Mom whispered to me. "It'll be fine."

The boy appeared on a chestnut horse, galloping across the property, then through the gate and down the road. We sat in silence as the sky darkened and the air grew cool. I shivered, but I didn't move to untie my jacket from my waist. I didn't move at all. I just studied the drawings I'd made on my arm in blue ink: the small flowers, the bear, the little planets. As I studied them, I wondered what Jamal was doing right this second—if he was cozy at the base, drawing in his room. Whatever he was doing, I hoped he was okay.

THE TEEN BOY didn't return until two hours later. By then the stars were out and the three of us were getting antsy on the porch. The boy rode right up to the house and nodded once at his father. "They ain't lying about the car," he said breathlessly. "Gas tank is empty."

His father nodded back. "So what do you think, son?"

The boy chewed his lower lip and studied me. "I think… they're alright. They don't seem sick to me."

The man opened the door and looked at Mom. "In that case, I'm Walt, that's Mitch. You can come help me with supper. "

"Oh," Mom said, rising to her feet. "Well, we're kind of in a hurry—"

"Don't test our hospitality," the man said as we stepped inside. "I doubt you'd survive the night out there alone, the way things are going. You staying or not?"

Mom hesitated, then nodded. "Show me to the kitchen."

Their house was old, well-lived in, almost abandoned-looking. The tan, floral wallpaper was peeling and the floor moaned underfoot. The furniture was sunken and stained—the wood-framed sofa looked a hundred years old.

"Shoulda seen the place when my grandaddy owned it," Walt said, leading us back into a small, orange kitchen. "Best ranch this side of the state before my father let it go to shit and left it all to me."

"It's just the two of you out here?" Mom asked tentatively, standing in the doorway with both hands around the suitcase handle, like she was ready to bolt at a moment's notice.

"Eh, Mitch's mom's dead. We had a couple ranch hands until last week, but they up and left once this flu bug started going around. Said they had to get home to sick family members or something. They're dead now, if you ask me."

Somewhere outside, a dog started barking madly. Walt groaned, set his rifle up against the kitchen counter, and stomped toward the back door. "Don't touch nothing!" he told us. "Be right back."

The screen door slammed, and Mom let out a long breath. She finally set down her bags and moved to see what was in the pot on the stove. Potatoes, not yet cooked.

"Why'd you tell him we're from Fernley?" I asked. "Where even is that?"

"It's a town we passed through yesterday. The car has a Nevada license plate, so I figure the less distance they think we've traveled, the better."

"Kinda weird they invited us for dinner ten seconds after having guns in our faces."

"Maybe they're lonely?"

Walt promptly returned with a black and white dog trotting at his heels. The dog came right up and licked my hand, but I jerked back.

"She's friendly, don't worry," Walt said, moving toward the sink. "You two like steak?" He picked up a wrapped frozen slab of meat that had been thawing in the basin and waved it in the air. "Local ribeye. Farm to table or whatever they say."

"Steak is wonderful," Mom said. She gave him a prim smile, and I wondered if she realized how unconvincing it was. Steak grossed her out.

I watched Walt gather the rest of the steaks, trying not to get queasy about how much blood was soaking through their wrapping. He nodded at the potatoes. "Boil those and mash 'em. I'll be out at the grill." Then he leaned his head out the screen door and shouted into the field. "Mitch!"

Mitch came running up to the back porch. "Yeah?"

"Take the little girl to the stable. She probably wants to see the horses."

I almost protested being called *little girl*, but I did love horses, and Mitch seemed alright. Plus, I didn't want to refuse Walt. It felt like so much as a glance taken the wrong way could send him over the edge.

Mom tried to cut in. "I'd rather Layla stay with—"

"I'll be fine, Mom. I want to see them." I stepped outside. "We won't be long, right?"

"No, ma'am," Mitch said.

Mitch started across the field toward the stable, so I hurried to follow. It was a weathered old thing with boards out of place and only remnants of red paint, and it leaned heavily to the left, but Mitch told me it had always been like that. It was sturdy as a rock.

My brow was sweating under the brim of my hat, so I pulled it off and ran a hand through my hair. I'd liked the cowgirl look earlier, but in front of these guys, I felt like a stupid girl playing dress up.

We stepped into the stable. I loved the smell of it: the hay, the horse sweat, even the manure. It reminded me of the ranch and Grandma's long stable, each stall holding a beloved horse with a name and a clean coat. The rafters high above, the sunlight pooling in. The hay crunching underfoot, the ornery orange cat that prowled for mice.

This stable was pretty small, just three stalls and a hay loft. Titus was in the first stall, and the other two were occupied by dirty white quarter horses.

"Titus is pretty," I said.

Mitch grinned and stepped inside the stall. He had a nice,

cozy smile. "Thanks. Raised him from a colt. You ever ridden one?"

"Oh yeah, I used to ride all the time at my grandma's ranch." I leaned over the half door and watched Mitch pick up a brush and run it along Titus' back. I was struck with thoughts of Preston, gently brushing Grandma's horses—the only time he was ever really calm—and suddenly I felt a jolt of kindred connection with this stranger. "Thanks for not shooting my brains out, by the way."

"Yeah…" he said. "Sorry about the guns. My papa gets, uh… territorial, I guess."

"Do you like living out here?"

Mitch stopped brushing and leaned against the wall. "Guess so. Never lived anywhere else. Mom wanted me to go to college,

but it's not for me. Doesn't matter anyway now that she's dead."
He looked at me sideways. "How old are you?"

I panicked. "Fifteen."

"Hm," he said. "You don't look it."

"Yes, I do."

He took a step closer, leaning over the other side of the stall door, just inches from me. "How old do you think I am?"

"I'm not good at guessing."

"Eighteen." He looked back at Titus. "You can pet him if you want."

He let me in so I could run my hand down Titus's smooth nose. Titus bobbed his head, nostrils flaring at my touch. I stepped back.

"He's just not used to strangers." Mitch tranquilly stroked Titus' neck. He had tough, working hands, but the rest of him seemed soft. His eyes were deep brown, almost doe-like, and his cheeks were pink. "I get along better with animals than people. Maybe that's why I don't mind living alone out here. We've got lots of animals for company. Sometimes I wish it was just me and them."

"And not your dad?" I probed.

"No."

"Why not?"

"He's not a good man, that's all." Mitch turned to show me his forearm, where small, pale, circular scars dotted his skin. "Those are cigarette burns. And this—" He lifted his shirt to show me a reddish scar along the soft side of his waist. "—this is from a belt. You understand what I'm saying?"

I nodded as he yanked down his shirt. His dad had given him those scars. "My mom never does *that* kind of thing, but I understand a little bit."

"Oh yeah? What does she do?"

I shrugged. "She just never listens. She freaks out all the time. I think she's worried I'll turn out rotten or something, but it makes her treat me like a baby." I sighed. "Sometimes I wish I could go live with my dad in Colorado Springs."

"Colorado Springs? Wow. Why is he all the way out there?"

"My parents are split up. So we're all spread apart, and we're just trying to get to my brother, if he's even alive. I don't know if we'll ever all be back together." The thought put a sick feeling in my stomach. Mitch watched me, his expression open and waiting. I felt myself melt into his gentle gaze, felt the words drip right out of me. "This is all my mom's fault in the first place. She's the one who sent him away."

"Sent him away? Isn't he just at camp?"

"It's not like that. It's a place for…for bad kids. But Preston's not bad, he just made a mistake." I rubbed my head. "The point is, my mom feels all guilty for sending him off, and I think she's trying to make up for it now."

Mitch's face sank. After a moment, he reached out and patted my shoulder. "Supper's probably getting close."

We walked outside and started across the dusty field toward the house. On our way, we passed a small wooden shed with a tin roof that was covered with different antennas and wires. The door was swinging open and shut, banging in the wind.

Mitch followed my gaze. "That's my papa's office."

"Office?"

"Want to see?"

We stepped into the dark shed, and for a second my stomach gave me that little gut feeling that something was off, but Mitch flicked on a lightbulb and my anxiety eased. The shed was full of junk and boxes, along with a few rusty rakes and shovels. But the main thing that caught my interest was a desk with a large, fancy-looking radio.

"That's Papa's ham radio. He can still reach the outside with it," Mitch said. "We get a lot of silence, but some people out there protected their equipment from the wipeout with Faraday cages and whatnot, so we've been trying to reach each other and share news."

None of that made any sense to me, so I only said, "News?"

"News on the situation. Military intel, mostly." He shrugged.

"Not everything comes through well, but Papa's been taking notes."

"Wow." For a moment, as I looked around the small, cluttered shed, I thought things might be okay. That we'd stumbled upon two people who might just give us a chance to make it out of this. "So…what kind of stuff do people talk about?"

"Well, a lot of what comes through seems to be encrypted. But there are civilian reports about military movement, or messages about what places are under quarantine, what places have been abandoned, what places to avoid. You know." He scratched behind his ear, eyes flicking to the shed door like he expected someone to come in. "Oh, and sometimes there are distress calls from people trapped in fallen cities."

"Fallen?"

"Yeah, like where the outbreak got so bad they had to bomb the cities."

My blood ran cold. "Wait, that happened? Like, recently?"

He shrugged and patted the big, stationary radio. "So they say."

"So you talked to those people on here? What else did they tell you?"

"Eh, it's not that simple. Here, let me show you." He sat me down in a scratchy, red chair and spun me toward the desk. "Okay, so," he said, leaning over my shoulder and pointing to the dial, "There are frequencies—channels. Papa's got a whole list of civilian ones, emergency ones, military ones. Some are just for listening, like broadcasts."

"Broadcasts?" I asked.

"Yeah, like that stuff the government sends out. They're not sitting there waiting for people to answer back." He twisted the dial a notch. "So you *can* talk on them, technically, but nobody's listening on the other end."

"Then how do people get help?" I asked.

"Calling channels," he said. "They're different frequencies. That's where people check in or send distress calls. You say what you need, and then you wait. If your signal's weak, you keep it real simple, like with Morse code or something." He reached for a black spiral notebook on the desk. "Papa keeps track of everything in here. What frequency, what comes through, and when."

To demonstrate, Mitch switched through a few frequencies until a voice came through. Just some guy talking about Seattle something-or-other. Mitch listened for a second, then turned the radio off without responding.

"Why didn't you answer him?" I asked.

"Because he wasn't asking for anything," Mitch said. "And even if he was, this isn't a channel I can talk back on. It has to be a calling channel to respond. Get it?"

"I guess. So you *don't* just talk to people."

He shook his head. "Nah. It's not a walkie-talkie. Frequencies all have their own purposes, and Papa says the key isn't just transmitting willy-nilly; you gotta know how to listen, too. Otherwise, you're just making noise."

I lost interest and spun in the chair. That's when I noticed a trap door in the middle of the floor. "What's that?"

"Uh, our stockpile. Food, fuel, you know. " His face twitched. "I don't know if I should tell you that."

"I'm not gonna steal anything."

He shrugged. "You never know, these days. Papa probably wanted you to have dinner with us so we could make sure we trust you before we help you. But I trust you." He blushed. "Anyway, we'd better go."

We returned to the house just as Mom was setting the table with mismatched plates. Walt had the steaks stacked on a ceramic platter with pictures of fat baby angels on it. "Well? Are we eating or what?" he said.

We didn't have much to say to each other over dinner, so the conversation inevitably turned to the virus. They told us they'd also lost signals and power on Halloween, same as us, but they weren't too affected by it. They'd always been pretty self-sufficient out here. Well water, propane tanks, and apparently a stockpile of supplies beneath the shed. But Walt didn't mention the stockpile part.

"Seems like you're well prepared," Mom said, pushing her dinner around her plate—the steak was chewy and the potatoes were bland.

"You gotta be." Walt sniffed loudly, his cheek full of food. The dog whined under the table and Walt dropped her a fatty piece of meat. "I was in the army. The stuff I saw, I knew it was only a matter of time before things fell apart. And here we are."

"I doubt you thought it would be this bad, though," Mitch mumbled. Walt gave him a dark look.

"I just wish I knew what was going on out there," said Mom. "It's scary not being able to talk to each other."

Walt laughed. "That ain't no coincidence."

Feeling smart, I said, "Our neighbor thinks Russia set off an EMP and implemented the virus as a bioweapon to wipe us out all at once."

Mitch's eyes darted to his father, then down at the table. Walt stayed mysteriously quiet for a moment, chewing. When he swallowed, he sat back in his chair and cracked a smile. "This ain't Russia's doing, sweetheart. This is a homeland problem."

"What do you mean?" Mom asked.

"I mean this is our own government's doing. Think about it. They find some virus in the hinterlands, send some scientists up there to conveniently get sick, then send 'em home to spread it to the rest of us before anyone can blink an eye. Those scientists were never quarantined at all. So the virus spreads and communications go down—and trust me, if that was Russia's doing, we'd have everything back up and running by now. But our government doesn't *want* things up and running. They don't want us talking. They don't want us to see what's happening."

"I don't get it," I admitted.

"Well, if they cut us off from each other, they control the story. They force us to stay in place and die where we're at." He looked between us. "What, you don't buy it? What about the safe zones? They set those up mighty quick, didn't they?"

"What safe zones?" said Mom. Under the table, her foot touched mine.

"There are some military safe zones popping up here and there," Mitch said. "Closest is Salt Lake City. You have to quarantine to enter the actual safe zone, but without power and gas, it's not like anyone can easily get to them, anyway."

Mom stared down at her steak.

"The government is sparing a select few groups of people," said Walt. "The ones that can get to the safe zones are the only ones that will survive. And those of us who know how to take care of ourselves, of course."

"Sparing them?" Mom said, her voice rising. "Are you insinuating what I think you are?"

Walt nodded firmly. "They're killing us off. They act like they have this under control, but they never wanted it to be under control."

"Population management," added Mitch.

"Right. This place has got too many damn people."

I glanced at Mom, expecting her to scoff or roll her eyes, but she looked pale as a sheet, fork sticking up in her hand, a little spot of potato in the corner of her open mouth. Walt took in her expression with a laugh.

"Don't you worry, sweetheart. The virus will conveniently 'die off' in a month or so, or they'll make up some vaccine they've had all along. Then, if you make it through all this, you can go on home to Fernley."

If we made it through.

"But before that happens," continued Walt, "this thing will be enough to wipe out a third of us. If not from the virus, then from the bloodbath that follows."

CHAPTER TWELVE

AFTER DINNER, Walt invited Mom to have a beer on the front porch. They sat in the rocking chairs and listened to the emergency broadcast, over and over, like they were waiting for it to say something new. The broadcast message would play three times, then be interrupted with a few minutes of classical music before it repeated again. Same thing every time.

Mom didn't seem like herself. I'd never seen her drink beer. Never seen her lie so much, steal so much. The last few days were turning her into some wild animal.

"Two days is all it takes," she said softly to Walt once the music started again. "Once you're infected, it takes two days before you turn."

Bugs whistled in the brush and moths flitted against the porch light. Walt had his eyes closed in the chair, but he was tapping his foot, so I knew he was still listening to the music. Mom stared off into the dark desert, listening too.

I tried to ignore what they were saying and sat on the porch steps with my comic book. I was sick of paying attention.

When Mitch joined me, I had just finished looking over Jamal's new chapter again and was starting to color the first page. "What's that?" he asked.

I was thankful for the distraction from the broadcast, but feeling shy, so I covered the pages with my arms. "Nothing."

But Mitch wriggled it out from under me and took a look. "Dang. Did you make this?"

"My friend did."

"What's it about?"

I told him briefly, then explained the new chapter—I'd found a sticky note in the back of the folder where Jamal had scribbled down the concept. On a quest to find a cure for Major Ursus, Leah tried to sneak into the Syndicate bunker alone, but she was captured. She realizes there are other human-animal hybrids there, and the scientists threaten to turn her into one too, unless she agrees to betray Major Ursus to work alongside their cause.

"So what happens next?" Mitch asked.

With a pang, I realized I might never find out. Never see Jamal again. I took the comic back. "I don't know. I just color the pictures."

He looked at my arms, at the drawings in blue ink. His finger traced the haphazard bear I'd doodled. "You must like bears, huh?"

I blushed. "They're alright."

His finger trailed down to the flower on my wrist. It was larkspur. Mom had planted them in the garden at our old house, tall and proud and indigo. Her favorites.

I glanced at her in the rocking chair, but she was just staring and staring, like she wasn't even there. The beer bottle clutched in her hand was only half empty.

Somewhere in the distance, a horse whinnied, and the sound startled me. With it came another memory of Preston: riding horses when we were little, him pulling me up behind him, me latching my arms around his ribcage as we trotted the perimeter of Grandma's sprawling property. The flowers, the river, the fog. All of it whirled through me like a storm.

I pulled my wrist back from Mitch's touch.

"I might get ready for bed now," I murmured.

Finally, like I'd uttered some magic word to break her hypnosis, Mom sat up and said, "It's getting late, isn't it?"

Mitch showed us to our room up the creaking staircase, down a wide, dark hall, and up another staircase into an attic room. It was warm and dusty, but surprisingly clean otherwise. There were lacy curtains, old wood furniture, and a watercolor painting of a lush, green ranch. On the two twin beds, there were white quilts with little embroidered roses.

"My aunts shared this room when they were kids," Mitch

said, "but they haven't lived here in about a million years, so… it's all yours. There's a bathroom downstairs. Try to keep the lights off, alright?"

He left us to get ready for bed.

After changing clothes, I sat on the edge of the bed and colored while Mom brushed through my hair. I could sense her nerves through her touch.

"I heard you telling Mitch about your comic," she said. "You've never told me about it."

"I've tried."

"When?"

"I don't know. Just…before."

"That girl in it is pretty. What's her name again?"

"Leah," I said. "She's a wildlife biologist who got caught up in some dangerous stuff. Major Ursus is always protecting her, but she protects him, too."

"Leah looks like you."

I rolled my eyes. "No, she doesn't."

"Yes, she does. Maybe Jamal did that on purpose. I think he likes you."

I pulled away from the hairbrush and scowled. "Can you not?" I tossed the comic onto the mattress. "Besides, I don't even like Leah's character. She's always making mistakes and Major Ursus always has to fix them."

"Maybe Layla is just learning as she goes."

"Leah," I groaned.

Mom laughed and ran her fingers through my smooth hair. "I'm just teasing you, Lay."

I rolled my eyes again, but smiled a little. "I'm going to the bathroom."

I left the attic and padded barefoot down the second-floor hallway. I didn't know where the bathroom was, so I peeked through the first doorway, but I realized too late that it was Mitch's room. He was on a bed that was too short for him, listening to music from an old silver iPod.

"Goodnight," I said.

He sat up fast and ripped out his earbuds. "Oh, sorry Layla," he breathed. "You spooked me."

"Sorry. Just…saying goodnight. Thanks for letting us stay and everything."

He nodded and smiled. "Yeah, no problem. It's nice to have somebody else around."

I tried to hide my smile as I hurried to the bathroom.

Back upstairs, Mom had switched off the lamp and was pulling back her covers. She tightly braided my hair again, then we both crawled into bed and murmured goodnights.

I stared at the beam of moonlight on the ceiling. The bed was plump and warm, and from the window, I had a clear view of the ranch and the starry sky. Outside, the bugs still chirped, but everything else was calm. I felt safe for the first time in days.

"Mom?" I whispered. "Maybe we should stay here a while."

She turned over to look at me. "What?"

"It's…it's not so bad. Mitch is nice. Plus, they have guns and food and…I don't know. Maybe we should stay here until communications go back on."

"Layla, don't be silly."

"I'm not being *silly*. I'm serious. I've been thinking about everything that's happened, and it could be weeks before anything gets back to normal, or longer. Weeks before we find Preston. Anything could happen out there, and we have no way of contacting him. For all we know, they took the campers somewhere else, or he's—"

"Don't."

"Okay. But I'm just saying…it's safe here."

Mom rolled back over with resolute silence, telling me this was not up for discussion. The whole reason we were out here was for Preston. We weren't going home without him, I knew that. But if we got to him, and all this was still happening, then what? Would we be able to make it home?

Would home even exist?

Suddenly Mom rolled back over and propped herself up on her elbow. "Layla, I need you to promise me something. Whatever happens, you need to get to Preston, then find a safe zone. *Whatever* happens."

"Why do you say it like that? Like you wouldn't be with me?"

"I will be. But if something happens, I need to know you'll be okay. Just get to Preston. Not your dad, not a stranger. *Preston.* I just need you to promise me that."

"Okay, okay."

"Promise it."

"I *promise.*"

She nodded and lay back down.

I sighed and turned toward the window.

Even with everything flying through my mind, I managed to doze off. I dreamed of school and the haunted maze. All my classmates were inside it, infected, and I couldn't get out. I had this gut feeling that Jamal and Preston were somewhere close, but I couldn't hear or see them, and I didn't know if they were okay. Mom's voice was calling me out of the maze. *Layla. Layla!*

I woke up with a start.

Something cold was touching my forehead. I blinked, trying to focus in the dark.

"Don't move unless I say so," said Walt's voice.

The barrel of his rifle was pressed against my head.

CHAPTER THIRTEEN

WALT AND MITCH yanked us out of bed and forced us downstairs, their cold rifle barrels jamming into our spines, their faces obscured by bandanas.

"What's going on?" Mom demanded.

"Just keep walking."

I had a jarring flashback to the night they took Preston. Those men didn't have guns, but my brother must've felt like this, getting yanked away in his pajamas. He must've felt this same burning, panicked feeling in his throat, his body clammy, his heart beating out of his chest.

They took us outside and walked us across the field to the stable. The sky was pale orange, dawn just breaking. The air was sharp, and the ground hurt my tender feet.

Inside the barn, Walt shoved Mom toward the loft ladder. "Climb."

I threw a desperate look at Mitch, but he just cocked his head, not meeting my eyes. His hands gripped the rifle tightly. I followed my mother up.

We sat on the scratchy, hay-ridden floor, and they tied us to a support beam with an old, long rope. Early light pooled from the slats in the roof. I was breathing hard, but Mom was hardly

121

breathing at all; her jaw was clenched so tight it looked like she could break her teeth.

Once we were tied tightly, Walt stepped back, hands shaking.

"You ain't from Nevada," he finally said. "And if you lied about that, there's no telling what else you lied about."

Behind him, Mitch went back down the ladder, then returned with Mom's backpack in hand. He unzipped it and spilled its contents onto the loft floor. The bean jar and tea canister clattered out, but so did the gun bag and Mom's knife. Beside them, her wallet.

"Oh," she whispered.

"Saw your license," Walt said. "You're from California."

"But we live in Fernley, I swear—"

"Shut up," Walt growled. "I know that ain't true. I went through the girl's backpack and saw her school ID, too. So admit it. Tell me where you're from."

Mom hesitated, eyeing the rifle. "North of Sacramento."

"Ah," Walt said, taking slow, careful steps as he circled us. "There's an Air Force base around there. You know it?"

"Yeah, Kerrick. What does that have to—"

"Given what happened there, it's hard for me to believe you made it *all* the way out here without being exposed. You should be turning any time now, and when you do, you're getting shot."

"Wait, what happened at the base?" I said.

Walt just grumbled in disbelief.

The rope burned against my skin, and I grimaced. I was starting to feel panicked. "We don't even know what you're talking about. Please, just let us go and we can talk."

"Nah, I don't listen to little girls."

Anger bubbled up inside me, but Mom's hand brushed the back of mine, and her touch made a cold reality wash over me. Walt might've been right: we could've been infected and just didn't know it yet. It could've been the rasher in the gold mine, or Pearl, or even someone else. There was no way of knowing until we got sick, and when we did, it would be too late. We'd turn. We'd become like the others.

"Mitch, stay here to keep an eye on them, but keep your distance," said Walt. "I'm gonna ride down and have a look at that car of theirs. Just need to be sure they're not hiding anything else before we take care of this."

They left us for a while, but every so often, Mitch's head would peek over the edge of the ladder to see if anything had changed. I didn't feel sick. Neither did Mom. And even after you got sick, it could take two days to turn. Were they going to quarantine us up here until we showed symptoms?

"Layla, you okay?" Mom whispered.

I struggled against the rope, feeling claustrophobic, feeling like it was cutting off circulation in my arms. I couldn't move them. The rope dug into my chest. "No."

"They'll realize we're not infected soon, and they'll let us go," she said. "Maybe they'll feel so bad that they'll give us some extra fuel."

"What was he talking about, Mom? He said something happened at Kerrick. What did he mean?"

"He probably doesn't know what he's talking about."

"But he has a radio thing. He can talk to people. Mitch showed me—what if he heard something happened at the base? What if something happened to Jamal?"

"Layla, breathe."

I was gasping, eyes burning with tears. I couldn't move. I had to get out of these ropes. "I can't."

"Yes, you can. You have to calm down. You're making it worse for yourself."

I took a couple deep breaths, head hanging. I tried to relax, to stop straining. The air made its way into my lungs, and I felt the oxygen pass through me and escape again. I pulled my feet up. The wood was rough and dry beneath them.

None of this made any sense. "Mom...why *aren't* we sick?"

"Hm?"

"I mean, I just did the math, and we've been on the road for three days, and we've been around plenty of people. Why haven't we gotten sick?"

Mom licked her lips. "I don't know, Lay. Luck, maybe."

I thought of Pearl again and felt nauseous. I had to get it off my chest. I had to get everything off of me, out of me. "I took a sip of Pearl's beer."

Mom gaped. "You *what?*"

"I'm sorry! I didn't know she was infected!"

"Layla, you're fourteen! You can't drink somebody's beer!"

"Shh," I said, worried Mitch would hear from downstairs. "I'm sorry. I didn't mean to...I don't know." I clasped and unclasped my hands. "I just didn't mean to."

I could tell Mom was angry, but in our present circumstances, she was trying to stay composed. She took a short breath. "One, you're lucky you aren't infected. Two, don't ever do that again. Alcohol is not a joke, and you know that. I don't need to remind you what happened to your brother."

I winced and turned my head away.

How could I forget Mom waking me up in the middle of the night and sending me to Margie's so she could go to the hospital? Hearing that the car had flipped, that my brother had broken his arm and split open his head. That he had internal bleeding, and they had to do surgery to save him. That Monty would never walk again.

Preston could've died that night. Sometimes it felt like he had, because he wasn't the same, and that made it worse. I was scared that when we got to him now, he'd be even further gone, and there'd be no trace of the brother I once knew.

Of course I remembered.

We stayed tied up there for a long time—a couple hours, at least. I had no sense of time passing except for the sun glaring brighter and brighter through the slats. It was getting hotter. My forehead was sweating, but I couldn't even wipe it away.

When Walt and Mitch finally climbed back into the loft, Walt stood over us with his gun, the scruffy ends of his beard sticking out beneath the bandana. "No signs yet," he said.

"No, because we're not infected," snipped Mom. She tried to sit up a little more. "Listen, I'm sorry we lied about California. We just needed help, and we thought you'd be more willing if—"

Walt held up a hand. "I don't take kindly to liars, virus or no virus. I let you into my home, I let you near my animals, I let you near my boy. And all this time, you were running around with a gun, and a knife, and sick, dirty blood."

Mitch clenched his jaw and looked away from his father.

"What do I do with you?" Walt said, glancing between us. "If I let you go, you'll turn and spread this thing further. Best thing we could do is take you out now, simple and clean." He looked at Mitch. "What do you think, boy?"

Mitch looked deeply uncomfortable, shifting on his feet, his cheeks deep pink. He took a tentative step closer to his father and pulled the bandana down. "Papa...maybe we should try to get them to a safe zone. Or at least give them gas to get there. I heard they're already working on that vaccine."

"Of course they are, you idiot. There's always been a vaccine. But they ain't giving it to no one until enough people die, I'll tell you that right now. So maybe we should help the government out and expedite the process, huh?" He looked back at us, both hands on his gun. "I knew we shouldn't have trusted you."

"I ain't an idiot," said Mitch.

"Not now."

"I *ain't* an idiot!"

Walt turned on him. "Mitch, I said drop it, goddammit! We have more important matters than whether you got half a brain cell in that empty skull of yours, don't you understand that?" He touched Mitch's chest with the rifle. "What am I saying? Of course you don't. You don't understand anything, you stupid, stupid—"

It happened in a flash. Mitch clenched the folds of Walt's shirt and charged, and they both went careening toward the loft's edge. Mitch shoved, and Walt flew back, his gun flailing. A shot fired. I screamed and shut my eyes. There was a thud, a bird flapping away, the soft sprinkle of dust over our heads where the shot had hit the roof. When I opened my eyes again, Walt was gone, and Mitch was staring over the edge.

He turned, eyes wide. "I..." he said, but he couldn't get anything out of his mouth. He looked back down for a second longer, then scrambled down the ladder.

Mom and I held our breath and waited for something to happen. For Walt to say something, for Mitch to say something.

But the stable was quiet. Mom's hand brushed mine, her skin damp with sweat.

Finally, Mitch climbed back up the ladder, the wood moaning under his weight. But when his head popped over the edge, his expression was as calm as the morning sky. "He's alive. Just out cold."

He clambered up, holding a rusty handsaw. I shrank back as he approached, but he only knelt to hash through the ropes. He was setting us free.

"Come on," he said, tossing the saw down. "I'm taking you to Oregon. We're all going."

Immediately, Mom moved to stuff everything in her backpack, but I sat for a moment, stunned, the sensation starting to prick back into my arms. Mom looked back at me, eyes frantic. She zipped her bag and tossed her head toward the ladder.

We followed Mitch down. Walt was sprawled on the ground, mouth open, rifle still in one limp hand. He was breathing, but it didn't sound right—it rattled. Mom took me by the elbow, pulling me close as we stepped around him.

Outside, the sun was rising higher in the sky. We followed Mitch to the back door of the house, and he waved us inside. "Go get your stuff. Hurry."

We rushed to the attic to change clothes and gather our things. I watched Mom tap a pill from her prescription bottle into her shaking hand, then turned to the attic window. There was a red pickup truck parked near the shed with a cap over the bed, and for a few moments, I watched Mitch run back and forth from the shed, carting supplies: four gas canisters and a funnel, a plastic jug of water, a cardboard box. All the while, the black and white dog frantically yipped at him.

"What on earth was that?" Mom said behind me. "He just *pushed* him. He pushed him right off. Layla. Help me pack."

I snapped out of my stupor and put on my hat. "Walt abused him, you know."

"How do you know that?"

"He told me. He has scars."

Mom blinked, no doubt as confused as I was. Mitch might've been crazy, or this might have been building up for years, and we'd just witnessed it explode.

"Are we really going with him?" I asked.

"We don't have a choice. We have to get to Preston."

Fear battered around in my chest, but she was right. Regardless of what we'd just seen, we had to go with him. We'd come this far, but there was no other way we were getting out of here. Walt would wake up and kill us, or we'd have to run off without a car, without a weapon, without any food but those stupid artisan beans and a handful of ice cream toppings. We'd never get to Oregon on our own. We'd never get *anywhere*.

Outside, Mitch already had the truck running.

"One of you can sit up front with me," he said.

Mom put her hand on my shoulder. "We're staying together. We'll both ride in the back."

So we ended up in the bed of the truck, lying on a scratchy blanket, staring up at the rusted metal roof of the bed cap. The truck jerked around as Mitch sped away, leaving his family ranch in the dust, and all I could see through the windows was the cloudless morning sky.

CHAPTER FOURTEEN

WHEN I WAS LITTLE, Mom was my best friend. I couldn't get enough of her. I wanted to sleep in her bed, braid her hair, hold her hand. Help her cook dinner, help her pick her clothes. Tell her about my day, full of crayons and dandelions and cartoon characters.

I wasn't sure when that changed, when I became more of an obligation than a daughter. But I started feeling inklings of it from a young age.

I wasn't very good in school. I ignored instructions, spaced out, doodled all over my homework. At my fourth grade conferences, I'd sat outside the room while my parents talked with my teacher, but I could hear everything. *She gets into tiffs with her classmates. She doesn't like working with others or being told what to do.*

Well, maybe she's just a natural born nonconformist, Dad said.

I just worry about her. She seems indifferent to everything, and she doesn't have many interests. She never wants to do any of the things we do in class, my teacher said.

Frankly, we're not too worried. She's probably acting out because of trouble at home with her brother, Mom said.

Ah, my teacher said.

And that was it.

They were right, in a way. I'd come to learn that if no one was going to notice me, it wasn't worth trying very hard to do well. On that car ride home from conferences, I cried quietly in the back seat, and neither of my parents asked me why. Maybe they already knew. I was crying because I wanted them to worry about me, but my problems just weren't worth worrying about. Not when they had Preston to fret over.

I didn't know why he got attention for being bad and I didn't. Maybe because he was *more* bad. Maybe because they only had enough energy to worry about one kid, so they'd have to concentrate their energy on the one who was getting into the *most* trouble. The one who didn't just argue with classmates, but with teachers, too. Who got detentions for it. Who slammed bedroom doors when they tried to discuss it with him. He was a *real* problem, not just a nuisance.

Any other kid might have tried to be exceptional. Step out of her brother's dark shadow and make some light in the world. But in my mind, if I ever went above and beyond, it would only make Preston look worse. So I made myself smaller. If I stayed in the background—if I was just difficult enough without being a real problem—maybe it would take some of the pressure off him.

The next year, my fifth grade teacher had us write a journal entry about someone we admired. My instinct was to write about my dad, because you were supposed to admire dads. But he had just moved to Colorado Springs, and my life was a flurry of confusion, so I wrote about Preston instead. Mom asked me why I wanted to be like my brother, and I told her to read the journal entry. *I want to be like my brother because he is nice. He is good at skateboarding. He is really funny sometimes. He loves me.* Didn't that say enough?

Preston, a seventh grader then, got into a fight in the school gym that same week. Some kid had taken his ball. It was so small, but it escalated until there was blood on the gym floor and phone calls home.

He got suspended for two days. He was grounded to our room. He was so quiet about all of it, unapologetic, yet I felt so sorry for him. I understood how anger piled up in his chest like a clogged pipe, how it all spewed back out at once, and when it was over, he was drained and empty and less of himself.

Mom and I ate dinner in front of the TV that evening. Later, I eavesdropped while she called Dad at his new place and admitted she didn't know what to do. Preston was thirteen and already so far off track. Dad just told her he'd shape up eventually.

The next day at school, I pushed a girl at recess. Just went right up to her and shoved her into the dirt for no reason. She didn't cry, didn't get mad. She just stared at me. Mom picked me up from the office and drove me home in silence. I wanted her to say the things she said to Preston. *You have so much more potential than this. I wish you'd just talk to me. I'm trying really hard here.*

But she didn't say anything. The way she looked at me sometimes, like she didn't like who I was becoming, was the same way she looked at herself in the mirror. She saw too much of herself in me—another aimless pushover—and she didn't have the energy for it.

That night, Preston and I were in our beds. He lay facing me, his face shadowy. "You don't have to do stuff like that, you know."

"Do what?"

"You know what. You don't have to get in trouble just because I'm in trouble. It's not worth it. Getting in trouble just pushes people away."

I held my blanket to my chin, staring at him, trying in vain to understand the enigma of his brain. "Then why do *you* do it?"

He rolled over to face the ceiling. "Because it's easier. If you don't try very hard, then you can't be disappointed when things don't work out. Like Mom and Dad. I stopped wishing they'd stay together, and suddenly it didn't hurt so bad when they separated." His lips twitched. "I don't want to pretend to be something I'm not. I've always been a screw up, and if I tried to change, I'd just disappoint everyone, including myself." His eyes locked with mine, glinting in the dark. "But you're not a screw up, Lay. So don't start acting like one."

CHAPTER FIFTEEN

WE DROVE north as the sun traced over the mountains, and I was lulled to sleep by the repetitive rumble of the engine. It was hot and uncomfortable in the bed of the truck, but I pressed up against the softness of Mom's arm and slept anyway.

I was awoken by the sound of a sliding window, the awareness that we'd stopped moving, and Mitch's whispering voice. "I'm pulling over to take a break," he said, talking to us through the tiny window between the truck cab and the bed.

I sat up and rubbed my eyes. Beside me, Mom was stretching her neck. She seemed dead tired, but I was sure she hadn't let herself fall asleep. The comic book folder was open in her lap—she'd been looking at it while I slept, and even though I had very little to do with those uncolored pages, it made me feel weirdly embarrassed to find her snooping.

I glanced out the window, half expecting to see some greenery, but the desert still loomed. We were now in the parking lot of a dinky truck stop, alongside a few parked cars and semi-trucks that looked abandoned.

Mitch got out and opened the tailgate for us, and we slid onto cracked asphalt. As my eyes adjusted to the brightness, I was shocked to find a large brachiosaurus statue staring down at us. It was painted a deep green color that had faded in the sun, and it was taller than the truck stop itself, standing over the place like a guard.

"Creepy," I said.

Mitch slung the strap of his rifle over his shoulder. "What, the dinosaur or the truck stop?"

"Both."

The side of the building said *Cafe, Slots, Beer,* and the front windows were bashed in. It seemed to be the only thing around, besides the road and the mountains. I was getting real sick of this landscape.

"Where even are we?" I asked.

"Eh, here or there." Mitch grabbed a couple cans from the cardboard box in the truck bed. "Why don't we go inside and have something to eat?"

"We can't stay long," Mom said. "I want to get to Jackpot by tonight."

My stomach was aching enough that even room-temperature canned pasta sounded good. We took our stuff with us, just in case we ran into another looting situation, and Mitch handed me the cans so he could keep his rifle at the ready. I took a quiet breath, trying to decide whether the weapon made me feel safe or nervous.

The inside of the building was ravaged. Shelves knocked over, glass on the floor, the Slurpee machine toppled with dried green sludge sticking to the tiles. Nearly everything was taken except some particularly nasty sour candies by the register. The worst part was the smell. As soon as we walked in, the stench burned my nose. It was the same smell from the mini golf place: something decaying and almost metallic. It put a sick feeling in the back of my throat.

Mitch noticed the same thing. "I think someone in here is dead."

His eyes scanned the room, and at once, we saw it: a rasher emerging from the shadows down the bathroom hallway, dragging itself over the floor. Its lower body was completely missing, just a bloody, torn mess cut off at his waist—I wondered if it had been run over or something. It hauled a slew of entrails behind itself, leaving a streak of dark fluid in its wake. Its skin was peeling to the bone, and its face was gaunt and white. It painstakingly crawled toward us over broken glass, eyes blank.

Mom yanked me behind her, and at that moment, Mitch raised his rifle and shot. The bullet went right through the rasher's skull, blowing his head clean apart, and sending a deafening ricochet through the small space. The body twitched for a second, then stopped.

I clung to Mom.

Mitch turned to us and laughed, but my ringing ears muffled the sound. "Put him out of his misery. I guess this means we can't use the bathrooms, though."

He took the cans from me and moved past us, deeper into the store, heading down a hallway that split the other direction. I didn't want to get too far from him—or his rifle—so I hurried after.

We came across the slots room. It was empty and dark, but there were a couple small, high windows, so the room was lit enough to see that there was no danger. I pressed against the closest wall, feeling like I was going to puke. I kept seeing that bullet go through that rasher's skull, his head breaking apart, his body thumping to the tile. No—*its* body. I had to tell myself it wasn't a person anymore, or I'd...I'd...

"You good?" Mitch asked, his voice still far away.

I nodded, hands on my knees, head hanging. I felt Mom's hand on my back. "She's fine," she said. There was a leather couch in the room wedged between two powerless machines, and Mom pulled me over to sit down. Finally, the ringing in my ears faded.

Mitch crouched on the floor, set out the cans, and pulled a Swiss Army knife from his pocket to pry them open. He didn't seem shaken. He carried this confidence around him, like nothing he did could ever go wrong. I hadn't seen it back on his ranch, but I saw it now. The way freedom radiated from him.

Like for once, he'd done what he wanted, and everything from here on out would be a result of that one moment.

After he'd popped open the last of the cans, he stared at the knife for a moment, and his expression shifted. "What happened back there with my dad...I'm sorry. Really. I want you to know I ain't a violent person. That's not me. It's just not."

He glanced at Mom, as if seeking approval. Mom shifted her jaw and nodded.

Mitch handed us our pasta, but we didn't have forks, so he ventured back into the store and scrounged up some plastic ones. Mom and I ate slowly, but Mitch scarfed his down, staring at the ceiling like he was fantasizing about something—about killing that rasher, maybe. I could sense that confidence quickly obscuring whatever softness we'd just glimpsed.

When he finished eating, he stood up and tossed the can aside. "I'm going back into the store. Want to come, Layla?"

My instinct was to say yes, but before I could get out a word, Mom cut him off coldly. "She's staying with me."

"I was just gonna look for something to drink," he said.

I met eyes with Mom, but she shook her head. So I slunk down bashfully on the couch and didn't argue. Mitch shrugged and left the room.

When he was gone, Mom reclined and closed her eyes. I expected her to mention the things that had happened today and turn them into some lesson, but all she said was, "I just need to rest for a minute. This has all been a lot."

I sat on the edge of the couch near her curled-up feet. Her hair was in her face, and I wanted to brush it away, but I held back. I didn't know why. "We must be getting close to the Oregon border, right?"

"We have to be." She cracked open one eye and gave a weak attempt at a reassuring smile. "We'll get to him soon."

I shifted in my seat, wanting to go out and explore with Mitch. He made something fluttery erupt in my chest, and plus, it wasn't like anything would happen to me out there if he was around. He had a gun. He knew how to use it. And that made me feel safer than sitting here.

"Can I please go out there?" I asked. "I saw some candy, and I thought maybe I could find more somewhere—"

"No, Layla."

"You can trust me. I'll be safe."

"It's not about trusting you."

"Well, *do* you trust me?"

Mom hesitated. "Yeah...I do."

"Doesn't sound like you do," I muttered.

She rolled her eyes and sat up. "You're still a child, Lay. I know you think you're grown, but you're not even in high school yet. The world is a dangerous place. Even more so now. It's not that I don't trust *you*, I just don't trust the world to not... not *swallow* you."

"I'm not talking about the *world*, Mom, I'm talking about looking for candy in a stupid gas station. It's not that serious."

"It is serious. It's *all* serious. I'm trying to protect you."

"You never tried very hard to protect Preston," I snapped. "Maybe if you had, he wouldn't have turned out the way he is, and we wouldn't be in this mess."

Her jaw tightened. "I've done everything on my own—don't forget that. Until your dad decided I couldn't handle Preston and sent him off instead of helping me. That was *his* idea." She blinked, her eyes suddenly teary. "When you're a parent, sometimes you feel like you've done everything you can and it's still not enough. You still do the wrong things sometimes. But this isn't what I wanted, and now I have to get to him and tell him before it's too late."

She wiped at her eyes and lay back down. My chest burned with anger, but also with guilt. I hadn't wanted to fight; it had just happened.

"Sorry," I muttered. "I didn't mean it."

"Yes, you did."

"I didn't."

She sniffed, and her voice came out small. "When I was a

little girl, all I ever wanted was a family. I got one and I screwed it up."

"You didn't screw up anything, Mom," I said. But she just shook her head and remained with her back to me, curled in on herself.

When I was little, there were days when she'd be so anxious that not even her garden could make her feel better. She'd lie curled on the couch by the window, bathed in sun, perfectly still. It was her habit to brush back our hair whenever we were feeling down, and so sometimes I'd do the same for her. Just run my tiny hands along the curve of her head, marveling at the way her red hair glowed in the sun, like she was an angel. A tired, fallen angel.

Her anxiety had gotten better over the years, and those unbroken hours on the couch had disappeared. But I sometimes wondered if she'd just learned to hide it better. If all that despair was still circulating beneath the surface.

I wiped my nose with my sleeve. "I'll keep watch if you fall asleep, okay?"

"I won't fall asleep," she murmured.

But she was out within seconds; I hadn't realized she was that tired. I watched her for a few minutes, her back rising and falling with breath. I thought I should be more angry with her, but I couldn't be. Like this, calm and sleeping, she looked like a little kid, and I knew she was just as scared as I was. She wouldn't stop being scared until we got to Preston. Until she knew both of her kids would be alright.

I could hear Mitch's footsteps out in the store. The slots room pooled with guilt, with words unspoken, and I couldn't just sit here and watch Mom sleep anymore. She would be okay. I would be okay. Everything would. But before I left, I reached out and brushed her hair away from her eyes. "You didn't screw up," I whispered.

I put on my backpack and crept down the hallway, past the counter and the slurpy machine and the overturned shelves. I didn't see Mitch. I turned toward the refrigerators lining the wall, and something flashed in my peripheral vision.

"I got you something."

I jumped so violently that I staggered back into the glass refrigerator door. It was just Mitch, holding up a pink stuffed bear.

"Geez, you can't scare me like that!" I put my hand on my chest to calm my racing heart. "There's, like, literal dead people walking around out here."

Mitch laughed. "Sorry. Here." He passed me the bear. It was the size of my hand, fuzzy and bubblegum pink. But it was for a kid.

"Why are you giving me this?"

"Just found it on a shelf over there and thought you'd like it," he said. I was about to protest that I didn't need toys until he added, "It's cute, like you."

"Cute?"

"Well, pretty."

My cheeks went hot. He looked at me, those doe-brown eyes glinting in the faint light from outside, and grinned. For a second, I forgot where we were. I forgot there was half a corpse on the tile just yards from us.

"Thanks." Flustered, I quickly zipped the bear into my backpack. "Maybe I should go back to Mom."

But Mitch took my hand. "Wait. I wanted to show you something else."

He pulled me over behind the counter. There was a pile of more stuffed animals on the floor, big plush ones and little fuzzy ones. A giant pink unicorn and a polar bear and a pale blue jellyfish. These were probably for truckers to buy and send home to children they never saw.

Mitch flopped down into the pile. "I made a nest," he said. "Come on, try it out. It's comfy."

It did look comfy, I had to admit, and I was tired. So when Mitch patted the spot beside him, I dropped my backpack off my shoulders and joined him.

As I settled in, I was very aware of the contrast of all this. Lying on clean, soft stuffed animals like a kid while there was a dead body on the other side of the counter. Maybe others somewhere else. There could have been infected drivers stuck out there in their trucks, and we wouldn't even know. I lay back, heart pounding, the back of my mind flashing the image of that woman's body in the outhouse, the man with the beard, the rasher in the mini-golf mine, and the bullet going through that skull, over and over.

Mitch put his hand on my arm. "Hey, it's okay. We're safe."

I realized I was breathing hard, and I tried to steady my breath. I'd never been as anxious as Mom, but things had changed so much in the last few days, and she was the one being calm now. Rubbing my back, telling me to breathe. It was like we'd crossed the border into Nevada and somehow switched nervous systems.

Mitch's hand stayed on my arm, cool and callused. I was sweating. I'd never been this close to a guy before, except Jamal, but he was hardly more than a boy. Not even fourteen yet.

"Sorry," I said.

"For what?"

I shrugged. I couldn't stop thinking about Mom back in the slots room, thinking I should get back to her, but something was clouding over the worry. It seemed impossible, but I felt safe down here with Mitch. Without the passing cars or the electric buzz of the machines, the world was muted and dim, and I felt like we were the only two people alive on the planet.

"I'm sorry about your dad," I said.

"I didn't mean to scare you. I didn't mean to push him. It just happened." Mitch looked away. "I hope he's okay."

"Well...you're free now."

He paused. "I don't like your mom."

I laughed a little, but he was stoic. "She's alright. Really."

"I've noticed how she treats you. Like you're weak."

"No, she's just...she's protective, you know? She wants what's best for us."

Mitch shook his head. "She belittles you. She's forcing you to be out here, putting you in danger, and she's making you think you have to go along with whatever she says just because she's your mom. That ain't being protective, Layla. It's emotional abuse."

My eyes widened. "Abuse?"

His tone was cold and level. "I've experienced it, so I would know. You change when she's around. It's like you're second-guessing yourself. That ain't normal. Moms shouldn't make you feel that way."

I glanced away, mind racing. Mom was fretful and tough, but she loved me. She pushed me because she loved me. At least, that's what I'd thought. But maybe Mitch was a little bit right. Sometimes I didn't know how to be myself around her, because nothing I ever did was right in her eyes. She didn't truly know me, and I wasn't sure I wanted her to. More often than not, I wanted space from her.

As much as it sucked that she sent Preston away, maybe he was happier without her.

"You deserve better," Mitch said. "And I know I haven't known you long, but if it counts for anything...I think you're a real cool girl."

I chuckled. "Thanks."

"I mean it." He looked me deep in the eyes. "You know, we could go to Colorado Springs. We could go to your dad. I could take you."

He had to be joking. The idea didn't make enough sense to be serious. "We'd never have enough gas to get there."

A sly grin crept onto his face. "We could steal a couple of horses and travel that way, like cowboys." I didn't respond, but I was trying not to smile. He nudged me. "Come on, I know you'd like that, horse girl."

I had to admit I was a little captivated. There was something romantic about the whole thing. We were lying on the floor of a ruined truck stop, but we were out here doing something, moving somewhere. The idea of being on the road with a handsome guy, riding horses through the wilderness, was rugged and real. It sounded like something Leah would do in the comic.

I stared at Mitch, my cheeks warm.

"What?" he said.

"Do you have a girlfriend?"

He sputtered a laugh. "Nah. But I know my way around."

"What?"

He smirked. "Don't play coy. You know what I mean."

I blushed harder and nestled deeper into our pile of animals. "I mean…I guess I know what you mean. But I don't…I've never had a boyfriend. I've never even had a first kiss."

I didn't know why I'd spilled that. I felt possessed.

"You're still young. Plenty of time for that."

Still locking eyes, he caressed my cheek with the backs of his fingers, and I froze. Light as a feather, his hand moved to my shoulder, then down my arm. I felt a swell of excitement or nerves or *something*, but I couldn't tell what it was. My heart rammed in my chest.

But then his hand slid to my waist, and I got scared. "I think you should teach me to shoot," I blurted.

He stopped. "Really?"

"Yeah. Never know what could happen out here." I sat up. "Can you show me?"

"Uh, sure."

So I threw on my backpack and led the way outside. I wasn't sure what time it was, but the sun was getting closer to the mountains already. It would be dark before we knew it.

Mitch opened the truck bed to get some more bullets, and I put my bag down in the back. When the rifle was loaded, he took me a few feet away from the car, closer to the dinosaur statue, which sat lonely in the fading sun. Behind it, I noticed a long wire fence and some horses grazing in the distance. Mitch lifted his rifle, and I covered my ears as he took aim. With a calm expression, he pulled the trigger, and the bullet splintered right through the dinosaur's large, white eyeball with a loud crack. I flinched. Behind the fence, the horses got spooked and dashed off across the open land.

Mitch lowered the rifle and smiled as I tentatively uncovered my ears. "Seems scary, but it ain't so bad," he said.

"I get why my mom doesn't want me to touch guns."

"Unattended, sure. But you're here with an expert. Ready to try?"

He handed me the rifle and showed me how to hold it, putting the butt against my shoulder, aiming it straight. He guided my hands around the body of it; I could feel his calluses against my skin. I aimed at the neck and pulled the trigger. The gun recoiled hard against my shoulder, and I nearly dropped it, but Mitch held me steady.

"I didn't even hit anything," I moaned.

"Go again."

I took a breath and aimed in the general vicinity of the dinosaur's body. My finger pushed against the trigger, and the rifle kicked back hard, but this time, I heard the bullet connect with fiberglass. When I pulled the rifle down, I saw an unmistakable hole in the dinosaur's stomach.

I beamed and turned to Mitch, but before either of us could say anything, the door of the truck stop banged open.

A wave of dread hit me as Mom stepped into the light. Her eyes were wild, her hair damp with sweat. She held a crowbar in both hands.

Something wasn't right.

"What have you done?" she said.

Mitch gently took the rifle from me and hung it over his shoulder. "Heather, calm down. We didn't do *anything*."

"I'm not an idiot," she said. She came closer, and Mitch took an instinctive step back. Her brown eyes flashed to me. "Layla, come on. We're leaving."

"Why, what's going on?"

"We don't know this man. We don't know what he's capable of. Step away from him, and let's go."

I didn't move—there was a crazy look in her eyes that held me back. Mitch was standing halfway in front of me, blocking my path. He looked down at me over his shoulder. His gaze was steady. Certain of something.

"What's she talking about?" I asked him.

He didn't respond, just shook his head.

"Tell her, Mitch." Mom's voice cracked. "Tell her where we are."

Mitch stayed quiet, even as Mom pointed the crowbar at him, hands tremoring. She swallowed hard. "He's not taking us to Oregon, Layla. He's been taking us east. I saw a map. We're hours off course." Her nostrils flared as she shifted her attention to him. "*Where* are you taking us?"

I hadn't even processed what she'd said before she swung the crowbar at Mitch with a *whoosh*. He ducked, narrowly avoiding the blow, and protectively shot his arm out in front of me. "Heather, stop!"

A horrible thought cut through my brain.

What if she was hallucinating?

Infected?

I was frozen in place behind Mitch, watching Mom's fingers adjust their grip on the crowbar, waiting for her to swing again. Or for him to take his rifle and shoot her.

"Layla, please," she said. Her voice was like a breath.

She reached for me. But in the split second I decided to take her hand, Mitch grabbed me by the waist and hoisted me up.

Before I could comprehend what was happening, he was throwing me in the back of the truck and slamming the tailgate shut. I crawled over and tried to push it open, but it was locked. I pressed against the window just in time to see Mom swing at him again.

Mitch sidestepped and scrambled backward, fumbling for his keys on his belt loop.

Mom lunged and caught his wrist. "Give me the keys!"

"Heather, just—"

"You're not taking her! Give me the *keys!*"

I was gasping, pounding on the window, trying to get out. The door wouldn't budge. Mitch struggled against Mom's grip until he finally knocked her to the ground. The crowbar clattered on the asphalt. Mitch swung his gun around.

"Don't shoot her!" I screamed.

He didn't. Instead, he lifted the barrel of the rifle and slammed it into her head with a crack. She slumped to the ground. I screamed, kicking at the door, trying in vain to get out and get to her.

Mitch didn't waste a second. He jumped into the driver's seat, started the engine, and floored it out of the lot. I banged against the back window. Mom was on the ground, and as the truck picked up speed, she grew smaller and smaller, just a lump on the asphalt.

A scream tore at my throat so violently it felt like being

ripped open, but barely made it past the glass—she couldn't hear me. There was only the engine, and the wind, and no air. No thoughts. Just my hands slapping on the window as she disappeared.

"Mom! Mom!"

"Layla!" called Mitch. "Layla, it's okay!"

"Go back! Go back, go back, go back!"

Mitch didn't turn around, didn't say a word. I crawled toward the window between the bed and the cab and hit the glass with my fist, getting jostled as we bumped down the road. I tried to pry it open, but it wouldn't budge. He'd locked it.

"Go back," I cried. "Please. Please, go back."

Mitch glanced back for just a moment, expression stoic, unreadable. His voice was muffled behind the glass, but it felt like ice. "I can't. We're going to Colorado Springs."

"But you said you were taking us to Oregon. You said you'd help us!"

He faced forward, eyes on the open, empty road. "I *am* helping you, but plans change. You need to trust me now. I'm trying to save your life."

I crawled to the back window again. We were moving so fast that the the truck stop was already far behind us, and all I could see now was a speck of green. Then it was all gone, swept into the haze of the darkening desert.

CHAPTER SIXTEEN

I'LL TAKE *care of you. I promise.*

That's what she told us after Dad left. The day we moved into our new apartment. Boxes everywhere, the walls stark white, the carpet dirty. Mom hadn't worked in years, but she'd just started training at a new hospital, and she wasn't going to accept any help from Dad aside from his legal obligations. So this was our new place. Modest and bare, but a place all the same.

Mom said we could each have our own room and she'd sleep on the pullout couch, but Preston wouldn't let her do that from the start.

"Layla and I can share," he told her. "We don't mind. We'll get a bigger place eventually, with a hot tub. Right?"

Mom smiled and kissed his head.

He was my age then, fourteen. He seemed so much wiser.

We sat on the couch that night, ate pizza, and watched a movie to christen the new place. It all felt so empty, but Mom seemed light. I leaned into her, trying to be okay with this new life as a family of three, but there was an ache in my chest. We watched *Finding Nemo*, and toward the end, when Nemo was back with his dad, my eyes blurred with tears. I looked over at Preston, and to my surprise, he was crying, too.

Mom turned off the movie and hugged us both in the dark. "It's okay. I'll take care of you. I promise."

I LAY CURLED UP, as if I could tuck away from reality, even though visions of it kept swimming through the murkiness of my thoughts. I hid like that until the truck squealed to a stop.

Mitch pushed open the little window. "Layla?" His voice was gentle. I didn't move. "It's getting late. Are you hungry?"

He waited, and I tried to pretend I was asleep, but he knew I wasn't.

He got out and opened the tailgate. I heard the clatter of cans as he rifled around in the box of food. Slowly, I lifted my head to look outside. We were on some potholed backstreet between a few long, low buildings; they looked like abandoned warehouses, with boarded windows and weeds slithering up the sides. The sun was nearly down.

"Where are we?"

"Right on the border of Utah." Mitch held up a can of baked beans. "How's this for supper?"

I slid out of the back of the truck. As soon as my feet hit the pavement, my instincts told me to run. But run where? Would anyone help me out here? We'd driven for a while—there was no telling how far we were from Mom. I'd never find her.

I felt dizzy. I sat back down on the tailgate, legs dangling.

Mitch opened the can and handed it to me, along with a plastic fork he'd taken from the truck stop. I ate the beans only because my stomach was growling, but I could hardly taste them. Mitch sat beside me.

"I'm sorry," he said.

I didn't reply.

"We're about ninety miles from the outskirts of Salt Lake City. There's a military safe zone there. I figure they might have comms and can help us find your dad, since there's a safe zone around Colorado Springs, too. Do you like peanut butter?"

I frowned in confusion. He reached into the back and pulled out a jar, along with a package of rice cakes. I didn't speak while he haphazardly spread the peanut butter on one and handed it to me.

"You should drink some water, too." He held out a plastic bottle. It was warm, but I tried to drink it anyway. Mitch sighed. "I need to go scout things out at the border. Want to come or stay here?"

I blinked down at the smear of peanut butter, the smell of it conflicting with the watery canned beans sitting in my stomach. It would be good to get my bearings. "Come."

We finished eating and closed up the truck, but we didn't scout very far. We walked to the end of the alleyway up to a connecting road. Across it, I saw an airport hangar and a vacant plane. We walked a bit further down until more came into view: to the north, a small town, and to the east, a vast and sprawling landscape. The ground was white and glistening in the setting sun. Far ahead stood a deep, blue ridge of mountains.

"Those are salt flats out there. And look." Mitch pointed north of us, toward a major road in the distance that led out of the town. I could see a bright line of cars. His finger spanned the horizon. "Over there is the border. I think that's a military checkpoint on the road, and we'll have to go through it to keep on toward Salt Lake City. They'll let us pass if we seem safe."

I didn't know what that meant, exactly.

We went back to the truck. I sat on the ground and picked at pebbles in the pavement while Mitch organized things in the bed. He was mumbling to himself—something about his dad's notebook—before he spoke to me over his shoulder.

"You ever think about how strange it all is? The world changed so fast." He closed the flaps on the box of cans. "And you know, it might sound crazy, but I ain't even scared. Are you scared?"

I didn't respond. I stared at the pebbles.

"Honestly, I just feel free," he said.

My gaze drifted back down the alley to the horizon, and I

thought of the cars on the far-off highway. The world *was* changing. I felt it slipping away from me, too big to grasp.

Mitch weighed my silence. "Sorry. I know you're upset."

I looked back down, this time at my boots. My stomach was churning. Mitch sighed and sat beside me on the ground, and his face twitched. "You know, I stopped being scared of my papa a long time ago. Because when you stop fighting the fear, it stops being so scary. You let it in to let it go."

I didn't know what he was talking about, but it sounded like a load of crap. He'd seemed very afraid of his father back there; he was just trying to be tough now. Trying to convince me that what he'd just done was for the best. For my good.

In a weird way, Mitch reminded me of my brother. Always trying to extinguish the things that burned up inside of him, but never being able to put the fire out. They were both burned from the inside out, raging. Mitch was what Preston could become. Burned beyond saving.

But Preston wasn't entirely like Mitch. He *wanted* to be good. He didn't want his fire to burn us, it just *did*, and I knew he hated himself for it. But when it counted most, he could reach into himself and find that gentle side. Maybe the difference was that he knew deep down that we loved him. I hadn't always done the best job, but I'd fight for him as much as he fought for me. Mitch never had that. For him, nobody had tried to put the fire out. They'd only added fuel, and now he was incinerated.

Preston never would've done what Mitch did.

Mitch's eyes were on me, waiting for me to respond, but I refused. So he pushed back to his feet with a grunt and mumbled that he needed to take a piss. There was a sharp edge to it; he was mad at me. He went off behind the nearest warehouse, and I picked at pebbles again, trying to ignore the sound of his pee hitting the side of the building. Trying to swallow down the taste of vomit in the back of my throat.

The quiet settled. The air grew heavy.

I was just about to get up and crawl back into the bed of the truck when I heard boots pounding on the pavement. Mitch came sprinting back toward me, zipping his pants, eyes wide. Immediately, I realized why.

There was a rasher behind him.

Then another. And another. Slinking out of the shadows, reaching for him as they crossed the weedy gravel. Their mouths hung open, expelling those ragged, wet gasps.

Mitch sprinted toward the truck. "Get in!" he yelled.

I slammed the tailgate shut and ran for the passenger door. As I climbed in, I found myself right next to Mitch's rifle, but he was still out there, car keys in hand. He'd only just flung open the driver's side door when a rasher grabbed him by the shoulders and yanked him back.

It was all rotting flesh and snapping teeth, its eyes clouded and white. Mitch twisted from its grip, but not before it clamped its teeth onto the fabric of his jacket. Mitch screamed and pulled, and his jacket ripped. They slammed into the side of the truck.

"Shit!" He rammed his elbow into the rasher's head, once, twice, three times. The thing stumbled enough for Mitch to throw open the car door, but the rasher recovered and grabbed hold of him again. Another came from the other direction and pounded its hand on the windshield. I jolted, frozen, useless.

Mitch wrenched himself free as the first one lunged again—I watched his keys fly from his hand and fall to the ground. "My gun!" he screamed. "Shoot them!"

I snapped out of it, grabbed the rifle, and leaned out the driver's side door. My hands were sweating, slippery. I struggled to hold it steady. The rasher fighting Mitch was too close to shoot without risking hitting him too, but there were others closing in —at least ten of them. I aimed at the closest one, hands shaking, and took a breath before I shot.

The recoil sent me backward and the rifle clattered to the truck's floor. My bullet had only grazed the thing's head, but it was enough to pull its attention from Mitch and onto me. I gasped and reached to yank the car door shut, but it was too late. The rasher was there, forcing itself in, screeching at me with bared teeth. Its jaw was unhinged, its saliva crimson and dripping.

I screamed and kicked at it, lying flat on the seat. Something hard dug into my spine. I reached back and found a can of green beans, and without thinking, I lobbed it as hard as I could at the rasher's head. The can hit hard enough to daze it, but it recoiled only for a second before it reached for me again.

I opened the passenger door and fell out of the truck.

There were others—so many more—spilling out from the alleyways between the warehouses, appearing from shadows, dragging themselves across the pavement.

Mitch was on his feet, holding his knife, his face scraped and jacket torn. He patted his pockets. "My keys," he gasped. "What happened to my keys?"

I heard a snarl behind me and turned. This one still had

hospital scrubs on, its stomach torn open. A woman. She was close enough that I could see the blood under her nails, smell her sour flesh, see her eyelashes, still dark with mascara. She reached for me, and the image of my mother flashed through my head. My mother, lying limp on the pavement. My mother, face to the sun. My mother in the garden. My mother, gone.

My body stiffened, and her cold fingers wrapped around my arm.

"Layla, move!"

Mitch whipped toward her, blade out, and jammed it into her temple. He kicked his foot into her hip and pushed, yanking the knife out as she reeled back. She gurgled. Blood sprayed. I stumbled away, gasping. I couldn't take it. I couldn't fight them. I broke into a run.

"Get back in the truck!" Mitch screamed.

But I was sprinting down the alleyway, dodging the rashers as fast as my cowgirl boots would carry me. Hands, bodies, teeth. A stench so vile it burned my eyes.

I didn't make it far. My boot caught, and I flew to the ground, scraping my hands. I pushed to my knees, but it was too late—one of them was upon me, lurching and reaching with dark, rotting fingers. It shoved me to my back, and my head hit the pavement. I grabbed it by the throat and pushed back, but it was strong, and it pressed down over me, its face inches from mine. I cried out. Its eyes. They were still a little blue. This one was fresh, new, barely unhuman.

Then *bang*.

Its head snapped back and burst apart, and it crumpled to the ground. I blinked through the splatter of blood.

Someone had shot it.

With a gasp, I looked back at Mitch, expecting to see him with the rifle, but he was still struggling with the knife. I looked the other way. I saw the figure before I heard its voice: a shadow, standing on the roof of a warehouse ahead of me.

"Get down!" he yelled.

I hit the pavement just as gunfire split the air. Bodies

smacked to the ground, gagging and screeching, and bullets hitting rock and metal and wood. I didn't dare move. I just flattened on the ground, hands over my head, pressing my arms hard against my ears to drown out the awful, bloody noise. All I could think of was Preston and Mom. I didn't want to go out like this, so far away from them, all on my own. I didn't want to die in this alleyway. Or get eaten. Or become one of *them*.

But as soon as it began, it was over. The noises settled until all I could hear was my breath, trembling against the pavement.

Carefully, I lifted my head. Though the light had faded, I could faintly make out that the figure on the roof was a man in army fatigues. Hope fluttered inside me. I was saved.

But as I rose to my knees, I realized the man wasn't alone. There were a few others scattered on roofs and a couple on the ground, some of them holding stocky black guns. But not all of them were in fatigues—most of them were wearing normal, tattered clothes.

Not the army.

Mitch came for me, dragging his leg but smiling. Behind him, at least a dozen rasher bodies lay scattered on the pavement, heads blown to bits. Blood was starting to pool, dark and congealed. He helped me to my feet, then looked up at the figures on the roofs. They'd saved us.

Mitch flinched. He touched my wrist and whispered, "Get to the truck."

"Why?"

"Just go."

We hurried back, but as soon we made it to the truck door, a woman emerged from behind a building and aimed her gun at us. "Drop your weapons."

Mitch only had the Swiss Army knife. He swore under his breath, placed it on the ground, and put his hands up. I put mine up too. That's when I spotted the car keys peeking out from beneath one of the tires.

The rest of her crew emerged, some climbing down from rooftops, the others circling us on foot. There were six of them.

The woman tilted her head toward the truck, and two of them moved in without a word. Scavengers.

I bent and snatched the keys from the ground.

"Not so fast," said the woman.

Mitch's face hardened. He looked at me firmly. "Get in and start the engine."

I jumped in through the driver's side and jammed the key into the ignition, but before Mitch could follow, the woman fired a shot into the air. "I said don't move!"

Mitch hovered by the door, four guns aimed at him. The other two scavengers peered into the truck bed through the cap windows, but they only had knives.

"They got gas," one of them said. "And food."

"Hey, that's my—" Mitch took a step toward them, but the woman shoved the tip of her gun into his chest. The man in army fatigues stepped up.

"Give us your stash and you can go," he said.

"No. It ain't yours," said Mitch.

The man in fatigues half-grinned and peered at me through the windshield. "There's a safe zone just over the border. You don't need any of that stuff anymore."

Mitch's face was hard as stone. "No."

"Alright," said the man. "We'll give you a couple of options, then. Either you give us your stuff, or you give us your little sister here as collateral."

My heart stopped. Mitch glanced at me, face still twitching. For a second, I thought he was considering it—handing me over to them, letting them do who knows what.

But then, he kicked the woman hard in the stomach, dove into the truck, and grabbed the wheel. Gunfire erupted.

"Go!" I screamed.

Mitch didn't even close the door before he slammed his foot on the gas pedal. The truck lurched forward and he swerved hard, slamming into the man in fatigues. The tires thudded over him. More bullets rained, and glass shattered over my head as the windshield blasted apart. I ducked and squeezed my eyes shut.

"Hold on!" Mitch said.

The engine revved, and we were off, cutting between warehouses, racing for the edge of the compound. Bullets pinged off the tailgate, the side mirror, the doors. But then we were free. Mitch picked up speed and drove right off the road, racing for the open desert across the border.

CHAPTER SEVENTEEN

WE AVOIDED the military checkpoint altogether. Mitch drove straight out, headlights shooting through the darkness, the tires bulldozing over rocks and shrubs. Then suddenly the land smoothed out, and we were driving through shallow water across a white landscape. The salt flats.

"I would've killed all of them!" he yelled. "Every last one of them!"

His hands clenched the wheel, but it felt like he was barely in control. I held my breath as we sped through the water, and at our sides, it splashed as high as the windows. Wind whipped through the broken windshield.

Mitch drove in raging silence. Drove and drove. The lights dimmed behind us, and ahead, the earth sprawled beneath a black, starry sky. Finally, the gas meter dinged. The dinging seemed to snap Mitch out of his fiery stupor—we were running on empty.

He let out a huff and let the truck come to an abrupt stop.

I sat very still as he turned the engine off, and when the headlights cut out, we were drenched in darkness. North of us, I could faintly make out the road stretching across the land, but only because there were a few minuscule lights from cars, heading east toward Salt Lake City. They blinked and disappeared.

"Here's as good a place as any to stop for the night. They won't follow us." He laughed to himself. "Clearly, they don't have the fuel to, anyhow."

I gripped the seat, trying to stop my hands from trembling. A small light clicked on—a flashlight on Mitch's keys. His face softened when he got a look at me. "Hey, we're safe now."

But his chin was scraped, there was a smatter of blood on the side of his face, and his jacket was all ripped up. My lap was sprinkled with glass. I stared at him in shock, unable to comprehend why he was being so calm. He smiled sympathetically, but I could still smell that *smell*. And why had I frozen back there when that rasher in scrubs had reached for me? Why couldn't I just run?

My gaze drifted into the black outside. I could run now. I could get away. My fingers twitched against the door handle. If I moved fast enough, if I didn't think, just ran—

"We should lie down," Mitch said.

My stomach sank. But I forced myself to nod, even though the thought of closing my eyes made me uneasy, and opened the door. Outside, we sloshed through the water, and Mitch opened the tailgate. I looked out, awestruck for a moment. The landscape unfolded around us, void and endless. The water was so still and clear that it reflected the stars, and I felt as though I was in between two worlds. I couldn't see much else. Not even the road now.

There was nowhere for me to go.

I crawled into the truck bed, balled up my jacket beneath my head, and faced the wall. My backpack sat an inch from my head, and I ran my finger down the canvas strap mindlessly as Mitch settled in. He stuck close. The space was cramped, and his presence loomed. My body didn't feel like my own.

"I was trying to protect you," he said. "From your mom, I mean. I think she was…infected."

"Why would you think that?" I whispered.

"She was so tired. She didn't seem all there, you know?"

Mitch breathed heavily for a moment, gauging my reaction. "Are you okay?"

I hesitated, scared to be honest. "I'm just…tired."

"You don't have to worry," he murmured. His fingers skimmed my arm, cool against my skin. "I'll protect you."

The words sank into my bones. My throat felt tight, my skin electric with the urge to run, but my limbs wouldn't cooperate. My shoulder pressed into the hard bed of the truck like I was glued there. *Protect me.* Like he hadn't just left my mother bleeding on the pavement.

I closed my eyes tight, head spinning. It was all catching up to me, everything from the last few days. The bodies, the news about the base, the uncertainty about my brother. And now, just like everyone else, Mom was gone too, and I was alone. All of this had become infinitely scarier. Infinitely more real, more urgent, more deadly.

I shivered hard. Mitch put his arm over me and pulled me close. "You're cold," he said.

His hand roamed over my shoulder, rubbing warmth into me. A knot of fear tightened in my stomach. "Mitch…"

His fingers tightened around my shoulder. He rolled me over and silenced me with a soft, demanding kiss.

"It's okay," he whispered.

My chest burned. His hands gripped me. The rush of everything paralyzed me, and I couldn't move, couldn't say yes or no, couldn't do anything but give in to the overwhelm. He kissed me again, and though my fists curled against the blanket, though everything inside me screamed *stop,* I went numb. I didn't want to disappoint him, set him on edge. I didn't want him to think I was a child.

But I *was* a child.

He moved over me, body pressing me into the blanket, his fingers digging into my skin. I felt a surge of panic. "Mitch, wait."

"Shh, it's okay."

I pushed his chest. "Please, I just…I just…" I was crying. "This is too much. Please—"

"Hey, hey," he said, looking down at me, eyes dark. "Don't cry."

"I want to go home," I whimpered, covering my face. "I want to go home. I want my mom. I want to—please, just—"

I started crying so hard I couldn't even choke out the words. Snot ran from my nose, and my chest heaved, and tears rolled down to my ears. Mitch got off and lay beside me. Then he pulled me to his chest. I cried into his shirt, shaking, so broken up that I couldn't resist being held, even when every fiber of me wanted to run.

"I'm so scared," I sobbed.

He shushed me and rubbed my back. "I know. But you're safe with me. I won't hurt you."

I knew that wasn't true, but I squeezed my eyes shut and let him hold me, because I didn't have any other options. I didn't have anybody left in the whole world. He put his cheek against my head, and I bit my tongue so I'd stop crying. I could smell that stench on him. Blood.

"We'll be okay. In the morning, we'll figure out what to do."

Relief coursed through me like a rainstorm. Morning. I just had to get through one night, and maybe I'd find someone to help me. "We'll get to the safe zone?" I asked.

Mitch didn't respond right away. He hummed a small laugh. "I don't know if they'll let me in, Layla." He lifted the remnants of his torn sleeve to show me his arm. The skin was broken, bleeding lightly, the edges of the wound already slightly green.

My heart stopped.

He'd been bitten.

"It's okay," he whispered. "Papa said they have a vaccine. They'll help me."

"Are you sure?"

"They have to have one. All of this…they planned it. They did."

His voice drifted off, and he closed his eyes, deeply tired after going so long without sleep. After everything. I stared at him warily, wanting to get away, but he still had his arms around me, holding me in place. I was stuck. I was going to die here.

His breath was hot against my head, his weight dense. I looked at his hand resting against my ribs, imagining it crawling up me like a spider. Fumbling and impatient, like he knew it was his last chance to take something before he was gone. But his hand was still.

I waited until his breath slowed and his arm fell limp over me. I had to get out.

I stayed put a little longer, just to be safe. When I was sure he was out cold, I slid out from under him and carefully got my bag and my hat, the only belongings I had left in all the world. That, and pages of an unfinished comic book that would probably never see the light of day.

I squeezed through the tiny open window into the cab, my hands pressing into shards of windshield glass. When I pulled my stuff through after me, Mitch stirred, but he didn't wake up. I didn't wait around. I stepped out into the shallow water of the salt flats, not even bothering to close the door behind me, and I ran. I headed for the light of the road in the distance as fast as my legs would take me, my bag thumping against my back in the same place where Mitch had put his hands on me. I ran, and I didn't look back.

PART III
THE SAFE ZONE

CHAPTER EIGHTEEN

THE WHITE GROUND stretched as far as I could see, glistening under the moonlight. It all looked the same. There was nowhere to hide while I ran. No rocks, no trees, not a single building in sight, just salt and shallow water for miles. Just the road stretching ahead like a beacon.

I splashed toward it until I couldn't run any longer, then slowed to catch my breath. It was only then that I felt a gnawing pain inside my cheek. I realized the pain had been there for a while, but I'd been too numb to notice it: a wire of my braces had snapped. The sharp end dug into my skin, filling my mouth with the taste of blood.

I pushed at the wire with my finger, but I couldn't bend it back into place. My eyes pricked with tears. It was so stupid. So small and stupid and normal. I should've been home. Mom should've been driving me to the orthodontist to fix this—I shouldn't even have *had* braces anymore. Instead, I was sloshing through a salt flat, completely on my own, hundreds of miles away. My mouth was bleeding, and Mom was probably dead.

Mom was probably dead.

I hung my head, stomach rolling, and threw up into the water. Beans and peanut butter and stale rice crackers. But when the nausea passed, I wiped my mouth and forced my legs to keep moving.

Back in the town with the abandoned warehouses, Mitch had said the safe zone was ninety miles away. I could walk for days out here and I'd never make it that far. I didn't even know if I could make it back to the town—even if I did, I'd risk running into those scavengers again. We were quite literally in the middle of nowhere, and whichever way I turned, I'd be walking for miles. Mitch would find me before I got anywhere.

I could see now how the smallest things could make the biggest difference. They build up and build up until you're stranded in them, sinking in your decisions like mud. That's what had happened to Preston. He wasn't a bad kid, he'd just made too many decisions that had sucked him under.

Maybe this wasn't completely my fault, but I'd put myself here. I'd put my trust in the wrong person. And whatever I did, there was no way out.

Keep moving, keep moving, keep moving.

When I reached the road, there were no cars, and no sign of civilization except a small, lonesome cell tower. I slipped into a trance as I walked along the shoulder, heading east. One foot in front of the other, hands tight on my backpack straps. I was so tense my neck hurt, and even though I was freezing cold, my skin was drenched in sweat. The leather of my boots was wet and salty, and my feet stung inside them, the blisters torn back open. I forced myself not to think about it. About Mom. Not to think *she was right, and I should've listened, and she's probably dead.* But I thought it anyway, over and over and over again.

I was only pulled to reality when a beam of light hit my back.

A car engine rumbled behind me, and my first thought was that Mitch had found me.

My legs started running again with a mind of their own. I didn't look back, but the light was gaining on me. I breathed so hard I was sure no air was reaching my lungs. He was going to get me. He was going to kill me this time, or do something worse to me first, and then kill me. I felt the wet burn of his lips, and I was blinded with rage and disgust and deep, choking fear. My foot caught. I tripped off the shoulder into the water on the side of the road.

Car brakes squealed behind me. A door opened and slammed.

I covered my head with my hands.

"Hey! Are you okay?" said a voice.

It was a woman. For a second, I thought it was Mom, but that was stupid. I pushed myself to my knees, soaked from my fall and washed in the headlights, and looked back at the road. The car had stopped—a big van, not a truck. A silhouette of a woman stood in the light. Yelling.

"Hello? Do you need help?"

I stood on shaky legs and tried to focus. The woman was wearing an old-fashioned dress, her hair in a poofy braid. Someone else was climbing out of the van to look at me, too: a man in a white button-up. I didn't know what else to do, where else to go, so I told my feet to move toward them.

The man stepped back as I approached. "God, she's covered in blood."

"Are you sick?" asked the woman.

I shook my head.

The woman put her hand on his arm and moved closer, her tone gentle. "Are you alone? Are you trying to get someplace? Are you in danger?"

I didn't know which question I was answering, but I nodded. I couldn't get my voice to work. I was still shaking hard, dripping water, the taste of blood pooling in my mouth.

"She can come with us," the woman whispered. The man looked like he was about to protest, but she cut him off. "God would expect us to help a child."

The man set his jaw and looked me over. "Have you been tested for the virus?"

"No," I whispered. "But I'm not... I just need..."

I stumbled and fell onto my knees. Without a second thought, the woman raced forward and put her arms around me just as I collapsed completely. She eased me to the ground.

"She *must* be sick," the man said.

"I don't think so. You remember what they said about children."

"Well, something is clearly wrong with her!"

They argued over me, their voices swimming. Finally, the woman convinced him they couldn't leave me here; God *would* expect them to help a child.

The next thing I knew, I was on my feet again, being guided to the van. The back door slid open. The inside was full of children: six of them, all dressed in old-fashioned clothes like their parents.

"Mary-Kenna," the woman said to the girl closest to the front, "make some room. Give her your blanket." She squeezed my arm. "Can you tell me your name, precious?"

"Layla."

Mary-Kenna, who seemed to be about my age, handed me a knit blanket from her lap, already warm. I glanced at the children behind me, spanning from teenagers to a toddler, and they all blinked back at me.

The couple got into the front. "We're going to Salt Lake City, to the safe zone," the woman told me. "Is that where you were headed?"

I nodded.

As we drove, Mary-Kenna scooted to the front of her seat and reached for her mother's hand. They intertwined fingers, squeezing so hard their knuckles were white.

WE REACHED the safe zone after about an hour. It wasn't within the city itself, but in the wide, grassy valley at the base of a mountain. We followed bright yellow signs toward the camp, the van rattling on the rough road. There was a small trail of cars with us now.

I huddled in the back seat, drooping with exhaustion, and absentmindedly ran my finger over the broken wire in my mouth. Up front, the couple spoke in hushed tones, and occasionally the mother would glance back at everyone. I clutched the blanket tightly around my shoulders and tried to ignore the feeling of all their wary eyes on me. I wanted to ask where they were from, why they'd ended up here, what had made them leave their home for the safe zone. But speaking seemed impossible.

Finally, we approached the safe zone entrance. There was a sign that had been painted over to say *Government Quarantine Zone*, but by the triangle insignia sticking out on top, I could tell it used to be a sign for a campground. There were long, white tents in the distance, lined up inside a perimeter fence. They were lit up by floodlights, which cast an eerie glow into the otherwise oppressive dark. It felt like the whole world had been swallowed up except for this one place.

"This is it?" said one of the boys in the back seat. "This doesn't look like a safe zone to me."

We drove along the dirt road and passed a sprawling field filled with parked cars. Mary Kenna leaned toward the window to look. "We visited here once," she whispered to me. "We came to visit the temple in Salt Lake City, and then we camped by a reservoir out here. Hard to believe it's..." She shook her head, her words tapering off into the void.

We pulled up to a gate, where a large group of armed guards in muddy green hazmat suits stood. Beyond the gate, a single white tent fluttered in the wind, and a line of people waited to get inside. The people were hemmed in by more fencing and more armed guards—they looked like convicts at a prison.

One of the guards stepped toward the van and motioned for the father to roll his window down. He peered into the back. With his hazmat suit on, all I could see of his face was his eyes, barely visible behind his bulky, protective mask. "How many?"

The father looked back for a second, like he had to count how many kids he had. "Uh, nine. Two adults, seven children. One of them isn't ours."

The soldier nodded, his eyes glossing over me in a clinical way. "Has anyone in your party exhibited symptoms of illness within the last 48 hours, including rash, fever, shortness of breath, acts of uncharacteristic violence, or hallucinations?"

"None, sir."

"Please exit the vehicle and proceed to the testing area to the left. Take only necessary belongings."

"But we have—"

"Only necessary belongings," the hazmat repeated. "All items will be searched and sterilized. Exit the vehicle and proceed to the testing area ahead."

The parents opened the back van door, and as the cold rushed in, the children piled out. But I hesitated. The mother reached her hand out to me. "It's going to be okay," she said softly. "They'll take care of you."

I swallowed and accepted her helping hand. The air was cold and still, and the gravel crunched underfoot as we were herded toward the line of many others, barricaded by fencing, and flanked on both sides by hazmats with guns. Floodlights buzzed above us and our breath showed in startled white clouds. I wrapped my arms tightly around myself, shivering so hard my knees knocked. I should've brought a better coat. Mom had packed one. It was still in the Yukon on the side of the road in Nevada.

The father stopped to say something quietly to a hazmat. The hazmat nodded and approached me. "You, come with me."

I wanted to stay with this family—the only scrap of safety I'd felt since losing Mom. Had that really been less than a day ago? Was I already that alone? But I followed the hazmat away. I was taken toward the tent entrance. We passed through the crowd of waiting people, all of them standing silently, some holding small children, some wearing masks that were probably futile.

When I reached the tent entrance, I looked back at Mary-Kenna, carrying her little brother on her hip. She offered a nervous smile. I was pulled through the tent flaps, and she disappeared.

Inside, the tent was bigger than it looked. It was partitioned into narrow stalls by translucent plastic curtains, stretching far back. The air smelled like disinfectant, like nothingness. Guards bustled around, herding people into rooms.

"Lone minor," my hazmat guard said, passing me off to a man wearing a protective suit, holding a tablet.

"Another one," grumbled the man. "Come with me."

I was immediately forced into a stall up front to be sanitized with some icy, chemical spray that made my eyes sting and my skin feel powdery dry. When I stepped out, the man slapped a plastic bracelet on my wrist with a barcode on it. My identification.

They took my hat and bag and pointed me forward, deeper into the tent. "Proceed."

I was directed into a curtained stall with a chair and a small table. There was another hazmat inside, this one a woman. She had an array of medical supplies on the table, swabs and vials and tools my pediatrician might have. I sat slowly as she arranged the tools, practiced and precise.

"I said, what's your name?"

I blinked and put my hands between my knees to stop the shaking. "Huh? Oh, uh…Layla Wise."

My chest heaved. But I wasn't going to cry. Not for Mitch, not for being so stupid. Not for the way it still felt like I was back in that car, pinned down, unable to breathe. Locked in that moment. Thinking of Mom.

She took my wrist and scanned my barcode with a small tablet. Then she asked me questions in a clipped voice. *Any exposure to NVS-1? Any fever, rash, hallucinations?* But I couldn't answer. My eyes stung. The stall smelled like bleach and rubber, like a hospital, but also like the earth. I looked at the dirt beneath my boots, my heart battering against my chest, my mouth burning with its open wound.

"Layla?" she said.

I blinked hard, tears spilling. "Sorry. It's just—I have—" I touched my lips. I didn't know what I was trying to say. There was so much—too much—and none of it seemed expressible. The tears poured, and I bit my tongue, trying to hold back. But the tears kept coming, and my shoulders shook, and a small, choked sound broke loose from my chest, like a wounded animal.

"I'm sorry," I said, folding over myself. "I'm sorry, I—I don't know why I—"

I couldn't even get the words out. I was a blubbering mess.

"You don't have to apologize." The woman sighed and lowered her tablet. "Did something happen to you out there?"

I nodded from the nest of my arms.

Then a dam broke, and the words wouldn't stop coming.

"My mom was with me, but there was this guy, and she told me to get away, but I didn't—I couldn't—and now I'm here, and—" I choked. "—and my braces. My braces broke, and I can't—my mom isn't—I don't know what to—"

"Hey, hey, hey." Very carefully, in a way that told me it was against the rules, the woman crouched and put a hand on my knee. "You're safe now. Whatever happened, it's not your fault."

She waited until my breath settled enough before she spoke again.

"I just need to do a few tests. It'll be over in a minute. Okay?"

I nodded.

"Good. Can you open your mouth for me?" She peered inside with a small light and hovered over the wound. "Ouch. Broken wire, huh? Let me finish your tests, and then I'll see if I can take care of that."

So she pricked my finger for blood, shone the light in my eyes, checked my temperature and heart rate, and took a nasal swab that made my eyes water. She asked me if I'd been in contact with any infected people, and I told her the truth.

The woman put my samples into a bag, labeled it, and whisked everything out of the room. She promptly returned with a small pair of wire cutters. "We're not supposed to give medical attention unless you've passed testing, but just don't tell, okay?"

Her voice was softer than it had been when I'd first come in. Like a woman who finds a lost little kid in the park and knows exactly what to do.

"I used to have braces," she said as I opened my mouth again. "I know the pain. Let me see if I can snip it. It won't fix it completely, but it'll at least feel better for a little while."

She cut the wire, and I sighed with relief, feeling the sore in my mouth with my tongue. It still hurt, but it *was* better. I felt a weight lift off my shoulders, like the world was a smidge more manageable. Like I could stand up without falling down. "If your test comes back negative, they'll send you through to the quarantine camp," she said. "There are medics there. They can help you and fix up that cut on your eyebrow."

I touched my face, unaware that I even had a cut at all. "I was supposed to get my braces off this week," I told her softly.

She didn't respond to that, just patted my knee, and I couldn't help but think her touch felt like Mom's. "Your test results should come within an hour. Good luck, Layla." And then she was gone.

CHAPTER NINETEEN

AFTER TESTING, a group of us was sent out back, where there were about fifty squares spray-painted on the ground. We were each told to stand in one square and not leave it—a miniature, temporary quarantine. A few armed soldiers in protective gear marched back and forth along the fence perimeter.

I went to my designated square and sat shivering on the cold ground, legs pulled to my chest. I sat for over an hour, rubbing my cheek. I never saw the family from the van and figured they were getting tested, or maybe even still in line. Somewhere, a baby cried, and in another direction, someone coughed. Everything else was still and quiet, and overhead, the moon hung heavy and low.

I had nearly fallen asleep on my knees when I heard a loud voice and jolted upright.

It was one of the soldiers, speaking into a megaphone by the fence gate. "Everyone up! Form a single-file line at the gate. Keep your distance."

There was a frantic scraping sound as dozens of people got to their feet. I stood shakily and followed as we were herded into a narrow chute of chain-link fence. I found myself behind a young couple with a baby, and I craned my neck to see around them. Up ahead, past the gate, there were two vehicles waiting: a dark, armored van to the right, and a truck with an open back lined with benches to the left.

As people approached the front, two soldiers scanned their barcode bracelets. I strained to see, listening to each *beep* of the scanners, watching as the soldiers then pushed people toward one vehicle or the other. Most of them were pushed to the right.

My heart started to pound harder. What did this mean? Who was infected? What if I was? Had it been from the incident by the warehouses yesterday, or from Mitch, or from before? I forgot how to breathe as I stood there, holding my arms so tightly around my chest that it hurt.

Finally, the couple ahead of me reached the front of the line and were scanned. *Beep.* The woman and baby were directed to the left, the man to the right. The woman tried to follow him, asking where they were taking him. No one answered her. She was pushed back. The man strained against the guards, but he couldn't fight them.

"I'll be fine!" he called to her. "Just get to the camp and I'll see you soon!"

And then he was shoved into the back of the vehicle with the others. The sound of its slamming door echoed across the clearing, and then it was gone, speeding off into the darkness of the valley.

The woman cried and sank down with her baby. A guard hoisted them up and pushed her toward the nearly empty truck.

There were still many of us left in line, everyone's faces shocked and white under the floodlights. Another van promptly pulled up to replace the one that had driven away.

A soldier nudged me forward, firm and impersonal. My breaths were labored with the knowledge that each one could be my last, that I had limited air here, limited steps. I was suffocating. He lifted my wrist to scan my barcode with his small device. *Beep.*

"To your left," he said. When I didn't move, he rolled his eyes. "You're clean. They'll take you to the quarantine camp."

Relief flooded me so intensely that I stumbled forward,

barely able to keep my balance as I climbed up into the truck. As I sat down, I glanced back at the quarantine squares. A new group was being brought out from the tent, and I spotted the family from the van, about to sit and await their fate.

I realized what a risk it must have been to let me in their car, not knowing whether I was sick or dangerous. But if they hadn't taken a chance on me, I'd still be out on the salt flats ninety miles away. Or I'd be with Mitch. Or I'd be dead.

We were driven away from the testing site, toward the other fenced-in area lined with long, white tents. Before we were let in, a new soldier stood at the back of the truck and gave instructions. "This is the quarantine camp. Before entering, you will be processed. Your bracelets will act as your identification; do not remove them at risk of being expelled from the camp. You'll be held in quarantine for five days, and then retested. Should you begin exhibiting any symptoms of the virus, you will be sent back to the testing site immediately. But if you pass the second round of testing, you will be granted access to the military safe zone, which is at an undisclosed location not far from here. Spots at the safe zone are limited, and should they fill before you are granted access, you will be asked to leave the area."

We were given a set of clothes in paper packaging to wear while ours were disinfected, then we were sent to small booths to shower and change. It was inside the booth, in a small, round mirror, that I finally got a look at myself. I almost didn't recognize the girl staring back at me.

Her eyes were swollen and bloodshot. There was dirt on her chin, a red cut through her eyebrow, a faint smear of blood on her face. Her hair was still in braids that her mother had given her, but they were so ratty you could hardly tell.

I turned away from the mirror and took the braids out. Then I looked through the camp-issued clothes in the paper bag—a gray t-shirt, sweatpants, and a crewneck—and began to undress, but my hands trembled so badly I could barely undo the button on my jeans.

The mirror caught the slope of my bare shoulder as I pulled

my shirt off. I couldn't stop staring. It wasn't that I hadn't understood what had happened back in that car, but there was something about seeing it on me—the faint, fresh bruise forming on my collarbone where his hand had gripped me—that made me realize just how violent it had been. Worse, somehow, than the rashers. Than all of it.

I curled forward, suddenly exhausted, the adrenaline gone. But I didn't cry again. I just crouched there, half-dressed and hollowed out, scared to look in the mirror again.

I shivered under the harsh stream from the showerhead, trying not to cry. As I scrubbed myself clean, the blood and dirt pooled at my feet and disappeared down the drain. I would have stayed beneath that stream all night if it hadn't turned off. Five minutes was all I got.

I forced myself to change—I even had to trade my boots for a pair of flimsy, slipper-like shoes—and then stepped out of the booth. My clothes and boots were swiftly labeled with my identification number and taken away.

Next, I was directed to a blue medical tent where a young medic rubbed the inside of my cheek with antiseptic, put a spot of wax on the end of my braces wire, and stuck a thin white bandage over my eyebrow. After that, he asked me all sorts of information. My name, my age, where I was from.

By the time I left the medical tent, the night had given way to cold, impartial dawn. I was handed a bundle of stuff—a scratchy blanket and a small hygiene kit—and brought into the camp. Although it was early in the morning, there were a few people in identical gray outfits meandering between the tents. I could tell this used to be a campground; there was a small, faded playground in the center, and toward the back, two cement bathrooms.

I was assigned to tent B. It was quiet and dark, filled with cots and sleeping bodies. Everyone inside was a kid like me. Lone minors. No parents. I chose an empty cot against the tent wall, unfolded the scratchy blanket, and wrapped myself up. I traced the ghost of blue larkspur on my wrist, still just visible, until my eyes grew heavy.

It was starting to sink in now. This was my life, and I'd have to go through it with no brother, no parents. If I made it through this week, I'd be placed in some government safe zone and never see my family again—maybe Dad, someday, somehow. But for now, I didn't see a way out of this.

I tried to sleep for a while, but couldn't. It was morning anyway. Kids started waking up when a few workers wheeled in a cart of breakfast trays. It came in steaming, sealed packages like TV dinners. I pulled off the plastic top to find a serving of bland oatmeal, sausage links, and two small, soggy pancakes. I'd eaten in the back of Mitch's truck last night, but none of that had stayed down.

The thought of him killed my appetite.

On an overhead speaker, they started calling identification numbers for showers. I waited patiently on the edge of my cot, hoping for another chance to rinse off the shame of the last few days, but my number didn't get called. I watched the other kids wander around in the meantime. Some of them seemed fine, playing card games or reading or drawing, like all they could do was distract themselves. But others were glued to their cots, stone cold, their breakfasts lying untouched at their feet.

I curled up on the cot, pulled the blanket over my head, and finally slept. I slept so hard that I only woke up when they began passing out dinner. It was green beans and potatoes and some kind of meat in a sealed package. My body ached with hunger now, but I ate mechanically, senseless and unfeeling.

I wished I had my stuff. The comic, at the very least, so I'd have something to occupy my mind. Maybe someone could help me find it.

I left the tent and found a young soldier daydreaming on a stool outside the door. "Excuse me?"

He blinked out of his stupor and smiled. He had braces like me, and acne, but was clearly a bit older judging by his scruffy attempt at a mustache. Still, so young. "Yes, ma'am?"

"Where can I find my stuff? Like, how do I get it back?"

He pointed to a wide shed off against the back fence. "There's a warehouse back behind the bathrooms. They keep everything there after it's sanitized."

"Seems disorganized."

"I guess. But it's not like we planned for this to happen." It reminded me of what Walt had said, about how this was all intentional, meant to get rid of us. How it was all in the government's plan. It was hard to know what was true. The soldier finished his thought. "Anyway, they'll call your number at some point, and you can go back there and claim your belongings."

"Oh," I said.

"Why, you missing something?"

I shrugged.

He glanced around the camp, at the people walking back and

forth from the bathrooms and the other soldiers marching around on duty. "I could probably take you in there."

"Really?"

He pushed off the stool. "Yeah, why not?"

As we walked, I realized he wasn't wearing any protection, hazmat suit, mask, or otherwise. Just his fatigues. "Why aren't you wearing a mask?" I asked.

"I'm mostly stationed around the kid tents, and kids aren't really getting sick. Don't know why. But I'm not too concerned being around you guys." He smiled kindly. "Are you alone?"

His voice sent a shiver down my spine. I took a shallow breath, burning with memories, with the feeling of being on my own.

"Sorry," he said. "I was just asking because I know a lot of kids here are alone. And I just wanted you to know you're not… you know. *Alone*, alone." He stared at me uncomfortably for a second, then ran his palms down his pants, like they were sweating. "You know, uh…in these trying times, I find comfort in faith. Have you heard of the Book of Mormon?"

"Um…I think so."

"Have you ever considered reading it? I can't help but think that with everything going on, it's a sign of the coming tribulations when the righteous will be caught up with Christ's return."

I hesitated, not sure how to respond. "I don't know what to believe, really."

He nodded empathetically. "I get it. But listen, if you ever want to talk through things, give me a holler, okay?"

We were approaching the metal warehouse at the back of the camp. I glanced out beyond the perimeter fence. From here, there was a view of that field of cars. It looked like a junkyard, abandoned and shining under the sinking Utah sun. Or a graveyard, more like. I wondered how many of those cars' owners were dead now. The thought made me shiver.

"By the way, what's your name?" the young soldier asked.

"Layla."

"I'm Gideon. Nice to meet you."

I bobbed my head toward the field. "All those cars…what will happen to them?"

"Not sure. We have a stockpile of keys, but not everyone will come back to claim them when this is all over. Those cars mostly belong to people who were sick. Not many people actually pass testing, you know."

"And what happens to those people?"

Gideon hesitated. "Well, there's no hope for them."

"So?"

"So we take them somewhere else to…you know. Die." He cleared his throat. "We better hurry and find your stuff. You can't be out of your tent after seven."

I obeyed and walked after him into the warehouse. It was bigger than I expected, like an old barn with high, beamed ceilings and lurid, yellowish lights hanging down. It was absolutely full of bags, suitcases, clothes, toys, laptops, phones, shoes. All of it was piled on plastic storage shelves, so tall you'd need a ladder to reach the tops. There was a peg board of hanging car keys on the wall, too.

A few soldiers were on duty inside, and they took a few minutes to hunt down my bag of clothes, my boots, my yellow striped backpack, my cowgirl hat. The soldier handed the hat to me last, and I ran my fingers along the soft, velvety rim.

"That's a nice hat," Gideon said.

"It was my mother's," I lied. I didn't know why I said it, but I had nothing of hers. I wanted something to hold onto her with.

I left Gideon in the warehouse and carried all my stuff back toward tent B, hugging it all to my chest. Everything smelled like antiseptic, the same smell as when they'd sprayed us down before they tested us. I didn't mind. In a way, it felt like all the stains of yesterday had been chemically stripped away, and now I could shove it out of my brain and start clean.

I got a little lost between tents on my way back. I entered what I thought was my tent and wove between the kids, who were either getting ready for bed or playing games. But when I went to the cot by the wall, I realized it wasn't mine—there was a Barbie doll on the pillow—and even in the dim light, I recognized that these weren't the same kids I'd been with before. This wasn't my tent.

I walked through, heading for the exit on the opposite end. But as I was heading out, I happened to look down and notice something lying on a cot. It was a comic book.

I stopped in my tracks and leaned in close, finding myself face-to-face with a detailed ink drawing of a bear named Major Ursus.

CHAPTER TWENTY

MY BREATH CAUGHT in my throat. I dropped everything to the ground and picked up the comic in disbelief. It was Jamal's. Clear as day, it was his.

That meant he was here somewhere.

I tossed the comic book down and took off, weaving through the cots and dodging kids, my heart thundering. I burst back outside. The compound was sprawling, tent after tent, person after person, soldier after soldier. A couple kids played on the playground in the center, and the sound of voices and running water from the bathrooms drifted through the camp. But I couldn't see him anywhere. It crossed my mind that he might be gone, taken back to testing. Or worse.

I stopped running, hardly able to breathe. "Jamal!" I shouted. I whirled around, searching the crowd, but I couldn't see him. Not his small frame, his dark hair, his stupid, impish smile. "Jam—"

"Layla?"

I turned quickly, my heart lifting, but it wasn't Jamal. It was Deepti. Perfect, pixie Deepti with her hair in wet knots, her face gaunt, her eyes dark. She hardly looked like Deepti at all.

We stared at each other for a moment, too stunned to comprehend it all. That we were here, that California and Ms. Henry and the Air Force base were back there, in an entirely different life than the one we had now. But then, at once, we flew forward on the stubbly, yellow grass and came together. She threw her arms around me and squeezed hard.

"Deepti," I gasped. "I can't—"

"I know."

She began to shake—she was crying. I pulled back. "What is it?"

She shook her head and wiped at her tear-stained cheeks. "I'm just so glad to see you. I can't believe it. My parents are gone. They're *all* gone. They took us here—"

"Who did?"

"The Air Force. Things went bad at the base, so they put a bunch of us on a plane and sent us out here. It was insane, Layla. You should've seen all the dead people. They were just lying there, and it was—" She couldn't finish her sentence without breaking into another sob. I pulled her in again. I hadn't realized how bad it could've possibly been for other people until I got here, to this tent full of parentless kids.

"How did *you* get here?" Deepti asked after a shuddering breath.

"I, uh…" I began, but I found it very hard to piece anything together at all. Seeing her break down—even just seeing *her*—had opened something inside me, and I felt the sting of tears again. I did *not* want to cry. "Doesn't matter. What about Jamal?"

She lit up. "He's here! Layla, he's here. He just went to the showers, but he'll be back."

Frantic hope fluttered in my chest. She took my hand and pulled me toward the back of the camp near the warehouse. There were those concrete bathrooms there, no doubt from the campsite days. It was nearly seven, and everyone was hurrying back to their cots, but we stood hand-in-hand, waiting and waiting as people filtered out, scanning each of their faces quickly. Deepti bounced on her feet. I felt like I was going to puke.

He finally stepped outside, wiping his face with a tiny white towel. When he lowered it, we immediately locked eyes. He halted, shocked. "Layla?"

I burst into tears and flung my arms around his neck, nearly knocking him off his feet. For a second, he was stiff, like he was afraid I might not be real. But then he laughed in disbelief, and the towel fell from his hand, and his arms closed around me. He hugged me so hard he almost lifted me from the ground. I was sobbing again like I had in the truck as we left Mom behind, falling apart all over him. But he just let me. We were too afraid to break it up with words. Too afraid to give attention to our reality. For now, I just wanted him close to me.

When he finally did let me go, he studied my face like he was trying to confirm this wasn't a dream. "How are you here?"

I smiled weakly and rubbed my teary cheeks. "It's a long story. I'm just so glad you're okay."

We hugged again, but before we could ask each other anything else, a low bell tone rang across the camp from the speakers, signaling curfew.

"I have to get back to my tent," I said.

He hooked me by the arm and pulled me after him. "They won't notice if you come to our tent for a little." We took a few steps forward, but then he slowed, his face contorted. "Is your mom here?"

I tensed. "That's part of the story."

Inside tent D, we sat on his and Deepti's cots. The camp dimmed the lights even more, and we leaned close to whisper so we wouldn't wake the kids who were already going to sleep.

I let them recount their stories first.

"The day you left, it all got really bad," Jamal said, eyes dark with the memory.

Not long after Mom and I had left town, panic about the outbreak spread. The power went down and things collapsed quickly. The supermarkets were scalped for food, storefronts were bashed in, fights broke out over supplies. Like nothing. Like a blink. Jamal heard that in the bigger cities, the military rolled in and started enforcing the quarantine mandate under threat of death. That's all he really heard, but things had turned violent fast.

That didn't even account for the violence of the rashers.

"Did you see any?" I asked Jamal.

He looked at his hands. "I was on the base the whole time but...yeah. I saw some."

Civilians thought the base was a safe place: locked down and heavily guarded, possibly offering evacuations. They had driven up in droves and swarmed at the gates. Families and acquaintances of military personnel, local government officials, and random, desperate people begging for a chance at survival.

By the second day, the situation worsened.

The story was that one of the technicians started showing

sudden symptoms, and an airman shot him, and then everyone panicked—who else was infected inside the base, and how could they stop it? As the Air Force tried to take care of their internal situation, things outside spiraled quickly. Jamal didn't know many details, but the crowd trying to get in only grew, and it was getting harder to control. Some of the higher-ups—his father included—made the call to evacuate non-essential personnel on the base and load up a plane bound for the nearest open safe zone: Salt Lake City.

But before they could, something happened with the crowd. Either someone was infected and started attacking, or the panic grew too severe, but either way, the defenses broke, and civilians got through the gates.

At this point, it was night and Jamal was sleeping, but the next thing he knew, there was an alarm going off and his father was standing over his bed, saying Jamal had to move. He only had time to grab his coat and backpack before he was ushered outside and put on a truck headed for the tarmac. But by now, civilians had made it to the tarmac too—some of them in cars— and they were swarming the planes, bathed in bright white light from the floodlights.

In the chaos, Jamal and Deepti and some other families were pushed toward a plane. Deepti was wrenched away from her family. All around, people were shoving their way forward. Then, there were gunshots. People screamed, and that's when Jamal saw a rasher for the first time. He wasn't sure when they'd turned or how they'd gotten on the base, but there were a couple surging through the crowd, biting and ripping and tackling people to the ground.

In the assault of gunfire, Jamal got onto the plane, expecting his dad to follow. But when he turned, his dad was lost in the crowd, and all he could see was bloodshed. As they took off, he looked down and saw hundreds of people fighting to survive. Some of them even hung onto the side of the airplane, only to fall to their deaths as it sped up and took off. His dad was back there somewhere. But he never saw him.

"So what do you think happened to him?" I asked.

Jamal shook his head and glanced at Deepti. "I don't know. Neither of us do. Our parents are gone."

"Maybe they just can't reach you right now," I said.

"The military bases got their communications back up already, Layla. If my dad was out there, he would've reached me by now."

Deepti's eyes were downcast. I knew she had an older sister too, but her sister was nowhere to be seen. It was hard to think they could be anywhere except the grave, but I didn't want to think like that. There was a chance for them. There had to be.

"Well, what about you?" Jamal asked.

Suddenly I was the one looking at my hands, feeling clammy, feeling that burn in my chest. I struggled for words. "It's hard to explain. We were on our way to Oregon, and we got stranded. This guy helped us, but..."

I trailed off, picking at my thumbnail.

Jamal tilted his head to get a read on me. "Layla, where's your mom?"

I shook my head. "He hurt her, and he took me. And I think —" I choked on the words as I forced them out. "I think she's gone."

"Gone, like..." Deepti said.

I nodded. They carefully asked me more questions then, like how I'd ended up in Utah, and what it was like on the road, and if I'd seen any rashers. I told them in the simplest way I could, and they drank in my words with wide eyes. When I could say nothing else, Deepti sighed.

"At least we have each other now," she said. "Two more days, and Jamal and I get retested, and then we can go to the real safe zone. For good."

"Four more days for Layla," Jamal said. That made me wince, and he noticed, so he took my hand and squeezed it hard. "I'll stay the extra days with you, okay? We're not leaving each other again."

That night, as I hurried through the crisp darkness toward

tent B on the edge of camp, I looked out through the fence. I could see the gate and the testing site down the road. Cars were lined up, waiting to be processed, all the headlights cutting through the dark in a line, heading toward the glowing site like moths.

THE FOLLOWING DAY, we tried to distract ourselves with whatever small activities we could find. We sat by the fence for a couple hours and watched more people enter the camp in their gray clothes, including more kids showing up alone. In the distance, we could see clouds of dust near the testing site as military vans drove off, taking the infected people to wherever they went to die.

In the afternoon, they called numbers on the intercom, and a group was taken into the medical tent in camp to be retested. After an hour, two vehicles showed up at the back gate of camp: an armored van and a bus. The group emerged from the medical tent, and all of them got onto the bus. We stood by the fence and watched it pull away from the camp, disappearing down the road.

"They made it through," Deepti said wistfully, her fingers hanging on the fence links. "They're going to the safe zone underground."

"How do you know that?"

"Another bus came yesterday," Jamal said. "It took another group that passed their five-day quarantine."

"Tomorrow it's our turn," Deepti murmured.

I leaned away from the fence and glanced back at the camp. It was getting fuller by the hour. "That was a big group on the bus. How many spots are even in the safe zone?"

This made Deepti stiffen, but her gaze stayed outward, toward the gate. Jamal met my eyes and discreetly shook his head, so I dropped the question.

But I was worried. Worried I wouldn't pass my second test.

Worried the safe zone would fill up and Jamal would lose his spot by waiting for me to finish my quarantine. It would be my fault, and I couldn't live with that guilt on top of everything else. But he'd insisted.

Jamal seemed different. He used to sort of follow me around like a puppy, and I'd never minded. But he seemed colder now, like whatever he'd seen had hardened him. And I understood. I felt the same way.

Deepti had changed too. She used to be one of the most confident girls in the eighth grade, but now she was fidgety, eyes always darting around, her hair unbrushed, her skin pallid. Whatever brightness she used to have had dimmed entirely.

I returned to my tent for dinner, and on my way to my cot, I ran right into Mary-Kenna, her little brother propped on her hip. She locked eyes with me. There was no light in them.

"What are you doing in here?" I asked. "Where are your parents?"

Her chin trembled as she spoke, but her words were clear. "Our father was taken on the first night, and our mother started showing symptoms late yesterday. They took her away before we could even—" She cut herself off, fighting tears.

"What about your siblings?"

She leaned her cheek against her brother's head. "They've put Amos and me here, and the others are in another tent."

"Are they okay?"

"The little ones don't understand. My oldest brother and I are trying to put on a brave face for them, but…"

But her mother was gone now, too.

I wanted to pull her in for a hug. I wanted to fix it all, bring our mothers back. I couldn't. "I'm sorry, Mary-Kenna."

"Don't worry," she whispered. "God will protect us."

Mary-Kenna left to find a cot to lay Amos down for a nap, and I followed her. She tucked the blanket beneath his chin and gave him a kiss, but he wouldn't sleep. The tent was noisy, and he was crying for his mother.

I thought of the pink bear from Mitch, still stuffed in my

backpack beneath my cot. Maybe it would make him feel better. I went to get it, and when I pulled it out of my bag, I expected a wave of disgust to crash through me. Instead, I only felt sad.

I carried the bear back over and knelt down to show him. "Look what I have, Amos. A friend."

Amos stopped crying just long enough to blink at the bear through his tears. His little lip quivered. I held it out toward him, and he took it tentatively.

"This bear is special," I said. "He...uh...he has powers."

Mary-Kenna raised an eyebrow, but didn't interrupt. My mind darted for a story, making things up on the spot. "See, he used to be a little boy, but someone turned him into a bear. But he loves being a bear, because bears are strong and tough. Are you strong and tough, Amos?"

He just blinked at me, then pulled the bear to his chest and closed his eyes.

Mary-Kenna smiled sadly at me and brushed her hand over Amos' hair until he sank into sleep. "I heard the safe zone is nice," she whispered.

"I don't know anything about it, really."

She watched Amos breathe, still petting his head like Mom used to do when I couldn't sleep. I wondered if that was just something mothers did. Mary-Kenna was like a mother now, with hers gone. I was glad I didn't have someone little to look after when I could hardly look after myself.

"One of the soldiers told me it's some kind of bunker under the mountain, and they have a vaccine. That sounds safe, doesn't it?" A lighter smile broke out on her face. "Maybe we can have beds near each other down there. And I'm sure all of this will be over before we know it, and we can go back home."

I nodded to make her feel better. "Sure."

Jamal had said things were bad back in California. But the longer I spent at camp—even with Jamal here—the more desperately I wanted to go home. To wash dishes for my mother. To lie across from Preston's bed, knowing he'd be home soon. To get cards in the mail from Dad. Things that had once been so minuscule were now unreachable.

I'd hated my old life, the one I'd had just days ago, but I wanted it back. More than anything, I wanted it back.

———

I REUNITED with Jamal after dinner. We sat on the playground, peering out at the camp from the top of the slide. From up here, I could see the graveyard of cars clearly, shining like jewels in the cold sunset light. It felt safe behind the fence, but it was starting to feel like a prison, too.

"Do you think my dad is dead?" Jamal asked suddenly.

I shivered; the air was brisk tonight. It was weird to think less than a week ago we were worrying about Halloween, the haunted maze, the kids from school who were going to be there. That's what we should have been talking about right now. Not this.

I decided to be honest. "I don't know, Jamal."

"I never thought anything could happen to him," he murmured. "Like Major Ursus. No matter what, Major Ursus always comes out okay."

I took his hand. We'd never done that before, but it didn't feel weird anymore. Ever since I'd met him, he'd been my only real friend in the world, and it was destiny that we'd ended up here together, half a thousand miles from home. We both knew it. So we held on.

"We're like orphans," he said.

"My dad's still out there," I replied, but my dad might as well have been in a different hemisphere. It hit me then, how little I really knew my father. Preston had been the one to walk me home from school, to come to the few volleyball games I had, to walk into the gym and yell at the coach when I got kicked off the team. He'd been the one to help me with homework when Mom was working. The one who always told me goodnight, no matter what. Without Mom, he was all I really had left.

I felt the magnitude of it all, pressing down on me from the wide open sky. "Preston's still out there, too. I need to get to him."

Jamal studied my face. "How are you going to do that?"

"I don't know. But I can't stay here."

"Well, whatever you do, I'm going too."

"You can't, Jamal," I said. "You're almost to the safe zone. You could go in *tomorrow*, and then you'd be safe. Like, actually, truly safe."

"I don't care. I'm not leaving you. You...you're the only family I have left. So I'm going with you." His eyes drifted over the cars. "We could drive."

I nearly laughed. "Drive?"

"I mean, all those cars are just sitting there. Nobody is coming back for them. Maybe one of the soldiers would give us keys, and—"

"And what, we drive to Oregon? We're in eighth grade, Jamal."

His hand slipped out of mine, but not because he was upset —it was more to get my full attention. He set his jaw. "We *were* in eighth grade, Layla. But things are different now, and we're already different too. So we'll figure this out and we'll get to your brother. But wherever you go, I'm going too."

JAMAL and I spent the next couple hours poring over my map in the dim tent light, mapping our route from this camp to Jackpot, Oregon. To Preston. The one thing my mother had made me promise was that I'd get to him. It had always felt a little impossible, but so many impossible things had happened in the last few days—Jamal and I were both alive, together—so who was to say one more impossible thing couldn't happen?

Deepti wasn't coming; she kept fretting over the safe zone, the test, the bus that would take her to safety. She was becoming obsessive about the buses, which had shown up at the back gate a few times that day to cart off new groups. Each time, she'd stood at the fence and counted the number of people getting on, trying to decide whether she had a chance of joining them tomorrow. But for as many people left the camp, twice as many seemed to trickle in, and I couldn't help but think that the elusive bunker must be getting pretty full.

"Are you sure you don't want to stay, Jamal?" I asked quietly.

He shook his head. "Let's just figure out how to get a car."

I decided to talk to Gideon, the Mormon soldier I'd befriended. I found him on his stool, picking at a loose thread on his sleeve. He smiled widely when he saw me. "Oh hey, Layla."

"I need your help."

"Uh oh," he laughed. But when he saw how serious I was, his mood sobered. "With what?"

I almost blurted out that I needed car keys, but I backpedaled. "I want you to tell me about that Mormon book stuff."

"Uh, really?"

I shifted my weight. "Uh, yeah. It's just like…this is all so crazy, and I'm having a hard time, and I guess I just wanted to hear what you had to say." I hesitated, then added, "But if you're busy, nevermind."

He jumped up from his stool and said, "No, no, I'm not busy. But why don't we go over where it's quieter?"

My heart pounded as he led me to a spot near the warehouse, where we sat on some overturned wooden crates. The sky was beautiful and crisp against the mountains, like a pot of deep blue ink, and it reminded me of Lake Tahoe, of night swimming, of my brother showing me how to put chips on sandwiches and eating in the firelight.

I blinked the memory away.

Gideon leaned forward, elbows on his knees. "So, what's troubling you? What do you want to know?"

I wasn't sure what I believed in, but I *did* believe he could help me get to my brother. I chewed my lip. "I guess I want to know if there's a reason for all this. Like, if God is real, why would he let this happen?"

"That's a big question."

"I have a lot of those."

He nodded, eyes scanning the sky as he gathered his thoughts. "I don't know why this happened. But I do know that even when things don't make sense to us, God still has a plan. He doesn't give us anything we can't handle. And if we trust Him, He'll guide us forward."

"What if this *was* his plan?"

"I don't think it was. Bad things just happen. We're creatures of free will, and we don't make the best choices for ourselves, which can lead us down roads like this. God only intercedes if we choose to follow the will of his Holy Spirit."

"So if I trust him, he'll...help me?"

"Yeah." Gideon rubbed his neck. "Sorry, I'm bad at this."

I was feeling more confused, but I put on a calm expression as I stood. "No, I guess...I guess I feel better. Thanks."

"Well, good," he said slowly.

He didn't seem satisfied with the speed of the conversation, but I was running out of time before curfew; I needed to keep this moving.

"Yeah. If God is with me, I'll feel much safer on the road."

I started walking away, but I heard the groan of the crate as Gideon jumped up. "Wait, the road?"

I glanced back. "I need to get to my brother. He's at a camp in Oregon, but...I keep thinking, if God has a plan, maybe it's for me to find him. So that's what I'm going to do."

His brows furrowed. "Layla, you're a kid. It's not safe out there."

"But *he's* not safe either." I lifted my chin, adopting the confidence I'd seen in my mother, in Jamal, in Preston—the clarity of understanding who you are in the world and what you have to do to survive it. I understood that I was a sister, and a daughter, and a friend. It was the only thing that defined me now. The only thing I had to hold onto. "I have to try to get to Oregon, even if it kills me. So you can help me, or you can let me die, but either way, I'm leaving this camp."

"Layla…"

I lowered my voice. "I just need car keys. You can get them for me."

"Layla, no. I'm not helping you put yourself in danger." He was pale as he spoke, his hands flexing at his sides, making him look less like a soldier and more like a nervous kid. "I can't do that."

I nodded, trying to let the disappointment show. I was angry, too. I needed him to understand that finding my brother was worth the danger. Worth dying for. I felt crazy for thinking it, but a life in a bunker, constantly wondering what had happened to the last piece of my family, was hardly a life at all.

I turned away again. "Yeah. I figured. Thanks for talking to me about God though. I hope he protects me without a car—"

Gideon grabbed me by the elbow and said, "Wait." He must've caught onto what I was doing, because he seemed conflicted. But I stared at him, silently pleading. There was no manipulation in the look, only desperation. Finally, he exhaled. "If I do this, it stays between us."

I nearly smiled, but held back, trying to be grown-up serious and trustworthy. "It will."

He sighed. "Meet me here tomorrow night. After curfew."

CHAPTER TWENTY-ONE

THE NEXT MORNING, Jamal and Deepti went to get retested, but instead of waiting for their results in the medical tent, which was normal protocol, they were sent back into camp. We sat on the floor near their cots and tried to play a card game to pass the time, but half the cards were missing from the deck, and Deepti stopped playing after a couple minutes.

"They said it'll only take an hour," she said, fidgeting with her barcode bracelet. "Then…then I can get on the bus."

We nodded comfortingly and went back to our game. We waited. And waited. Two hours passed, and they never called any numbers over the speakers. I could sense the nerves practically seeping from Deepti's skin.

"Why isn't anything happening?" she whispered, sweating despite the cold, her fingers hooked around her bracelet.

"I don't know, Deep," I said. "I'm sure there's just a delay."

But when I went outside to use the bathroom, I took a trip to the edge of camp where the bus should've been waiting. But I didn't see it at all. It simply hadn't arrived.

I returned to the tent and decided not to tell Deepti this.

THE ENTIRE DAY passed and no numbers were called. We ate a dinner of steamed rice and vegetables, we then waited for Deepti to fall asleep before Jamal gathered his things and crept to tent B; we'd told her we were leaving, but she didn't want to hear it, and she absolutely didn't want to come.

There were no spare cots in my tent now—it was at capacity —so Jamal lay on the ground beside mine. Across the tent, Mary-Kenna seemed wary of us, like she knew we were planning something, but she just snuggled Amos and let it rest. There was no energy left for questioning things.

Soon the tent was filled with the sound of shifting bodies and the pervasive silence that fell thick every night out here in the middle-of-nowhere, Utah. Everyone was asleep.

Jamal and I snuck to the bathrooms to change out of our gray quarantine clothes and back into our street clothes. I pulled on my spare outfit that Mom had folded into the bottom of my bag when we left home. It felt like putting on a layer of myself again, and even if they smelled sterile now, there was still the faint scent of home. I left the other clothes—the ones I'd worn when I was with Mitch—behind in a pile in the bathroom stall. That shirt had once been my favorite, but I wouldn't miss it anymore.

Once we were dressed, we gathered our bags and crept outside.

Gideon was waiting for us exactly like he'd promised, standing in the shadows by the crates near the warehouse. He was wearing a t-shirt and what looked like military-issued sweatpants, with a loop of keys in hand.

"I don't technically have clearance for this," he whispered, leading us around the back of the warehouse. "If I get in trouble, I'm holding you personally responsible."

He let us into the dark warehouse but didn't turn on the lights. Instead, he pulled out a flashlight and swung the beam across the shelves, making stark, jarring shadows of the objects on them. The place was much more full than it had been when I'd arrived.

We went to the board on the wall where the car keys hung. "Uh, any preference?" Gideon asked.

I didn't know a thing about cars. I looked to Jamal, but he looked mildly clueless too. He leaned in, studying the sets of keys like hieroglyphs on a tomb wall. Then something glinted in his eyes, and he reached for a set of keys that said *Porsche*.

"These," he grinned.

Gideon plucked them from his hand and hung them back up. "That probably won't have the best gas mileage. You want something efficient, like…" His eyes scanned the board, then landed. He grabbed a set. "A Hyundai, maybe?"

Gideon searched the rack and grabbed a few more sets of keys for us, because there was no telling which of those cars out there even had gas in the tank. We ended up with about twenty sets, all dangling with quirky keychains and gym passes and house keys, which would never be used again. I tried not to think about it as I dumped them into the front pouch of my backpack.

"Thank you," I told Gideon. "For real."

He didn't look very happy, but he nodded. "Be safe out there. I'm serious." He cocked his head toward the door. "Alright, let me show you the best way to get out of camp unseen."

But the second we walked out of the warehouse, something was off. There were voices. A lot of them.

We rounded the corner and saw a group of people gathered by the back gate under the floodlights. The same gate people used to get on the safe zone bus, which had never arrived. The three of us tentatively walked closer to listen.

"What do you mean full?" a man shouted. Behind him, there was an eruption of agreement from the crowd. I spotted a few soldiers with guns standing before them, guarding the gate.

"I've been here over five days—I'm clean! And you're saying that means nothing? You're just going to leave us here?"

Gideon drew a sharp breath. "Oh no."

"What?" I said.

He pulled us back into the shadows of the warehouse, chest heaving. "I knew this would happen."

"*What?*" I repeated.

"The bunker is full. They have to start turning people away."

More voices crashed together by the gate. I could hear feet moving, the clatter of the fence. I peered back out at the crowd. They were surging forward, forcing their way through the gate, all of them shouting. *Let us in! We deserve to be let in! I have kids! I want to survive!*

A gunshot cracked.

The man who led the charge fell to the ground with a thud. The crowd drew back in horror, parting around his limp body. Even from a distance, I could see blood pool from his chest, saturating his gray clothes and the hard ground beneath him.

Jamal grabbed my wrist, and at that second, everything fell apart.

The crowd scattered, some still charging for the gate, others screaming and tripping over each other as they tried to get away. More gunshots fired. *Bang. Bang. Bang.*

Jamal yanked me to the playground, and we dove underneath it to hide behind the slide. I looked behind us—Gideon was gone. "What's happening?" I gasped. Another round of gunfire pierced the air, and Jamal pressed close to the ground.

"We have to get Deepti," he said.

People were running everywhere now, lost in a panic. Jamal's hand was still clamped on my wrist. He looked out behind the slide, waiting for the gunfire to pause. When it did, he said, "Now," and pulled me out from beneath the playground.

We raced for tent D at the front of camp, but as we approached, we saw that the front gate was blocked too. Soldiers were on guard, guns ready. A cold realization swelled over me: if this was some kind of riot, then no one was getting out of here now.

People were pouring out of the tents, wide awake from the gunfire. Panicked screams echoed across the camp. We pressed against the side of the nearest tent. *Bang. Bang. Bang.*

"Where was Gideon going to take us?" I breathed. "He said he had a way out."

Jamal didn't get the chance to answer. A surge of people rushed past, and someone hit my shoulder so hard I fell to the ground. I looked up, blinking through the panic, just in time to see three people sprint toward the soldier at the front gate. Shots fired, no remorse, and they dropped to the ground one by one.

Jamal hauled me to my feet. We ran the other way, feet skidding in the dirt, splotches of it already soaked in blood. We found his tent and burst in. Kids were up, scrambling everywhere, most of them crying. An older kid—Mary-Kenna's brother—was yelling over them, telling them to stay calm and get under their cots. I looked for Deepti but couldn't see her.

"There!" Jamal said.

She was huddled by a cot near the end of the tent, hands over her ears. Jamal dove in front of her and grabbed her by the arms. "Deep, you have to come with us."

He tried to pull her up, but she shrieked and recoiled from his touch. "I'm not going out there!" she cried, tears rushing down her face. "I'm not, I'm not—"

This must have felt so similar to what had happened to them on the base. The surge of people, the panic, the gunfire. I knelt in front of her. "Deepti, they're not taking you to the bunker. They're not letting anyone in. People are rioting. You have to come with us."

She locked eyes with me, dark brown, deep as an abyss. "I don't want to go back out there. I won't."

I didn't know what else to do, so I just hugged her. I'd never liked Deepti much. She was snobby and sharp-tongued, and she had always made me feel small. But that was an entirely different life, and nobody was the same forever. Nobody could be in this world. So I hugged her and held her tight, knowing that it might be the last time anyone ever did.

Jamal hugged her too. Outside, there was more shooting, more screams. We didn't want to leave her, but we had to go. Before we ran out, I turned and yelled at her, "Don't leave the tent!" hoping she'd listen. Hoping, in another life far away from this one, I'd see her again.

We didn't know where to go, so we raced back toward the warehouse when the coast was mostly clear. Bodies littered the ground, blood pooling in the dirt, and my lungs forgot how to breathe. We skirted around a woman who had been shot, and she grabbed at our ankles, but we couldn't stop—there was nothing we could do. We just had to move. If they saw us trying to escape, they might think we were attempting to get to the bunker, and they'd shoot us too.

But where could we go?

We were running past the bathrooms when Gideon leapt in front of us. His face was splattered with blood, and it didn't look like his. "There you are," he rasped. "Come on."

We followed him blindly to a far edge of camp, a part I hadn't been to, hidden behind the warehouse. There was a jagged hole in the fence. The edges had been wrenched apart, the links splayed outward like broken ribs. I was about to ask Gideon how he'd done this without being seen, but then I saw something in the corner of my eye: a soldier lying motionless in the dirt with his rifle. I halted, feeling sick. But Gideon nudged me toward the fence and pressed his flashlight into my hand.

"I was going to take you through a back gate, but it's guarded now. This will have to do. Now move. Crawl out, go left, keep going until you see the cars. Don't stop running, okay?"

We didn't question it. Jamal went first, shoving his bag through the hole then army-crawling after it. When he was out on the other side, I fed my bag and my hat through to him and followed. But before we ran off, I looked at Gideon through the fence. I wanted to say thank you, I just couldn't find it in me. I couldn't say anything at all.

Jamal stepped in, lacing his fingers through the fence links. "If someone comes looking for Layla Wise and Jamal Hardy, tell them we went to Jackpot, Oregon."

Gideon nodded. "If I make it out of this, I will."

And then he was gone.

The ground was uneven with rocks and brush, but we picked up speed and cut through the dark, blazing into the unknown that lay before us. Whatever waited out there couldn't be much worse than what we'd already left behind.

CHAPTER TWENTY-TWO

WE SPRINTED out to the car graveyard, but it spread even further than I'd thought. We stopped by the first line of cars, struggling for air. I gave Jamal a handful of car keys from my bag. "Start pressing buttons."

We split up the keys, separated in the sea of cars, and each ran off down the aisles, trying to set off car alarms with the key fobs. There were hundreds of cars to search through, parked haphazardly across the field. Hundreds of lives and families, just gone. In another life, it might have been parking for some kind of sporting event, and I could imagine people walking across the lot together, about to go have some fun. But most of these people were dead.

Every time one of the fobs worked, the sound of a car horn would blare across the field, and I'd set off running toward the sound. The moon was high now, hanging yellow over the mountains. I felt exposed and frantic, worried that someone would come stop us any moment. But no one ever came.

When I found each car, I'd get inside and start the engine to see if it had any gas. Most were near empty. No one had been able to fill up for days, and I was sure lots of these people had traveled pretty far to get here.

As I sat in the driver's seat of a shiny pickup truck and stared at the empty gas meter, a chill ran over me. I knew someone who had fuel. Someone who might still be exactly where I'd left him.

After five more tries, I ran out of keys. I hurried back through the field, eyes peeled for Jamal. He yelled my name, and I followed his voice to a beat-up silver Jeep with a dented back door. It had a Utah license plate, and it was thick with dust like it had been out here a while. Jamal climbed into the driver's seat.

"Please, please, please," he whispered as he turned the engine. The dashboard lit up—the tank was half full. I cheered, but Jamal said, "This will probably only get us out of Utah. If that."

My heart started to hammer at the thought of going back into the salt flats. Of seeing Mitch again, of telling Jamal how we'd ended up out there. But we needed those gas canisters. I took a steadying breath. "I think I know where we can get some more fuel."

We threw our bags in the back and Jamal put the car into reverse. It was quickly obvious that he'd never driven a car, but I couldn't hold it against him, because I never had either. Mom was weird about driving, and when Preston got his learner's permit last year, she would freak every time he was behind the wheel. Since he'd been in an accident, she'd probably never let him drive again, let alone *me*.

What was I even saying?

Jamal pulled out of the parking space, only mildly scratching the car beside us in the process, and raced to the road. We passed a row of military vehicles speeding toward the quarantine camp, but they ignored us. We were free.

As we left the camp behind and got back onto the main road, I opened up the atlas and squinted at the maps in the dark, trying to figure out how many miles we were from Jackpot. It was impossible to tell. I didn't know how anyone ever used these things. "I don't know how long it will take us to get there."

"Doesn't matter if we don't have gas."

"Just keep going. I'll tell you where to pull off." I turned to look around the back seat. There wasn't much there. A carseat, a couple toys scattered on the ground, an empty bag of chips. With a pang, I thought of little Amos and hoped he and his siblings would make it through the night.

As we drove closer to the salt flats, the knot in my stomach grew tighter and tighter. Mitch had killed my mom. He'd killed her, and if he hadn't, we would've been in Jackpot with Preston by now. I could feel his hands on me still, cold yet blazing. His wet lips. Infected. Hungry.

"You okay?" Jamal said. "You look like you're going to be sick."

"Just keep driving," I snapped.

"Well, I don't see anything out there," he replied, but he could barely see over the steering wheel as it was.

We drove for a long while. The landscape was dark; there was no way of knowing exactly where the truck was, but I remembered that small cell tower nearby. From there, we'd driven about an hour before we'd reached the quarantine camp. My eyes flickered between the clock and the road, trying to keep track of where we might be. There were no cars, nothing out there. We were alone.

I was starting to worry we'd never find the tower. But then, there it was—a black skeleton against the indigo sky. I gasped and pointed. "Wait, drive out that way!"

Jamal pulled off the road, and suddenly I was thankful we'd found a Jeep, because the flats were still covered in water a few inches deep. Jamal gasped every time we hit a bump, his hands tight on the wheel. I couldn't help but imagine that one of these puddles was going to be deeper than a few inches, and it would swallow us whole. I sat on the edge of my seat, looking through the light of the headlights, searching for a dark spot on the land that resembled a truck. But the closer we got, the more things came into focus, and I could feel it all over again. That choking horror, that sense of being utterly alone.

I glanced at Jamal. I'd found him. That was worth something.

"I see it!" he exclaimed.

My stomach dropped, and I saw what he saw: the dark red splotch of a truck in the distance. "Cut the lights," I said.

The Jeep crawled through the dark until we were just yards away. I held my breath, not sure what to expect or what I'd do if Mitch was there. It was hard to know for certain, but it looked abandoned. I let out a breath, but deep down, I knew he might still be inside.

"So this is the guy who hurt your mom?" Jamal whispered.

"Yeah."

That's all I was able to say. Jamal understood. "Let's get out and get this over with."

I grabbed the flashlight and stepped out into the water. It was deep enough that it swallowed the tops of my boots. I moved toward the truck and shined the light into the bed. My heart lifted when I saw the four gas canisters and no Mitch. The passenger door was still open like I'd left it, but when Jamal tried to open the tailgate, it was locked. He circled around to the driver's side, but then I heard his feet stop.

"Layla?" he whispered. "Come look."

I circled around and stopped short when I saw Mitch's body facedown in the salt water, his dark hair fanned out around his head. His skin was bloated and pale, with a sickly green tinge where the water had soaked in. The salt had crystallized over his clothes, leaving a thin, white crust along the folds of his shirt and the edges of his hairline.

I swallowed hard. "Is he...?"

"He has to be," Jamal whispered. Then he lit up. "Hey, the keys."

The keys were hooked to his belt loop with a carabiner, half-submerged in the water. With shallow breath, I leaned forward, but as I reached out, my hand shook. I took one more step, the water lapping at my boots. *Just grab them.*

But the moment my fingers touched the metal, Mitch twitched.

Before I could move, he jerked violently, rolled, and shot his arm out to grab my ankle.

I screamed and fell backward. He pulled me toward him with a distorted, wet moan, and I wrenched away, but I couldn't get out of his iron grip. Water spilled from his mouth, and his eyes were milky and vacant—no longer human.

Jamal burst forward and kicked Mitch's head as hard as he could. It didn't do much, but it loosened his grip enough for me to wriggle out of my boot and get away. Jamal reached down and yanked the keys from Mitch's belt loop, then tossed them at me. "Go!" he yelled.

The keys plunked into the water, and Mitch shot back up. Jamal splashed behind him. "Come and get me, dingbat!" he shouted.

Mitch's attention snapped to him. Jamal waited for him to rise to his feet, all crusty and wet, and slosh toward him before he made a mad dash to the side.

I swept my hands through the dark water, frantically feeling for the keys. My fingers closed around them. I gasped, almost delirious enough to laugh, and quickly shoved my boot back on before I ran for the tailgate.

I fumbled with the keys. Behind me, there was splashing—Jamal running, Mitch thrashing—but I didn't stop to look. I just got the stupid thing open and dragged out the gas canisters one at a time. They were heavy in my arms, but I ran each of them to the Jeep and heaved them into the back seat.

Sweating, I ran back to the truck to look for supplies. I could see Mitch and Jamal's figures streaking across the flats, Jamal shouting and taunting—I didn't have much time. I searched the bed for whatever food I could find, but only came away with two cans of baked beans.

Back at the Jeep, I leapt into the driver's seat and turned the key in the ignition. The lights and engine turned on. I touched the gear shift, but it wouldn't move. My mind blanked.

Jamal was still running in circles, now bathed in the headlights, but he was losing steam. Mitch was close behind.

I sat on the edge of the seat and hit the gas pedal, but the engine revved angrily. I hit the brake pedal instead. I pushed the gear shift again, and it finally moved into drive. I stepped on the gas, and the car jerked forward so fast that my head hit the seat. I grabbed the wheel to regain control, flying through the shallow water, then drove as close to Jamal as I dared before I slammed on the brake.

"Get in!" I screamed.

Jamal threw himself toward the car, Mitch close enough that his fingers brushed the back of his shirt. He jumped into the passenger seat and yanked the door shut just as Mitch slammed up against it. I floored it.

We skidded across the salt, splashing up waves as we headed for the road. Jamal let out an explosive, shocked laugh and turned in his seat to watch Mitch vanish behind us.

When he sat back, his breath was shaking. He wiped saltwater from his cheek. "Hey, Layla? Try to actually catch the keys next time, okay?"

I wrapped both hands tightly around the wheel. "Deal."

CHAPTER TWENTY-THREE

THE LAST FALL we spent at Grandma's ranch was just before I turned eleven. Earlier in the trip, before we knew the ranch was going under and Grandma was going with it, she sent Mom and me out for a trail ride. Grandma wanted to spend some time with Preston, so it was just the two of us. We packed a lunch, put on our muddy boots, and saddled up our horses, then headed out on the narrow, rocky paths that led off the property into the wilderness.

I could feel the newness of the absences in our lives. The absence of Dad, the absence of my brother, who was still right there, just farther away somehow. The absence between my mother and me, where there had once been more love than we knew what to do with. But on the trail, it all seemed far removed.

We went pretty far that day. I was riding an older white mare who was so big I couldn't even get into the saddle on my own. Mom was riding a black and white Appaloosa with a habit of stopping mid-trail to nibble at tree branches. She always let him have his way.

We rode until my hips hurt, until the ranch grew distant and the mountains stood sturdy like a promise around us. I'd never been so far out; it felt like we'd crossed into some new, wild frontier like gold-digging pioneers. The hills were thick with wild grass, and it swayed in the early fall air. That was one thing I loved about northern California. The weather was never over-bearing, just calm and foggy and sweet like dew. Like the whole landscape was breathing.

Mom took me to a higher point where we could overlook the valley, which sprawled below in the bright daylight. We stopped to rest on some rocks along the trail and ate our turkey sandwiches.

"You know, your grandma used to see herds of wild horses in this valley when she was a kid," Mom said.

I gasped, delighted, and looked around, half expecting to see them come galloping across the hills. "Really?"

She took a bite. "Really."

"Are they still here?"

"I don't think so. I don't really believe in them."

"What do you mean you don't believe in them? They're not ghosts."

Mom leaned back in the grass, and the wind rustled her red hair. She looked very pretty then, with the sun on her pink cheeks, brown eyes squinting in the light, lips pursed in thought.

"When I was a kid, my parents took me and my siblings on a camping trip out here. We wanted to find those horses. We searched for three days, and every single day, I held out hope that I'd finally see one—just *one*. But it never happened." She shrugged one shoulder. "They used to be around, but I just don't think things like that can survive long."

"Things like what?"

"Wild things. They were here before you and me, even before grandma's town. But land management rounded them up and sold them. People don't like things they can't control."

"So you never saw one?"

Mom shook her head. "No. But there was something so beau-tiful about it. You know, the idea of it. Something that didn't belong, but had found a place anyway, despite everything telling them they shouldn't live free." She took another bite. "I should've known it sounded too good to be true."

AT DINNER THAT NIGHT, Grandma asked about our ride, and I asked her about the wild horses, if she'd really seen them out there.

"Sure did," she said. "I was on a hunting trip with my big brother, and we saw a herd of about twenty of them, just galloping and galloping."

"Mom said land management got rid of most of them because they couldn't control them. She said they caused soil erosion and…and erasure of native plant species," I said, trying to remember what she'd told me. How she'd justified people herding them up and taking them out of the wild, where they'd never belonged in the first place.

"She's just mad she never got to see one," Grandma said teasingly.

But when I looked at Mom, she was staring at her plate. I

could picture her as a little girl, her red hair in braids and a hat on her head, gazing out into that valley with an expression of extinguished hope.

"Not everything wild is bad, Layla," Grandma said. "Remember that."

Across the table, Preston locked eyes with me, then looked away with a tiny grin.

CHAPTER TWENTY-FOUR

JAMAL and I headed for the border town where Mitch had gotten bit.

The military checkpoint was gone now, and the town was deserted. I wondered where the military had gone, or why they'd given up on their border patrol. Maybe no one was traveling anymore. Maybe no one was left out there *to* travel. Either way, we crossed back into Nevada without a problem.

We stuck to the highway, but as we drove past the town, Jamal slowed to look. It was just a small place wedged in the desert, but although there wasn't much there, I knew it wasn't empty. "Just keep going," I told him, fists tight in my lap. "There are scavengers out here."

"Scavengers? Like people who want to take your stuff?"

I nodded. "We ran into them before." Or ran *over* them, actually. Maybe they'd all been infected by now. I hated that part of me hoped so.

When the town was behind us, we stopped to fill the gas tank. We stood in the dark on the shoulder of the road and lifted the canister, carefully pouring gasoline down the funnel. As we did, we realized we were both still wearing our barcode bracelets. We ripped them off and left them at the border, hoping we'd never have to go to Utah again.

THE ROAD WAS DARK, the desert vast and watchful. It was late, and I knew Jamal was getting tired, so I reached for my backpack and pulled out my pages from *Major Ursus*. They were a bit bent and dirty, but still intact. Just something to talk about on our long drive.

"I didn't get much time to work on them," I said, turning the pages in the moonlight.

"I mean, I don't blame you."

"So…they were captured. What happens next?"

Jamal, a boy of so many answers and ideas, said something I didn't expect. "It doesn't matter."

"What? Why?"

"Just doesn't. Look around. Who cares about a stupid comic book anymore?"

I do, I wanted to say. But I didn't say it, because something else grabbed my attention. I almost didn't see it in the dark, not until we were passing right by it and the headlights caught it in their gleam. The long green neck of a brachiosaurus.

"Stop!" I cried.

Jamal slammed on the brakes in the middle of the road. "What the heck, Layla? What is it?"

I didn't respond. I was already unbuckling my seatbelt and grabbing the flashlight from the cupholder between us. I jumped out and ran across the road toward the truck stop, and Jamal called after me, but I hardly heard him. My thoughts were too loud. *Mom, Mom, Mom.*

I burst inside the shop, swinging the light around. "Mom?"

When no one responded, my heart fell into my stomach. All this time, I'd assumed she was dead, and it was stupid to reignite the hope that she wasn't, but I couldn't help it. I hurried back to the slots room, kicking aside trash as I went.

The slots room was empty. I aimed the flashlight everywhere, toward the couch, between machines, into the corners, just in case she was hiding in a shadow, just in case I'd missed her. Glass crunched behind me. My heart erupted and I spun.

My light landed on Jamal.

"Ow." He shielded his face. "What are we doing here?"

I stepped backward and fell onto the couch, lightheaded. The flashlight fell from my fingers onto the cushion. "This is the last place I saw Mom."

"Oh." Jamal sat next to me slowly. In the dark, his face was all shadows, but I could make out his concern. "I'm sorry, Layla."

I realized I was crying and wiped my eyes. "I thought maybe she'd still be…"

"I'm sorry," he said again.

My flashlight beam was aimed at the floor now. There were pasta cans, remnants of our meal here with Mitch. But there were more food wrappers too—honeybuns, sour candies, a couple energy drink cans. Things we definitely hadn't eaten that day with Mitch.

I got on my hands and knees to get a closer look. Jamal crouched right next to me, his arm touching mine as I sorted through the cans and wrappers, as if I'd find a message hidden amongst them. That's when I noticed the empty packet of wildflower tea.

"She was here," I realized. She'd been here, alive.

I sat back, breathless, and held the empty packet with both hands. This didn't change anything. She wasn't here now. She wasn't with me, and for all I knew, she was still dead, just somewhere else. But she hadn't died that day at the hands of Mitch. In a strange, unsettling way, sitting in the glow of the flashlight in the abandoned slots room, I found comfort in that.

We stayed until dawn, trying to get a little sleep on that couch. When we woke up, we searched the truck stop, both for signs of my mother and for anything salvageable. When I glanced behind the counter where the stuffed animals still lay, my chest felt like a clenched fist, and I had to turn away.

We didn't find much; whatever food was left had no doubt

been eaten by my mother. But I did find a thick black marker in a drawer behind the cash register, and I used it to write on the counter before we left, just in case.

We were here.

Going to Oregon.

Layla + Jamal

———————————

JAMAL and I hit the road again, but we took it slow, stopping every so often to refuel, stretch our legs, and painstakingly study the map. We tried to stay far from towns, but it wasn't always possible. Sometimes there were so many cars stalled on the road that we had to drive on the shoulder, and other times the road was empty for miles.

By the time we passed a sign that said *Welcome to Oregon*, our stomachs were aching for food, but we'd eaten the beans from Mitch's truck, and we didn't have anything else. We hadn't planned that far ahead.

Southern Oregon was bone dry and dusty yellow. I'd been to Oregon once, but it was to the coastal part, where the forests were lush and dense, where the ocean crashed against the rocks. But on this side of the state, there were timid, scraggly mountains that hung low to the earth. The ground was covered in shrubs and rocky outcroppings, and the trees were sparse. They looked sort of spooky, jutting out over the endless, grassy plains. But I was so sick of those endless plains, those desolate waves of hills, that small, angry sun in the white-blue sky. I was so sick of it I could've cried.

We had nothing to talk about, so inevitably, my mind wandered to dark places. I thought of Mitch, and when I thought of him, I couldn't help but imagine Preston in his place. Preston lying in the salt flats, having pushed away everyone he loved, but having been abandoned by them at the same time. Preston, dying alone. Him and Mom, hundreds of miles apart, both slowly losing life and wondering why no one was there to save them.

But I *was* coming for my brother. I'd take care of him, and he'd take care of me, because that's what Mom would've wanted. I tried not to let myself think of what would happen if we got to JAWS and he wasn't there.

We were on our final stretch of the trip. It was late afternoon now, but the November light was already fading faster than I'd hoped it would. I could sense Jamal's uneasiness too. The gas meter was getting dangerously low again, and this time, we were out of fuel.

"I want a turn driving," I said. I just needed something to do.

We got out and switched, but even in the passenger seat, Jamal couldn't relax. He held the atlas in his lap, examining it over and over. He'd fiddle with the car radio every twenty minutes or so, too. We'd been on the road for some six or seven hours, traversing miles, but every time he turned it on, it was the same thing: the emergency broadcast and static.

Tomorrow, we'd have to figure out how to get up to the JAWS camp in the mountains, because we didn't have enough gas to get up there, let alone get back down. We'd have to find another ride. That meant we'd have to find someone to help us. As wary as I'd become of just about everybody in the world, I held onto the hope that somewhere, somebody was willing to help two lost kids.

I drove along a shallow, winding river—a good sign that we were almost to Jackpot, according to the map. "We're getting close," I said. "But I don't know how to get to the camp from town. There's got to be some road—"

"Did you see that sign?"

I looked out the window, but all I saw were hills thrown in shadows. "What sign?"

"A hot spring resort," Jamal said. "I always wanted to go to a hot spring."

This isn't a vacation, I wanted to say. But we had to stop *somewhere* for the night to regroup, so that wasn't the worst idea.

"Doesn't sound bad, as long as it's not in the middle of nowhere where we'd get eaten by bears."

"Better than getting eaten by rashers."

"True."

We passed another sign a couple miles ahead that said *Jackpot, 5 Miles*. My heart lifted, but as we crossed those five miles and approached town, something didn't feel right. I smelled it before I saw it: smoke. Ashy, chemical smoke that stung my nose. The sky thickened with it as we got closer, clouds of white drifting over the trees.

"What the heck?" Jamal muttered.

We crested a hill, and the town unfolded below us—or what was left of it.

The entirety of Jackpot, Oregon had burned to the ground.

I slowed to a stop on the hill, taking in the corpse of the town. Dark skeletons of buildings, collapsed to rubble and ash. Teetering frames of houses. A church steeple scorched to a horrible shade of black, barely visible through the unforgiving white smoke.

"Keep driving," Jamal said. "We don't have the fuel to stop."

I rolled to the bottom of the hill, where we passed a gas station. Its shop was completely gone, its metal awning was melted, and the fire was still burning across the parking lot, fed by leaking fuel.

As we continued deeper into what I thought was the downtown area, it was apparent that everything—absolutely everything—was gutted.

"Do you think this was intentional?" Jamal said. "Like, maybe there were too many rashers."

"Or maybe Russia did it," I muttered. Joking, mostly. But Jamal didn't laugh.

The Jeep crawled forward, tires bumping over debris in the road. The air was so thick with smoke it was hard to see more than a few yards ahead. Still, I looked intently for signs, anything that could direct us to the camp, or at least to somewhere with clear air and standing buildings.

Then, through the haze, something moved.

On instinct, my foot hit the brake. At first, I thought they were people. Living people, who had survived the fire. But as their figures emerged from the smoke, I saw the sluggish, jerking way they moved—and they were moving toward us.

My pulse quickened. "Jamal?"

"Just keep going," he said.

I tapped my foot on the gas and we crawled forward. My stomach flipped as the rashers moved toward the car and I got a better look at them. Their bodies were blistered, their skin charred like the ruins around them, flaking away to the raw muscle underneath. They must have been drawn to the sound of the car engine, because suddenly there were droves of them, dark and bloody and burned.

A large man tumbled into the street and slammed into the front of the car. I gasped and hit the brakes.

"Don't stop!" Jamal said.

A woman in nun's clothing smacked against my window. Eyes white, skin singed to nothing. Her face was marred with a long gash, right down the middle. Her hands left streaks as they slid down the glass.

"*Drive*, Layla!"

I stomped on the gas pedal, crushing the man who had hit the car just moments before. The Jeep jostled over his body, and I shrieked, but I continued down the street, past remnants of shops and bars and restaurants, past the graveyard of lives these people had had just days ago. But the rashers were everywhere—*everywhere*—and we were out of gas. We'd be trapped.

"Jamal, what do I do?" I wheezed. "What do I *do*?"

Jamal looked around quickly, then pointed right. "Go that way. It looks clearer."

I picked up speed and swerved onto an adjacent street. We zoomed blindly through the smoke, jerking over potholes and debris, until suddenly the smoke broke. It was as if we'd come to the end of a wall, and like a breath of fresh air, the periwinkle sky appeared again. I looked in the rearview, watching the rashers vanish in the haze behind us.

We had entered another part of town, mostly houses now, many of them still damaged but not utterly destroyed. The worst of the fire hadn't spread this far.

Jamal's breath shook, and he covered his eyes. "Jesus."

I saw what he'd been looking at. A rasher up ahead, dragging itself across the road, leaving a streak of dark fluid behind it, its legs charred to the bone. It was that sight, and the reality that he used to be a person, and the jostle of the Jeep that I could still feel in my bones when I ran that guy over back there, that made me burst into tears. I swerved around the rasher in the road, drove another fifty yards or so, and then stopped the car completely.

This time, Jamal didn't tell me to keep driving. He peeked out from behind his hands. "Are you okay?"

I pressed my forehead against the wheel, sobbing like an utter, snotty mess. "I killed that guy."

"What guy?"

"The guy back there! I ran him over!"

"Oh, Layla," Jamal sighed, half-annoyed, half-empathetic. "He wasn't…it's not a person. It was already dead, you know?"

I shook my head and hiccuped another sob. Jamal carefully touched my shoulder.

"I think we're both just tired. We should find the hot springs. The sign said it was a resort; maybe we can find beds to sleep in."

"What if it's burned down too?" I whispered.

"The sign pointed north of here. Maybe it made it out. Just keep heading this direction."

I started back down the road and kept to it until the town thinned out. As the road grew shadowy with tall pines and the smoke grew distant behind us, I started to wonder if this was a bad idea. There was no telling what we'd find out here, or what would find us.

But then, sure enough, we passed another sign for the resort. It was on the furthest outskirts of town, away from the damage, hidden in the trees and the hills. There was no other option.

I followed the signs, my palms sweating, until Jackpot Hot Springs Resort appeared.

CHAPTER TWENTY-FIVE

THE RESORT LOOKED like something out of a postcard, but a really old one. Sun-bleached white paint flaked off the siding, exposing splintered wood beneath, and the front porch sagged under a rusted metal roof. The windows reflected the drowsy evening light.

I pulled into the weedy gravel lot, and the place looked promisingly abandoned—another casualty of this strange new world—until I saw a Subaru parked to the side. "Someone might be here," I said

"Maybe, maybe not. Let's go."

We left everything in the car in case we had to book it out of here. I really wished I'd thought to grab Mitch's rifle; I obviously wasn't a good shot, but it would've been better defense than nothing. All we had were our fists, and we were two scrawny eighth graders who couldn't pack a punch.

We stepped onto the porch, and I tried the heavy wooden door. It wouldn't budge, so Jamal gave it a hard knock, and we stepped back and waited. After about a minute and a few more knocks, Jamal sighed. "Maybe we can try to find an open window, or—"

"Can I help you?"

We jumped and turned around. A woman stood in a wet

bathing suit, a towel slung over her arm. She was older, heavy-set with gray streaks in her dark hair. Her expression was cautious, but she didn't seem scared. We *were* just two scrawny eighth graders, after all.

"Um…hi. We're just trying to find a place to stay the night," I said.

The woman frowned. "Traveling at a time like this?"

I hesitated. "Long story."

The woman looked us over for a few seconds longer, picking at something in her teeth with her tongue. Finally, when she decided we were no threat, she climbed the steps, moving with a limp. She unlocked the door with a key that hung around her neck. "Tell it to me inside. I have to get out of this bathing suit."

Jamal met my eyes behind her. "Are you sure?" he said, and I wanted to smack him for asking, but the woman just shrugged.

"I don't have much to lose, hon. Come on."

She pushed the door open and we followed her in. The interior of the resort was dim, but an oil lamp burned at the front desk beneath a stuffed buck head. The woman told us to stay there while she changed, and we obeyed. She promptly returned in a robe and she took us to the restaurant just off the lobby. It was a skinny little place with a paneled bar counter and squeaky green stools.

She poured Jamal and me some lukewarm soda. "You like tuna?" she asked.

She got to work making us some sandwiches of canned tuna mixed with packets of mayonnaise. Her oil lamp cast long, flickering shadows across the walls, and I looked around at the memorabilia hanging there. Photos of famous people who had visited this dump, supposed sightings of Bigfoot, and other relics like license plates and postcards. A TV was mounted in the corner. I tried to imagine a time when this place was thick with voices and the sound of the news or sports games, but it seemed crazy. Too far gone.

She placed a plate before each of us. "I'm Rosalita, by the way."

"I'm Layla and this is Jamal." I pulled the plate toward me, starving, but oddly not very appetized. Too much was on my mind. "You didn't seem very surprised to see two kids out here."

"I don't know if anything would surprise me anymore."

"Have other people passed through?"

Rosalita shrugged and started making a sandwich for herself. "I tried to take care of people when I could. I figured it was better to be a charity than a victim of looting. But it's been quiet since the fire."

"How'd that start, anyway?" Jamal asked.

Rosalita's tired eyes lingered on his face. "Lord knows. It started a few days ago and just now settled, and only because we had a storm last night. I bet anyone who survived left town. *If* they survived." She pursed her lips. "Most of them were already sick, I suppose. I don't know why I never got that damn virus, or why my place is still standing for that matter. Guess some of us are just lucky, huh?"

Jamal took a bite and looked at me funny since I hadn't touched my food. I let out a breath to ask another question—a more important one. "Have you heard of Jackpot Alternative Wilderness School?"

Rosalita scoffed. "Awful place. Why?"

The bittersweet buzz of validation pricked across my skin. "My brother is there." Then my voice cracked, and suddenly I wanted to cry again. "He's the only family I have left, and I need to know if he's still...you know. If he's still alive and everything. That's why we're here."

Rosalita sighed through her nose. "I don't hear much news out here, except for that stupid broadcast. But I can tell you one thing: I haven't heard a word about any of those boys, so I'd think they're still up there. And to be frank with you, they might be better off away from all *this*." She gestured vaguely with one hand, eyes focused on her sandwich.

"Can you help us find the camp?" I asked.

"I've got maps of the area around here somewhere. We could

look tomorrow. Tonight, I think it'd be best if you stayed put. They get more active at night."

"The…rashers?" asked Jamal.

Rosalita laughed thinly. "Is that what you kids are calling them? Cute."

She turned away from the counter to put her mayonnaise knife in the sink, which was piled with dishes. I thought of Mom. The apartment. Those dishes I'd never washed.

Before the guilt could eat me alive, Rosalita turned back to us and leaned over the counter. "You got gas in that car?"

"No, we're out. Maybe a few more miles in the tank," Jamal said.

"Ah, that's okay. Don't think you'd make it up there in a car anyway. After the storm, I'd expect heavy treefall and whatnot. Thankfully, it put out the fire before it ate the whole mountain, but Lord, it felt like the end times." Rosalita's eyes flicked between us. "You two know anything about riding horses?"

My heart fluttered. "Why, do you know where we can get some?"

She paused. "I might. But I'm just not sure you should go up there at all, hon."

"We have to find him. We'll do whatever it takes."

"I'm sure you would. But...I had a child once, and letting you two go off into the mountains alone just grinds against my maternal instinct. I've seen things. People who've lost themselves to the sickness, acting like animals. It's not safe out there."

"We know," Jamal said. "We've seen it too."

"You used to be a mom?" I asked.

Rosalita nodded solemnly. "I'm still a mom. My son died several years ago, but there's nothing—nothing in the universe—that can take away the identity of a mother. I will always be one, no matter what happened to my boy, or what will happen to me." She ran her tongue over her teeth and looked at the sandwich in her hand for a moment. Then up at me. "Where are you two from, anyway?"

"California."

Rosalita whistled. "I assumed you were from nearby, but you've come a long way. You must be determined."

I nodded firmly. "We are."

"You could come with us," Jamal said. "I mean...if you wanted to. If you could."

She shook her head. "I've got a bum foot, hon. Can't go very far on it. I'd probably just be a burden." She slapped the counter and straightened up. "We'll talk about it tomorrow, okay? In the meantime, want to go for a swim before it gets too dark? There's a hot spring just up behind the lodge, fenced in. Well, I call it a *warm* spring, but hot spring does better with the tourists."

For the first time all day, Jamal smiled.

We finished eating, and Rosalita led us out back. The hot springs were pools of water nestled in a small, secluded clearing, circled by rugged trees and low, rolling mountains. The smoke wasn't blowing this way, so the air was cool and crisp with the faint scent of pine and earth. Steam rolled off the surface of the water.

Rosalita went back inside, saying she wouldn't be far if we

needed her. We pulled off our grubby clothes and floated in our underwear, steam rising above us. In the past, I would've been mortified for Jamal to see my bra, but it was hard to care anymore. It was hard to care about anything.

The sky was violet now, the sun descending fast. Jamal rested against the smooth, eroded edges of the spring, eyes closed and face skyward. It was calm. A rare feeling.

I tilted back, letting my hair spread out in the warm water, and closed my eyes. For a moment, I was small again, floating in the bathtub. Mom's gentle hands gathering my tangled hair, her fingers running through it with soap. Working slowly to get through the dirt, the knots. I listened to the leaves rustle. I could almost feel her touch, light and careful, like I was fragile. Hear her voice fluttering above me. *Squeeze your eyes shut so they don't sting.*

I held my breath and sank beneath the surface to make the feeling go away.

She'd always treated me like a baby, as if she could save me from becoming something out of control. But I'd have given anything to have her here right now, even if we were arguing, or she was telling me what to do. Because she cared. Because she knew best. Or at least, she was trying to do what she *thought* was best. Either way, I didn't want to be on my own like this. I really *was* just a baby in so many ways, and I wasn't ready to grow up without her.

I ran out of air and erupted back to the surface. Jamal was watching me. He smirked, then swept his arms through the water to splash me.

"Hey!" I sputtered. "What was that for?"

"I don't know. You looked dirty. I was trying to help."

I grinned and I shoved water back at him.

He ducked. "Oh, I see how it is."

He lunged forward and tackled me around the waist. We plunged in. It was warm and invigorating, and our laughter garbled underwater. When we came up for air, it was like we'd resurfaced as kids again. I could forget the absences, the loneliness, the fear. I could forget it all, just for now. We kicked and thrashed, sloshing water all over the rocks, and our voices echoed across the clearing and the pines. In this moment, we were still young, still here. There might still be lives ahead of us.

We played until the sky grew black, until our bodies grew tired, until our breath settled.

And then, suddenly, we remembered who we were.

The air had grown sharper. I shivered, staring at Jamal across the water. The heaviness came back down like an anchor, and just like that, the night was quiet again.

ROSALITA SET us up in a suite, one of the best ones, she said. It came with a little kitchenette and a bathroom with a giant tub, plus a massive TV—not that it was usable without power. There was a master bedroom, which I took, and a room with bunk beds where Jamal set up.

After we settled in, Jamal sat on the wooden balcony outside our suite, watching the stars come out. I pulled out the comic book folders and joined him. The air was cold and goosebumps rose on my arms, but it felt nice. We sat in silence for a while, and I played with the corner of the papers, trying to think of what to say.

"I really liked your new chapters, even without words," I said. Jamal let out a breath and leaned his head back, but he didn't respond. The paper was rough against the edge of my finger. I swallowed. "Can I ask you something?"

"What?"

"Is Leah based on me?"

That, of all things, made him crack a smile. "What makes you think that?"

"I don't know. She looks like me."

"Well, she's not you. For one thing, she's nice, and you..." He trailed off, but I knew he was teasing. But then he looked down at his hands and grew serious. "Leah's got your hair, though.

Before we were friends, back in fifth grade, I saw you at lunch, and I liked your hair."

I snorted. "Really?"

"Yeah. I drew a picture of you, like a cartoon, kind of. And I liked it so much that I used it for Leah's design." He shrugged. "I guess she's kind of you, in some ways."

I studied his expression, trying to read the emotions behind his words. He'd always been hard to read, but it felt impossible now. "How?"

"She doesn't take anyone's bullcrap. And she cares more than she shows."

I blushed and flipped through the pages. I was holding the first issue, and I caught an image of a brave bear roaring in a lab, surrounded by terrified scientists. "Well, what about Major Ursus? Is he based on you or something?"

Jamal didn't answer right away; he was staring back out at the hills and the stars. "Major Ursus was based on my dad. The comic is really about him."

"I didn't know that."

"He was stronger than anyone, like a bear. That's why I made Major Ursus like that. He's tough, and he'll do anything to protect the ones he loves."

I felt a lump in my throat. "I hope he's still out there."

"Me too," he said. He glanced at me. "I'm just glad I still have you."

Warmth spread through my chest, and I reached for his hand again. Things were so uncertain now, and there was no room for hesitation when it came to showing love. Jamal was my brother as much as Preston was, and I wanted him to know.

We sat in silence for a bit. Then Jamal let go of my hand and went inside.

That night, I wrestled with the sheets in bed, unable to sleep. It was the first time I'd slept in a real bed since Mitch's attic, and I didn't even know how many days ago that was now. It felt like too many to count. Like if I counted, I'd go crazy. But as I lay there alone, tossing and turning, it all replayed in my head anyway.

My door creaked open. I tensed and sat up, but it was only Jamal, looking half asleep. Without a word, he crawled into the bed next to me and pulled the covers over his shoulders. We rolled away from each other, but I could feel his heat at my back. Finally, with him so close, my heart rate settled, my eyes grew heavy, and I slipped away from the world.

CHAPTER TWENTY-SIX

ROSALITA'S NEIGHBOR HAD HORSES. Well, what *used* to be her neighbor had horses. He was long gone, ravaged by the brain rash, but his horses were snug as bugs in a stable down the road. Rosalita, being the self-proclaimed good neighbor she was, had been feeding them and letting them out to graze.

"They aren't mine," she told us, smearing mixed fruit jam onto stale bread for us while we sat at the barstools for breakfast. "But no one is coming back for them, I promise you that. So if you can handle them, you can take them."

While I'd ridden plenty of horses, I'd never been responsible for one of my own. "I can handle them," I said.

This morning, having slept so deeply, I'd woken up thinking I was home again, until I rolled over and saw Jamal, and it all crashed into me again. I knew what lay ahead wouldn't be easy, but today, I'd see my brother again. We'd find safety together, like Mom wanted. That was worth all of it.

Rosalita showed us a local trail map while we ate, marking our route with a red pen. The camp was sixteen miles from town, wedged between mountaintops, west of the river. There were dirt roads and some trails we could take, but between the fire— which had gotten halfway up the mountain—and the storm, she couldn't promise good conditions.

After we ate and packed up, Rosalita walked us down the road to her neighbor's farm. She'd made some jam sandwiches for us; it was the last of her bread, but she had a bit more food to survive on.

On the farm, we passed the neighbor's aged, gray house, and I thought I spotted a smatter of blood on the siding before Rosalita steered us away. "One thing I've learned," she said, "is never look too closely at things you don't care to know about."

The stable was long and brown with some riding pens out back. Rosalita told us her neighbor had trained his horses to help kids with disabilities, so they were all pretty gentle-tempered. But as Rosalita unlatched the door, Jamal twiddled with the zipper on his jacket.

"You good?" I asked.

"Uh, yeah," he breathed. "Just…horses are so big. They make me nervous."

I chuckled, but the moment we stepped inside, my confidence wavered. The stable was like any other, with stalls and the heavy scent of manure and hay. But my stomach clenched with the memory of the ranch in Nevada, of the rope on my arms, of Mitch's mouth. I stopped in the doorway.

Jamal paused beside me. "What's wrong?"

I shook my head. "Nothing."

Rosalita beckoned us to follow her down the length of the stable. "It's going to be a tough ride up there. The roads are steep, probably muddy from the storm. These are good horses, but they're probably only used to the ground around here. You understand?"

We both nodded. She stopped in front of a stall of a palomino horse, golden with pale hair. The nameplate on her door read *Sandy.*

"From what I've gathered, this one is the most stubborn of the bunch, but she's strong. You said you can ride, Layla? I'd take this one."

Rosalita brought Jamal to a black horse with a white star on her nose. "You can ride Lunabell. She's sweet." She reached out to stroke Lunabell's nose, and Lunabell snorted. Jamal stepped back warily, and Rosalita laughed. "Don't worry, hon. She won't bite."

Rosalita and I saddled them up and led them out of the stable. The leather reins felt solid and familiar in my hands, like I'd been at Grandma's ranch only yesterday. Like that entire other life wasn't so far away, just at a different vantage point I could only see from the back of a horse. Once I started riding again, it would all come back to me.

Outside, the sky was gray, and Rosalita said it looked like snow was coming. My heart raced with fear, but going up that mountain and getting to my big brother was the right thing to do. The only thing.

"You best get a move on," Rosalita said. "I'll point you to the road."

"Thank you for helping us. I mean it," I said.

She nodded sadly. "I know you do. But are you sure about this? It doesn't rest well with my conscience, letting you go alone."

"We came all this way," I said. "We'll be okay. Once we find my brother, we'll come back down and stop by to let you know we made it."

"Stay safe, and stay alert, you hear me?"

I surprised myself by stumbling toward her, arms reaching for a hug. She let me, and I closed my eyes against her shoulder, thinking of Mom. Letting myself pretend for a moment.

"I don't know why God let me live," she said softly, "but maybe this was why."

WE SET OFF, me in the lead with Jamal riding skittishly behind. We followed Rosalita's directions carefully, knowing one wrong turn could set us off course by miles. *Ride a mile past the farm, turn left onto Junction Road, and follow it another mile. There'll be a sign for JAWS, and another narrow gravel road. Follow it, and you'll find your way—but be sure to stop by the river to let the horses rest.*

The first leg was easy, but once we reached the sign for Jackpot Alternative Wilderness School, things started to get rough.

The mountain road had been weathered by the storm. The forest around us was scant at first, and many of the trees had been charred from the fire. But once we got past the line where the fire ended, the forest grew a little thicker. The trees soared high overhead, and the ground was littered with their broken limbs. The gravel was loose and mucky, so wet that water trickled down the rocks in some places. It started to rain as we rode, mostly mist, but it was enough to make things slick.

After a mile, we found our first fallen tree. It was thin enough that our horses could skip over it, but it wasn't promising. The temperatures were dropping, and I couldn't help but worry that all this water would soon turn to ice. Or that we'd have to stay the night out here, hunkered under some tree in the freezing rain. Or that we'd run into someone—something—bad.

I held the reins tight and kept my face toward the distant, hiding sun.

Our only consolation with the storm damage was that it might have meant Preston was trapped up there. Unless they'd walked or someone had come in with a helicopter or something —which was highly unlikely—they had to be there. Hopefully still healthy. Still in one piece.

It was hard to believe we were so close. After all these months, after all these *days,* I was going to see my brother again. The anticipation helped block out the fear.

I leaned forward as Sandy huffed up the hill, trying to stay balanced. Every few minutes, I'd look back at Jamal. His face was pallid, his legs tight around the saddle.

"Loosen up or you'll kill your back," I called to him. But it seemed like he only stiffened.

We came across the river after a few miles, flowing slow and wide, and got off to let the horses drink. We drank some water too, and ate our sandwiches before we got moving again.

I tried to be confident for Jamal's sake, since I'd brought him into all this. Jamal followed my lead up the mountain, carefully steering around obstacles and picking through the mess. The horses snorted in frustration, hooves sinking into the rocky, muddy ground.

"We're getting close," I shouted back at him, sliding on the slick leather saddle. My jacket was damp, the brim of my hat dripping with rain. We felt high up, far removed from everything else in the world. "We have to be."

The road grew steeper toward the end, the forest thicker. My legs burned as I clenched Sandy's sides, and my hands were cramping from nervously holding the reins too tight. But the crest of the hill was in view. The sky was dark, the air cold.

We'd made it.

We reached a clearing at the top of the hill and stopped, breathless, to look over the wooded mountaintop. To the east was a wide, winding valley, but just ahead of us was a pair of modest cabins and a log-built lodge, a lazy plume of smoke curling into the air from its chimney.

My breath caught in my throat.

They were still here.

I kicked Sandy into a trot, hurrying toward the camp, my eyes scanning for Preston—for anyone. It seemed empty. But it couldn't be. After everything, it couldn't be. Everyone was inside because of the rain, that was all. I knew it.

I rode up to the lodge and slid off Sandy, not even stopping to see if Jamal was with me before I bounced up the porch steps and moved to the door. My heart was hammering. *Preston, Preston, Preston.* It was all running through my head. The reunion, the way he'd run out of some cabin, beaming, and pull me into his arms after so many months apart.

I reached for the door handle, but it turned before I touched it. The door swung open. I expected a counselor, but it was a boy with dark curls, not far from my age, holding out a knife.

"Who are you?" he snarled. "What do you want?"

I stepped backward. "I'm...I'm looking for—"

The words were torn from my mouth as another boy stepped up behind him, looking far older and more rugged than I remembered him. He put a hand on the dark-haired boy's chest, telling him to stand down, then stood over me with a startled expression.

"Layla?"

PART IV
THE MOUNTAIN

CHAPTER TWENTY-SEVEN

"YOU KNOW HER?" said the dark-haired boy.

"She's my sister," Preston replied softly.

I gaped, hardly recognizing him. He'd grown—he was sixteen now—and his golden brown curls, which were once long enough to cover his ears, were now buzzed. His face was thinner, but his body looked strong and lean. One of his arms was in a makeshift white sling, and his cheekbone bore a purplish bruise.

We faced each other for a long moment, neither of us sure what to do, how to be. Everything was so different now. Things had changed so drastically since that night they'd taken him away, and we were both irreparably changed. Not only by what was happening in the world, but by the way we'd been torn apart in the first place, when all we'd ever really had was each other. I looked at my brother, and I didn't know who he was.

But I couldn't hold back anymore. I slammed into him and wrapped my arms tight around his chest. He staggered backward on the porch. He didn't hug me back.

"Layla, you shouldn't be here," he said. There was urgency in his voice. He put his hand on my shoulder to push me back. "Wait, is that Jamal?"

I turned to see Jamal flopping off Lunabell into the grass. Before I could say another word, Preston took me by the sleeve and pulled me into the lodge.

"You get in here too, Jamal!" he yelled, and Jamal scurried

inside after us. The boy with the knife followed, shutting the door hard behind him.

The lodge creaked with age, and it smelled like aged wood, smoke, and sweat. There wasn't much to it. We passed by a long wooden table with benches, and a counter for serving meals from the kitchen, and into a common space at the back, where there was a roaring fire and two sagging plaid couches in an L shape. Drawings and notes lined the wall, and the ceiling was strung with little multicolored fabric flags. Two red-painted wooden doors lined the other side of the lodge, leading into closed-off rooms.

"Sit down," Preston said.

We were the only ones inside. It was quiet except for the crackling fire and the rain pattering on the roof. Jamal and I sank onto one of the couches, sticking close. I realized we hadn't tied up the horses; I hoped they wouldn't wander off.

"Preston, I—"

"How did you get here?" he said. Beside him, the kid with the knife paced. He was young, his head full of unruly black curls, his face deeply freckled. His eyes were so dark brown that when he looked me over in the firelight, they seemed black. Preston took a breath. "And where's Mom?"

I hesitated, then just shook my head. "I don't know."

He sighed and flopped down onto the other couch, hands to his forehead. "What do you mean you don't know? Did you come to Oregon alone?"

"Mom was with me, but we got separated in Nevada. I don't know where she is now, or if she's..." I tapered off, not wanting my voice to break. I shook my head. "But I ran into Jamal later, at a safe zone, and we didn't know where else to go, and Mom made me promise to get to you. It's a really long story."

"You made it to a safe zone and you *left?*"

"You know about the safe zones?"

"Why the hell did you leave?"

"Things went bad. Does it even matter now? I'm here."

"And Mom..."

"I don't *know*, Preston. She's gone."

Saying it to him felt like plunging a knife into his chest. He clenched his jaw, and his face looked the same way it had that night our grandma admitted she was sick, or the day our parents told us they were splitting up. It was his *I can't process this right now* face. He'd worn the same expression in the early days of the divorce, when Mom would try to talk to him about it. When anyone would try to break past the surface of his trouble and dig underneath. He was good at shutting down, avoiding the conversation. Avoiding reality. That part of him was still the same.

He glanced at Jamal. "Where's *your* dad?"

Jamal didn't say anything, and Preston looked away quickly, understanding. We were all on our own now.

"I can't believe you came here," he mumbled.

I scooted toward the edge of the couch, looking at him imploringly, trying to get him to connect with me. His face was deeply tanned, also dirty, and his eyes looked hollowed out, like he hadn't gotten a good night's sleep in months. He didn't look like my brother, but he still was. "Of course I did. You're all I have left in the entire world, Pres."

He didn't respond.

Jamal glanced around. "Where is everybody?"

"In our cabins," Preston said. "Antonio and I were just in here going through rations for dinner. We're on our own now. Our counselors left us."

"*Left* you?"

"About a week ago," Antonio said, leaning over the back of the couch. He wriggled his nose. "We were on a wilderness excursion. We woke up and they were gone."

Preston nodded. "We found our way back to base camp, and they'd taken all their stuff, got in their trucks, and left. The generator was still running, but communications went down. I found this radio in a locker that they'd somehow missed. I could hear a few people on it, but none of them could help. Mostly all we could get was this message, repeating over and over."

"The emergency broadcast," Jamal whispered.

I looked around the lodge, feeling creeped out, like someone would step out of one of those red doors. "They really just... abandoned you?"

"If you knew them, you wouldn't be surprised," Preston sighed. Then he pushed to his feet and reached out with his good arm. I let him help me up, thinking we were going somewhere else now, but he just pulled me close. I pressed against his chest, surprised, and listened to his frantic heartbeat.

"I'm glad you're okay," he whispered.

"At least it's safe here," I said after a moment. "You guys have power, and food, and—"

"We're not safe," Antonio said. "We've never been safe."

"What does that mean?" asked Jamal.

Antonio wriggled his nose again—a nervous tic. "There are others. Other guys, out in the woods. We kicked them out, but they're trying to get the camp back."

Preston went very quiet and looked me in the eyes. "You really shouldn't be here, Lay."

ANTONIO WANDERED off to finish preparing dinner. Preston brought Jamal and me to the window. It was dark now, and the rain had finally turned to snow, drifting in wet flurries across the clearing. He pointed out the cabins across the field. He lived in cabin two, but half the time, their counselors would take them on treacherous hikes for miles and miles and make them sleep on the ground. Over the summer, it was sweltering hot, and now that it was late fall, it had been freezing.

"Why didn't they let you have tents?" I asked.

"This isn't Boy Scout camp," Preston said. "Everything here is a lesson. It's supposed to wear us down. At least, that's how it was before the counselors left." He wiped his nose with his sleeve. "I hope they're dead."

I winced at the cool conviction in his voice, but then I thought of his phone call. How desperate he'd been to come home. He'd probably never tell me what had happened that day, and I'd never understand what it was really like here, but I could feel it.

There were two cabins outside, each housing sixteen boys—or they *had*, before six of the boys split off, one was killed, one went missing, and three went down the mountain and never made it back up. That left twenty-one boys still at camp, all scared out of their minds.

We sat back down, this time at the long table, and Preston told us the situation. He didn't get too deep into the details, telling me only what I needed to know.

Preston and the others had been on an excursion, but they were abandoned in the middle of the night, left alone in the wilderness, miles from base camp. They'd thought it was some kind of test of teamwork or survival skills or something, and that they'd find their counselors at base camp like nothing had happened. But when they made it back, they were met with the dark reality: the counselors were gone, communications were off, and there were limited resources. Winter was coming.

They decided to wait for the delivery truck that came once a month. It was scheduled to arrive the next day with propane and a replenished food supply. While they waited, they did whatever they wanted, eating the food, sleeping in, and living without the harsh rules they'd been forced to follow for months. But the truck never arrived.

When they realized no one was coming for them, Preston decided to go down the mountain and figure out what had happened. There was a van on the property, but no keys anywhere—he'd scoured the place and come up with nothing. So he, Antonio, and four others set out on foot. They'd hiked the sixteen miles down the mountain, and what they discovered at the bottom was a ravaged town full of violent, sick people. After finding shelter in a church, they learned about the military's safe zones from a small group of survivors, but the safe zones sounded too good to be true—too unreachable, at least. Before Preston could learn much more, the fire broke out.

Three of the boys didn't make it out of Jackpot. The others rushed back up to camp, trying to outrun the fire as it licked its way up the mountainside. If that storm hadn't come, the camp might've burned too.

Back on the mountain, Preston told the other boys what they'd seen, then tried to make a plan. He rationed the food and assigned chores, like gathering firewood and washing dishes and clothes in the cold well water. He made rules: no fighting, no violence. Curfew at sundown. Stay on the property, because there was strength in numbers.

He became obsessed with trying to reach a safe zone on the radio, but he had no idea how. All he could do was sift through channels and try to respond when he heard messages. But it never worked.

"You need a calling channel," I said.

"A what?"

"A calling channel. Some frequencies aren't for talking, so you can't just respond back, or no one will hear you. If you couldn't get through, you probably had to find a calling channel and hope someone was listening."

Jamal squinted at me. "How do you know that?"

I shrank in my seat, not eager to tell them where I'd learned it, or that I really didn't know what I was talking about. "I don't know."

Preston rolled his eyes. "So, what, no one heard my messages? How was I supposed to know what channels were the right ones?"

I shrugged, because I didn't entirely understand that either. Walt's black spiral notebook back on that ranch had been full of information he'd been gathering for who knows how long, but to me, all this radio stuff felt like some secret knowledge I hadn't unlocked. I wished I had.

Preston sighed and went on with his story. "Well, it doesn't matter anymore anyway."

He'd decided that until he figured the radio out and contacted help, they'd all be safer up here. Sooner or later, someone would come. Until then, they had to work together, or they'd die alone. Most of the kids willingly agreed to live by Preston's rules until things went back to normal or they were rescued. Others weren't so eager.

"There's this guy, Trent," Preston told us. "He's the one who made it all fall apart.."

Trent, who had been at camp for thirteen months—longer than anyone—didn't want to be rescued. He didn't want to live by anyone's rules ever again. He wanted whatever freedom he could get his hands on, no matter who he hurt in the process. Just last night, Preston had been alone in the lodge with the radio. He'd fallen asleep, but someone woke him up and told him there there was a problem outside: Trent and his friends had stolen rations.

He'd gone out to confront them, and that's when all hell broke loose. Punches were thrown, people were injured, and Preston's shoulder was dislocated. But when a young kid got killed in the crosshairs, the fighting stopped. Trent, and the five boys who had stood with him, were driven from camp by the rest, splitting off into their own faction in the woods.

It was only after they were gone, when Preston returned after helping bury that young kid, that he realized the ham radio had been stolen.

"So Trent has it?" Jamal said.

"Yep," Preston droned.

"But what if someone tries to communicate and save you guys?" I asked.

"That's exactly it," Preston said. "They don't want to go home. It's complicated to explain, Lay. But there's nothing for them there, and here, they can be in control." He glanced at the floor and scuffed the wood with his boot. "We haven't had much of that."

I knew that living at a wilderness therapy camp for months couldn't be easy. Especially if they'd been treated as badly as I thought they'd been. But how could anyone want to stay here?

"You said you heard people on the radio sometimes. What did they say?" I asked.

Preston's brow furrowed. "I've heard a few people—I even talked to one—but none of them could help us. If I just had a way to know what channels I could reach people on, maybe..." His expression softened briefly, then hardened again. "Doesn't matter unless we get the radio back, anyway. We aren't getting rescued without that thing."

"It's okay. Jamal and I have horses," I said. "You can come back down with us. We made a friend, and maybe she can help us—"

"No, Layla," Preston said.

"But winter is coming, and you'll run out of food soon. You said it yourself." I stood up. "You can't stay here."

"Layla," he said slowly, firmly. "I'm not leaving." He pointed out the window, toward the cabins. "Some of those boys are hurt, and not all of them can make it down the mountain. Plus, it's no better down there. We need to get that radio back, and we need to get a distress signal out. Until then, I'm not leaving any of them behind. I'm sorry you came here for nothing, but I need to stay. I told them I'd protect them until help comes, and that's what I'm going to do. For the first time in my life, I have people looking up to me. They need me."

"Well, I've always needed you."

That shut him up. His eyes flashed, sticking to mine for a long second, searching deep for what to say. It felt like he didn't believe me, even though I'd said it with my whole chest. Finally, he looked away. "Well, that's your fault for putting your trust in the wrong person, Lay."

Beside me, Jamal fidgeted with his zipper. "What if help doesn't come?"

Preston clenched his jaw and took a steadying breath, but didn't speak. We all knew the answer. If help didn't come, we would eventually die up here. All of us.

CHAPTER TWENTY-EIGHT

WE WERE INTERRUPTED by the lodge door swinging open. Preston shot to his feet as a group of boys poured inside, shivering from the rain but chatting noisily. Their voices faded when they saw us sitting there.

Preston glanced at me, then walked toward them, his voice dipping so low I could hardly hear. I caught only words. *My sister—long story—be nice.*

He stepped back and the boys gathered around the table slowly, all eyes on me and Jamal. There were over a dozen of them, dressed in dirty jeans and flannels and jackets that probably wouldn't get them through winter. I looked at the wood grain as they sat, embarrassed. I should've been a hero for trying to rescue my brother from this stinkhole, but instead, I was being gawked at like an idiot.

"So what the hell is she doing here?" one of them finally said.

Standing at the head of the table, Preston looked embarrassed too. I thought he'd berate me in front of everyone, but he said, "Something happened to our mom, and she didn't know where else to go." He locked eyes with me. "Don't underestimate her. She's tough."

The boys looked over me and Jamal gruffly. My cheeks burned.

Antonio, Preston, and a couple others soon served dinner: rice, beans, and some rabbit that had been caught with traps. Someone plopped a metal plate in front of me, and I'd never thought I'd eat rabbit in my entire life, but I was so hungry I didn't care what it was.

The boys talked in low voices, but no one spoke to me or Jamal, and I could tell the tension was high. The boys scarfed down their meals, heads hanging over the table. Whatever was going on with this *other faction*, it was serious.

When he was done passing out food, Preston joined me at the end of the bench with his plate. Several boys glanced at him, but kept their mouths shut.

"You can sleep in here for the night," Preston murmured. "Don't go into the cabins."

"Why not?"

His eyes briefly drifted down the table, passing over all the boys, and although he didn't say it, I could tell what he was thinking—he didn't entirely trust them. He shoved a bite of rabbit into his mouth, swallowed, and said, "Just don't, okay? I'll stay in here with you."

When everyone was done eating, a couple boys carted off all the plates into the kitchen, apparently on cleaning duty. I felt like I needed to prove something to stay here. "Can I help them?" I asked Preston.

"You don't have to."

"I want to."

He nodded his head toward the kitchen door. "Fine. Go in there and help them dry dishes. They'll show you where to put them."

One boy in the kitchen was a little older with unshaven scruff on his face, but the other was closer to my age, with rusty-colored hair that had grown out past his ears. They didn't acknowledge me, but spoke quietly to each other. I could hardly make out their voices over the clatter of dishes and water, but I strained to listen.

"I say you go sooner than later," Rusty whispered.

"But what about what Preston said? Strength in numbers and all that—"

"Who gives a damn what Preston says? What does it matter if he isn't going to *do* anything?" Rusty perked up, and his gaze drifted toward me. He clenched his teeth. "We'll talk about this later."

They set me up at the end of a long metal counter with a towel. They washed the dishes in a deep basin—with only frigid water since the soap had run out—and then slid the dishes down to be dried and carefully stacked on a shelf. With me in the room, they stopped talking altogether.

I finished my job with my head down, then returned to the common area. Many of the boys had stuck around. There were stragglers at the tables, some playing cards, a couple writing and sketching. One boy with glasses, who seemed even younger than me, was setting up a board game, but it didn't seem like he had anyone to play with.

I returned to the fireplace. Jamal was sitting cross-legged in front of it, holding all three of his comic book folders and staring into the flames. I sat beside him slowly. He looked on the verge of throwing the folders into the hearth.

"What are you doing?" I said.

"What's the point?"

"The point?"

He lifted the folders. "Yeah, what's the point? I don't know what to do with the story, and no one is ever going to read it anyway."

I licked my lips, feeling the warmth of the fire roast my cheeks. "Well…you said it's about your dad. What would your dad do if he were in Major Ursus' situation? How would he get out of it?"

Jamal stared ahead darkly. "He wouldn't."

The flames snapped, but despite the heat, a chill ran down my spine. I knew what he meant. His dad could fight all he wanted, but it didn't mean he'd make it. He wasn't invincible. Even if he was still alive right now, there was no telling what situation he was in, or if he'd ever get out of it. Like Major Ursus —and like the story—he didn't know what his future looked like. He was trapped, and so were we.

But I didn't want to say that to Jamal.

"You have to finish," I said.

"Why? I don't have any inspiration left."

"Because I said so." I took the comics from him. They felt thick and heavy in my hands, nearly a year's worth of work. I thought of all the nights Jamal had spent at my house, drawing over the coffee table while we watched movies. All the discussions we'd had about the story at lunch. I thought of the day he asked me to work on it with him. *I have this idea I started, but it'll take me too long to do on my own. Do you like coloring?*

It was his comic, but it was mine, too. I cared about it now more than ever, and I couldn't bear to see it so close to the flames. Maybe because it felt like a part of us. Of who we were not so long ago, before we got torn apart and mangled by the world. I cared because it was something we did together when we had so little else to hold on to.

"Jamal, do you remember when my dad left?"

"Kind of," he said. He'd only just moved to the base, just met me at school. We were only acquaintances then, until we ended up at the same lunch table one day and everything changed. He didn't know it then, but that day had been hard. Dad had sent us a picture of his new couch in his new place that morning, and it left my stomach feeling all tangled up. Jamal and I had found our way to that same table, and we'd talked about trivial stuff like our science quiz, and the Sacramento Zoo, and adult cartoons we technically weren't allowed to watch. And so I forgot about the couch. I forgot about Dad, just for that moment. Because although he had left my life almost completely, someone else had suddenly appeared.

The first time I went to Jamal's place on the base, his dad made chili and let us watch *Family Guy*. He complimented my spice tolerance. He told me stories about being stationed in Korea when he was younger. Of meeting Jamal's mom in an after-school book club in high school. Of summiting Mt. Shasta on his thirty-fifth birthday. He was climbing the ranks and didn't have much free time, but whenever he had time to make chili, he made sure Jamal invited me over.

"When my dad left, I felt really alone," I said. "But you came to town, and you were there for me. And so was your dad. I don't know what happened to him, but I don't think he'd want you to be so lost without him that you'd forget the things you love."

Jamal took the folders back from me, wordless and serious for a moment. Then he scoffed. "You better finish coloring, then. We can't finish if you don't do your part."

"Goes both ways, pal. Finish the stupid story already."

That finally got a faint grin out of him. "I had one idea to end it," he murmured. "Major Ursus manages to turn back into a human one last time. He escapes captivity, frees Leah and the hybrids, and then...he dies."

"You can't end it like that."

"Why? He sacrifices himself because he loves her."

I shook my head. "Major Ursus always comes out okay, remember?"

Jamal glared at the folders, then set them aside, frowning deeply. "That's just not realistic, Layla. You should know that by now."

THAT NIGHT, Preston and I put the horses away in a large garage near the lodge. The vehicles were gone except the one van with no keys, so there was plenty of room inside.

After that, Preston wanted to check on one of the injured kids, so I went with him. It was more out of curiosity to see the cabins than anything, but the minute I entered cabin one, I regretted it. The air was stale and hot from the wood-burning stove by the door, but it smelled like sweat and the metallic edge of blood and infection. I knew those smells well by now.

The cabin was long and narrow, lined with eight bunk beds. The beds were unmade, clothes were on the floor, and there were photos and letters and drawings taped on the walls. A paper banner hung from the ceiling that said *Long Live Cabin 1! Counselors Can Die!!*

The cabin was nearly empty except for a few guys, including one in bed at the very end of the room. I hung onto Preston's sleeve as we approached him.

"Hey Tyshaun," Preston said. "This is my sister. She came all the way from California."

Tyshaun nodded at me, seemingly too tired to really question my presence. "So you're Layla."

"Yeah," I said with a small smile.

"Luke brought you dinner, right? You doing okay?" Preston asked.

Tyshaun grumbled in response. His skin was clammy, his lips dry. I didn't know what was wrong with him until Preston carefully peeled back the sheets from over his leg. I gasped and stepped back, instantly nauseous. His leg was wrapped in bandages, but they were soiled with yellowish, bloody stains.

"What happened?" I gasped.

"Uh, bear trap in the woods," Preston whispered. "Our friend Luke has been trying to take care of it, but we think it's infected."

Tyshaun smiled weakly. "Sucks for you idiots, since I'm one of the only guys who can actually hunt."

Preston returned the smile. "How do you feel?"

Tyshaun just shook his head. "You have to get me out of here, man."

"I'm trying. I promise." He replaced the sheets over his leg. "I'll tell Luke you need some fresh bandages, alright?" He put his hand on my back. "Come on, Layla."

On our way out, we passed a bunk that had photos taped all over the bedposts. I paused to look. One photo was of a blonde boy with a wide smile, and some younger boys who looked a lot like him—little brothers, maybe.

"That's Luke," Preston said. "This is his bunk."

"Did you keep the pictures I sent you?" I asked.

Preston's eyes flicked to the floor. "They wouldn't let us. We were allowed to see them when they came in the mail, but then they'd keep everything in the office because they thought they'd make us lose sight of why we were here or something."

"Bullshit!" Tyshaun exclaimed weakly.

Preston laughed. "We broke in when they left and took all our stuff back. Letters, pictures, books, everything."

"What about the candy we sent for your birthday?"

Preston snorted. "I'm pretty sure the counselors ate it."

We headed back outside. The snow was coming down heavier now. Although it wasn't sticking yet, by morning the ground would probably be covered in white. I wanted to go warm up, but instead of going to the lodge, we walked into the fringes of the woods. There was another cabin tucked there, just past the treeline at the far end of the property.

Preston was the one holding onto me now, like he thought I'd be snatched away in the dark. As we walked through the trees toward the cabin, I said, "Is Tyshaun gonna die?"

Preston's face darkened. "I don't know. We keep trying to dress the wound, but we don't know what we're doing. I'm not a doctor. I was never supposed to be in charge of all this."

The wooded cabin was slathered in chipping green paint, and there was a covered porch with rocking chairs chained down, like they were at risk of being stolen. Out back was a lopsided tool shed. To the side, there was a pile of firewood under a tarp, slowly getting buried in snow.

Preston drew a key from his pocket and unlocked the door. Inside, the cabin was different than the others: bigger and cleaner. The center room was a common space with a little kitchen, couches, and a TV, and it was surrounded by open doors into bedrooms.

"This is the counselors' cabin," Preston said. He stepped into the nearest bedroom; it was pretty basic, but nicer than the bunk rooms the boys slept in. There were folded, scratchy red blankets on the bed, and Preston took a few.

"Why don't you guys sleep in here?" I asked.

"Feels cursed, somehow." I thought he was joking, but his voice sounded serious. "Plus, we have lower visibility out here in the trees. Trent and the other guys are out there now, and they're unpredictable. I just don't want anything else to happen to anyone, you know?"

"You said people died. But you didn't really say how."

Preston swallowed, eyes downcast. "A few got killed by the infected in Jackpot. One guy, Kaden, up and left yesterday. He got pissed and went off into the woods to confront the others, but he never came back. I have a bad feeling something happened to him. And Jamie…" Preston sighed. "Jamie was only twelve. He got in the middle of the fight, but he shouldn't have been out there."

"So he's…?"

"Dead," Preston snapped. "Yeah. Trent killed him, and I had to bury him."

He looked guilty. I wanted to tell him it wasn't his fault, but I held back. I didn't know what had gone down since this all started, and as much as I trusted Preston, I knew he had a darker side that I didn't always see. Anything could've happened here. I knew he'd never kill someone, but maybe part of it *was* his fault.

He handed me a blanket. "Let's get back to the lodge."

Outside, Preston walked briskly through the snow dust, but I glanced back through the woods. The trees were dark and foreboding, curling in around each other like claws. I slowed, feeling watched. I'd seen too many dead bodies to count now, and I knew that would stay with me all my life. But there was something about this that felt darker—imagining boys lying dead in these very woods, not much older than me. Boys who hadn't been killed by rashers or nature, but by each other. Boys who never should have been out here in the first place. It was so violently primal and tragic, and it sent fear crawling down my neck.

I turned away from the trees and hurried after my brother.

BACK IN THE LODGE, Jamal and I spread the blankets out on the couches, and Preston made his bed on the floor at the foot of my couch. Before he settled in, he double-checked the locks on all the doors, all the windows. He threw a couple more logs into the fire, carefully took off his sling, then finally lay down with a huff. A kitchen knife rested on the floor beside him.

Jamal fell asleep quickly, snoring lightly. But Preston and I both lay awake.

I never minded sharing a bedroom with him. It made things complicated when we had friends over, when we needed privacy, or when we wanted to listen to music or watch a show without headphones. But when he left, I wasn't used to the silence. The lack of his breath and his consistent, murmured *goodnights*. I didn't like being alone.

Being back with him now felt alien. I'd spent the whole summer and fall on my own, wondering what it would be like when he got back. If he'd be different.

Looking at him now, he *was* different. Colder. He'd never been the warmest kid, but I'd always been able to see through that. Now, I couldn't. He was nothing but a shell.

"Preston?" I whispered.

He took his eyes off the ceiling and turned toward me. "Yeah?"

"I'm sorry for coming."

"You didn't know what else to do." He chewed his lip for a moment. "You never told me what happened to you out there. Or Mom."

As glad as I was that he was asking, the thought of it made me shiver. "There was this guy we thought would help us. He said he was taking us to you, but he got it in his head that I wanted to go to Colorado Springs. When Mom realized we weren't heading to Oregon, they got in a fight and he...he hit her. Then he took me." I blinked back tears. "He scared me a lot."

My brother went very quiet. "What did he do?"

I closed my eyes, pretending we were back in our bedroom at home. That he was still the same brother I could talk to about anything. Who tried to toughen me up, but never pushed me too far. Never wanted me to *have* to be tough. Pretending I was in my own bed and Preston was in his made me feel a little more okay. "He was going to hurt me, but I got away."

Preston exhaled hard and spoke through his teeth. "He was *going* to hurt you? But he didn't?"

"I got away," I said again. "I'm...okay."

"And Mom? Do you really think she's..."

"I told you, I don't know."

Across the room, Jamal stirred and rolled over. Preston sighed and closed his eyes tightly. "I'm sorry all this happened, Lay. Seriously, I am."

"Me too."

I briefly told him the rest of it. Leaving home with Mom, the Wild West town, the ranch. What happened after I escaped Mitch, how I'd found Jamal at the quarantine camp, and how we'd stolen the Jeep and made our way here. I told him about the truck stop, too, how Mom might have survived for a little while—but if she had, she could be anywhere. She might still be dead and probably was.

Preston was silent, mulling it all over. He'd seemed surprised that Mom had wanted to come get him at all. Like being sent away had hardened him so much that no one would see him as worth saving anymore. But he was.

"I've missed you a lot," I whispered. "I kind of pictured this going differently. Like, seeing you again. I guess after all this time, I got an idea in my head of how it would go, but it didn't feel the way I wanted it to."

"I know. I missed you, too. All I could do was send you those stupid postcards."

I chuckled. "I told Mom they didn't sound like you. She always told herself you were better off here, but deep down she knew you weren't."

"I don't give a shit what she told herself." Preston looked back at the ceiling, and his voice cracked. "I know I've done a lot of messed-up stuff, but I didn't deserve this. None of these kids deserved the things that happened to us here."

I curled into my blanket, almost too scared to ask. "What kind of stuff?"

He shook his head. "I don't even know where to begin. That day I called you, Trent started a fight with me. So they made us go to the pit—this clearing out in the woods—to haul rocks and chop wood for hours. Neither of us were allowed to eat anything or talk at all."

"Seriously?"

"Seriously. There were so many rules here, Lay. You wouldn't believe it. You know, my friend Luke got put on silence for two days. That means he couldn't talk to anyone, all because he got into a dumb little argument. When I first got here, this kid was talking about how he wanted to kill himself, and he tried to write it in a postcard to his parents. The counselors told the kid he was being manipulative—they didn't want his parents to come get him, because then what happens to all that money they're getting from him, you know? But then he snapped his ankle on an excursion and got to go home anyway. We all thought he was so lucky. Sometimes I think he broke his ankle on purpose."

I watched Preston's gaze flicker across the ceiling as he spoke. None of this was my fault, but the guilt was so deep it felt like it was flowing through my bloodstream.

"That first day after the counselors left felt like paradise, even with our impending doom," Preston said. He smiled a little, but it quickly disappeared. "Then suddenly it was like *Lord of the Flies*."

"I've never read that book."

"You'll witness it yourself soon enough."

The way he said it so calmly, so certainly, made me nervous. But I didn't want to talk about it anymore. I was thinking about Mom, desperately wishing she'd gotten to see Preston. To say goodbye, at least. To tell him sorry. Now she'd never get the chance. But I didn't want him to hold onto that anger forever, especially now that she wasn't coming back.

"This whole camp thing was Dad's idea, you know," I said. "Not Mom's. She just didn't know what to do with you after the accident, and…"

Preston's eyes stayed glued upward, and the muscle in his jaw tightened. "I know it was his idea, and I don't forgive him. But she signed off on it, too."

"She's been trying to get to you."

"But she's not here. I needed her. I called her, and she didn't answer. *You* did. So it doesn't matter what she's been *trying* to do, not after everything she already did."

We both went quiet, letting this settle into our chests. I hesitated, blanket pulled to my chin, cowering from my own thoughts. "Maybe we should try to get to Dad."

Finally, Preston looked at me. "You can't be serious."

"I am."

"Colorado Springs is a thousand miles away, and Dad doesn't care about us." Preston sighed and faced the fire, his back to me. "Goodnight."

I watched the back of his head for a minute, blinking back the sting of tears. "I'm tired of fighting," I whispered.

After a moment, he rolled back over. His good hand reached for mine and gave it a squeeze. "I know, Lay. Don't worry. I have a feeling it'll all be over soon."

CHAPTER TWENTY-NINE

IN THE MORNING, the field was white with snow. The boys started a bonfire in the middle of it and huddled around to stay warm, holding thick, sharpened sticks as weapons. I wondered aloud to Jamal why they didn't just stay inside the cabins. He said they were probably trying to stay vigilant.

We sat by the fire as the sun came up. The air warmed a little, but not enough to melt the snow. Preston wanted us to stay inside, but I was enjoying the fresh air, and from here, I could keep an eye on the horses as they grazed the field. Two of the younger boys were petting Sandy while she munched on the long bits of grass peeking through the snow.

I gazed off into the woods, trying to picture the fight that had broken out here just days ago. This morning, camp was peaceful, the boys meandering and leaving footprints in the clean white snow. It was hard to imagine anything else. This other faction sounded like a fable, like Bigfoot, just figments of a collective imagination; even though I'd been told that kids had died, it was hard to comprehend just how bad this other group could be.

I knew taking the radio—the only chance for rescue—was serious, but why couldn't they talk it out? Why didn't the other boys *want* to get rescued?

Preston and Antonio were over at the woodpile by the garage, talking in low voices, Antonio holding an axe that looked too heavy for him. He didn't strike me as a very tough kid, but it seemed like he was trying to be. Preston looked upset.

"I'm so hungry. We need to go hunt more," said a boy across from me. He had shaggy blonde hair pulled into a short ponytail; I recognized him as Luke. He was speaking to a tall Asian guy who was scraping a stick through the dirt.

"Preston said no," the Asian guy muttered.

A third boy, who had reddish-brown hair and tan skin, said, "Who cares? We're going to starve out here."

Just then, Preston came over with an armful of wood scraps under his good arm, and he dropped them in a pile by the fire. The boys went silent and watched Preston toss a couple pieces into the flames.

"Preston," Luke finally said, "we need to hunt. We're out of meat. I can set a few traps on the hills east of here, out by the valley, and—"

"It's not safe," Preston said.

"But Trent's camp is west. If we just stick to the east, then—"

Preston straightened up. "They could be anywhere. And after what happened to Terrance and Jamie, and maybe even Kaden, we know they're capable of violence, and I'm not taking any chances." He glanced at me. "Especially not now."

The Asian guy stood up to face Preston. "I know you're trying to protect us, man. But there comes a point when we have to stop being scared and just go back into those woods. There are twice as many of us as there are of them. "

Preston hesitated, jaw tight. "I'm not scared. Just cautious."

"Then we'll be cautious in the east."

"I can help," Jamal said. Everyone turned to look at him. He blushed, hunching down, and added, "I'm in Boy Scouts."

"I can help too," I said.

Preston groaned. "You aren't going out there."

"I'm not a baby. You have no idea what I've seen the past week."

"Yeah, well, you have no idea what I've seen *here*. So listen to me. I'm serious."

"Okay, okay," I mumbled, slinking down on the log. "I was just trying to help."

"You don't need to help. You just need to stay put and stay in the background." He huffed and turned back to Luke. "I'm just saying, hunting's probably not worth it. Not until we make a plan to go back out there and resolve things."

"You're not making a plan though," said the boy with reddish-brown hair. "Why are you so scared of him?"

"Because, Mason, he killed Jamie!" Preston said. "Are you all forgetting that, somehow?"

Luke put up his hand and spoke calmly. "A lot of things happened that night, Preston, and it was messed up. I get that.

But he's one guy. You can't let him have this much power over you."

Preston wasn't having it. "You're the one who said he's trying to bait me with the radio. You know him. He won't just let this go."

"Then just make a plan and do something!" Mason said. "I'm sick of just sitting here waiting for something to happen, and if you ask me, this whole radio thing sounds like it's between you and Trent anyway."

"So what do you want me to do?" Preston yelled.

"If you want the radio back, man up and go out there! If you don't, let it go. But don't make it our problem," Mason said.

"I hate to say it, Preston, but he's kind of right," the Asian guy said.

Luke breathed in deeply, his expression sort of reluctant, like he felt bad for not taking Preston's side. "We have to hunt. Are you more scared of Trent, or more scared of starving?"

"What's Trent gonna do with one axe anyway?" the Asian guy asked. "*If* he even has it."

"He'll go all Jack Torrance on us, like *The Shining*," Mason said.

They all laughed, but Preston was pale, his teeth clenched. "Glad you guys think it's funny. Really. I'll make sure to remind Trent it was all a big joke when he shows up in the middle of the night to take back the lodge."

"Okay, paranoid," said Mason.

Preston kicked a log, sending it into the bonfire. The whole structure teetered, but didn't fall. With that, he stomped off, muttering about needing to make breakfast. Everyone watched him go. The fire crackled. Then slowly, people rolled their eyes and went back to what they were doing.

Luke sat down beside me. "Your brother is a good dude, Layla, but damn. He freaks out sometimes."

I didn't want to talk bad about my brother, so I laughed it off. I was trying to think of something nice to say to ease the tension when someone else interrupted. It was the young, rusty-haired kid, hobbling over with a slight limp.

He motioned to Jamal. "Hey Luke, you should show him how you make your traps. We could use the help."

Luke sighed, probably still annoyed at Preston, and reached out to help Jamal to his feet. "Yeah, sure. What was your name again, kid?"

"Jamal. I've made traps before, actually."

Jamal eagerly went with him, heading back toward the garage and chatting all the way. I was going to follow, but Rusty stopped me. "By the way, I think one of your horses wandered off," he said. He pointed across the field. "Someone said they saw it over by the counselors' cabin."

"Oh, shoot. Thanks."

He sat down by the fire, so I scurried off across the field, heading toward the counselor's cabin just past the edge of the woods. I kept my eyes peeled, both for Lunabell and for any sign of trouble. Sandy was still munching on the grass, but Lunabell was nowhere to be seen.

I stepped past the treeline, down the trail that led to the cabin. The woods were thin here, but behind the cabin, they deepened and darkened. I slowed, suddenly nervous. Over my shoulder, I could still hear some echoes of voices and an axe cutting through wood. If something happened, they'd be able to hear me from the camp. Wouldn't they?

I searched all around the cabin, circling the back where brambles clung close to the siding like claws. I even considered climbing up the firewood onto the roof to get a better view, but that sounded dangerous, and Preston would kill me, so I just looped around the area a couple times. How hard was it to find a horse?

"Oh, Lunabell," I called softly. "Where the heck are you?"

I'd just given up and started back down the trail when something rustled behind me. A sharp crack, a foot snapping a branch. Thinking it was Lunabell, my spirits rose, and I whipped around. But there was nothing there.

The hairs on my arms stood up, and instantly, I got that gut feeling that told me to run.

In the split second it took for me to turn around, it was too late—an arm hooked around my waist and yanked me backward, out of nowhere. The world lurched. I sucked in breath to scream, but a cold hand clamped over my mouth before I could.

Something hit me hard in the skull, and everything vanished.

CHAPTER THIRTY

MY FIRST CONSCIOUS thought was that my hands were numb. I blinked, blinded by daylight, only seeing hazy orange and green overhead. As my eyes adjusted, I realized they were leaves, and I was staring up from the forest floor. Actually, I was moving.

"Hurry, she's waking up."

My arms were stuck over my head, and I felt the tug of a rope. I was being dragged, scraping against pine needles, rocks, snow. My head swayed. I closed my eyes again.

"She's heavier than she looks," someone grumbled.

"Here's far enough. Let's stop."

My arms were dropped and my head hit the ground. I winced and looked up. This time a face was peering over me: a teenager with a patchy beard and a black eye.

"Where'd she come from, anyway?" he asked.

"Supposedly she showed up on a horse," someone else said.

Another voice responded, just out of view. "Doesn't matter. Let's just hope they notice she's gone soon so we can start negotiations. I'm sick of this."

My heart skipped a beat. Negotiations.

Things were slowly coming back into focus. I strained to see the other faces—three teenage boys total, standing around me, all of them dirty and almost manic looking. One was broad-shouldered, standing with arms crossed. Black Eye was bouncing anxiously on the balls of his feet, eyes darting, like he was ready to flee at a moment's notice. Or fight.

The third guy crouched down in front of me. He had a dark buzz cut and a long scar that cut across his skull in a white line. "Hey," he said. I was breathing hard, my heartbeat thundering in my ears, but he smiled. He had a southern accent and a voice that was surprisingly honey-soft. "Oh, relax. You're gonna help us fix this mess, that's all."

I glared at him, my mouth dry, my head spinning. "What mess?"

"The mess your brother created, Layla."

It dawned on me that they knew exactly who I was. Preston's

baby sister. Ransom. That's why they'd taken me here—wherever this was. My heart raced, and I struggled against the ropes, but it was no use. The buzz cut boy laughed.

"I'm Trent. I don't know what the others told you about us, but we didn't do anything wrong. Everything that happened at camp was because of Preston's decisions."

The other two boys murmured in agreement.

Trent sniffed, then spit into the snow. "When our counselors left, he thought he could take their place as leader. He started speaking for all of us, trying to run things his way. But a lot of us didn't like that—"

"Most of us," the broad guy piped in.

"Yeah, most of us, but *most* of us were too wimpy to actually do anything about it," Trent said. "You understand, right, Layla? We spent *months* living by shit rules that none of us deserved. The last thing we want is another prick to make decisions for us. We were the only ones brave enough to say that out loud, and it got us banished. But we're out of food, and it's getting cold out here, and we want the camp back. We're going to use you—" he pressed my nose with his finger "—to get it."

A bitter feeling washed over me. "They just want the radio," I said.

"That ain't gonna happen, princess."

I opened my mouth, but before I could say anything, I was yanked up by the broad-shouldered boy. I protested weakly, but my head was still spinning, and I couldn't stop them if I tried. He and Black Eye pushed me against the nearest tree trunk and untied the long, braided rope from my wrists, only to then wrap it around my body a few times until I was tied tightly to the tree.

"I can't breathe," I said, tears pricking my eyes—I felt like I was back in that hay loft with a gun to my head. "Please, can't we just—"

"Shut up," Trent said. He seemed to be the oldest, maybe older than Preston. He looked at the others. "I bet Greyson approached him with the trade by now. It shouldn't take long for him to realize she's gone. We better move into positions."

"Are you sure he'll come out here?" Black Eye asked. "He wouldn't before."

Trent cracked a smile. "Of course he will. It's his sister."

As he began to walk away, panic rose in my chest. "Please don't leave me here," I cried. "Please just talk to them. They'll listen. *Please*."

Trent backtracked and pulled a bandana from his back pocket. "One last touch," he said. He shoved it in my mouth and tied it around the back of my head. It tasted like dirt and sweat, and it made me choke.

"Don't get any funny ideas," he said, and then he darted off into the trees after his friends.

Left starkly alone, I tried to steady my breath. I felt myself sinking into panic, and it was hard to get air into my lungs. But now I could see my surroundings better. I was in a wide clearing, and the ground was torn up with a shallow trench that cut through the dirt like a scar. There were jagged piles of rocks and half-cut logs scattered in the snow. Maybe this was the pit, the place Preston had mentioned. The place they'd put him to work as punishment.

Tears burned in my eyes, so I squeezed them shut.

Preston was smart. He wouldn't walk into a trap, would he? I wondered who Greyson was—probably that kid with rusty hair who'd lured me to the trees. He was supposed to be approaching them with the trade, but what was it? *Give us control of the camp or we'll hurt your sister?*

Would they go so far as to kill me if Preston didn't agree?

I kept my eyes shut, trying to calm down. I couldn't say how long I was alone, but it didn't seem like much time had passed before I heard at least two pairs of footsteps rushing through the woods. I jerked my head up and strained to see around the tree, both praying it was my brother and praying it wasn't.

"Layla!"

No.

My eyes widened as Preston burst through the brush to my left. He rushed to my side, skidding in the icy mud, and immediately got to work on the knot in the bandana—he wasn't wearing his sling anymore. Antonio was with him, brandishing his serrated knife. He started sawing through the rope.

I strained to speak, to warn them, but everything was muffled.

"Hang on," Preston murmured, his hands shaking as he fumbled at the knot. I squirmed and screeched and nodded my head toward the trees, desperately trying to tell them they weren't safe. Preston saw the panic in my eyes and cursed under his breath. Finally, the knot came loose. He yanked the fabric down, and I sucked in a breath of cold air.

"It's a trap," I gasped. "They're going to ambush you. They're going to—"

Preston cut me off. "I know. It's okay." He threw a quick glance at Antonio, and then out at the trees. "We'll get you out. As soon as we get these ropes off, run."

But before I could say another word, a branch snapped to my left. Preston straightened up and put his hand to his waistband, as if reaching for a weapon, but nothing was there.

As the other group emerged from their hiding places to surround us, the forest became very small. I counted seven of them now, circling like a pack of wolves. Greyson was there too, limp and all.

Trent grinned, holding a knife. "Hey, Wise-guy. Thanks for coming."

As he took a small step toward Preston, Preston stepped in front of me. Meanwhile, Antonio was still dutifully working on the ropes, as if it would matter now. We were outnumbered. They could kill us all in minutes.

Preston glowered at Greyson. "I can't believe you," he spit.

"You have to give this up," Greyson said. "The guys at camp are getting restless. They're sick of the rules."

The circle tightened; they were closing in.

"The rules keep us *safe*," Preston said. His hand reached back to touch me. "Just give us the radio, and you can come back to camp. We can work through this. We just need to hang on until things out there settle, and then we'll get rescued. It will be okay, I promise."

"I already told you, that ain't gonna work for me," said Trent. "You act like if we get rescued, they're just gonna let us all go on with our lives, like nothing here ever happened? Some of us can't go back. Some of us don't have places to go back *to*. You know that."

I recalled Preston saying Trent was the one who got Jamie killed in that fight. I wondered if he was scared to go back to the real world—or what was left of it—for fear that he wouldn't be welcome. I wanted to tell him it didn't matter, but maybe it did. Global outbreak or not, it's hard to kill a kid and then expect everyone to just move on.

"You can have the camp back, but I'm not leaving. We can work this out," Preston said.

Trent twisted the knife in his hand. "Maybe I don't wanna work it out. Maybe I'll just *take* the camp. Take something from you, after everything you took from me."

Preston sucked in a tiny breath—Trent had struck something inside him, something I'd probably never understand.

"Here's my offer," Trent said. "Take your sister and her friend, and leave. Hell, take anyone who wants to go. But the mountain is ours now. If not..." He lifted his knife, reflecting the sun. "...we'll just have to come to some other agreement."

"You know we'll die out there. And I'm not leaving anybody behind. I'm gonna get us rescued, whether you like it or not."

Trent's expression darkened. "You willing to die on that hill, Wise?"

The air felt stretched thin as they stared each other down. A cold fear pricked at the back of my neck, but at that moment, the ropes fell to a pile at my feet and the blood rushed back into my arms. Antonio had freed me.

Trent froze. "Don't move!" he barked, aiming the knife at all of us. "None of you move or I'll kill you, I swear to god I will."

We were surrounded. I looked at Preston's back, silently willing him to do something. To say the right thing. To give them the camp if that's what they wanted, and leave with me. Instead, he took a little breath. "No, you won't. You're not that bad. I know you're not that bad."

Trent's jaw muscle bulged. "Why don't you ask Kaden what he thinks?"

Preston stiffened. "Where is he?"

Trent didn't respond. It was answer enough—Kaden was dead.

Trent had killed him, too.

Preston let out a war cry. He dove for Trent, weaponless, hands reaching for his throat. But Trent was faster. His blade slashed. Preston sucked in a breath and staggered back, blood blooming across his forearm. Trent shoved Preston down and wedged his knee into his back.

From the ground, Preston's eyes found mine. "Run!"

I stumbled forward, but two rough hands caught me, and a sharp edge pressed against my throat—one of Trent's guys. His arm was locked around my body, his knife cold against my skin. At the same time, two others grabbed Antonio and wrestled the knife from his hand.

Preston was pressed to the ground, Trent bearing over him, and Antonio's arms were pinned behind his back. My brother's chest heaved. He looked ragged with fury.

"Let her go!" he screeched.

Trent wiped Preston's blood off his hand and said, "Nah, I think we're done talking. What'll it be, Wise? Leave or die? Speak now or sissy gets it."

The blade pressed harder on my throat, my pulse pounding against it. Preston looked at me desperately, lips parting to speak. Everything around us slowed, sharp as a razor's edge, and all I could sense was metal, and blood, and anger. I clenched my fists, trying not to shake. Trying to be brave. Preston and I met eyes. If this was how it ended, after everything, at least I'd made it to him. My brother. One last time.

Then an explosive sound ripped through the clearing.

Trent screamed and recoiled, falling flat on his back.

Everyone cowered as the sound ricocheted. Trent touched his shoulder in shock, and blood seeped between his fingers.

It was a gunshot.

All at once, we looked through the trees.

There, sitting tall on the back of a horse, the sun glowing down on her hair and her handgun still aimed, was my mother.

CHAPTER THIRTY-ONE

SHE STORMED INTO THE CLEARING, gun raised. I felt the knife leave my throat, heard it clatter to the ground. Heard footsteps and screams as boys fled from the clearing. I fell to my knees, but I couldn't take my eyes off of her. My mother. *Alive.*

She rode toward Trent and aimed the gun at his head. "Get out of here."

Trent scrambled backward, slick with sweat, his shoulder bleeding heavily. The remaining boys were quick to follow suit. They scattered into the trees—Antonio ran the other way—and suddenly it was just my family and the wind in the leaves.

The horse huffed. Mom slowly lowered the gun. Her eyes found me.

"Layla," she breathed. Then, bursting into tears, she threw herself off the horse and ran to me. "Layla!"

She dove to the ground and wrapped herself around me, but I didn't hug her back. I couldn't even breathe. It felt like I'd been cracked open. I looked over her shoulder at Preston, who was still on the ground, holding his arm to his chest and staring at her like she was a ghost. Part of me wondered if I was dead. If I'd just had my throat slit, and I was bleeding out in the clearing, and this was some final, dying dream.

But her arms were solid. I could feel her heartbeat stutter, and feel her breath against my head as she shook with cries. She pulled back, and her cold fingers brushed my cheek. "Oh, Layla. Oh my god. I thought you were—"

"Me too," I whispered.

She was close enough that I could see the texture of her flushed cheeks, her smile lines, the flecks of gold in her brown eyes. She smelled like leather and rain. I gripped the folds of her flannel and fell back into her. My voice cracked. "I'm sorry. I'm so sorry."

"Hey, you don't have to be sorry, Lay. I do," she said. I started sobbing, but she just held me for a long, long moment.

Preston's voice broke the silence. "What are you doing here?"

Mom pulled back. Her eyes flicked to the trees, still wary. "We can talk at the camp. We should go before they come back."

"Layla thought you were *dead*."

"We'll talk at the camp," Mom repeated. She let me go and gently brushed pine needles off my shoulders. "Let's go."

Preston's brows were locked together in a deep frown. He didn't seem to want to move, but we had to. Mom helped me onto the horse's back, and Preston clambered up behind me, and Mom took the reins and led us quickly out of the clearing. It was a sturdy chestnut horse I'd never seen before, and I wanted to ask where she'd found it. I wanted to ask a lot of things, but in the shock of the moment, I couldn't find the words. As we broke into the woods, I just held tight to the saddle and watched the back of her head.

The wind cut through our clothes, even beneath the trees. We hadn't gone far, but Preston was breathing hard behind me, clinging to my jacket for balance. I looked down and saw his arm was still bleeding, cut deeply.

"We need to stop," he breathed.

"We should just get back to camp, and—" I said.

"No, we need to stop. Mom, stop, please."

She walked us into a sparse grove of trees, which butted up to a gentle cliff. From the edge, I could see the wide valley spread below, the grass long and yellow, the sun gently melting the snow. As we slid off the horse, Preston stumbled, holding his arm to his chest. His shirt was soaked with blood.

Mom stepped toward him, but he pulled away. "Don't," he said.

"*Preston*. Let me look. I won't touch it, I just want to see."

I stayed on my feet, feeling too scared, too disoriented to rest. Mom and Preston sat on the ground as she examined his arm, her hands hovering, careful not to touch the wound. Preston flinched. "I didn't ask you to come."

"Well, too bad. I'm here."

He rolled his eyes, then glanced at me, still nervously shifting on my feet as I looked through the trees. "Layla, we're fine for now. Come sit."

I joined them and pulled my knees to my chest. Mom paused to look me over. "Are you okay? Are you hurt?"

I shook my head, even though my skull still ached. "I'm just…I'm so confused. How did you get here?"

"It's a long story. For now, we need to get this taken care of. Is there a good first-aid kit at the camp, Preston? You might need stitches."

He nodded.

"Good. For now, we'll wrap it."

Preston pulled away again. "Not until you tell me what the hell is going on. What happened to you? How could you let Layla be on her own like that?"

"It wasn't her fault—" I said.

He cut me off. "It *was* her fault. Whatever happened out there, to her, to you, it was entirely her fault. She shouldn't have brought you with her in the first place."

"It was my choice, too!"

"Well, it was a stupid choice." He looked between us. "I didn't ask you to do this. Now you're both in danger, and that is *not* on me."

His eyes were starting to get red, his breath unsteady. Mom put her hand on his leg and used that calm voice she always used when he'd start to get upset. "Sweetie, no one is saying it's your fault. *None* of this is. But we're here anyway, because we're family, and I'm your mom. That's what moms do. Now let me wrap your arm before you bleed out."

He stubbornly held out his wound, his expression stiff and broken as he desperately tried not to cry. Mom retrieved a knife from her backpack, then took off her flannel and cut off the sleeve to wrap it around his arm. He winced as she pulled it tight and knotted it, but there was a tired, motherly gentleness in her movements, like putting a Band-Aid on a scraped knee. When she was done, she used the rest of the flannel to carefully wipe the blood from his skin. I could picture her with him as a toddler, wiping food from his face, snot from his nose.

With her flannel off, the bottom of her shirt was slightly lifted, and I could see a patch of gauze on her hip. An injury. "What happened to you?" I asked.

She smiled, pulled her shirt down, and pushed to her feet. "Don't worry about me, Lay. Come on, we need to move."

Mom pulled a sweatshirt out of her bag and tugged it on while Preston helped me back up onto the horse. He climbed up after me, but Mom hesitated to take the reins. She stood beside us, one hand resting on the horse's neck.

"What are you doing?" Preston said. "We have to go."

"It's just...over the last few days, I kept thinking about everything I'd never get the chance to say to you two. So, I need to say this."

I was surprised by the gentleness in her voice. Earlier she had seemed so fierce—a way I'd never seen her. She'd changed since we left home. But underneath it all, she was still the same. Still our mother.

She couldn't seem to look at us. "I know...I know I can be too hard on you sometimes, and I've made mistakes. A lot of mistakes. But I don't ever want you to feel like I don't care. I know I pushed you both away, and I'm sorry. That's what I'm trying to say. I'm sorry."

I swallowed the lump in my throat. "I never thought you didn't care."

At that, she looked up at me. There were tears in her eyes again. "When I rode into camp looking for Preston, Jamal told me you were out here, too. And I thought to myself, *Of course she found her way here.* I should've known you would find each other."

Preston sniffed. "She's not a baby."

"No, she's not." Mom put her hand on my knee and

squeezed. "Layla Elizabeth Wise, you are so smart. And you are so much stronger than I give you credit for. I think I've always needed to just trust that, and let you live your life."

I laughed. "If there even is a life after this."

Mom didn't laugh. She turned away and gathered the reins in her hand. It was only as she guided the horse back into a walk that she spoke again, and I felt the composure in her voice ring through my bones. "There will be."

WE RODE BACK INTO CAMP, right to the center, where the bonfire still raged. There was a large group of boys gathered there, and Antonio was in the middle, talking wildly with his hands. As we approached, they fell into a hush. The second the horse came to a stop, Preston slid off its back, hit the ground, and started to storm away, looking ashamed. Before he could make it far, Antonio shot through the crowd and threw his arms around Preston's neck.

"You made it!"

I saw Jamal at the back of the crowd and jumped off the horse to go to him.

"Oh my god," he said, pulling me in. "It was crazy. This kid brought Preston a ransom note, and the next thing we knew, Preston was running off into the woods with Antonio. I thought you'd died or something. And your *mom*. I couldn't believe it when she showed up. Literally, like fifteen minutes after Preston ran off. She thought you were dead, and I told her you were here, but you'd gone missing, and—"

"I know, Jamal. All that matters is we're all still alive."

He quieted, and we turned to look at my mom, who was standing close to the horse, like his form could hide her. She surveyed all the boys, but I couldn't tell what she was thinking. Did she feel guilty, looking at them? Knowing their parents had sent them away like she had? Some of them as young as twelve?

But as I scanned their faces, they didn't seem angry at all. They seemed like they were just waiting for her to explain herself.

Finally, she stepped out and cleared her throat. "I'm Preston's mom. Listen, I know things aren't great, and I'm probably not someone you care to see right now, but I want to help you however I can. What do you need?"

"We *need* the radio," Mason said from the crowd. "We have the numbers to take those guys."

Preston shook his head. "I'm not going back out there. We can't risk—" His voice broke. "Look, they killed Kaden. I don't know how or why, but Trent admitted it. They won't back down. It's not worth it."

At this news, there was an eruption of shocked murmurs, until a boy cried out from the crowd, "I told Kaden not to go out there! That stupid idiot!" He burst into tears and ran off, and one of the others followed after him.

Preston took an unsteady breath. "Trent wants me to leave. The way I see it, there are only two options. Whoever wants to can head down the mountain and risk whatever's out there, or you can stay and let Trent have the camp. But I'm done fighting. I can't lose anybody else."

"But we have a gun now. We can take them!" Antonio said.

"No."

"But what about getting the radio back? What about rescue?"

"No one is coming."

Antonio's eyes drifted to Mom. "She did."

Everyone was quiet, eyes on our mother. Preston's chest rose and fell hard for a moment before he shoved through the crowd and walked off. Mom lifted her chin, trying not to let it get to her. She knew he was wounded in more ways than one, and it wasn't something she could fix in an instant. But she was here now. In time, things would be okay. She let Preston walk away and turned back to the boys.

"Can you show me where the first-aid kit is?"

"You know first-aid?" asked one of the boys toward the back.

"I'm a nurse," she said. "I have some medicine in my suit-case, too, if you need it."

There was a murmur in the crowd. I heard the name repeated a few times. *Tyshaun, Tyshaun, Tyshaun.*

So Mom fetched her yellow suitcase from where she'd left it in the grass, and a few of the boys brought her to cabin one while Luke got the first-aid kit from the lodge. I was about to follow sheepishly, not sure what else to do, until I spotted Preston sitting on the steps of the lodge. He was scowling, cradling his arm in its makeshift bandage. He looked like he needed me.

I walked over. The flannel was seeping with blood, but he didn't seem bothered by that. The wood steps groaned as I sat beside him. "Are you okay?"

"Not really," he muttered.

"I told you she wanted to come."

He didn't respond.

"She loves you. She loves both of us. I know she does."

"She was supposed to protect us."

"She's trying, Pres," I said. "You should've seen her back in Nevada. When that guy took me, she was swinging at him with a crowbar. I almost couldn't believe she was Mom."

He scoffed, on the verge of a smile. "Really?"

"Yeah, for real." I bit my lip, feeling like I had Preston balanced on a very thin ledge of forgiveness, scared to push him back over the edge. I looked out past the camp, over the valley, all washed in daylight. I searched the skyline for smoke from the town and only saw the mountains, rolling on and on.

"This place reminds me of the ranch," I said. It made me sick to think of how viciously everything had changed.

Preston nodded. "One of my counselors heard I liked horses and told me there used to be a herd of wild ones out here. That made me think of Mom. She always wanted to see them."

"Did *you* see them?"

He shook his head. "But I bet they're out there. Sometimes

wild things survive better because they know how to fight for it."

"Fight for what?"

"You know. Fight to live."

I looked back over at cabin one, wondering what Mom was doing in there, and hoping she'd be out soon so she could fix her son—not just his arm, but all the broken things between them. "Pres, when I lost Mom, the only thing that kept me from giving up was knowing you were still out here. That's what kept her going, too. This whole time—even when she thought she'd lost me—all she wanted was to get here so she could tell you she's sorry and take you home."

"There is no home," Preston said.

"Maybe not. But she is sorry."

Preston let out a slow breath, but he didn't say anything else.

AFTER MOM HELPED TYSHAUN, she stitched and bandaged Preston's arm, showing Luke how to do it just in case anyone else got hurt.

That evening, someone made instant mashed potatoes and watery canned ham for an early dinner. That's when the power went out.

The room cut to black and fell silent as the heater turned off. No one said anything about it, they just kept eating in a hush. Luke pulled out some lanterns from the office like he'd been waiting for it to happen, and Mason started a fire. Even then, the dark felt overbearing, the air cold.

After dinner, the boys went back to their cabins, sticking together as they walked, like they were afraid. If Trent would kill two campmates and a fourteen-year-old girl who had no part in this, there was no telling what he'd do to anyone else who got in his way. He'd slipped past the point of sanity. He was almost like the rashers: too far gone.

Once they all left, Mom asked Preston to see the camp office.

There wasn't much in there. Empty file cabinets, a desk, a beige landline phone. There was also a locker that had once held rifles, all taken away, and another one that held some walkie-talkies and other low-grade equipment. Preston told Mom that none of it worked. Only the ham radio had, and it was gone. There was nothing of use here.

Later, when the others had gone off to bed and we were alone, we sat on the couches, and Mom finally told us what happened to her out there. Jamal sat by the fire with his back to us, working on the comic book, pretending not to listen.

After Mitch had attacked her, she'd woken up in the parking lot alone. She stayed at the truck stop for a while, hoping we'd come back—or hoping I would, at least. She stayed as long as she could, but she couldn't survive there, so she moved on. She saw the horses on the property behind the truck stop and hopped the fence, hoping she'd find someone more welcoming than Walt and Mitch. But she didn't find anything but an empty house. There were bottles of medicine left open on the kitchen counter; she assumed they'd gone to the hospital early on and never came home.

Although there wasn't much salvageable food, there was a generator, running water, and a bed to sleep in. She stayed for a couple days, still nursing her concussion and grieving me. It was unfathomable to accept that I was gone, that I could be anywhere with anyone. But she knew that I wasn't coming back. She decided the only thing to do was get to her remaining child —what she'd set out to do in the first place. She couldn't let this be for nothing. At the very least, she had to tell him what had happened to me so he wouldn't spend his whole life wondering. She had to try, even if it was the last thing she ever did.

She'd scrounged up whatever supplies she could, saddled one of the horses, and set off for the Nevada-Oregon border. She'd arrived in Jackpot just before dawn today.

"And then I made it up here," she said. "Those boys told me you'd headed into the woods, so I went out there and..."

"You shot Trent," Preston said from the couch opposite her.

She met his eyes. "He would've killed you."

"Do you have any bullets left?" he asked.

"Only two."

He exhaled hard, then buried his face in his hands. "I don't know why I even asked. It's only a matter of time before this is over. You shouldn't have come."

"I had to."

"Why?"

"Because—" she said, suddenly flustered. "Because I love you, Preston. I know you don't think that, but I do. And I just needed to tell you that. I love you, and I'm sorry."

He kept his face buried.

I wanted to tell her what had happened with Mitch. The rashers, his bite, the way he'd pinned me down in the car. I knew it would fester if I didn't get it out. But I knew it would hurt her, too, telling her the things that had happened to me after I slipped from her grasp. I didn't want her to think it was her fault, so I didn't say it. Someday, maybe, when the time was right.

"What now?" I whispered.

Mom rested her head on the back of the couch and let out a tired breath. She seemed weak, almost far away from us, like even though she was just feet from me, she was trapped behind some barrier. After a moment, she said, "I think I know what to do."

She dug in her backpack at her feet. Preston looked up from his hands as she pulled out a black spiral notebook. Walt's notebook.

I gasped. "Where did you get that?"

"I took it from Mitch's stuff before we got to that truck stop. I was looking through it on the drive and I thought it might be important."

"What is it?" Preston asked.

"A notebook with ham radio stuff," I said. I grabbed it from her and flipped through, heart lifting when I saw all frequencies and notes jotted down. "Now we can find a calling channel. We just have to get the radio back!"

Mom nodded. "I'll do it. I'll take the gun, find those boys, and make them give it back. And then you three…you can get help and get out of here."

I laughed in giddy disbelief and looked at her, my brilliant, thieving mother. But she wasn't smiling. She'd sunk back into the cushions, like there was a weight pressing down on her. She absentmindedly reached under her sweatshirt to touch her hip.

"Are you okay, Mom?" I asked softly. I dropped the notebook and reached out. "You should let us look at it—"

"No." She slapped my hand away so forcefully that even Jamal turned around. Then, seeing the shock on my face, she sighed. "I'm sorry. I'm…I'm fine."

Recognition crossed Preston's face. "You got bit, didn't you?"

I tensed. "What? No, you didn't."

She didn't respond. Her fingers brushed the bandage, then her hand fell into her lap. Her silence was damning.

"No," I said. "You *didn't get bit*. Tell him you didn't."

"Scratched," she whispered. "A few days ago."

I sat down hard on the couch opposite her, feeling like I was falling out of my body. Like I was slipping away into some other reality, like I was slipping into a dream. Because this couldn't be real. Mom had survived everything. She'd gotten this far. She was going to take us home.

"No," I said again, tears pooling. My voice broke, and I shook my head, wanting to rewind time and erase it all. "We can fix it. We can fix you. We just—we—"

"Layla," Mom whispered. She sounded too gentle. Like a mother. "We can't fix this."

I looked at Preston in disbelief, but he was sitting still, face blank. He knew what this meant. "How long?" he asked, voice hollow.

"A day. Maybe two."

The silence that sank over us then was unbearable. I wanted to scream just to break it. I wanted to throw something. I wanted to make the world stop, because how could it just keep spinning like this when everything around us was crumbling, when she was going to die?

She studied Preston, but he wouldn't look at her. "I should've gotten you out of here a long time ago. And not because of everything happening, but because in my heart I knew you weren't okay here, and I should've listened. I listened to your father instead, and that's not an excuse. After being on my own out there, I realized I can make my own decisions, and I should've realized that a long time ago." Her lip quivered. "All I ever wanted was for you to be a good man, and you are. You have been. I see that now."

"Stop," I said.

"And Layla—"

"Stop! How could you do this?" I shouted. I knew it wasn't her fault, but in all the confusion, I just needed someone to blame. "You can't leave us."

Mom smiled. It was a resigned smile. A lifeline. "For tonight, I'm still here."

For tonight.

Only for tonight.

Wait—hadn't she said it happened a few days ago? "How have you not turned yet?" I asked.

She looked at a loss. "I'm not sure. For a while, I didn't even realize I was infected, I just thought I was weak. Then I thought maybe I have some kind of immunity, or that it was only a scratch so it wasn't so bad, or…" She shook her head. "Or maybe it was the tea."

"The tea?" Preston asked.

"We found some wildflower tea while on the road. After I got scratched, I started feeling sick, so I made some, and I actually felt better for a little while. I thought maybe it had medicinal properties or something—"

"What was it?" I moved to the edge of the couch. "What kind of flower? We can find some more. We can grow some."

"Layla…it's November."

"But what was it?"

"Fireweed, probably." She read the hope on my face and knew she had to extinguish it before it overtook me. She shook her head and reached for my hands. "But the tea is gone, Layla. I drank the last of it last night. Maybe it helped me, maybe it didn't, but either way, it's gone. And fireweed doesn't bloom again until June."

Nobody replied. The fire crackled. Her hands were warm and dry in my hands, and I could see it now. The rash. Red and flaky, peeking out from her sleeves, her collar. How had I not seen it before? It was so subtle, but by morning it would surely be worse. I could see it *all* now. See it in her glassy eyes, her drooping body.

"I know I won't make it, and I'm so sorry," she said. "But tomorrow, I'm going to get you that radio, and you're gonna get out of here. I will do whatever I can to keep you safe, one last time. Do you understand?"

"No," I cried.

"I'm sorry."

"No!" I was sobbing now. "No, no, no—"

Preston got up and scooped me into his arms. I cried against his chest, and when I looked at Mom, I could tell she wanted to join us, but she wouldn't. It was only a matter of time, and she was afraid to get too close, like the blood in her veins would tarnish us. Turn us, like her.

Preston brushed his hand on the back of my head. From the fire, Jamal stared at me, his eyes wet with tears of his own, but he didn't move. He just held our comic book tight, fingers trembling.

I didn't want Mom to go out into the woods. She'd never make it—not with her body shutting down. Tomorrow would be too late. I didn't want her to put her life on the line, even if it was going to end soon anyway. Not after all this. Not after what we'd been through with Mitch—

My stomach dropped. "Wait, what about the vaccine? Mitch said there's one!"

"Oh, Layla…" Mom said.

"No, remember, Mitch and Walt said the government was making one. What if we can get rescued, and they can save you? What if it's not too late?"

Mom watched me sadly. For a moment, I thought she would tell me it wasn't true, that it was all a delusion in their heads, and there was no such vaccine. That even if there was one, it would be too late, and just like the fireweed, it was a futile hope. But instead, she looked at me and said, "Okay."

"Okay, what?"

"Tomorrow, I'll get that radio, and we'll all get rescued, and they'll save me, too. Okay?"

I knew she was lying to me. I knew she didn't believe there was a vaccine, and that she was going to go out into those woods and get us the radio, even if she died trying. Because she was our mom, and that's what moms did. But if we could just get the radio without her being harmed, then find the right channel to send out a distress signal, maybe the military would hear us. Maybe they'd get to us in time, and it wouldn't be too late. For her, for any of us.

Preston held me close, and while he did, I looked down at the comic in Jamal's hand. The drawing on top was of Leah, her brow furrowed, no doubt thinking up some plan to get back to the one she loved. Suddenly I could see the ending of the comic in my mind so clearly. It wouldn't be Major Ursus who played the hero in the end; it would be Leah. She'd free everyone, no matter the cost, and this great act of love would break Major Ursus free. He could now turn at will, and he'd use his power to destroy the Syndicate once and for all. Because Leah was fearless too—just as fearless as him. So fearless with her love that it was sacrificial.

I pressed against my brother's chest and listened to his heart pound.

I knew what I had to do.

CHAPTER THIRTY-TWO

I WAS tired of being pushed around, tired of things just happening to me. I wanted to have control again. I had to do something, and for once in my life, I *could*.

Mom had chosen to sleep in the office, far away from us, because she could feel herself fading fast. I watched the firelight flicker on the ceiling and waited. It took a long time for everyone to go to sleep. At one point, Preston got up to check on Mom, and I pretended to be asleep until he returned. I waited for his breath to steady, then crept out of bed. Preston stirred as I put the notebook into my backpack, slipped his knife into the side pocket, and put on my boots, but he didn't wake up.

I hurried outside into the darkness. The air was bitter, and flecks of snow whirled down from the indigo-gray sky. I crept across the field to the garage, saddled Sandy, and gently led her outside. Once I rode her to the edge of the field, I stared ahead at the dark woods before me.

I was going to save everyone.

There wasn't much of a trail, but I tried to follow the route we'd taken yesterday. I found my way back to the cliff over-looking the valley, and soon after, to the pit where they'd tied me up. From there, I went in the direction the other group had run off in after Mom had shown up with the gun.

I rode in circles for what felt like an hour, continually hitting dead ends: piled rocks, an impassable stream, the edge of a cliff spilling down into a ravine. But then, finally, I saw the faint orange flicker of a fire in the distance, and my heart leapt.

I kept Sandy at a slow walk and went closer. The fire came into clearer view, and through the trees, I could make out their shelter. No tent, just two tarps stretched between the trees. Six boys were piled under it in sleeping bags, but there was also a cardboard box between them. I couldn't see clearly enough to know if the radio was inside it.

The only person not beneath the tarp was a boy slouched by the fire, probably on watch. I realized it was the one with the rusty-colored hair—Greyson. I slipped off Sandy and crept closer, peering through the brush. He was asleep. Perfect.

The wind rustled the tarp. I crouched into the camp with my backpack, staying low to the ground as I approached. The radio had to be down there. The boys were huddled close for warmth —an impenetrable dragon guarding its treasure.

I stayed in the shadows, peering in, weighing my options. The air smelled like bad breath, dirty hair, armpit sweat. As I looked at them—even Trent snoring in the middle, his shoulder bandaged—I felt surprisingly sorry. I shoved the feeling away. I couldn't start feeling sorry for these guys now, knowing what they'd done. But still…they were only a few years older than me. Abandoned. Sleeping in the snow.

Focus.

I traced their sleeping forms with my eyes, and then—there. A small black case tucked between them. That *had* to be it. But that meant I had no choice but to go in.

I let out a quiet breath, willing myself to just get it over with before Greyson woke up and found me. I took off my backpack and slipped out of my boots, hoping I could move more quietly that way, and crept under the tarp in my socks. I crouched over two boys, struggling to balance, struggling to place my feet just so between them.

Trent was right beneath me, slumbering in the middle. The

black case was right by his head. I bent over and strained to reach it. When my fingers closed around the handle, I froze, waiting. But nobody moved. I dashed out, back into the shadows.

That had been too easy.

Feeling accomplished, I returned to the bushes and opened the case. The radio was handheld, bulky and black, with numbers on the front like an old cell phone. I'd done it. I'd done *something*. I was going to get us rescued. I clicked it on, and it blinked with a small orange light, and I nearly laughed.

But then it hissed with loud, grating static.

I turned it off fast and sucked in a breath. Too late.

"Trent!"

Greyson was wide awake by the fire, staring at me through the bushes. Beneath the tarp, some of the boys sat up, but I shoved the radio into my bag and booked it. I left my boots, raced to Sandy, flung myself over her back, and set off into a gallop.

I held tightly to her reins, my backpack thumping at my back, my socked feet slipping in the stirrups as we tore through the woods. Sandy snorted, running hard. As she dashed between trees and brush, branches whipped past us, and I winced against their sharp fingers. The cold air bit at my cheeks. I urged her to go faster, but she couldn't see, and I could barely hold on.

As we neared camp, something spooked her. Her ears shot back, her muscles tensed, and I had half a second to brace myself before she reared.

"No!" I cried. I tightened my legs and clutched at the reins, but my socks slipped in the stirrups, and I couldn't hold on. I slid and hit the ground, landing on my backpack with a thud. Sandy thundered off through the trees, leaving me in the snow.

"Layla!" someone screamed, their voice echoing hollowly. Trent's voice.

I gasped, chest tight, and searched the dark. I couldn't see them, but they didn't sound far off. How they had gained so much ground? Maybe they knew some shortcut I didn't, or maybe I'd gotten turned around in the dark. But either way, I was close—the trees were thinner here. Base camp couldn't be far.

I staggered to my feet and kept running.

My heart leapt when the dark silhouette of the counselors' cabin finally appeared through the trees. The clearing wouldn't be far beyond it, with the scattered buildings, the snow bright under the moonlight. But the lodge was a football field away. And the boys—they knew these woods better than I did, and they couldn't be far behind.

They'd get me and take back the radio before I made it to the lodge. It was now or never.

I crouched behind the cover of the small tool shed, swung my backpack off, and took out the radio. My heart fluttered with hope as I clicked it on again, but it only hissed.

I wracked my brain for what Mitch had told me back in that shed. I'd spent days trying to scrub him from my memory, and now everything from the last week felt like a blur, but he'd told me what to do. I just had to remember.

The key isn't just transmitting willy-nilly. You gotta know how to listen, too.

But I didn't know how to listen. I had no idea what I was doing with any of this.

This radio was different from Walt's. His was bigger, stationary, but it had to work the same. With numb, fumbling fingers, I raised the antenna. I just needed to find a channel, a message, and then I could respond. As I turned the dial on top, switching to frequency after frequency, all I got was more static.

Still, I pressed the call button and sent out my voice to nothing. "Uh, hello? This is Layla Wise. If anyone can hear me, I'm at Jackpot Wilderness Alternative School in Jackpot, Oregon. We need help, please."

I waited, but there was no response, only the hum of dead air. I was being reckless with this—I needed to find a calling channel. I yanked Walt's notebook out of my backpack and flung it open, flipping through pages by the faint orange light of the radio screen. I leaned close, scanning his scribbled numbers, codes, notes, my hands shaking. Finally, I found a list of frequencies, pages long. But which ones could I call on?

My gaze landed on one labeled *AF Ops – Emergency Freq.*

AF. Air Force.

I could still hear the boys, far off but closing in. I squinted at the numbers, but that's when I saw something else, just below it. *AF Emergency Beacon – KERRICK? Broken evac call 11/1.* Kerrick was the base where Jamal had lived—where Sergeant Hardy had been. Kerrick was home.

I inhaled and turned the dial slowly, carefully matching the numbers.

A voice broke through the static. It was faint, barely there, but I could hear words. I held the radio close to my ear, straining to listen. There were footsteps now, breaking branches nearby. It was a man's voice on the radio, but it was warbled and indistinct, and I couldn't make out a single word through the static.

I needed higher ground.

I looked at the counselors' cabin beside me, the wood piled beside it, the roof sloping over the porch.

With the radio in hand, I hurried to the woodpile and gingerly climbed it, the logs wobbling beneath my feet. The boys were right behind me now, tearing through the trees. I clawed my way up the cabin's side, stretching for the damp roof shingles, barely reaching, but I dug my fingers in and hauled myself up with a grunt. Then I crawled to the peak of the roof.

"Where is she?" someone said.

I gasped and pressed myself down, hoping they wouldn't see me in the dark. I could hear them moving down below now. They'd no doubt hear the radio. I turned the volume down and pressed it to my ear, desperate to understand that small voice out there.

Static.

Static.

Static.

"Please," I whispered. I squeezed my eyes tight, wishing at the sky, at whatever was up there, to give me something. To give us a chance, after all of this. It couldn't be for nothing.

"Look, there's her backpack!" a boy said below.

I adjusted the antenna one more time. At once, a voice cut through the air. *—stay put—find you.* The words crackled, and I didn't know how to make it any clearer, but I was too afraid to lose it. I listened hard.

—Kerrick Air Force Base, for Little Cub. Little Cub, if you can—switch to civilian emergency—one-two-one-point-five mega—high ground. Stay put. I'll find you.

I gasped and sat up.

"Up there!"

I'd been spotted. Three boys were surrounding the cabin: Trent, Greyson and Black Eye, who wielded an axe.

The message had ended—it was now or never. With trembling fingers, I turned the dial until the screen said 121.5 MHz, like the message had told me. Then I pressed the button and sent my voice into the darkness. "My name is Layla Wise. We're at Jackpot Alternative Wilderness School—"

Something crashed below. There was the thud of boots against wood.

Panic swallowed me, but I forced the words out. "And Little Cub is here. But people are hurt. Please, if anyone—"

A hand closed around my ankle and yanked.

I screamed as I slid on the shingles, the radio dropping from my hand and clattering out to the far edge of the roof. A figure towered over me in the dark, holding the knife from my bag. Trent.

I kicked at his shin, making him stagger just enough for me to roll away. I scrambled after the radio at the edge, and Trent stalked after me, slipping on the old shingles.

"Give it back, you little freak."

I got to the edge first and grabbed the radio tightly. The ground was so far below it made me dizzy. But Trent was almost upon me again. There was only one way I was getting off this roof.

I dropped to my stomach, gripping the shingles. Trent lunged for me, but I let go and flew toward the ground. I crashed to my feet and my knees buckled underneath me, but I swiftly got up and broke into a sprint, radio in hand. I had to get back to the lodge. I had to tell them what I'd heard. *Little Cub.*

The boys were hot on my heels, and the radio hissed with static, and I wanted to send out another message, but it would only slow me down. "Preston!" I screamed. But I was so far from the lodge, even from the other cabins. No one would hear me.

There were only three of them; maybe I had a chance. I ran harder, lungs on fire, and broke into the clearing. I'd nearly reached the bonfire pit, and the lodge was in sight. But before I made it, someone grabbed me by the collar and yanked hard.

Next thing I knew, I was staring at the sky, lungs heaving, head spinning. I gasped and tried to sit up, but someone's knees pinned me down: Greyson. I wheezed in a breath to scream again, but his hand slapped over my mouth, and I was so winded I couldn't fight him.

Trent snatched the radio from my hand and tossed it to Black Eye, who dropped it into the snow. In horror, I watched him swing the axe down hard.

With a series of sharp cracks, the radio splintered into shards of plastic and wire.

My message—what if it hadn't gone through?

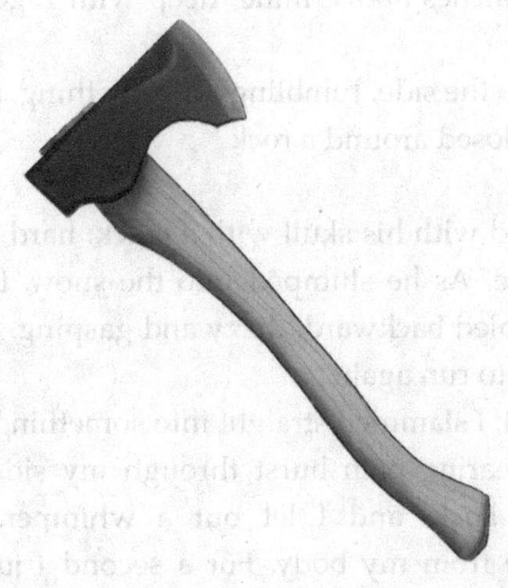

Greyson stared up at Trent, his knees digging into my upper arms. One hand on my mouth, the other clamped around my wrist. "What now?" he said.

Trent thought for a second, breath curling in the cold. "Go wake up Preston, tell him it's over. For real this time."

"But his Mom has a gun," Greyson reminded him.

"She won't kill kids."

"She might if she thinks they're gonna kill her daughter."

"It doesn't matter. With this idiot and no radio, it's an easy negotiation. We should've destroyed it a long time ago. Here, take the axe."

Greyson let go of me to reach for the weapon. That was all I needed. I slammed my knee up between his legs and kicked him in the nuts. He grunted and doubled over, giving me the sliver of space I needed to get out from under him. I lunged to my feet and sprinted for the lodge.

I didn't make it far. Black Eye's arms wrapped around my legs, tackling me down hard. I hit the ground, and before I could scream, he'd pinned me back down. His fingers clamped around my throat. I choked, clawing at his hands, kicking wildly. His face hovered inches above mine, deep with rage, his black eye shining.

I reached to the side, fumbling for something, anything.

My hand closed around a rock.

I swung.

It connected with his skull with a crack, hard enough that he toppled off me. As he slumped into the snow, I shoved to my feet and stumbled backward, dizzy and gasping, trying to orient myself, trying to run again.

But as I did, I slammed straight into something else.

A sharp, searing pain burst through my side. There was a hand on my back, and I let out a whimper as something wrenched free from my body. For a second I just stood there, trying to process the feeling. My fingers traced my right side and found the sticky warmth of blood seeping through my clothes.

The world tilted, and I was on my knees before I even realized I was falling.

CHAPTER THIRTY-THREE

TRENT STOOD OVER ME, my knife in his hand. It glinted in the moonlight, dripping red, but all I could focus on was the pain. Hot like a brand, but creeping through me like poison.

Trent's eyes widened as he looked down at the knife, like he couldn't believe what he'd just done. He was breathing hard. "I didn't—I didn't—" he stammered. "You should've just listened to us. This is your fault."

I coughed, unable to speak, and rolled over.

Footsteps pounded, a voice screamed my name, and then a dark blur slammed into Trent, sending him flying. I heard a thud as they hit the ground.

Preston.

There were other footsteps now, running through the darkness, but I didn't know where they were coming from or what side they were on. I curled into the snow, burning with pain. I could hear fighting, hear fists landing. Trent yelling.

I turned my head to see that Trent had my brother pinned between his knees. He was relentless, hitting and hitting with a fury so hot I swore he glowed.

"Layla!" Mom skidded to her knees beside me, gun in hand. "Layla! Layla, baby, don't move!"

My body was heavy, yet I felt as if I was drifting like ash, like smoke. I focused my gaze upward, trying to find her face. "Mom?"

"Oh, god, Layla."

I coughed and tasted blood. Her hand caressed my cheek. Finally, she came into focus. She'd worsened overnight, her skin paper white and reddish-green with rash, her eyes foggy. Her fingers shook against my face. She was turning.

"Jamal!" she screamed over her shoulder. "Go get a towel or something. I need you to press her wound." She looked back down at me. "I can't—I shouldn't touch it. I'm infected. I—" She sounded panicked, and she just kept running her hands over my face. I could hear something to my left. Grunting. Fists connecting with bone. I closed my eyes.

"You have to stay awake," she said. "*Layla.*"

I forced my eyes open again, just in time to see Greyson coming up behind her, axe raised.

Mom registered the look in my eye and turned fast, whipping her gun toward him.

"Back off!" she screamed.

Greyson staggered back, and things went deathly quiet. There were more boys from the other faction running toward the bonfire pit now. They were holding makeshift weapons, but when they saw the gun, they faltered. Though she was weak, Mom held the gun steady. The gun with only two bullets—but they didn't know that.

"All of you, back off!" she said. "If you so much as breathe wrong, I will put a bullet through your skull."

Jamal rushed to my side and pressed a towel down hard. I panted in pain.

There was a groan a few yards to my left, and I looked over to see that Trent had Preston pinned. His body weight was pressed to Preston's back; they were half-sitting, half-splayed out, struggling for control. Trent had one arm locked around Preston's throat, and the other had Preston's wrist pinned back. Preston thrashed, his feet scraping against the snow, his breath labored.

"Let him go," Mom said to Trent. "You have to stop this."

Preston's fingers desperately clawed at Trent's arm, his face going red. "Mom, I can't—I can't—"

"Let him go," she said again. I noticed her hand start to shake, and Trent didn't defer. Mom swallowed. "This is about survival now. You have to stop fighting each other. All of you."

Preston struggled, but Trent just held him tighter; he could kill Preston right now if he tried. Preston blinked back tears, looking at our mother, scared. "It's no use. He won't—stop. Look what he did—to Layla. You have to. You have to."

I didn't know what he meant until my eyes drifted back to the gun in Mom's hand. *You have to shoot him.*

Around us, boys stood still, watching. Trent's eyes flicked across their faces, then landed on Mom with a sneer. "Go ahead. I know you won't."

Mom clenched her jaw, bringing her other hand up to the gun now, aiming it straight at his head. But she didn't pull the trigger. She didn't say anything.

"You're *weak*," Trent spit. "Just like your son."

"Mercy isn't weak," she said. "It doesn't make you weak to stop fighting. You don't have to fight anymore."

"Mom," Preston choked. "Please."

Mom shook her head. All around us, the boys were wide-eyed, their faces bright white in the moonlight. They were looking at Preston, at me, at the bright red blood blossoming through the snow beneath me. One of them took a tentative step backward.

Jamal pressed the towel tighter to my stomach. I gasped at the pressure, vision going dark. At the sound of my labored breath, Mom winced. She kept her eyes on Trent, but let go of the gun with one hand to squeeze my arm. Her hand was cold, but it felt like it was barely there. "Just hang on, baby," she whispered to me.

She weakly moved closer to Preston and Trent. The other boys watched warily, hands on their weapons, but still, they didn't move. I thought she'd shoot him, but slowly, she knelt and lowered the gun.

She looked in Trent's eyes. Her hand stayed clenched around the gun, but she didn't seem angry, just exhausted. Like she was holding a weight so much heavier than this fight. It was the weight of this camp, her kids, her reality. The way her body was shutting down and turning on her. Her time had run out, converging to this one final night, and it was all she could do to not let the sickness overtake her.

"I'm sorry," she said. "I'm sorry your life turned out like this."

Trent's body went rigid.

"You're here because along the line, somebody failed you, and you didn't deserve that. But you have a chance to do something good, now. To *be* good, even after all the bad that's been done to you."

Trent was quiet, still trying to keep hold, but he was listening. They all were, gathered around in the snowy darkness, watching with bated breath. But her head tilted to Preston for a brief second, and I understood that wasn't just speaking to Trent. She was speaking to her son.

"It wasn't right for you to be sent here," she said, "and I know that makes it hard to believe there's anyone out there that you can trust. I *know* it makes you angry. But you can't let the anger win like this, or the fear, or the guilt. Believe me. You have to let it go."

Mom leaned toward my brother, crying, still locked in Trent's arms. "Preston, look at me. I was wrong to ever let them take you. I should've fought harder for you, because you've always been worth that. *Always*." Then she looked at Trent again, shaking her head. "You're not the enemy. You're just a scared kid who feels like no one is looking out for him, and I'm sorry. I'm so, so sorry."

Preston was heaving for air, face deep red. Trent shook, and for a second, I thought he would explode out at Mom. Instead, he shuddered and took a breath. It came out as a cry. His fingers released their desperate grip around Preston, and unable to hold on any longer, he let him go.

Preston rolled, coughing. Trent slumped forward and buried his head, like all the life had drained out of him. He stayed like that, arms around himself, face hidden in the snow. Nobody moved.

Mom was the one who finally reached out. Her free hand crept toward his shoulder, seeking to comfort him. Trying to be the mother he didn't want, didn't have.

Her hand brushed his back.

Then he snapped.

With howling rage, he surged forward and grabbed for the gun. Mom fell back with a startled gasp, Jamal screamed, Preston lunged forward. I squeezed my eyes shut, and there was a rush of noise and blood and white light as a shot exploded through the night.

Everything stopped.

I opened my eyes again just in time to see Trent collapsing backward. He sputtered for air. A dark shadow spread across his chest. Mom was splayed on her back, still holding the gun, her index finger loose on the trigger. She wheezed, mouth hanging open. Her face was splattered with blood.

Preston crawled to Trent and hovered over him. He tried to lift Trent by the shoulders, but Trent's head slumped, and his weight fell back toward the ground. Mom didn't say anything. The gun dropped from her hand and sank into the snow. She bent forward, curling over her knees, hands pressed to her mouth.

Trent lay still. Blood dyed the snow, black in the night.

Preston gripped Trent's jacket, knuckles bloody and white. He stared down at his slack face, his glassy, open eyes. It was hitting him. Everything. I could see it, like how he'd been so hard and cold during the divorce, until that night on the couch when he'd just fallen apart and let Mom hold him. Everyone was watching, but Preston didn't care.

He looked at Mom and broke into tears.

"Oh, Pres," she said.

She opened her arms, and he finally let Trent go and fell into her. He sobbed into her shoulder, hands grasping her sweatshirt tightly. Even still, they shook. She shushed him and stroked his head and did all the things a mother does, and around us, the world fell silent and dark.

The boys from the other group stepped back. There were more appearing now, running out of their cabins at the sound of the gunshot. They slowed when they came upon the scene, their expressions searching and confused as they took it all in. Trent lying still. Jamal holding a towel to my stomach. Preston collapsed in our mother's arms—our mother, who was so afraid of turning into something vicious, but who had become that very thing already. A killer. A savior.

"What happened?" Luke cried.

Jamal turned to the boys, his hands all bloody, still pressing into my wound. I couldn't feel the pressure, couldn't feel the pain. The world was slipping now. I felt so cold, like I was sinking beneath the snow.

Jamal's voice cracked. "I think she's losing too much blood."

Those words awoke something in my brother. He left Mom, crawled back to my side through the snow, and sank to his knees by my shoulders. His hands pressed around my head. I looked into his eyes, trying to hang onto them, but above him, the stars twisted and blurred. "Why the hell were you out here, Lay?" he asked.

Suddenly I remembered what I was supposed to tell them. "I got the radio. I tried to—to get out a message, but Trent—the radio—I don't know if it went through."

He almost laughed. "You're an idiot."

Jamal pressed the towel down again. I squealed and writhed, and Preston's face fell as he tried to hold me steady. "I just wanted to help," I gasped. "I thought—"

Preston wiped at my forehead. "Hey, hey, hey. I know. It's okay."

My body felt frozen and numb, but beneath the shock, my

heart still raced with panic. My eyes found my brother's, and I forced the words out. "Little Cub."

He and Jamal leaned closer. "What?"

"I heard a message. For Little Cub."

Jamal's face lit up. "Wait, what? Was it my dad? What did he say?"

"I tried...I couldn't..." A tremor ran through my body, and I felt myself fading. I just needed them to know I'd tried. "I just wanted to help. I'm..."

"Layla, come on," Preston said. I thought he sounded like Mom. *Come on, Layla. Come on.* I opened my mouth to tell him, but instead I coughed, and it came up tasting like blood—thicker now. I realized Mom wasn't beside us.

"Mom, what do we do?" Preston looked over his shoulder. "Mom."

She was still off to the side. One hand was pressed to her head, and the other held the gun. Her breath was unsteady and quick, like she was fighting off something inside herself. She was getting sicker by the minute.

Luke ran over, oblivious, and put his hand on her back. "Hey, are you—"

She pushed him away and hunkered down. She was murmuring something—I couldn't understand.

"Stay away," Preston said. "She...she got scratched. She's turning."

Luke scrambled back. "What?"

We watched Mom tremble in the snow, fighting back against whatever raged through her mind. After a long, excruciating moment, her body seemed to settle. She straightened up a little, breathless and wavering.

"Jamal's right," she panted. "Layla's going into shock."

Preston went pale. "You have to give her stitches or something, to stop the bleeding. Right?"

"I can't touch her. I can't risk it. You'll have to do it. I'll...I'll tell you what to..."

"Mom, I can't."

She crawled toward him, dropped the gun, and took his face in her hands. Suddenly her voice was clear, like she'd found it inside herself. "I need you to take her in, and I need you to stitch her up. Luke can help you."

"Mom."

"You have to keep it clean or it'll get infected. If it gets infected, she dies. Do you understand?"

"*Mom*," he said, crying.

"Preston, do you understand?"

"Please, just come with us. Please. I can't do this. I can't—"

She held his head firm, jaw clenched. "You can. You have to." She kissed him between the eyes. "I love you, Pres. I'm always with you. No matter what happens to my body and soul, I will never stop fighting for you."

He broke into sobs, but Mom let him go and looked down at me. "Preston's going to take care of you. You're going to be okay."

"What about you?" I whispered.

She shook her head. Her hand crept toward the gun again. "It's too late for me, Layla. If I stay, I'll turn, and it'll only put you in danger. I'm sorry."

"Please."

She pressed her lips to my clammy forehead. "I love you."

"Mom, no—" I cried. "I won't—I can't make it without you. I—"

"Layla," she said, in a clear, rigid voice that made me know she meant it. The same voice that told me she'd ground me if I didn't wash the dishes, the voice that said she hated my impractical shoes, the voice that said she was on my side, always, no matter what. She took my hand and squeezed it tight. "Layla, you can do anything. You are capable, and you are brave. You've proven that."'

It was my mother's voice. It would always be my mother's voice, from here until the end of time.

Preston scooped me up into his arms and shakily got to his feet. I screamed, but not because it hurt—I screamed because we were walking away, and Mom wasn't going with us. I screamed because I saw the gun in her hand, one bullet left, and I understood what was going to happen.

"Come on," Preston said, crying. "We have to get you inside."

I kept screaming, too weak to fight him, too weak to get out of his arms and run back to her. All I could do was reach out and cry for her. The world was getting darker. I felt myself falling away. But I had to hang on, to reach through the void and get back to her, my mother, my savior.

The last thing I saw was her face, teary and smiling, watching us leave her behind.

I slumped against Preston's chest, and then I was gone.

CHAPTER THIRTY-FOUR

I WAS LOST IN AN IN-BETWEEN, floating somewhere just beyond my body. Voices slipped through my feverish haze: *Little Cub, Little Cub, Little Cub. Layla. Layla, you can do anything. You've proven that. I'm sorry.*

The pain in my side was a constant throb, and every breath sent a sharp ache through my ribs. I felt heat. Cold sweat on my skin. When I opened my eyes, everything was hazy and orange. My fingers curled against the couch cushions beneath me.

A shadow hovered in my peripheral. My heart stuttered. "Mom."

"It's me." Preston's face came into focus. He smiled, relieved, but at the sight of him, my chest caved in.

"Where's Mom?"

He shook his head. "Don't worry about her, okay? Just rest."

"But—"

"Shh." He traced his hand along my damp forehead, through my matted hair. He'd never touched me like that before. He'd hardly ever hugged me. But his touch was so sharp and warm and real, pulling me back to the earth. I needed him, my brother. The one I'd come all this way for.

"You're okay," he whispered. "They won't hurt you again."

Pain ebbed through me, and I gingerly lifted my shirt to look at my torso. The wound was deep and long, slashed across my body in an ugly, jagged line. My skin was shiny and swollen, haphazardly stitched.

Preston winced. "I was about to redress it. We did the best we could; at least we stopped most of the bleeding. We'll get help soon."

My head fell back against the cushions; I could hardly hold it up. "Help from who?" I whimpered.

He hesitated. "Our only hope is that your message went through." He took in the stress on my face. "But don't worry. We're going to send out some hunters for food, and then once you and Tyshaun are back on your feet, we can figure something else out. You just need to rest, and we'll take care of everything."

"What happened to Mom?"

He shook his head. "I don't know."

"How can you not know?"

He just shook his head again. He wasn't being honest with me. He knew exactly what had happened to her and where she was. "We brought you inside, and by the time Luke fixed you up, she was gone," he said.

"Don't lie to me, Preston. I swear to god. Not after everything. I deserve to know where she is."

His eyes closed softly. "She…she took the gun and went into the east woods, heading for the valley."

"Why?"

"She wanted to get away from us." His voice broke. "She was losing control, and she didn't want to hurt us."

I was starting to get pissed. "Why didn't you try to stop her?"

"I *did*. I went after her, but she made me turn back, because I had to take care of you, not her. There was nothing we could do for her." He huffed. "You never should have gone out there, Lay. You should've let Mom go instead. She was dying anyway."

"She never would've made it."

"What does it matter?" Jamal said. That's when I realized we weren't alone; he was sitting across the room, his stoic face glowing orange from the fireplace. "Either way, your mom is gone, and so is the radio."

PRESTON TOLD ME TO REST, but I couldn't.

Luke had sent out two scouting parties at dawn after the fight. They all met back in the lodge to debrief that afternoon, and although they stayed over by the tables across the lodge, I strained to listen.

One party had gone looking for what remained of Trent's faction. After he died, three of them had blended back into the larger group, but the other three—Black Eye, the broad-shouldered kid, and Greyson—had slipped back into the woods. Tensions were still high, but everyone was too worn down, and nobody would make it through the winter if things kept going the way they had. So, hoping to somehow make amends, the scouting party had set off into the woods. All they found was the clearing where the camp had once been; everything was packed and gone, with only my discarded cowgirl boots left behind. The fire pit was still warm. But the three boys had disappeared into the wilderness.

They also found Kaden there, buried in leaves. He had a stab wound to the throat. He'd only been fifteen. The scouts carried him back in a sheet they'd brought along just in case they came across him, and now he was lying in the east woods, waiting to be buried.

The other party had gone looking for Mom. Or her body, at least. They found nothing.

"So she might still be out there?" I called out from the couch. She would've turned by now. I couldn't bear to picture her like that, but I also couldn't bear to think of her using that gun just to make it end before she lost herself.

"Maybe she's just…wandering," Antonio said.

I didn't know what was worse.

Preston left the debrief and joined me on the couch. "I need you to rest. There's nothing we can do now."

I stared at him pleadingly, needing him to be straight with me. "Do you think she shot herself?"

He swallowed. "I don't know. Does it matter?"

"Yes, it does! Because if she's still out there, we have to find her. We can fix her. They have a vaccine—"

"You don't know that."

"They do!" I started crying, and hot pain shot through my side. "They do, Pres. Why don't you believe me? They can fix her, I swear. We can grow those flowers. You have to find her." He got up, but I grabbed his arm. "Pres, you have to find her! Please!"

"She's gone, Lay."

"Shut up!" I screamed. "Shut up! Shut up! She's out there, and you have to—we have to—we can fix her. You can't leave her. You can't—"

My lungs were struggling for air, and it felt like someone had me by the throat. I was so angry I saw red. Why didn't he believe me? Why wasn't he still out there looking? Why had he let her go? He put his hands on my shoulders, and I cried and thrashed, trying to get up, but I couldn't move.

He spoke over his shoulder. "Antonio, go into my mom's backpack over there. Look for a pill bottle. And get some water."

Antonio came back with an orange bottle—Mom's pills, still half full. Preston tried to press one into my mouth, and I fought him, turning my head, sweating hard, screaming. Finally, Antonio held me down, and Preston forced my mouth open and got the pill down. He gave me a drink, and I swallowed it through my tears.

Finally, I settled enough to breathe.

He knelt down and held my head to his chest. "I'm sorry, Lay. I'm so sorry."

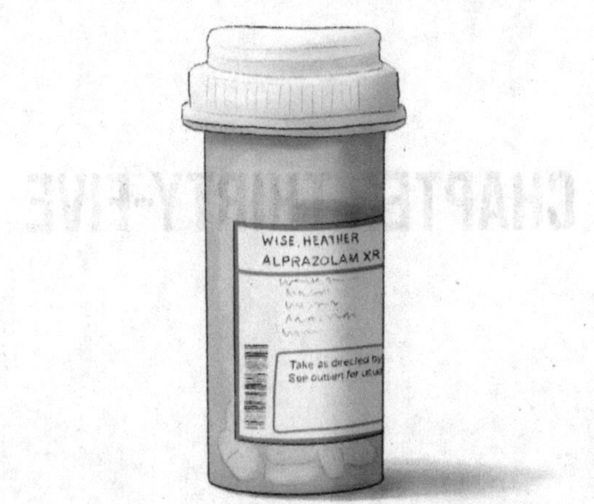

WISE, HEATHER
ALPRAZOLAM XR
Take as directed by
See outsert for usual

CHAPTER THIRTY-FIVE

I DRIFTED in and out for a while, but I wasn't sure how long. Here and there, I felt a hand on my head, or someone coaxing me to sip water. When I truly woke up again, daylight was pooling through the windows. I was lying in a puddle of sweat, but my body trembled with cold.

Jamal was sitting beside me, drawing. When he heard me stir, he said, "Hey."

"Hey," I whispered. Preston was at the other end of the room, carrying three dead rabbits to the kitchen, his hands covered in blood. I winced and looked toward the window instead. The sky was bright, and flurries of snow hit the window. I thought it would've been nighttime. "How long have I been asleep, Jamal?"

"A couple days, in and out. You should try to eat something, or at least drink some water. I'll go get you some."

I grabbed his sleeve. A couple days. Too much time had passed and we were still here. "So my message...it didn't go through."

Jamal ground his teeth together. It was only then that I saw how hollowed-out he looked. How dim his eyes were. It had sunk in that his dad could very well be alive out there, but there was no way of truly knowing, no way of reaching him anymore. I'd tried, and I'd failed.

I was starting to wonder if I'd even heard what I thought I had.

"If that really was my dad on the radio, he didn't hear you," Jamal said softly. "He'd be here by now. He's not coming."

We were silent for a moment. I listened to the fire snap, thinking of that first night back in the woods with Mom as we realized what we were really in for. It felt like years ago. It had only been about two weeks. So much had changed so fast, and there wasn't anything I could do about it. It made me so angry, but I was tired, too. So, so tired.

Jamal chewed his lip. "Some kids left today, Antonio too. They took the horses with them. Sorry you didn't get to say goodbye."

"Oh. Maybe they'll see Rosalita."

"Maybe," he said. He was quiet for a moment, then rubbed his nose. "I know it doesn't matter that much anymore, but I thought of a better ending for *Major Ursus*. I thought you'd want to know. Leah finds the cure for the hybrids. She releases them, and they help her escape and find Major Ursus. She cures him too, and then…it's over."

"Like, the whole comic is over? That's it?"

He shrugged. "I think I just want it to be happy. I need it to be happy. So that's it."

I smiled weakly. "That's good, Jamal."

"I know you're dying or whatever, but you're not off the hook. You still have to color for me, okay?"

I gasped a laugh and closed my eyes.

The boys came in for dinner soon after. There was no more rice, only canned black beans, rabbit, and some fish that Luke had caught after finding a counselor's fishing pole and hiking down to the river in the valley. Preston tried to get me to sit up and eat, but my body was shaky and weak, and I wasn't hungry.

After dinner, Preston tried to clean the wound again. My

abdomen was still swollen, almost greenish. It looked like Tyshaun's leg.

"It's infected, isn't it?" I asked as he wrapped a clean bandage around my torso; we were running out of bandages too.

"That word feels a little loaded now," Preston said with a smirk, but I didn't think it was funny.

"Stop trying to hide stuff from me. Just tell me what's going on."

"Yeah, I think it's infected."

"So what does that mean for me?"

He sniffed, hands slowing down as he came to the end of his roll of gauze. "We don't have any more medicine. I don't know how to fix this. Any of this." He stood up and wiped his nose with his sleeve. "Hey, I forgot. I have something for you."

He reached into his pocket and pulled out a polaroid. It was of Mom and me, one I'd sent Preston in the mail months ago. In fact, it was the first one I'd ever sent. Mom and I were outside, standing beneath the purple blooms of a jacaranda tree, smiling cheek to cheek. It had been one of those rare days we really got along. School was almost out, it was Sunday afternoon, and we had nowhere to be, so we'd gone to the park. The tree had been so beautiful, and I'd wanted Preston to see it.

He'd only been at camp for a week then. I was angry, but it hadn't settled so deeply into my chest yet. The anger hadn't marred us. And maybe it hadn't been entirely anger, but also righteous love. All of us were only trying to do the right thing for each other. Mom wanted Preston to get better. She wanted me to be okay. She wanted her own life to start fresh again. She wanted to be strong enough to do it all on her own, so that we could all be taken care of.

Things didn't always work out the way she wanted. But I could see now how hard she'd tried. I could see it in that smile, and the glow in her cheeks, pressed against mine beneath the jacaranda tree.

"She wanted me to tell you not to be afraid," he said.

"Thanks, Pres," I whispered.

He put his cold hand to my hot, sticky forehead and half-smiled. Then he turned away quickly, and I knew it was because he was about to cry. It almost made me happy. It almost felt like he was the old Preston again, who felt things deeply and let it show.

CHAPTER THIRTY-SIX

I DIDN'T SLEEP much at night. I was feverish, and my head was full of visions. Bullets through skulls. Blood pooling over dusty wood. The voice on the radio, the growl of static. Broken glass and green Slurpee sludge, crowbars, cold lips and dirty cars. It repeated over and over in my dreams. The second I thought I'd gotten out, it would all happen again. All the while, I kept looking for my parents, and I couldn't find them anywhere.

"Layla, wake up."

I cracked my eyes open, thinking I'd still be lost in the dark. But it was Preston. The room was dim, the fire depleted. I tried to look around, but I could hardly move my head at all.

"You're burning up a lot," he said. "I'm gonna take you outside for some fresh air, okay?"

"No," I muttered.

I nestled back into my pillow, but Preston scooped me up, blanket and all, and carried me away. I gasped with pain, but was too weak to protest. We walked past Jamal, sleeping soundly, and went outside.

The air was bitter, the field covered in snow, bathed in the cold pinkish light of dawn. There was more snow than I remembered, but I wasn't sure how many days had passed. I curled my head into Preston's neck to hide from the wind and listened to his heartbeat as he carried me away from the lodge.

Across the clearing, he set me down and propped me up against something hard, so I finally opened my eyes. I was resting against a tree, and in front of us, the valley stretched between the mountains. Preston sat beside me and held me up.

"You've been inside for days," he said. "I thought you might want to see outside. The fresh air might help with your fever."

I rested against his shoulder gingerly, feeling my body object to even the slightest movement. I knew what this was about. I was dying, and my time was limited. This was the end of the road, and Preston didn't think I needed fresh air. He thought I needed something pretty to look at, to get away from all the horror in my brain before the end.

I glanced up at him. His eyes were teary again, for the millionth time in recent days. "What?" I croaked.

"You should've seen this valley in early summer. So many wildflowers you couldn't believe it." His mouth twitched into a smile. "Mom would've loved it."

"Is she really gone?"

"I think so," he whispered. "But I can't wrap my head around it. It happened so fast, and…and I was so angry before, but now I feel so…"

"Empty."

"Yeah."

"Are you going to miss me, too, when I'm gone?"

"Don't talk like that, Layla."

I'd sort of been joking, but I was clearly not very good at making jokes these days. I nestled close to his neck, my body aching and cold. "Sorry."

He shook his head. "I should've left with you when I had the chance. I never should've let you get caught up in this. I—" He choked on a stifled sob, cutting off his thought. I didn't want him to finish it anyway. I didn't want him to feel guilty.

I just wished there was a point to all of this. When I'd left with Mom, I thought it would be easy to get to him, and then we'd all just go home. But now Mom was gone, and soon I would be, too, and Preston would still be stuck on this mountain.

"I'm sorry," I said again. I didn't know what for. For coming here, for failing with the radio, for dying, for making him lose another person. Maybe all of it.

"Well, I'm glad you came," he murmured. "I don't know how long any of us would've made it out there, the way things are. But you got to me, and now I know—now I *really* know—that she loves me."

I lifted my head weakly to get a better look at him. He was talking about Mom. "You said loves. Like she's not dead."

"I don't think that love is going anywhere. No matter what happens to us."

I shut my mouth and gazed out over the valley. The sun was rising over the hills in the distance, faint and yellow. Down below, the pines swayed in the wind, sending snow flying off their limbs and over the dry grass. Even as winter crept in, the river water still rushed, determined and alive. I wondered if Mom was out there somewhere, wandering. Or finally at rest for the first time in all her life. I wondered if there was any fragment of herself left inside her body, and if that fragment felt at home in the wild. If that fragment would hang on until springtime, just to see the flowers bloom one last time.

"I'm so tired," I said.

"But you're still holding on."

I was, because I was scared. Because I didn't know what would happen if I let go. "Was Mom scared when she left?"

Preston thought about it. "No, I don't think so. She knew we'd be okay as long as we were together."

"This is the end, Pres. Isn't it?"

His breath made trembling clouds in the air. I loved listening to him breathe. It made me feel like I was back home, my bed feet from his, falling asleep beneath my warm covers. Mom on the other side of the wall. The TV chattering softly. The kitchen faucet dripping. His breath was home.

"No, it's not," he said. "As long as we're still here, it's not the end."

I closed my eyes, unable to keep them open. Preston adjusted to cradle me, and he held me close, my head in the nook of his shoulder. As I lay there, my body finally settled, and the sound of his heartbeat lulled me back into a cold, flitting sleep.

Somewhere in my dream, there was a deep, thumping sound, echoing from somewhere far off. I was standing in a field of swaying, golden grass, and the sky was a pale blue. My body shivered, but I felt the sun on my cheeks, and I heard that *thump, thump, thump*. I turned around in the field, and I saw them: a band of horses, running hard, hooves pounding, backs gleaming in the sun. They galloped across the field in perfect tandem, racing toward the snow-capped mountains that stood in the distance.

"Layla."

I turned, and there was Mom. She smiled—she looked better. In fact, she didn't look sick at all. Her long, red hair fluttered like the grass did. I reached for her, but she was too far away.

"The horses, Mom! Did you see them?" I glanced over my shoulder, and the horses were still there, rugged and wild, running somewhere I couldn't make out through the tall grass.

"Layla," Mom said again. I turned back toward her, and saw that her hand was outstretched. But it wasn't her voice speaking anymore. It was my brother's.

I reached for her, and then jerked awake.

My eyes struggled to adjust to the light, but Preston was still holding me. I blinked, coming back to reality. He was staring down at me. Beaming.

"Layla, wake up!" he cried. "Look!"

His face turned skyward. As I struggled to follow his line of sight, I realized I could still hear the *thump, thump, thump*ing. It wasn't horses at all.

There, on the horizon, was a long, gray aircraft, veering over the tall pines, its blades cutting through the sharp, November air.

Preston let out a howl at the sky, then kissed me hard on the cheek. "Your message," he said with gleaming eyes. "They heard it, Lay. They heard it!"

I smiled faintly and leaned back against his chest, wondering if this was all still a dream. If it was, I didn't want to wake up. I felt him pick me up, and I felt the wind. I let it take me, listening to my brother's heartbeat until it all slipped away.

CHAPTER THIRTY-SEVEN

THE WORLD WAS RUMBLING and cold. I heard voices, muffled beneath the sound of an engine. My body swayed and the ground shuddered beneath me. Someone took my hand. I curled my fingers in.

"Lay?"

I cracked open my eyes to a blur of red light. I couldn't make out the face above me, but I knew it was Preston. As he leaned closer and brushed back my hair, I tightened my grip on his other hand. It was hard to hear him over the roaring sound, but he pressed close to my ear so I could just make out his voice.

"Hey. You did it, Lay. You got us out of here."

There was a mask strapped on my face. I was lying on a stretcher in some kind of metal room. My body swayed again, and I realized we were flying. We weren't in a room, but in the aircraft; Preston was on the ground with me, not buckled in. I wanted to sit up, but I was strapped down. My side ached with the effort.

"Who?" I croaked. But Preston couldn't hear me.

He didn't have to answer, anyway. The rest of the aircraft came into focus. There were boys on either side, buckled into pull-down seats, dirty and traumatized, their bodies shaking in unison with the airframe. But sitting near the middle were Jamal and Sergeant Hardy. Jamal's head was on his father's shoulder, and his eyes were closed, and he held my hat in his lap. Sergeant Hardy sat in all black clothes, chin up as he looked straight ahead.

My heart raced.

He'd found his Little Cub. Against all odds, he'd found us. He'd heard me after all, across miles, through the darkness.

"There's a lot to explain," Preston said into my ear, straining against the noise. "But he heard your message, and they're taking us somewhere safe now. I don't know where—not home. But you're gonna be okay, I promise."

Tears blurred my vision. I breathed in deeply and held tightly to my brother's hand, feeling the uncertainty press in on me. But his hand was cold and firm, and it was the realest thing I'd ever felt. I knew that my brother didn't lie to me—he was the only one I'd always been able to trust with my entire heart. So if he said we'd be okay, then that was the honest truth.

There was an unfamiliar man in the seat just behind Preston, wearing black clothes like Sergeant Hardy. He took Preston by the shoulders and hoisted him up, trying to get him to buckle back into his harness. Preston did, but the whole time, he was just looking down at me with glassy eyes, smiling through the red gloom.

As we left that lonely mountain behind, I thought of Mom. I could hear what she'd say to me now—the same thing as Preston. *You're going to be okay.* It was because of her that we were still here, really. She'd brought us that notebook. She'd saved Preston's life. She'd used her last breaths to get to us.

Preston looked so young as he hovered over me. Sometimes I forgot he was just a kid. But we didn't feel like kids anymore. Not really. So much had changed, and would keep on changing.

I didn't know what would happen to us now, but I did know that my brother had been right: this wasn't the end. We'd be safe again. Someone would patch us up, and give us food to eat, and take off my stupid braces. And maybe the power would come back on, or maybe we'd get used to the dark. Maybe the darkness was just a part of us now.

I looked at my brother, still smiling, and closed my eyes.

We'd be different forever—both of us. Something would always be missing, reduced to memories of gardens and horses and sun on the road. But maybe we were never meant to stay the same forever. Maybe that was part of growing up. It wasn't fair that it had to be this way, but at least we had the chance to grow up at all.

As long as we were still here, it wasn't the end. It was only the end of the world we knew. Only the beginning of something else.

ACKNOWLEDGMENTS

First and foremost, thanks be to God for giving me the gift of writing and the means to pursue it.

Thank you to my family (especially Mom and Dad) for supporting me as a writer and artist from the very beginning. I'm thankful for a family that has cheered me on and taken my dreams as seriously as I have. Thank you to my sister Savannah for the constant design advice and for inviting me on the road-trip that sparked this story. To my sister Sierra…you didn't do much, but you can still be included because I love you.

Thank you to Katie Childs, my dearest friend. Thank you for your involvement in editing this book and always giving me the most brutal, useful feedback (and noticing things no one else does). You are an astounding writer, editor, and friend, and I am so happy we get to do life together.

To my editors. Haley Chapman, I'm so thankful to the Columbia Publishing Course for bringing us together. You've been a great friend and an amazing line editor. Thank you, thank you, thank you for the work you've done on this book. And Landry Parkey, proofreader extraordinaire, thank you for catching all my typos and being a very cool friend. I'm so grateful for your generous help.

Thank you Taylor, Elle, and Lola. You are the *best* writer friends, and I am beyond grateful to NovelBound for bringing us together. Thanks for being this book's biggest fans since the beginning (and always letting me yap about it).

To Madi Baldwin, my co-founder, and to our community NovelBound. Madi and I created this community for others, but it's been such a help to me personally. I love each and every person who is a part of it—and this book would not exist without your support. Thank you also to my beta readers. There were quite a few of you, but all of your enthusiasm got me so excited about this crazy story I wasn't so sure about.

Thank you to two authors, Courtney Walsh and David Arnold. Courtney, thanks for all your self-publishing help (and for convincing me to pull the trigger and just do this thing on my own). I've always admired you as an author and I love getting to work with you. David, you may not have realized it, but some advice you gave me back in 2021 helped me be confident enough to write a book that felt way out of my wheelhouse. Your continual advice since then has been so appreciated.

Thank you to my most impactful writing teachers, Katie Volk and Kristina Erny. Katie, in 7th grade you inspired me to write my first ever novel, and you've been cheering me on since—even as we became coworkers. I hope to be half the creative writing teacher you were. Kristina, as my former professor, you have been one of the most influential people in my writing career. Your belief in me has been so important throughout the tumultuous journey I've had so far, and I would not be the writer I am if it weren't for you.

And finally, thank you to my readers. You are all I've ever wanted and I'm so glad you're here.

ABOUT THE AUTHOR

For more books and updates, visit sophieriley.com.

Sophie is an author and illustrator from Illinois, USA with a B.A. in creative writing and art & design. She attended the Columbia Publishing Course at Oxford and co-founded a writing community called NovelBound, which offers retreats, events, and resources to writers around the world. When she's not writing, you can find her traveling, hanging out with her sisters, playing video games, and starting too many creative projects she'll never finish.

From young readers to adults, Sophie loves to write stories with messy, enduring relationships at the center. This is her first published novel.

THE WILD SIDE

COMING SOON

IT'S NOT THE END OF THE WORLD

SPOTIFY PLAYLIST

www.ingramcontent.com/pod-product-compliance
Lightning Source LLC
Chambersburg PA
CBHW021806130726
47987CB00010B/3032